ENCHANTED

A CHRISTMAS COLLECTION

MELISSA TAGG

LARKSPUR
PRESS

BOOKS BY MELISSA TAGG

Walker Family Series
Three Little Words
From the Start
Like Never Before
Keep Holding On
All This Time

Enchanted Christmas Collection
One Enchanted Christmas
One Enchanted Eve
One Enchanted Noel

Enchanted: A Christmas Collection (compilation)

Where Love Begins Series
Made to Last
Here to Stay

A Maple Valley Romance (e-novella)

ONE ENCHANTED CHRISTMAS

CHAPTER 1

*O*nce upon a time—specifically, last December—author Maren Grant had what she thought might be the most perfect night of her life.

Actually, the word she used was "enchanted"—because she's a writer and writers tend to get dramatic like that. She also might've said something to her best friend Remy about "being able to die happy now."

But let's be honest. She was only 29 at the time. She didn't really want to die.

She did, however, want to relive that night. She talked about it all the time—at first to Remy and her other friends. And later, when they got sick of the story, to her dog Gilmore.*

Why was it so ~~perfect~~—ahem—enchanted? Well, it all started when...

Never mind. Let's just show you . . .

---

*NAMED after her favorite TV show. Also, a stuffed animal, not a real dog. Because she teaches in addition to writing which means she's crazy busy and she travels on weekends and so as much as she loves dogs, she's very aware she'd probably be the worst pet owner ever.

* * *

LAST DECEMBER

There had to be more ridiculous things in the world than an author falling in love with her own cover model.

Maren Grant simply couldn't think of any at the moment.

"All right, what are you going to say when you meet him?" Dayton Harris reached for the travel mug in the console tucked between car seats. Seemed the editor hadn't been joking about his tea addiction back when they first met—via phone, thankfully. He'd called to talk about her manuscript, and she'd been so nervous her hands shook.

Almost as nervous as she was now.

"I'd bet money you practiced in a mirror." Dayton's tone sashayed with enough amusement it should've earned a glare.

But Maren couldn't possibly muster one—not with Colin Renwycke mere yards away in the downtown Minneapolis park, tossing the photographer's camera his flawless granite stare while a breathy wind curled snowflakes around his feet. The man couldn't have been closer to the character in her imagination if she'd somehow channeled Rembrandt and painted her fictional detective herself.

Ethan Whitney, P.I. More Sam Spade than Sherlock.

That's how she'd pitched the main character of her mystery series back when her publishing dream was still just that—a dream.

And now here she was, watching it come true right in front of her while Dayton's Honda idled under her fur-trimmed boots. Jeans layered over long johns and one of those puffy marshmallow-looking coats would've been the smarter apparel of choice for this afternoon's Minnesota cold. But a girl didn't meet a man who might be the love of her life dressed like an Eskimo.

Thus the black leggings that wouldn't stand a chance

against the chill once she stepped out of the car, the striped skirt that barely reached her knees, the cropped jacket. She'd hidden her usual mess of uncooperative brown hair under a cranberry red knit hat.

Dayton had already pointed out the others at the photo shoot as they drove up—the photographer's assistant, a stylist, the cover designer. She'd have met them all in person by now if a combination of afternoon snowfall and rush hour hadn't delayed her drive across the Twin Cities. By the time she'd met up with Dayton and they'd trekked a few freshly plowed streets to the park, the shoot was nearly finished.

"Well?" Dayton tapped the steering wheel. "What are you going to say?"

"I'm going to say, 'Hi there, I'm Maren Grant, author of the book you're going to appear on the cover of and I think I might be in love with you.'"

Dayton sputtered on his earl grey. "Try again."

"Hey, nice to meet you. I'm Maren Grant, and there's a very good chance we're soul mates." The car's heater chugged, and she leaned into the tufts of warm air.

Dayton rolled his eyes. The editor had less than a decade on her, but his expression now was pure paternal, if exaggerated, disapproval. "You're hopeless."

Maren grinned. Hopeless or simply the most starry-eyed romantic since Doris Day in . . . well, basically any movie but especially the ones with Rock Hudson.

But who could blame her? Her debut novel, the first in what she hoped would be a long-running series about a cunning detective, would release nine months from now. Reason enough to trade in common sense for continual giddiness. But then a couple weeks ago Dayton had emailed the headshot of the model the publishing team had decided to use for the cover.

And it'd been like seeing a sculpture come to life.

3

Cue: instant fascination.

'Course she'd mostly been joking when she'd sent Dayton the gushing reply with enough exclamation marks to make her old college writing prof hyperventilate. She hadn't really expected to be here today, the day of the photo shoot . . . to get to actually meet the man she'd forever picture from here on out as her beloved detective.

Outside the windshield and across the snow-quilted lawn, Colin Renwycke now perched against a lamppost under a wash of pale winter sun, powdery white dusting the air around him and the breeze lifting the shock of dark hair over his forehead. The upturned collar of his charcoal trench coat reached toward a shadowed jaw line.

And then there were those eyes. Even from a distance, their frosty blue could wreak havoc on a girl's heart.

"Leg warmers." She propped her elbows on her knees, chin on her fist.

Dayton notched up the heat. "What?"

"Something more ridiculous than an author falling in love with her cover model. Leg warmers. Why're those a thing? Who decided ankles deserved more warmth and coddling than any other body part?"

"It was the 80s. Fashion went off the rails."

"Yeah, but they're back in style now. And it's only a matter of time before I slip from making fun of them to wearing them myself. It always happens. Skinny jeans. Ankle boots."

"Now this conversation is off the rails." Dayton sipped from his mug. "You do realize this is about a hundred kinds of unusual? An author getting to watch her own cover shoot, I mean. Especially a debut."

"But you invited me to see it because you're secretly a closet romantic?"

"Sure." Dayton let the word dangle with faux agreement.

"Because I only live twenty-five minutes away and it was

about time I visit the publishing offices anyway?" She'd met Dayton a couple times since signing with the publisher, but never at his office.

"Closer."

Another grin. Another glance out the windshield. "Because I texted you that photo of Colin Renwycke's headshot hanging on my fridge and you wanted to make sure, in person, I haven't gone completely out of my mind."

"Bingo."

So maybe she'd developed an unreasonable crush. So what? Wasn't Remy always telling her she needed to give romance a chance again?

Forget Dean. Forget the way things ended. Move on.

For half a year she'd put up with the well-meaning lectures, pretending to appreciate the advice all the while knowing her heart still needed space to heal.

Maybe a silly infatuation with a man she'd never met—a model of all things—was the first sign it finally had. Maybe that set-aside dream of finding a love like what her parents shared—one full of big, enchanted, magic moments—wasn't such an impossibility.

After all, if her publishing dream could come true . . .

"Hey, Dayton?"

Outside, the photographer was unzipping the bag slung over his shoulder and dropping in his camera as his assistant lowered the flash umbrella. Done already?

"Yeah?"

"I know I've said it a dozen times already, but thank you."

"You haven't met the guy yet. He could be a creep."

"I don't mean for today. I mean for picking out my story from your slush pile. Liking it. Making my publishing dream come true."

She'd poured her heart into the book and *oh*, she'd fallen hard for her own main character. A paradox of a detective—

rugged and still somehow soft, a lover of logic and justice and answers, with enough of a dreamer in him to woo even the hardest of hearts.

Except Dean's.

And there it was again—the question she could never quite silence: If she hadn't been so intent on her writing career, so enthralled with her own made-up character, might they still be together?

Dayton turned the key in the ignition now, and the car's rumbling stilled. "Wasn't just me that made it happen. The editorial committee, sales and marketing, the pub board—lots of people were in on the decision."

"Yeah, but you're the one who took the first risk. And the timing . . . " She'd still been in a post-breakup haze when her agent had emailed to let her know a publisher was interested in the story. Still numb.

There'd been a six-month wait while the book sat with the publisher, its fate waiting to be determined. Time for Dean's words to fade into mere whispers, only murmuring to the surface in weak moments.

"If the man you described in your notes and what little I've read of your story is what you want, Mare, good luck finding him. You'll need it 'cause he doesn't exist."

"Well, anyway, just . . . thanks." Maren reached for the scarf she'd abandoned earlier.

If Dayton heard the snag in her voice, he didn't let on. Only tucked his travel mug back into the cup holder and pocketed his keys. "You're welcome. For the dream-come-true *and* for today. Just promise me you won't impulsively propose to the cover model?"

Bag packed, the photographer was walking this direction now, Colin Renwycke not far behind him. His trench coat whipped behind him in the wind.

Maren wound her scarf around her neck and reached for

her door handle. "Promise I won't propose. Can't promise I won't fall on a patch of ice, though. Or forget my name. Or spill something."

"Say again?"

She opened her door and a blast of wintry cold pinched over her. "I may write mystery, not straight romance, but trust me, my dear editor, I know how meet-cutes work." She slipped from the car.

Dayton followed suit, tossing his next words over the Honda's hood. "This isn't a Hallmark movie, Grant."

The breeze sent her scarf fluttering as she reached back into the car for her purse. "I wish I had a dog. We could've done this *101 Dalmations* style." She gathered her purse over her arm, turned while fitting on her gloves. "You know, where the leash gets all tangled around our feet and we're thrust together—me and the model, I mean."

With a backward kick, she closed the car door and started forward . . . then instantly jolted back, one end of her scarf stuck in the door. At the strangling pull, her arms flew into the air and her back hit the car.

She heard Dayton's snort as her purse landed in the snow with a splat and the other end of her scarf matted itself to her face.

And then the voice.

"Is this the author I'm supposed to meet?"

And the sound of her own groan.

And Dayton's laughter.

"Indeed. Colin Renwycke meet Maren Grant."

* * *

OKAY, *you get the point, right? Thanks to the handiwork of her editor—who by the way, definitely IS a closet romantic—Maren got to meet the handsome model that would be appearing on the cover of her very first book.*

And it was, in her words, akin to sipping a peppermint mocha by a fireplace while watching the first snowfall of the year with Bing Crosby singing a baritone ballad in the background.

Again, remember . . . writer.

But she didn't only meet Colin Renwycke. After that not-at-all-cliché meet-cute, the couple actually went out for coffee . . . which turned into dinner . . . which turned into one of those horse-drawn carriage rides through downtown Minneapolis. Colin regaled her with stories of his idyllic childhood in the charming town of Maple Valley, Iowa, and didn't once yawn when Maren babbled about her writing.

Hmm, so maybe "enchanted" isn't such a stretch, after all.

Alas, the evening eventually came to an end. Although Maren entertained hopes of seeing Colin again, she only heard from him once after their whirlwind evening. A postcard arrived shortly before Christmas with a wintry scene on the front and a couple scribbled lines on the back.

Thanks for the date and best wishes for your book.
Don't forget my open invitation. -C

I know what you're thinking: "Open invitation? What's Colin talking about? Why didn't you let us see that part of their date? Or, for that matter, any part of their date other than that first adorable moment?"

But this is a novella, dear reader. There's simply not time to show you everything.

And thus, we skip ahead to present day . . .

CHAPTER 2

THIS DECEMBER

To hear his neighbor talk, Drew Renwycke was about to throw away everything. Lose both his savings and his sanity in a doomed endeavor.

But what was so crazy about resurrecting his grandparents' dream?

And how could Byron Pratt be so sure he'd fail?

Drew tromped through the span of yard leading from the farmhouse he'd never stopped calling home to the machine shed where he honestly didn't know what he'd find. A shovel, hopefully, if nothing else. His work boots—a size too big, but the only ones he'd located in the house—sunk into soggy, dirt-packed snow. Probably if he'd just wait another day, the snow might melt away. Save him the chore of shoveling.

But he needed the physical labor today. Needed something to stave off the force of Byron Pratt's words. *"You're not up to the task, son. This places needs more than you've got to give."*

His neighbor trailed behind him, consternation hovering even now in his silence.

"Mr. Pratt—"

"Byron."

Right. The man had told him two times already to call him by his first name. Iowa manners—hard to shake even after a decade away from Maple Valley. Still, if he was to win his neighbor's approval . . .

"Sorry, Byron. I appreciate what you're trying to do here, and I understand what this means for you. You've been working Renwycke land for years now." Ever since Mom and Dad moved away. Byron had likely planned to go on with the arrangement indefinitely.

Drew reached the shed, its curved metal handle rusted and loose, white paint peeling and weatherworn. A perfect match for the farmhouse's stripped siding and the barn's faded color —spring rain and hot summer sun, the bone-chilling breaths of winter too much for its once cheery red.

The whole farm seemed to sag under the weight of age and neglect.

And he had a mere five months to turn it all around in time for planting season.

He yanked on the shed door, feet sliding against his over-sized soles. He should get some boots that actually fit if he was really going to pull off this Farmer Drew thing.

The door barely budged.

"It's not just the land I'm concerned about." Byron stepped up beside him. Even with Drew's six-foot-one height, the man nearly towered over him, his shadow gulping up Drew's against the shed door. One hefty shunt and the door creaked open.

But Byron stopped him from walking inside with a hand on his shoulder. "I watched you and your siblings grow up, Drew. I heard your father say more than once he didn't foresee any of his children following in his footsteps."

Yeah, well, there was probably a lot about his children Dad hadn't foreseen.

Flashes of memory shoved in. The night that started it all. The barn crowded with teenagers, thumping base and humid air thick with the smell of cheap alcohol. Leigh with tear-streaked cheeks and desperation etched into her hollow eyes. And Colin...

A dangerous mix of reckless frustration.

They'd fallen apart at the seams, his family.

But surely it wasn't too late. It's why he was here. Why he'd moved back to Maple Valley four months ago and poured himself into repairing as much of the house as he could before winter trundled in.

But how to make Byron understand?

"I have to do this." Feeble words, perhaps. But their weight trekked through him, the same resolve that'd prompted him to walk away from his contracting job in St. Louis coaxing him inside the shed now. He'd already talked Leigh into moving into her old bedroom, had given his niece, Winnie, the one that used to be his parents'. She'd been plenty surly about it, but she was thirteen. Guess that was par for the course.

If he could just get Colin home for Christmas he might be on his way to putting his family back together. And he still had time. The snow, the holiday decorations all around town made it feel closer to Christmas than it actually was. But today was only the first of the month.

He blinked to adjust to the dim lighting of the shed, wan rays of light streaking through cracks and highlighting floating dust particles.

Byron's voice echoed off metal walls. "This the first time you've been in here since you came home?"

Drew nodded, picking his way across the dirt floor strewn with abandoned tools. He'd spent plenty of time in the woodshop next door, but had so far avoided this cavern. The shadows of old tractors, a combine, other equipment, clambered up the walls. Maybe it would've been quicker to run into town, buy a plastic shovel from the hardware store. Better yet, a snow blower.

Byron stopped in front of a grain wagon. "Tires are flat."

Which was probably only the beginning of the repairs he'd need to find a way to pay for. Sure, living the life of a bachelor for the past decade since college meant he'd had plenty of years to build a tidy little savings account.

But no way could he afford to pay out of pocket everything getting the farm up and going again would require.

No need for Byron to know that, though.

"Tires can be replaced."

Byron only sighed, stuck his hands in the pockets of his Levi's, tan coat with the John Deere patch stretching over his torso. "All right, son. I've said my piece, and my offer stands. If you decide to sell your land—"

Drew felt his jaw tighten. "I won't." Never mind how peculiar it still felt to even think of it as *his* land, *his* house. It had been less than a year since his parents had signed over the property—a gift he'd not asked for, one so unexpected it'd taken more than half a year to make the decision to actually move here.

And the longer he was here, the harder and harder it was to believe he could make a go of this. And the easier and easier it was to wonder if whatever divine nudge or guidance he'd thought he'd felt earlier this year was just his imagination.

"But if you change your mind, I hope you'll see me first." Byron pulled a pair of gloves from his pocket. "Or if you decide you need to hire on my boys to work it again this year, give me a call. Have a good afternoon, Drew."

The man turned, bulky form silhouetted by the sun outside the shed's entrance.

And for an uncertain moment, Drew had to fight the temptation to call after him. Just give in. Because what did he know about running a farm? Byron had said earlier that most area farmers had already purchased their spring seed by now. Drew didn't even know what kind or how much or where to buy seed.

What in the world was he doing?

You're being an older brother. You're helping your siblings.

He was finishing what Grandpa and Grandma had started. What Mom and Dad had given up on.

The farm, yes. But mostly, the family.

"Oh, and Drew?"

Byron had turned at the shed's entrance and he stood now, one hand at his hip and the other straightening his ball cap.

"Yes?"

"Almost forgot. My daughter wants to know if you're available."

His daughter? The scrawny kid with the freckles and high-pitched voice who used to play house with Leigh?

Correction, not a kid now.

"Available?"

"As in, I'm pretty sure she's making a pie right this very minute with every intention of getting dolled up and bringing it by."

"Actually, I'm . . . " What? He couldn't say "taken." He'd been on all of three dates in as many years.

"I'm not big on desserts," he finally said, an uncomfortable twinge in his voice. Only thing he could think to say and a complete lie, at that. He should feel guilty.

So why, as Byron chuckled and walked away, could he only feel the scratch of unease?

Because you're worried Byron's right. Worried this is too much for you.

Worried all the repairs in the world wouldn't fix what was really broken.

But then, as he angled around a tool cabinet, he saw it . . . not the shovel he'd come looking for, but something better.

Grandpa's old table saw. Somehow, despite its age and possibly only because of streaking sunlight poking through a hole in the roof, its gray metal glinted, almost gleamed with promise.

And suddenly he was nine years old again, wearing goggles too big for his face and ears buzzing with the sound of the saw's hum, its vibration shaking his arms as his grandfather talked him through the movement.

"Always make sure you're using a sharp blade. Dull blades bind in the wood and it can kick back at you. And never push the wood into the blade, just feed it slowly. There you go...you've got this, son."

With a steadying breath, Drew turned and made his way back across the shed. *Okay.* He'd head in to town. Buy a shovel. Come back and get the drive scooped before Leigh and Winnie got home.

"I've got this." A whispered promise.

But he didn't make it to his car before his phone blared into the quiet. And the ID on the screen stopped him. Maple Valley School District. On a Saturday?

"Hi, this is Drew."

Winnie?

"Drew, this is Principal Hardin from the middle school. I've tried your sister three times already—"

"She's at work and when the restaurant's busy—"

"I just need one of you to get to the school." A hard edge sharpened the principal's voice. "Now."

* * *

IT COULD'VE BEEN Maren in the back seat of the antique Ford, its black exterior shined to perfection and the words "Just Married" scrawled in white across the back window.

"I can't believe you stayed for the reception." Remy's voice reached over the cheers of the wedding crowd. "If it was my ex-boyfriend's wedding, I would've escaped after the ceremony." Sleet tapped against the canopy of umbrellas outside the church, the winter-white sky overhead smudged by gray clouds.

Not a pretty day for a wedding.

But at least the gloomy weather would make for a cozy evening. Tonight called for a crackling fireplace, mug of hot chocolate and a Christmas movie. Preferably one in black and white.

Yes, Maren would go home and crash—her reward for making it through Dean's afternoon wedding, composure in tact.

That is, after returning the call from her agent she'd missed during the reception.

"Scratch that." Remy tilted her umbrella so it shielded Maren. Her best friend's pitch-black hair was cut in a cute 1920s-ish bob that somehow defied the wind and rested in place. "If it were my ex, I wouldn't have attended at all. Who goes to their ex's wedding?"

"Mature, well-adjusted adults, that's who."

Or maybe more accurately, ones who still saw the guy at church each Sunday and moved in the same circle of friends. Ones who knew how obvious it'd look if they didn't attend.

Remy hooked her arm through Maren's "No one would've blamed you."

Maybe not, but she hadn't spent over a year and a half putting up an amicable front to blow it now. Besides, she'd made it through the day, hadn't she? Managed to smile at all the right moments and pretend to be truly happy for Dean and his new bride.

And maybe she wasn't pretending at all. Maybe a piece of her truly was happy for him. Just because she hadn't found her own version of happily ever after yet didn't mean she'd begrudge him his.

Maren leaned in to her best friend. "Regardless, I'm glad you came with. You're the perfect 'plus one.'"

"Of course I am. I remembered an umbrella, for one. And I totally pretended not to notice when you dumped a handful of those table mints in your purse, for two."

"You saw that?" So much for covert.

"Yeah, and I made it a point to distract the rest of the table."

The wedding crowd had begun to disband as Dean's car disappeared around the corner. That man loved his antique cars—rented a shed on the edge of town where he stored three of them. She'd loved taking drives on county blacktops in the early days of their relationship.

But she'd never quite understood how he could spend thousands of dollars and possibly as many hours on his hobby and then turn around and call her writing dream "too consuming."

And eventually use it as a reason to break up.

"Maren Grant?"

The astonished voice behind Maren sounded at the same time as her phone buzzed again from the pocket of her knee-length winter coat. It gaped open in front, cold creeping over her legs and through the fabric of her dress. She'd welcomed the chill after the crowded warmth of the church's reception hall. But now it scraped through her, harsh and jarring.

"I knew you'd RSVP-ed but I didn't realize you'd actually . . "

The voice trailed as Maren turned. Dean's sister. The only

thing she'd worked on harder than her plastic smile during the wedding was avoiding Elaine.

She tugged her coat closed, cinching the belt at her waist. "Nice to see you, Elaine." Not entirely true, but polite, anyway.

"Yes." Under her pink umbrella, Elaine combed her fingers through russet waves before nudging her hair over her shoulder. "And Remy. It's been awhile. I never see you anymore."

Remy tensed. "Well, you know how quickly social calendars fill. I can barely keep up with Maren here."

Oh, please, let's not do this, Rem—

"I mean, she's a famous author. Always on the go." Remy waved one hand. "You've read her book, haven't you?"

Elaine's magenta-tinted lips pinched. "I'm afraid I really don't have time for pleasure reading."

"You're one of the few then. Her first book has so many five-star reviews it's like . . . constellations or something. That many stars. Between her writing career and changing students' lives during the day—seriously, think *Dead Poets Society*—and dating a male model—"

Elaine lifted one eyebrow. "You're with a model?"

Now hold on. One magical date did not a relationship make. She reminded herself of that fact every time she looked at the postcard Colin Renwycke sent eleven months ago. But oh, the temptation to exaggerate right now . . .

"Actually, he's an actor. Modeling is just a side gig." That much was true, even if the implication wasn't. Colin had told her all about his acting aspirations that night in Minneapolis, his plans to eventually move to Hollywood.

Maybe that's where he was now. Maybe he'd landed one role after another and that's why she'd never heard from him again. Why they'd never had his promised second date.

Her phone buzzed again. A text this time. And the perfect out.

"I'm sorry, Elaine, but my phone's been going crazy all afternoon. I should probably get going."

Remy's expression turned *I-told-you-so*. "See, she's annoyingly popular."

Elaine only shifted her umbrella. "Yes, well, good day."

The second Dean's sister was out of earshot, Remy snorted. "Did she seriously just say 'good day?' When did we land in a Regency novel?"

Maren started toward her car, pulling her phone from her pocket. "You shouldn't have done that, Rem."

"Done what?" Her heels clipped on the sidewalk.

"Made me out to sound like Minnesota's It-girl. The only reason I have a busy schedule is because I juggle substitute teaching *and* online teaching to keep from financially flailing. I write and I work, which doesn't entirely scream social butterfly. And I've been on exactly one date in the past year."

She lifted her phone, scanned the text: *Dayton okayed the extension. But this needs to be the last time.*

She sighed as they reached her car, sleet streaking down its windows. At least it wasn't cold enough just yet to freeze.

Remy lowered her umbrella. "Bad news?"

"The opposite, actually. My editor's giving me another extension on my second book." January 15. A full month and a half.

If only the good news didn't come with a sour aftertaste.

"Problem is, this is the second extension I've asked for. And I still only have a few chapters written." And she couldn't ditch the nagging thought that maybe the first book had been a fluke.

That this series and an initial string of great reviews were fleeting.

That her writing ability might have an expiration date.

She dropped into her car, turned to Remy who was already warming her hands in front of the heater. "It's more than writer's block. It's . . . I don't know. Who peters out after only one book?"

"You're not petering out, Mare. You're just tired. You're basically working two full-time jobs, maybe three considering those online classes. You're constantly making trips to see family and attending writing conferences and I don't even know what all."

Outside, a streetlamp flickered to life as the last of the day's pallid sun waned.

"You need a break."

"I don't have time for a break. Whether or not I get to keep writing Ethan Whitney books, whether or not I get another publishing contract, basically my whole future—it all depends on how well this second one sells. It needs to be amazing, and I keep telling Dayton it's going to be. Ethan Whitney is going to his hometown for the first time in ten years and facing his past and falling in love . . . at least, he's supposed to do all that. But I'm . . . stuck."

And her ex-boyfriend had just gotten married. She could tell herself all she wanted that she was fine with it. That she'd moved on. That she was happy for him.

But it'd be a lie to say "stuck" didn't extend beyond her writing life.

She sunk her key in the ignition, but Remy's hand on the gear shift stopped her from turning it. "Hand over your purse."

"Why, you want a mint?"

Remy ignored her and pulled the purse from her lap. She unzipped it and reached inside, a couple mints spilling out as she pilfered through its contents. "No, I want this."

She held it up—the postcard.

Maren's jaw slackened. "How did you know—"

"That you still carry this thing around with you? I'm your best friend, Mare. Do you know how many times in the past year you've told me about Colin's invite? 'What if I actually took him up on it, Remy? What if I just showed up in Iowa?' Do you know how often you've muttered that?"

Probably not nearly as many times as she'd replayed the night in her imagination. Coffee in a little shop that overlooked a bustling street. Dinner at a ritzy Italian place. That carriage ride.

And Colin—enigmatic and talkative—telling her all about his childhood, his hometown, playing with his brother and sister on the farm. She could've listened to him talk all night.

"It sounds so idyllic," she'd said. And so different from her own upbringing—the private schools, the constant moves, Mom and Dad traveling so often.

"I guess it was in its own way. Lots of good memories. And...I don't know." Colin had shrugged. "Actually, December's my favorite month on the farm. Everything's white and calm and peaceful. The house gets drafty, but that makes the fireplace all the better."

"Sounds like a great writing spot."

He'd helped her out of the carriage then, one hand lingering on her waist as they'd stood on the sidewalk, snow salting the air around them and the faint cadence of music from a nearby restaurant drifting over the street. And for a few intoxicating seconds, his eyes held hers captive "You should come sometime. Seriously, spend a week at the farm and write your heart out. If I'm there, we can have our second date."

She might've agreed to pack all her belongings right then, up and move to Iowa at his beckoning.

But then his hand had dropped and he'd stepped back, the magic moment broken. "Although, most likely, you'd have the place to yourself."

"Wait, no one lives there now?"

"Not since my parents retired and moved to Arizona. The house just sits there empty most of the time. A neighbor farms the land.

Drew keeps hounding us to get together at the farm for Christmas, but . . . " He'd looked to the ground. *"Anyway, consider it an open invitation."*

Remy propped the postcard on the dash in front of them now, covering the clock, its corners frayed and Colin's scribbled words staring back at her.

"You always say your favorite scenes to write are the big moments. The ones that change everything."

"Rem—"

"Make a big moment happen. Stop asking 'What if?' and actually do something."

"Like what? Randomly show up at a farm in Iowa?"

"Yes, exactly. If nobody's there, great. Take Colin up on his invitation and spend some time writing there. That's the joy of substitute teaching. You're scot-free if you want to be. You can teach your online classes from anywhere. And if someone is there, if Colin's there . . ." Remy grinned. "You get yourself that second date."

The thought bubbled through her. What if . . .

No, it was a completely daft idea.

Except sometimes the best things came from daft ideas. Like when she'd written a book and hoped against hope for a publishing contract, even when the industry blogs and experts and everyone said the chances of breaking out as a debut author were scant. Like when she'd joked to her editor about wanting to meet Colin and then it'd actually happened and . . .

What if . . . ?

"I don't have any way of contacting Colin." She'd actually gotten brave enough to try his phone number once back in February. Disconnected. "I guess I could Google him. I could dig up an email address or maybe he's on Facebook."

"Or you could nix wasting any time and hit the road, baby."

"I don't even know where the farm is."

"You know it's in Iowa, so basically next door, and you know the town name and Colin's family's last name. The internet can take it from there." Remy reached over to turn the key in the ignition.

"What are you doing?"

"You're smiling that author-picturing-the-perfect-scene smile. Only for once it's a real life possibility you're picturing. So we're getting this show on the road. Literally." Remy buckled her seat belt. "Drive, Grant. My iPhone and I will figure out the farm's address. You're going home to pack a suitcase and you're leaving today, before you change your mind."

* * *

WINNIE WOULDN'T EVEN LOOK at him.

"You just can't go breaking into a school, Win."

Winnie's only answer was to cross her arms. The same stony silence she'd greeted Drew with when he found her in the principal's office had accompanied them all the way home. He'd waited for her to bolt from the passenger seat of his truck as soon as he pulled into the circle drive in front of the farmhouse.

But she hadn't even taken off her seatbelt.

At nearly seven-thirty p.m., frothy stretches of sunset's color had long since given way to star-dotted black. He studied Winnie's profile—she looked so much like his sister. High cheekbones and stick-straight blonde hair currently knotted behind her head with a pencil poking through.

"I know it's hard getting used to a new school—"

"How would you know? Mom said you guys went to MVS your entire life."

Finally, words. Never mind the sarcasm. "Speaking of your mom—"

"Don't tell her." Winnie swung her gaze to him with the plea. Bangs slanted over her forehead and the sky's remaining wedge of sunlight tinted her cerulean eyes. And suddenly it wasn't Leigh he saw in his niece.

But Colin.

Restless. Frustrated. Trapped.

He swallowed. Hard. No chance he was letting her end up like his little brother.

"She's your mom. I have to tell her."

"She's a flaky mess."

"Don't say that—"

"And anyway, she won't care."

He couldn't have deciphered the emotion in his niece's voice if he tried. Maybe a bunch, all knotted together.

And he wished he had any idea how to begin untangling them. He'd known Winnie wasn't excited about moving to Maple Valley when Leigh had agreed to the plan. But had she really been happy in that cramped apartment in Omaha? The huge school?

So many reminders of what she'd been through?

"Your mom loves you, Win."

Winnie's focus reverted to the window. Tire tracks dirtied the snow. So much for shoveling. "My mom loves pills."

All the breath seeped from his lungs. "She's clean now. You know that."

"For now."

"For good." Maybe he said it with more conviction than he felt. But he wanted to believe it. For Leigh, for Winnie.

For himself. And the conscience that could never quite let go.

If you'd just paid attention . . .

"Why'd you do it? Break into the school, I mean. Just tell me that much."

No answer.

"I want to make this work, Winnie. I want you to be happy here."

"How am I supposed to be happy in a stupid small town that has eight thousand antique stores and not one single bookstore? Sleeping in a lumpy bed that's like sixty years old? Eating your horrible cooking?"

"Man, tell me how you really feel, why don't you?" He tried to joke, but she only grabbed her backpack from the floor and pushed her door open.

He climbed out of the truck and followed her stalking form toward the house. Why couldn't he make this better? Find the right words to connect with her? Get her to see he only wanted to help?

"Winnie—"

"I've got homework."

He clamped down on a retort about the irony of her being concerned about homework when she'd just barely escaped suspension. "I have to tell Leigh."

"Whatever." She flung the word over her shoulder before suddenly halting, her head tipping back. "What the—?"

He stopped short just before running into her, followed her upward gaze.

And saw what she saw.

A figure perched on the lattice that climbed up the side of the porch. "Is someone seriously breaking into my house?"

Winnie's backpack dropped into the snow. "Finally, some excitement around here."

CHAPTER 3

Maren's limbs went numb the second she heard tires crunching over snow and gravel.

Bad enough she'd taken Remy's advice, let spontaneity or maybe just desperation get the better of her and hit the road for the three-hour drive. She'd started chiding herself as soon as she crossed the Minnesota border into Iowa and didn't stop until she reached Maple Valley. Surely Colin Renwycke had never meant for her to actually take him up on his invitation.

Besides, what if the family had sold the farm sometime in the past year? Or what if it sat abandoned—no water, no electricity? How was she supposed to write if she couldn't pop bags of microwave popcorn—her "inspiration food"—or charge her laptop? Writing a book by hand might sound quaint and poetic, but please, the hand cramps alone would take her down.

'Course none of that mattered now that she was probably about to get arrested for trespassing. While dealing with temporary paralysis. Her gloved fingers gripped the lattice, both feet propped in the gaps between criss-crossed wood that suddenly felt about as stable as a tightrope.

"Can we help you?" A man's voice—baritone and hovering somewhere between curious and irritated.

She angled her head just enough to see him. He stood with a wide stance, arms folded over a stretching plaid flannel shirt. No coat. Dark hair, dark eyes, stern jaw. He almost looked like—

"Well?"

A gust of wind clamored through the lattice, jostling the rickety structure. Her grip tightened. "C-Colin told me there was a key hidden in the rain gutter. Which seems like a weird place to me but the door was locked and I . . . " *Rambling.* Another whoosh of cold air and she slapped herself against the lattice. When did the ground get so far away?

"Colin?"

"Uncle Colin?"

The voices sounded in sync, the second one coming from the girl that stood a foot behind the man.

Three thoughts registered then:

1. Colin had a niece.

2. Which probably made the guy her dad, which made him the older brother Colin had mentioned on their date.

3. And this lattice wasn't going to hold her weight much longer.

"When did you talk to Colin?" Intensity pulled the man's tone, his expression taut.

"Maybe we could continue the interrogation after I get down?"

He dropped his arms. "No one's stopping you."

She tested one foot, tried to lower herself to the next gap in the lattice, but the movement shook the entire structure and she froze all over again.

If this is how she was going to die—trying to extricate

herself from an unsteady trellis while an angry handsome man watched—

Her thoughts cut off at the feel of a hand on her waist. She willed her neck to turn. While she'd huddled into a helpless state, he'd climbed onto the outside of the porch. His feet were perched under the base of its railing and one hand held on to the lattice beside her.

"People who are scared of heights shouldn't go scaling a house."

She gritted her teeth. "Not scared of heights."

"Could've fooled me."

"I'm great with heights. It's just that this thing's unsteady."

He held the lattice in place while she descended until they were face to face on the outside of the porch railing. "That's because it was meant as a decoration, not a climbing wall."

This close, she could tell he had a few years on Colin. And unlike his brother's sky blue irises, this Renwycke's eyes were darker, inkier. If he'd shaved today, he didn't look it now.

Stop staring.

"When did you talk to Colin?"

"Why aren't you wearing a coat?"

His eyes narrowed. "What are you doing here?"

"Not much with the warm welcome thing, are you?"

Impossible to tell whether that was a grimace or a smirk. "I can be perfectly welcoming when I know who I'm welcoming. And when they knock on the front door like a normal person. I found you trying to break in."

She shook her head. "Not breaking in. I told you, Colin said there was a key—"

He gave an exasperated grunt and swung one leg over the porch railing, then the other, and faced off with her across the wood barrier. The tips of his shoes touched her boots and his hands griped the railing on either side of hers. He stood so close she could smell a faint rustic hint of aftershave or cologne or . . . she didn't even know but "nice" didn't come close to doing it justice.

But suddenly there wasn't a hint of joking or amusement or even curiosity in his expression anymore. Only a glint that demanded answers edged by something else—what, she wasn't sure.

"Please, just tell me when you talked to Colin. We haven't seen him since last Christmas."

She pinpointed it then, the softness rimming his features. Concern—maybe even worry.

"Almost exactly a year ago." Why the urge to apologize? To do something to erase the disappointment lurking over his face? She didn't even know this man.

Just like she didn't really know Colin, much as she'd liked to pretend over the past months. Oh, what in the world had she been thinking, coming here?

You were thinking you'd find Colin and he'd sweep you off your feet all over again. Ha.

Yeah, well, apparently she wasn't the only one wondering if he'd fallen off the face of the earth.

The girl who'd stood in the yard now climbed the porch steps, floorboards creaking under her shoes. No missing the family resemblance or the spark of recognition playing over her face. "Hey, you're . . . " She stopped beside Colin's brother. "You're Maren Grant, aren't you? Uncle Drew, she wrote that book, the one Colin's on the front of."

Uncle Drew? Not her dad then.

The man's Adam's apple bobbed as he swallowed, his flicker of emotion evaporating as if forced.

The girl pushed around her uncle, and she reached for one of Maren's hands, motioning her over the railing. "I recognize your picture from your website. I loved your first book. I've already got your second one pre-ordered online. Usually I like to buy my books in store but this dumb town doesn't have any bookstores." She flashed a look at Drew. Other than the tick in his jaw, his face had gone unreadable.

She should leave. Just drive away and pretend this never happened. Go ahead and let go of any fantasy involving a future with Colin, too. Because if his family ever *did* get ahold of him and they told him the story of finding her climbing up the lattice . . .

"I can't believe I'm really meeting you." The girl again. "If I go get my book, will you autograph it?"

"Of course."

She pivoted and at the slap of the door, Maren turned back to Drew. She couldn't quite look him in the eye, but even so, she knew he stared.

"I really am sorry about how you found me. It's just Colin said no one lived here. He told me if I ever needed a place to write, I should come here. My second book is a wreck and it's due in a month and a half and I've got a few weeks off teaching so . . ."

Drew didn't say a word, only watched her from behind midnight eyes.

"I didn't really plan to come. It was pure impulse. I have this best friend and she tends to talk me into doing things I wouldn't normally do and she told me to stop asking *what-if* questions and make my own big moment happen, which probably doesn't make any sense to you, but . . ."

Rambling. Again.

It'd help if Drew would say something. Anything to keep her from babbling. But he just stood there . . . mute.

The door squeaked open and the girl returned, the familiar spine of Maren's first book visible from under her arm and a Sharpie in her hand. She budged past her uncle and passed it to Maren, Colin's face glinting on the cover.

Maren cracked open the cover. "What's your name?"

The girl handed Maren the Sharpie. "Winnie. Stupid name, I know."

"I don't think it's stupid." She made the inscription out to Winnie, then signed her name.

Winnie stared at the signed page as if entranced. "I seriously can't believe this is happening."

"At least something good came of me showing up here, yeah?" She chanced a peek at Drew. Still with the folded arms, the probing stare.

Apparently not a talker, this one. Not at all like Colin.

But then, "You were just going to squat in someone else's house?"

"Yes?" She squeaked the answer. And oh, how ridiculous it sounded. Because that's exactly what it was. Who drove three hours on a whim, actually packed a suitcase with enough clothes for a couple weeks, planning to camp out in a house that might or might not be abandoned?

Of course, she'd told herself on the way here she could always find a hotel instead. If nothing else, spend a few days in the town Colin had talked so much about. Maybe find inspiration for her book's setting, Ethan Whitney's hometown.

Drew spun, raking his fingers through wind-tousled hair, voice lowering to mutter. "That's just like Colin. No thought . . ."

Winnie ignored her uncle. "Are you still writing the second book now? Is Ethan Whitney really going back home? He kept saying in the first book he'd never go back and I'm dying to know why. Can you at least give me a hint?"

"To be honest, I'm still figuring it out. I'm only a few chapters into the new story. I was going to work on it here, actually." Drew still had his back to her, his stance rigid. "But um, I should probably get going. Is there a hotel in Maple Valley?"

"No way. Uncle Drew, you can't make her go stay in a hotel. We have plenty of room here. Let her stay tonight."

At Winnie's protest, Drew turned. "Win—"

"I'll tell Mom what happened today, the whole thing. I'll stop complaining about my bed and Maple Valley and everything. Please. This is the only cool thing that's happened since I moved here."

She could practically see it happen—the unraveling of Drew Renwycke's resistance. His shoulders dropped as he sighed and he turned from Winnie to her. "Do you have any luggage with you?"

* * *

HE BLAMED WINNIE'S SMILE.

How was Drew supposed to say no to letting the author stay the night when Winnie's grin—the first he'd seen in weeks—sparked with genuine delight?

Drew plopped Maren's suitcase on the bare mattress in the sprawling attic space that still smelled of freshly sanded wood. Built-in bookcases flanked a curtain-less window that peeked into the yard, the window seat underneath piled with clean sheets and a quilt.

Maren's whispered "whoa" sounded behind him as she ascended into the attic. "What a cool room."

"An empty room, you mean." Because he hadn't planned on a guest. Not until Christmas anyway when Mom and Dad had promised to fly in from Arizona.

But that was still weeks away. Right now he had his hands full enough with a niece who didn't want to be here, a sister who was still trying to settle in while working too many hours at the restaurant, a farm in desperate need of attention.

"It's not entirely empty." Maren strolled past him. She

walked to the window, brushed her hands over the shelves. "These are beautiful. And the window seat? It's so cute."

Not the word he would've chosen, but all the same, he couldn't help a swell of pride at her words. He'd only finished sanding the oak shelves last week. One of these days he'd stain them to match the beams running overhead. And then he'd make a desk for the opposite wall. Maybe see if he could cut a window over there, too, one that overlooked the grove and the west fields. Eventually he'd add a wall and install a master bathroom.

Maren sat in the window seat now, legs stretched out in front of her. Her pale pink scarf hung loose around her neck and her white coat, unbuttoned, had slid off one shoulder. Did she know dirt streaked her jeans from her attempted climb up the trellis? "This is so perfect. The window seat and the view and the quiet. Colin was right. All I'd need is my laptop and . . . " She clamped her lips shut, turning a guarded gaze his way.

And for a solid, uncanny second, the concerns of this day dropped away—Byron's words, Winnie's problems at school, even the strangeness of this author showing up tonight. Because sitting there in front of the attic window, she just looked so . . . right.

Some of her brown hair framed her face in unruly strag-gles, the rest of it pulled into a messy ponytail. Pale green eyes, a smattering of light freckles and pink cheeks. Probably from the chill in this room.

"I can, uh, get a space heater from downstairs. The house is drafty. It might get cold up here tonight and—"

"That's what Colin said." She stood as she interrupted him.

He hadn't noticed how tall she was earlier—almost enough to look him in the eye without craning her neck. "What'd he say?"

"He said the house was drafty, but he liked it that way. He said December is his favorite month here."

There was actually something Colin liked about this place? The thought grappled through him. She had to have seen Colin just before he had last December. Before the argument . . .

"Anyway, I realize this is probably a major imposition, me being here tonight. Like I said, it was a total whim, even showing up here and I had no idea what I'd find and I certainly didn't expect this or . . . or you. I really can stay in a hotel."

He nearly cut her off. "You don't need to stay at a hotel." Because suddenly, for a reason that made absolutely zero sense, he didn't want her to.

"Well, I'll leave in the morning."

He nodded, except now he had the stray temptation to argue that, too. Tell her to camp out in the attic as long as she liked.

It was an impulse he couldn't shake. Not as he helped her make up the bed. Not as he explained where to find the second floor bathroom. And not as he walked her through the rest of the house—the narrow hallway with the cluster of bedrooms on the floor below the attic, the living room and dining room downstairs with the original crown molding and French doors.

Maren stopped at the upright piano that took up half the living room wall—a monstrosity of a thing in dire need of tuning and a new keyboard. Cheaper, probably, to replace the whole thing.

But Drew couldn't make himself. Not with so many memories written into it like swirls in the wood's grain. Lessons with Grandma. Colin's once a week pleas to quit. Leigh's collection of recital ribbons. He'd kept the piano as much for her as anyone, hoping it might bring back the same memories it did for her as it did for him.

She hadn't mentioned it, though. Hadn't tipped open the lid like their guest did now. Maren ran her fingers over yellowed keys as voices drifted from the kitchen. Leigh must be home from work.

"I love pretty old pianos."

"Do you play?" He stepped beside her.

She lifted her gaze. "Barely. I took lessons as a kid, but we moved so often I never made it very far. But I don't need to play well to appreciate an antique like this." She tapped out a scale.

"Well, if you like antiques, you've come to the right place. Maple Valley has more antique stores than churches."

"Colin mentioned that." Her thumb landed on a high C. He could hear the key stick, its tone flat and muted.

"Actually, can I ask, how do you know Colin? I mean, I know he's on your book cover . . ."

She seemed to sigh her words. "We only met once—on the day my publisher did the cover photo shoot. But we got to talking and we went out for coffee and that turned into dinner and . . ."

And of course. He should've known. Colin had wooed her. Because Colin was Colin and that's what he always did. "But you haven't seen him since?"

It was like watching a balloon deflate. "No."

Had she hoped to find his brother here? For all Colin had apparently told this woman about Maple Valley and the farm, had he bothered to tell her he didn't actually live here? That he'd been town-hopping for years?

But before Drew could ask another question, the voices in the kitchen ramped.

"You did *what*?"

Definitely Leigh. Winnie must've made good on her promise to confess.

"Where's your uncle?"

He hurried into the kitchen. Winnie slouched at the small table in the corner of the room. "I'm right here, Leigh." His sister still wore her coat, blond hair pulled into two half-undone braids and a paper sack over her arm. Dinner, probably.

"She broke into the school? And no one bothered to call me?" Exasperation—or maybe exhaustion—strained Leigh's voice.

"The principal called you several times, and I called on my way to school. But we knew you were working, and I figured it'd be best if I went ahead and handled it. I already paid for the window she broke."

Leigh's eyes flashed. "Win, what possessed you to do such a thing?"

"I left my science notes in my locker."

Drew leaned against a counter and blinked. Why hadn't she told him that? Or the principal, for that matter? She'd let them think it was all a rebellious prank. 'Course, either way, she'd thrown a baseball through a window.

Leigh dropped the paper sack on the table, her voice ragged. "I really don't know what to do with you, Win. I though this was the answer, moving here. But I really don't know."

He yearned to reassure his sister. Tell her of course it was the answer. That it'd get better. They'd settle in and Winnie would loosen up. That she didn't have to work so many hours at the restaurant. He could help with their expenses and—

The words gummed in his throat.

And then Winnie jumped from her chair. "Maren!"

His gaze jerked to the doorway. He'd left her standing at the piano. She looked as uncomfortable as he felt, hands hidden inside the long sleeves of her green sweater, only the tips of her fingers poking out.

"Mom, this is Maren Grant. She's the author of that detective book. The one Uncle Colin is on the cover of."

Winnie tugged Maren into the kitchen and he watched as the author's eyes traveled the room. He'd just finished remodeling last month, right before Leigh and Winnie moved in. He'd sanded and painted the old cupboards until they looked brand new—white with frosted glass inserts. He'd built an island for the middle of the room, replaced the old countertops and installed a new farmhouse style sink.

"Mom brought dinner from The Red Door—that's where she works. It looks like an old bank because that's what it is, but this guy named Seth Walker—everybody knows who the Walkers are around here—turned it into a restaurant." Winnie walked a still clearly discomfited Maren to the table. "Mom always brings way too many leftovers home, so there's plenty for you."

Leigh offered Maren a "nice to meet you" before sidling up to him as Winnie continued chattering. "What's she doing here?" she whispered.

"Long story." He shook his head. "Actually not that long. Just weird."

"She's staying?"

"Just for the night. In the attic." Unless he acted on that impulse from earlier and let her stay longer. Pathetic as it sounded, she felt like a link to the brother he hadn't seen since Colin stormed out last Christmas, right after Mom and Dad had made the announcement about their plans to give Drew this property.

Whatever rift had divided Drew from his brother before only intensified in that moment. And he'd been wondering for months if it was a pipedream, thinking he could convince Colin to return.

But maybe if Colin knew Maren was here . . .

"He said December is his favorite month here."

"Yoo-hoo."

The knock on the back door nabbed his attention.

"Drew? It's Diana Pratt. From next door."

Next door? The Pratt Farm was three miles away. Reluctance anchored his steps as he moved to the door, Leigh's knowing chuckle following him across the room.

He dragged the door open. "Hi, Diana."

Her full-wattage smile competed with her flaming red hair for attention. And why was she wearing a dress and heels . . . while standing on his doorstep . . . while holding out a pie?

"Blueberry." She said it without displacing her grin. "Fresh from the oven."

"Well, thanks, but—"

She crowded past him. "You don't know what I had to go through to get Dad to keep his hands off this. He kept asking for a piece, and I kept saying, 'Oh no you don't. I baked this for Drew Renwycke and Drew Renwycke only and—" She cut off at the sight of Leigh and Winnie.

And Maren. Who held a French fry halfway to her mouth, something a little too close to amusement in her emerald eyes.

"Why, Drew . . . " Diana shot him a questioning look. "You already have company?

He looked from Maren back to Diana out the back door window to the woodshed. What he wouldn't give to escape out there.

"Aren't you going to introduce me?"

While he was still cobbling together an answer, Maren crossed the room. She was at his side, arm extended before he could say a word. "Maren Grant. I'm Drew's friend. His good friend."

Um, what?

And why the heck was she lacing her arm through his? Looking up at him as if they hadn't just met an hour ago?

"Well, I . . . that is . . ." Diana stuttered, focus flitting from their threaded arms to the pie in her hands. "I guess . . . here."

She thrust the pie toward Maren, who dropped his arm to accept it, and then Diana retreated from the doorstep as quickly as she'd appeared, the door behind her closing with a wallop.

And his gaze sloped down to Maren. *"What* was that?"

She had a nice laugh—low-pitched and lilting. "I couldn't help it. You looked so uncomfortable. Like you were wearing a shirt three sizes too small."

"But I . . . you . . . she thinks . . ."

"That was kind of the point." She gave his arm a consoling pat. "But I didn't lie. All I said was we're good friends. Way I see it, you found me climbing up the side of your house and instead of calling the police, gave me a place to sleep for the night. That pretty much makes us friends, doesn't it?"

She grinned and held up Diana's offering. "And now we've got pie."

* * *

It's funny how life works, isn't it?

You see, if Diana Pratt hadn't brought over a still-hot blueberry pie on the same Saturday night that Maren Grant found herself sleeping in a farmhouse attic in Iowa, then Maren might never have snuck down from said attic in the middle of the night to eat a second piece.

She might never have found Drew Renwycke already in the kitchen, halfway through a slice of his own.

They might never have argued over whether blueberry pie is best served hot or cold.*

And Drew might never have found himself maybe kinda sorta

liking the author from the attic. Enough that an unbidden, spontaneous side of him took over and he surprised himself with his own words.

But Diana did bring over a still-hot blueberry pie.

Maren did sneak down from the attic.

She did find Drew and they did argue over pie temperature.

And Drew did surprise himself when he said, "Hey, you can stay. In the attic, I mean. To write. If you want. If it's helpful. However long you need to."

And so she did.

---

*For the record, Maren voted hot. Drew voted cold. They both voted á la mode. Because, honestly, what's the point of pie without ice cream?

CHAPTER 4

*M*aren was beginning to think Drew Renwycke had secrets.

Either that or he was out to give "strong, silent type" new meaning.

"So you really aren't going to tell me what's happening right now?"

A snappish, winter air carried his answer. "Just wait. You'll see."

The wind grappled with the awnings hanging over quaint storefronts and tipped the tinseled decorations dangling from old-fashioned lampposts. They stood in the center of the town square. Glistening snow ribboned over craggy branches and capped the buildings that wrapped around the oblong block of white-swathed lawn. Christmas greenery traced the band shell in the corner and twinkle lights wrapped around every tree trunk in sight.

So this was Maple Valley. A week in Iowa and this was the first Maren was seeing of the actual town.

If only she had any idea what was going on. The crowd gathering around the square hummed with anticipation. And next to her, Drew seemed to be growing more agitated by the second. He'd zipped and unzipped his vest at least a dozen times.

"Well, if you won't tell me what's about to happen, at least tell me about Maple Valley. We drove past a sign for a historic railroad and museum. What's that? And I heard Winnie talking about the restaurant where Leigh works. She said it's inside an old bank or something?"

"Tell me again how tagging along with me today counts as work?"

There he went with the zipper again. Did the man never wear an actual coat? How many times had she seen him from the attic window traipsing out to the barn, the shed, that smaller building Winnie told her was his workshop, never more than a fleece pullover or the navy blue puff vest thing he wore now? Couldn't possibly be enough to keep him warm. At least he wore gloves—even if they were the kind without the fingertips.

"It's 'work' because I'm researching your town, Drew. The bulk of my second book takes place in Ethan Whitney's hometown. I need inspiration."

She'd managed to eke out a good six chapters in the past seven days, but as soon as her fictional detective had stepped foot in his still unnamed town—first scene of chapter seven— he'd gone as silent as the man standing next to her.

"In the first book, I built up Ethan's hometown to be this intriguing, almost mysterious place."

Drew rubbed one hand over his stubbled jaw. "Hate to tell you this, but Maple Valley's about as mysterious as a dandelion."

Maybe not, but it was charming all the same. As if the town founders had crawled inside Norman Rockwell's imagination before setting up camp. And it wasn't just the town square. On the way into town they'd driven over an arched bridge, the cobalt waters underneath tussling against chunks of ice. Drew had broken his quiet streak long enough to tell her about the flooding this past fall—how the whole town had pulled together to line the river's banks with sand bags.

"Maybe it's not mysterious, but I bet it has personality. That's what Colin said."

Was she imagining it or did Drew's already dusky eyes darken? "Huh."

The clumps of people around them seemed to be forming into a fanning shape in front of a man with a megaphone. Wait, a megaphone? Beside him, two other men were moving a pristine bench—had to be brand new—into a freshly shoveled slat of ground underneath an unlit lamppost.

Drew's focus was on the activity in front of them. And when he spoke, his tone echoed with distance. "It's just interesting, I guess—and a little unbelievable—that Colin would talk so much about Maple Valley when he hasn't bothered to come home in so long. And last time I talked to him . . ."

She knew it was coming even before it happened. The trail of thought cut off before it reached an end. Drew always did that, clammed up when conversation approached Colin.

Not that they'd had *that* many conversations in the past week. She'd spent most of her time holed up in the attic.

And Drew? Well, the man would make an Olympic athlete look lazy. The light hadn't gone out in his woodshop until after eleven last night, long after she'd set aside her laptop in favor of a book.

On past nights, she'd happened upon him in the second floor hallway on her way from the bathroom—or down in the kitchen when she'd popped her nightly bag of popcorn. Chance encounters.

But last night she'd purposely waited in the stairwell to hear his footsteps. When he'd appeared, smelling of sawdust and soap, she'd seen the weariness etched into his eyes. And wondered, not for the first time and certainly not for the last, what it was that haunted him. And what it had to do with Colin.

And maybe, truly, that's why she'd really invited herself along today. Not just to explore this town, but to figure out this man who lived with his sister and doted on his niece and clearly worried about his brother.

"Drew—"

Almost as if sensing she was about to ask a question he didn't want to answer, Drew dropped his arms and turned to her. "Okay, I'll tell you a fun fact about Maple Valley. If you're anywhere in town where there's a crowd of people and you start singing a song, everyone will eventually start singing. Doesn't matter what song it is. Someone will know it and join in and then pretty soon, everyone's singing."

"Like in a musical?"

"Just like."

"Don't know if I can believe that. I mean, I get that it's quirky here. Or in Winnie's words, 'insanely weird,' but that seems improbable."

He nearly smiled. "You could start singing something and see for yourself."

"And risk the chance that you're just pranking me? That everyone won't turn to stare at the stranger?"

The breeze riffled through his hair. "Oh, you're definitely not a stranger. You've been here a week. You've been spotted by a neighbor. Most people here probably know your life story by now."

"Too bad for them it's not a more exciting—"

She was interrupted by the sound of a man clearing his throat into the megaphone. "Attention, folks. Attention, everyone."

"Do you really need the megaphone, Milt?" a voice called from the crowd, laughter following his teasing question.

"That's Case Walker." Drew leaned down. "Probably the most well-known person in town. Which isn't saying much 'cause everyone knows everyone here. But he's a fixture."

"And the guy with the megaphone?"

"The mayor. Milton Briggs."

"So this is like a town meeting or something."

Drew folded his arms again. "Or something."

"We're here today for a wonderful reason." The mayor's voice boomed, must've come out even louder than he expected. Because he shrugged and tossed the megaphone into the snow. "As you all know, in the tornado this summer, every single bench in the town square either disappeared or was damaged so badly it ended up in the bonfire."

Maren inched closer to Drew. "Wait, there was a tornado this year, too? In addition to the flood?"

Drew only nodded.

"But thanks to a talented townsperson—a recently returned townsperson, at that—the square will be bench-less no more!" The mayor spread his arms at the announcement.

"Are we supposed to clap?" She whispered the question to Drew.

But before he could answer, the mayor was talking again, gesturing, and then, suddenly, pointing at...Drew?

"And this is the fine young man who's made it happen, folks. Drew Renwycke delivered this bench just yesterday. And has promised six more just like it by the Christmas carnival."

Maren felt her own jaw drop as the applause started. "This whole thing is about you?"

The applause started then—and in earnest. People clapped him on the back, the mayor kept talking, and Drew—poor Drew—looked ready to bolt.

"Come up here, Drew. I want you to be the first one to sit on the bench."

Drew held up one hand. "That's really okay. I—"

"Nonsense. Get up here. Bring your girlfriend, too."

Wait, he didn't mean . . .

"That'd be you, Maren," Drew's exasperated whisper warmed her cheeks.

"But—"

"Remember? Diana Pratt? The pie?"

The next five minutes passed in a blur of hilarity. Drew was practically pushed to the front of the crowd, Maren with him. The mayor made a show of insisting Drew be the first one to sit in the new bench. Again, with Maren. A reporter named Amelia took their picture.

Drew turned a hundred shades of red.

The mayor kept talking.

And Maren could hardly hold in her laughter.

"Don't giggle," Drew hissed through a barely contained grin. "Not while Mayor Milt is waxing eloquent. If you laugh, I'll laugh."

"Can't help it." Her whisper crackled with amusement.

"Think about something serious. Tornadoes. Cavities. Bee stings."

"Bee stings?"

He turned his navy eyes on her, gaze saturated with exaggerated gravity. "Deadlines."

"Ooh, good one." She swallowed another laugh. "I just had no idea your 'errand' included being honored in front of half the town."

"Believe me, I didn't either." He rubbed his hands over his jeans. "Seriously, any chance to make a fuss about something, this town jumps at it. If it's not festivals and fairs every weekend, it's silly impromptu ceremonies in the park and—"

"But you built this." She heard the awe infused in her whisper. "It's really pretty, Drew. And you're making more? And . . . " And the realization whooshed in then, as the townspeople clapped at whatever the mayor had just said. That window seat in the attic. The shelves. The completely remodeled kitchen.

"It's all you, isn't it? All the renovations at the house." Why hadn't it registered before?

He only shrugged. "I like building things."

"Well, you're good at it."

His arms might be folded, his stance stubborn or maybe just embarrassed. But the crinkles at the corners of his eyes, that almost-smile again, told her he liked hearing it. "So how long do we have to sit here?"

"Eh, Milt usually cuts off after thirty minutes or so." He leaned toward her then, voice still low. "But there's a coffee shop on the riverfront. It's called Coffee Coffee. Owner is this young girl—kinda sarcastic, pretty much like how I bet Win will be at twenty-one—but anyway she makes good coffee."

"Yeah?"

"If you want, we could grab some. Then I could give you a tour of the town. You can do all your research or whatever."

She had no clue why he offered.

But no way was she turning him down.

* * *

How had he let Maren talk him into this?

Drew stood in the doorway of the century-old church at the corner of Oak Street and Pine. Behind him, the breeze whirred through wrinkled branches and shuffled over the ice-clogged waters of the Blaine River.

The door clanged shut behind him.

"We shouldn't be here."

Maren's laughter echoed off the walls of the church sanctuary. Excitement radiated in her eyes and she spun on her heels to face him, already halfway up the aisle leading to the front of the church, where a side door opened into the bell tower.

He should never have told her about the bell. Probably shouldn't have spent the entire day carting her around town either. They'd had lunch at The Mandarin—his favorite local hole-in-the-wall, a Chinese restaurant run by a Scottish expat named Alec. They'd visited the library, housed in an old mansion, stopped at a couple antique shops and he'd even driven her past the railroad and museum.

And somewhere along the way, he'd told her about the church bell.

Shadows huddled against the walls and a branch rapped into the stained glass window up front. "Are you scared, Drew?"

He stalked down the aisle, footsteps like cannon booms in the quiet. "Do I look scared?"

Sometime during the day, she'd given up on the barrettes that'd held her hair away from her face this morning. It hung in willful twists over her shoulders now. She loosened her scarf as he reached her. "No, you don't look scared. You do, however, look wholly disapproving."

"Because I am. I tell you one silly story about the church bell tower and suddenly we're breaking in—"

She flopped her mitten in front of his face. "Not breaking in. The door was unlocked."

"Still. If we get caught and arrested—"

"Then that infamous Maple Valley rumor mill will have its story of the week." Her smile lit her up her face.

Oh, probably the Maple Valley gossip superhighway already had plenty to say about the Renwyckes. Big enough news that a bestselling author was camping out at the farm. But after this morning, he was pretty sure the whole town already had them married off.

Too bad no one knew of Maren Grant's affection for her

cover model. Drew might not be the most intuitive guy in the world, but he didn't have to be an Ethan Whitney type—that was the name of her detective, right?—to pick up on the fact that Miss Author had a thing for Colin.

AKA the brother who couldn't deign to answer even one of Drew's slew of phone calls.

He'd really thought that first night when Maren showed up that maybe if his family wasn't enough to get Colin home, she might be. Maybe that's why he'd made such an impulsive invitation for her to stay.

But a week's worth of unanswered calls and texts and he'd long since abandoned that wishful thinking.

"Fine," he said now. "I give. We climb the tower. We ring the bell. And then we get out of here."

Maren tucked her mittens in her pockets. "Don't forget the make-a-wish part."

It was Maple Valley lore—the old church's broken bell and its mythical ability to grant wishes. The bell was more for show than anything—no pull-rope or controls. Only time it ever rang was when someone climbed the tower and gave it a heave by hand. Usually bored teenagers.

Well, and tonight, the unruly author currently living in his house.

In the past week and a half, she'd become a fixture in the attic—her form in the window seat visible from the wood-shop, the machine shed, pretty much anywhere in the farmyard.

And it hit him now—as he followed her toward the side door leading into the sliver of bell tower room—he'd gotten used to seeing her up there. To not being the only one home during the day. To the late night snatches of conversation when he finally abandoned the woodshop and she crept downstairs for her nightly bag of popcorn.

She was an odd mix, this author. Intensely focused on her

writing and insistent it was her much more spontaneous friend Remy who'd talked her into her spur-of-the-moment trip to Iowa. But she was impulsive enough to stay. Not just willing but delighted to set aside her work for a day of exploring his peculiar little town.

Maren stood now at the base of the ladder leading up to the bell. Chilly night air tunneled down the tower, the glint of starlight barely visible through the opening at the top. Pale moonlight slicked over her form as she tipped her head to stare up the ladder.

"Remembering a certain climb up the side of my house, are we?"

He shouldn't enjoy it so much—teasing her, watching her green eyes flash and her nose wrinkle as she searched for a comeback. "I'm not scared, if that's what you're insinuating."

"In that case—" He held out one hand toward the ladder. "After you."

Hesitance slowed her movement, but she grasped a rung with both hands and started her climb. He hefted himself up behind her. Leigh and Winnie probably wondered where they were. And it was supposed to snow again later this week—which meant he really should've been home tonight finishing up the patchwork to the machine shed roof. And...

And he could think of a hundred things he *should* be doing.

But he couldn't remember when he'd had such a carefree day. Certainly not since moving back to Maple Valley. Maybe not since Mom and Dad had closed up the farm and moved to Arizona and whether they'd meant to or not, left him with the weight of family responsibility.

Maren reached the top of the metal ladder and with nimble movements, stepped onto the ledge jutting from the tower's interior brick wall. He climbed off after her, the metal under his feet clanging.

The gap between the narrow ledge and the bell was like a gulf, and he could sense Maren's enthusiasm slipping, almost hear the uptick in her heartbeat.

Or maybe that was his own heart murmuring that this here—the close quarters, the vanilla smell of her hair, and the very real desire to protect her—it was messing with his common sense. He cleared his throat, shucking away any stray sparks for the nonsense they were.

He was just tired. Too many fourteen-, sixteen-hour days making repairs to the house, trying to learn his way around the machinery in the shed, convincing himself he could make this work on his own. "All right, Grant, we came this far."

Her gaze was on the shadows below. "That's an awfully big drop."

"You climbed all this way. Don't chicken out now." With barely a thought, he reached for her hand. Her fingers were ice cold but they grasped his like a lifeline. "I gotcha."

She looked from him to the bell and back to him again. "Promise?"

His grip tightened and he nodded.

It must have been enough for her because she reached out then—tentatively at first and then with the same look of resolve he'd seen on her face this morning as she filled her notebook with notes about Maple Valley. Her hand connected with the bell and she gave it a push.

The clash reverberated through the narrow tower, brash and echoing. Maren thrust herself back against the wall, one hand still clinging to his as the other came up to grab his arm. Her sigh of relief released in a whoosh and he couldn't help a laugh.

"Well done." He had to shout to be heard over the bell. "What'd you wish for?"

"Can't tell you or it won't come true."

"This isn't candles on a birthday cake. Come on, you

dragged me all the way up here. Least you can do is tell me what you're going to get out of it."

"Fine. I wished I'd get this book done." The bell's clatter slowed and her voice lowered. "And that my editor would like it and it'd do the series justice and readers would eat it up. And that I'd somehow figure out how to balance both writing and teaching so I could have more free time. And . . . " She took a breath. "That I'd know what to write next."

The bell's last echo gave way to silence. "That's all?"

The wry comment drew a laugh. Good, because she'd almost started to look . . . he didn't know, sad or something. Wistful, that might be the word.

Maren tipped her gaze to meet his. "Although if I get this book done, it'll be more thanks to you than a bell tower wish. I hope you know I know that. Letting me stay on the farm, it's exactly what I needed." Her pause stretched as the breeze tugged on the strands of hair around her face. "He said you were like this, you know."

"Who said I was like what?"

"Colin."

Drew released her hand.

"I asked him about his family and he mentioned both you and Leigh. He said you're the kind of person who sees a need and makes sure it's met."

Didn't sound like Colin. But maybe he'd been feeling extra gracious the night of their date.

"That's why you agreed to let me stay, isn't it? And why you spent all day showing me your town when I know you had work to do. And it's what you're doing for Leigh and Winnie, isn't it? You're helping Leigh get back on her feet and trying to give Winnie the stability she's never had."

He took a breath and let it out slowly. "How much has Winnie told you?"

Her hair brushed over his arm as she shook her head. "Not much. Just that Leigh did a couple stints in a recovery center."

"More than a couple. Pretty much the first decade of Win's life, Leigh was in and out of facilities."

The acknowledgement was enough to bring too many memories to the surface. Sobbing phone calls in the middle of the night—calls Leigh didn't even remember making in the morning. The smell of her apartment after her latest binge. The pit in his stomach whenever he left her at another recovery center in another town in another state.

The look in Winnie's eyes.

The wind howled through the tower's opening. "Win's been shipped around from relative to relative for years. This past year is the longest she's been with Leigh."

"What about her dad?"

The pit in his stomach threatened to rise up and choke him. "Leigh's high school boyfriend. Winnie stayed with him a few times, but last I heard, he lives in California now. If we're all lucky, he'll stay there."

And Drew wouldn't have to see him again. Wouldn't have to remember . . .

If I'd just paid attention.

Cared more about his siblings than his friends, the party, the thrill of attention...

"I wasn't all the way honest." Maren's voice cut in.

He blinked. "Huh?"

"About my wish. I didn't just wish to finish my book. I also wished to know I belong in a place as much as you know you belong here. Or maybe . . . " Her voice was soft. "To know I'm wanted in a place as much as you want your family here."

Her honesty hovered in the quiet, gliding past the swell of his memories and landing under his skin.

"It's so great, Drew. What you're doing for them."

"Yes . . . well . . . " No words. Only a warmth he didn't understand.

And then Maren elbowed him. "Your turn." She nudged her head toward the bell.

"We came up here for you, not me."

"In your own words, 'We came all this way. Don't chicken out.'" She grasped his hand. "And I promise not to let you fall."

He laughed then and with a lightness that felt foreign, he reached forward and rang the bell.

Only when it quieted did Maren turn to him.

"What'd *you* wish for?" Her voice was soft and he let himself look down at her. Under the ogling eyes of the stars, her own appeared luminous, watchful. As if his answer might unlock the door to secrets.

And he didn't know why he said it. But he did. "I wished Colin would come home. That we could all be together for Christmas."

He couldn't make himself look away as she let his answer linger in the cool night air before placing one hand on his arm. "Then let's go get him."

* * *

UNFORTUNATELY, *our famous author and aspiring farmer were not able to leave that very night. In fact, it would be another week before they would set out to find our elusive book cover model.*

Five things happened in that week:

1. Inspired by the charming town of Maple Valley and the mysterious aura of the bell tower, Maren added another twenty-three thousand words to her novel.

2. Drew called his brother's former talent agency . . . only to discover Colin was no longer with the agency. He did, however, obtain what he hoped was a current address.

3. Drew and Maren both attended Winnie's school choir

Christmas concert. It was, to put it nicely, rather long. But this is what you do when you're a doting uncle and an author-in-resi-dence-who-is-beginning-to-feel-like-family.

4. Drew introduced Maren to the wonder of stove-popped popcorn, forever ruining her for microwave popcorn.

5. Diana Pratt gave up.

CHAPTER 5

*I*f all went according to plan, after twelve months of pining and nostalgic mental replays, Maren would see Colin Renwycke again tonight.

If only Drew seemed half as hopeful.

In the driver's seat of his truck, Drew flipped down the sunvisor. The winter day glowed under a white sun, nothing but snow-packed fields stretching on either side of the highway. "Des Moines. One measly hour away and he couldn't even call to let us know he's that close? What's he even doing there?"

It had to be the sixth or seventh time he'd muttered the question since the silhouetted lines of Maple Valley faded in the distance fifteen minutes ago.

And for the sixth or seventh time, Maren pilfered past a canned response for something to sway Drew's skepticism. "Maybe he signed with a new talent agency. Maybe there's some great community theater there. He wants to be an actor, so . . ."

Drew only tipped his sunglasses over his eyes. But the tick in his jaw told her what his words didn't: He wasn't nearly as hopeful. He was worried about the kind of state they'd find his brother in.

It just didn't make sense—all his doubts about Colin. The Colin Renwycke she'd met this time last year was outgoing, confident, practically charismatic. He'd had plans and goals and enough verve to convince her he'd reach every one.

Then again, she'd only spent one evening with Colin. Drew had grown up with him. Clearly *something* had gone awry in this family. And despite his uncertainty, Drew was doing all he could to right whatever had gone wrong.

She had to admire the man for that. Even if he did make for a gruff road trip companion. She should've been prepared for his bordering on brooding company when he'd argued with her over the merits of flavored coffee at Coffee Coffee this morning.

[Narrator]

Oh, this is good. Let's backtrack . . .

Maren: Peppermint mocha, extra whip, lots of sprinkles.

Drew: Just coffee, please. Black.

Maren: You don't even want any creamer? Or a shot of hazelnut or raspberry or something?

Drew: You've lived in my house for two weeks now, Grant. We've had coffee every day this week after Winnie went to school. Did I ever once doll it up?

Maren: No, but this is a special occasion. We're road-tripping.

Drew: We're driving an hour and fifteen minutes.

Maren: Have you ever even had a mocha?

Drew: I had a cappuccino from a gas station once. It was like drinking a melted candy bar.

Maren: That actually sounds amazing.

Drew: It was gross. And lukewarm.

Maren: And not at all the same thing as a mocha made by a barista who knows what she's doing.

Yes, this went on for ten minutes.

For reals.

What had been amazing, though, is that after just two weeks in town, Maren had recognized at least a half-dozen faces in the coffee shop. Like the raven-haired owner, Megan, just as surly as Drew had claimed but likable all the same. And Raegan Walker, cousin to the man who'd opened the restaurant where Leigh worked, and her dad, Case Walker, the guy Drew had pointed out at the bench unveiling in the park. The man could've been a stand-in for John Wayne. She'd spotted Amelia from the newspaper, Sunny Klassen, who ran the hardware store where Drew shopped, and a high school kid named Webster Hawks, who'd apparently become a late-season football star.

It'd grown on her, this town and its people. Or perhaps not grown so much as promptly attached itself to her heart. Ever since that day Drew had shown her around and followed her up the bell tower.

"So." Drew steered his truck around a curve. "How's the book coming along?"

"The book's fine. I'm actually pretty happy with it at this point."

"Good."

Not one to prattle on, this man, but he had a way of saying more in one word than most could in rambling replies. And in his "good," she heard his hint of gratification, same timbre in his voice when Winnie came home with a pleasing grade report or Leigh mentioned she might apply for an assistant manager position at the restaurant. He felt a part of it—didn't he?—their lives, their progress.

And he was. It was his attic where she'd finally found the productivity she'd needed. It was seeing his work ethic that pushed her to fit in more writing hours each day than she would've normally. It was his town that'd inspired a new depth in Ethan Whitney's latest storyline.

"Listen, I should probably . . . " Drew's hands slid down the steering wheel as he fumbled for words. "I should probably warn you about what we might . . . "

He pressed his lips together and reached up to pull off his sunglasses. The sunlight turned his eyes such a strobing blue, she had to look away to keep from staring.

"I should just tell you," he finally sputtered. "The last time I saw Colin...it wasn't good. We argued and it got ugly. Actually most of the times we've seen each other in the past few years have been that way. He might not be all that happy to see me."

"He didn't seem overly antagonistic toward you when he talked about you."

Snow flurries twisted in the air outside the car. "Of course he didn't. He was on a date with a pretty girl."

In other words, Colin was too suave to air his dirty family laundry in front of her. Fair enough. But still. "I just think if it's been that long since you've seen him, you should hold out hope. A lot can change in a year. He might not be the same person." Who it seemed, reading between Drew's sparsely uttered lines, must've been something of a party guy. "He's probably changed. Matured. People do that, you know."

Drew didn't reply so much as grunt, his grip tightening on the steering wheel as he avoided a curling snow drift.

She waited minutes before speaking again. "Are we going to hit bad weather?"

"Maybe a little snow. Nothing I can't handle."

She believed that. She'd watched from the attic window a couple days ago as he attacked the latest round of snow with a snow blower. And she'd seen him throw tire chains in the truck bed before leaving.

Silence pattered through the front seat then, accompanied only by the rumble of the engine and the swiping of the windshield wipers as the snow picked up. Too, the chugging puffs of warm air from the heater.

And the first hint of her own doubt whispering in.

What if the Colin you met last year, the man you've pictured in your daydreams ever since, isn't the person you think he is?

What if he wasn't anything like the man she remembered? Nothing at all like Ethan Whitney, the man he portrayed—solid and dependable, the kind of man a person could count on?

What if men like Ethan Whitney don't even exist?

Just like Dean had said.

She leaned her head back against the headrest, closing her eyes against the memory but it barreled in anyway.

"You spend hours locked away working on this thing." Dean had held up the story notes he found scattered on her couch. *"I swear, you care more about this fictional person than me."*

"That's not true—"

"He's not even realistic. Look at these notes. He's a flippin' caricature."

"He's not. Yes, he's a good guy, but he's also layered. And flawed. He has weaknesses. You haven't read the book."

"This isn't working, Mare."

It'd unraveled from there. A year-long relationship, done, just like that. Because the real man in her real life resented the fake one in her fictional world.

But what if Dean had a point? Maybe even more than one? She *had* spent crazy amounts of time on that book, let it consume her. She *had* started to see this made-up character as the key to her publishing dream coming true. She'd known Ethan Whitney would make readers swoon because he'd made *her* swoon.

But in the process of writing him into existence, had she unintentionally made Dean feel less-than?

"I'm just worried that . . . maybe you're hoping for something that isn't going to happen."

Maren's eyes opened to see Drew's probing gaze on her once more. Right, they were talking about Colin. Not Dean.

A howling wind brushed a wave of white over the road in front of them. "I'm just hoping we make it to Des Moines safely. That's all."

Another quiet minute passed, then two, her what-ifs fading as weather worry took their place. If the wind kept up and the snow fell any thicker, they could be on their way to a whiteout.

"You sure you're okay driving through this?"

Drew only nodded, his quiet confidence almost enough to smooth her concerns.

"You know, my parents met in a blizzard." The cold of the near-storm outside seemed to claw through the passenger window.

"Oh yeah?" Drew turned up the heat at her shiver.

"They were at ski lodge in Colorado. I heard the story over and over growing up Dad was working at the lodge, his first job out of college. Mom was a junior on a winter break trip with friends. There was a snowstorm on the last day of the trip, so instead of skiing, Mom spent the whole day with the cute ski instructor."

"And they lived happily ever after?"

Maren laughed. "Actually, Mom went back to college and Dad went back to his everyday life. They wrote a couple letters, but that was it. And they didn't meet again until two years later when Dad got a job managing a lakeside resort in Minnesota. Just happened to be in Mom's hometown. They instantly reconnected and get this, got married just two months later."

Drew whistled. "Growing up with a story like that, I'm

surprised you don't write romances for a living instead of mysteries."

"But the best is when Mom talks about the moment they first met, back in that ski lodge." Maren reached for the lever on the side of her seat that tipped it back. "According to her, she knew even back then that Dad was the man she'd marry. That even when the trip was over and the letters stopped, she just knew—the moment was that magical and unforgettable." She propped her feet on the dash.

"You believe that?" It wasn't doubt in Drew's voice so much as curiosity.

"Yes, but I'm a writer, Drew. We tend to believe in grand romance and enchanted moments." She downed the last of her mocha. "Probably sounds silly."

The car's heater filled the air with warmth even as the snow hurled outside. Drew looked over. "Not so silly."

* * *

AN ANGRY WIND flung itself against Drew's truck, plastering his windshield with white. The near-blizzard had charged in seemingly out of nowhere, swift and harsh. His headlights barely cut through the storm—sheets of snow twisting in the wind to turn the road treacherous.

At least it wasn't dark. And if his GPS knew what it was talking about, they'd be at Colin's place within minutes. Stripped trees bent over the Des Moines street, branches iced and weather-weary. Through hazy white, he could see snowdrifts covering porch steps and slanting along rooftops.

He'd tried calling Colin one more time this morning. Left one more veiled message.

"Hey, Col, it's me. I'm to the point of thinking maybe this isn't your number anymore. But if it is and if you get this, we're on our way—Maren and I. Maren's the author I told you about a few

messages ago. I'm sure you remember her. Um . . . so maybe we'll see you in a couple hours?"

"You don't understand, Drew." Maren's voice cut into his thoughts, her jaunty tone pushing back at the reluctance needling through him. "Every single Starburst in this package was pink. Every single one. I saved the wrappers as evidence." She nudged his arm with her elbow, motioning to her purse sitting open in her lap. "See? Proof."

"I believe you, Mare. I just can't believe we've been talking about Starbursts for twenty minutes now." Ever since she'd pulled a bag from the backseat and announced, "Roadtrip snacks!"

Snacks for a drive that barely maxed at an hour and fifteen minutes. She was way too excited for this.

And way too naïve about his brother.

"All. Pink. Has that ever happened to anybody ever?"

"I don't know. Maybe we should be calling CNN. Or at least the *Maple Valley News.*"

The truck lurched just then as his tires hit something—a snowdrift, a patch of ice, he didn't know and didn't have time to think as the vehicle whipped into a spin. His gasp was lost in the sound of squealing tires and his foot slamming into the brakes. The curb came careening into view.

He winced as he heard the clunk of Maren's head hitting her window as his antilock brakes kicked in. Maren's computer bag and purse, the bag of snacks, everything went flying, and the tread of his tires growled over slick road. But as quickly as the truck had spun out, it shuddered to a stop. For a shocked, silent second, his heart pummeled his rib cage . . . until he jerked against his seatbelt to face Maren. "Are you okay?"

Eyes wide, face white, she nodded.

"Are you sure? I think you hit your head." He reached out one hand to brush her hair away and let his fingers feather over her forehead. No cuts but he could already see a splotch of red that would likely be a bruise before morning.

His gaze dipped down to meet her still-wide eyes. She swallowed.

"It's . . . it's not even just that all the Starbursts were pink, but also the fact that that's my favorite flavor." Her grin started in one corner of her lips before filling out.

And despite his truck sitting at an angle in the road, idling against a curbside snowdrift while the wind pounded outside, and his white-knuckled grip on the steering wheel, he laughed. "You're a nut."

"And you're the calmest driver I've ever met. I'd have panicked and driven into a tree if I was in your seat."

"Well, I need to keep you safe. Winnie would kill me if something happened to you before you finished your next book."

With a shaky breath, he shifted into reverse and fought against spinning tires until he'd freed them from the snowdrift. The truck slogged forward then, and he peered through whipping snow, scanning the numbers on houses that look as fatigued as he was beginning to feel. Worn siding and crumbling brick. A strand of Christmas lights had detached from the house on the corner and dangled to the porch floor.

But maybe . . . maybe this wouldn't be as bad as he was imagining. Maybe Colin had simply lost his phone and that's why he hadn't returned any of Drew's calls. Maybe he was doing well and had put last year's tussle behind him and would welcome Drew with open arms and . . .

And maybe Maren is seriously rubbing off on you.

One block more and he found it. *1226 Cedar Street.* Plastic covered the windows, flapping in the wind. Snow layered the lawn and edged up to the house—no sign of footprints or shovel tracks.

Maren had her seatbelt off before Drew had even parked

in the unshoveled driveway.

"I think I should probably go in first."

If Maren wanted to argue, she must've thought twice. Because she only nodded and settled back against her seat.

He opened his door, a blast of frosty air barreling in. "Go ahead and keep the truck running and the heat on." He closed the door and tromped through snow that reached his knees. It trickled into his shoes, dampening his socks by the time he reached the front door. He knocked, then reached down to brush the snow from his pants.

Nothing.

He knocked again.

The storm door swung open.

His brother's disgruntled form stared at him on the other side of the screen door—wrinkled t-shirt and sweatpants, a beard, tousled hair. And not even a hint of welcome.

"Drew."

Wind chimes from the porch next door clashed. Had Colin just woken up? After one in the afternoon? "So you, uh, didn't get my messages?"

Colin didn't answer, only turned away from the door, padded footsteps sounding over hard floors.

"Ooo-kay." The word came out a drawled sigh.

But at least Colin hadn't slammed the door. Apparently that was as much of a welcome as Drew was going to get. With one last glance over his shoulder to where Maren waited in the car, he slung open the screen door and stepped inside.

Colin sat at the bottom of an open staircase, pulling a pair of socks over his feet. Drew's gaze roved past the stairs into the living room—open pizza box on a coffee table crowded with magazines. Garments hanging over a couch, a couple chairs. A muted game show flickered from the TV that took up half of one wall.

"So what do you want? Life update?" Colin stood now, raking his fingers through his hair. "Highlight reel: Booked two commercials and a magazine spread earlier this year. Lately? Nothing. So I'm working in the theatre department at Drake University and playing cell phone salesman in my off-hours."

A row of beer cans lined a living room windowsill. "And throwing parties for students?" Drew regretted the words the second they slipped out.

Colin swiped a sweatshirt from over the bannister and yanked it on. Ire laced his laughter. "One year and you haven't changed a bit, big brother."

And obviously Colin hadn't either.

Not fair.

Just because this place looked and smelled like a frat house didn't mean Colin was still living that life.

He doesn't need your judgment. He needs . . .

Well, Drew didn't know what Colin needed. And maybe that was the problem. When Mom and Dad had moved south several years ago, thrown up their hands and cut Colin off, Drew had tried to step in. He'd paid Colin's rent for a full year, for one thing. Sent money when his brother was between modeling gigs. Called and visited and did all he could to wheedle Colin into something resembling adult-hood, maturity.

But clearly he'd always gone about it wrong. Because Colin had clung to the same-old, same-old. Wild parties that led to damaged property and fines. Lavish spending. Wasting the few good job opportunities he'd had.

"If it's been that long since you've seen him, maybe you shouldn't assume he's the same guy he was back then."

Maren's words. Idealistic and hopeful. Maybe . . .

"Look." Colin pulled a water bottle from between two

couch cushions and uncapped it. "If you're here because you heard about me and that student—"

"What?"

"It's all a stupid misunderstanding. It was just one dumb kiss at one cast after-party and she goes and blows the whole thing out of proportion. I'm appealing the college board's decision and—"

Drew couldn't listen to this. "And you think I'm the one who hasn't changed?"

Colin capped his bottle and chucked it at the beer cans in the windowsill. "Why are you even here?"

Drew moved across the room, booting a paper plate out of the way. "Because I had the crazy thought in my head that maybe—just maybe—you'd like to actually come home for Christmas. See your sister and your niece. See the farm and all the work I've done—"

"You're wasting your time on that place?"

"And because I've got an author out in the car who happens to think you're some kind of dreamy Prince Charming. Man, if I ever had any doubt of your acting skills . . . " He cut off at the sight of Colin scratching his beard.

"An author?"

"Maren Grant. You went on a date with her. You were on the cover of her book and . . . " He shook his head. "You don't even remember her, do you?" Whatever disappointment he'd felt in the past few minutes, it was nothing to the disenchantment he knew Maren would feel if she realized Colin Renwycke didn't even recall her name.

"I remember the book cover shoot." Colin shrugged. "And yeah, I hung out with the author afterward, but . . . " Another shrug. "Why's she with you?"

He should just lie to Maren. Go back out to the car and tell her Colin wasn't home. That the man who'd answered the door was someone else. They could find a restaurant or hotel or something, wait out the storm and then go home and pretend this never happened.

"Stop it, Drew." Colin moved around the couch.

"Stop what?"

"Stop looking at me like I'm a colossal disappointment."

"I'm not—"

Colin jerked forward. "You are. You always do."

Too familiar, this argument. Like an echo of the past. And suddenly it was last year, the day after Christmas and they were standing outside the farmhouse—Colin having just returned home after a night of partying and Drew picking the wrong time to lecture him.

He should've known to stand down. Should've known he was probably the last person Colin wanted to hear from, considering it was just the day before Dad had made a show of handing him the deed to the farmland. Colin had walked out—wordless—soon after.

But instead of guarding his words, he'd let loose.

Can't you see what you're doing to yourself? Haven't you learned anything from what Leigh's been through?

Colin, still hung over from the night before, had thrown the first punch.

"We don't have to do this again, Colin."

"I'm not the one who showed up out of the blue."

"I'm trying to help you."

"I never asked for your help." His brother shoved him backward.

The bookcase behind him rattled as he slammed into it. And the next thing he knew, he had Colin by the shirt, swinging him around until it was his back up against the shelving and—

"Drew!"

The air seeped from his lungs.

Maren.

CHAPTER 6

She shouldn't have pushed Drew into coming here.

Maren sat on the couch in Colin Renwycke's living room, hands twisting in her lap, while Drew perched rigid on the arm of a chair. Colin had disappeared up the stairs a minute ago. His footfalls sounded in creaks and groans in the ceiling overhead.

"Drew—"

"Don't ask."

"You were fighting."

He dropped from the arm of the chair onto its cushion. "I tried to tell you it wouldn't be pretty."

"And what were you going to do if I hadn't come in? Throw a punch?"

Drew's shadowed eyes refused to meet hers.

She stood, angled around the coffee table and sidestepped a tipped over ottoman.

"Where are you going?"

She stopped at the base of the stairs. "I'm going to talk to him."

Drew lurched to his feet. "Maren."

Sure it was ridiculous following Colin upstairs, thinking anything she might say could soothe whatever had just happened down here. But Drew had been too riled to see what she'd seen when she walked in.

The haunted look in Colin's eyes as Drew held him against the bookcase. As if . . .

As if he'd wanted his brother to go ahead and hit him. Knock him out and put him out of his misery.

"Maren," Drew's voice softened. "He doesn't even remember—" He cut off his own words. And then simply shook his head, letting her go.

The second floor hallway was a series of doors, dark wood wainscoting climbing up the walls underneath stifling burgundy paint. She peeked in the first door—bathroom.

Thumping movement sounded from the second.

She lifted her fist and knocked.

"Go away, Drew."

"It's not Drew."

Silence.

Then padding footsteps and the door swung open. And . . .

And her throat clogged. Could this really be the same man she'd met last December? The one with the model's pose and vibrant eyes, the brilliant conversationalist who'd reeled her in with his hometown anecdotes and stories of his childhood?

His eyes were still that disarming shade of blue and probably underneath the beard there was still the sculpted jaw. He'd changed into jeans, but not out of the faded t-shirt—the one Drew had fisted in their scuffle. The circles under Colin's eyes and the slump in his stance, the emotion lurking behind his gaze.

Drew was right.

She didn't know Colin at all.

"Hey." It was the only word she could get out.

"Maren, right?"

She tried not to flinch at the realization that he barely remembered her and towed her focus away to take in the room behind him. Rich, espresso-colored furniture, rumpled blue bedspread in a pile at the foot of the bed. A shelf hanging over his dresser with several comic books on display.

Oh right. He loves comic books. He'd told her that last year.

So she did know something.

"It's all coming back."

Colin was studying her now, and oh, in that moment, despite the glaring differences, the family resemblance was uncanny.

So like Drew. So not at all like Drew.

"We went out for dinner, didn't we? I had this amazing ravioli. And then we went on a carriage ride and it was snowing."

She nodded mutely.

He turned back to his room, disappeared into the closet and returned with a sweater. "That was a good gig, that cover shoot." He peeled off shirt. Her gaze flitted around the room until he spoke again, fully clothed. "And it was a good date, too." He stepped toward her, the grin he'd offered in generous portions last year finally breaking through now. "And now you're here."

"You invited me to the farm and I . . . well, I took you up on it. Total whim."

"Total whim is totally how I like to do life."

It's the kind of thing he would have said on their date. And she would have laughed and made a mental note to have Ethan Whitney say something similar in her next book. Because it sounded fanciful and fun.

But now . . . after what she'd just seen downstairs . . . ?

"I know this is weird me being here and—"

He leaned one hand on the doorframe over her. "Not that weird."

"And you weren't expecting us, but Drew drove all this way because . . . well, I think he misses you. And he really wants you to come home for Christmas. He's been doing all these renovations and working like crazy and . . . " And where was she going with this?

And why were Colin's eyes darkening? "Look, it's cool to see you again. It's bringing back fun memories of that date. Truthfully, I would've called you if I hadn't moved down here so soon after that. We should've had a second date." His posture straightened. "But Drew and me, we're not a *Lifetime* Christmas special. There's crappy history there."

"But you're family. He's your older brother—"

"Which he loves to remind me of. Older, wiser, smarter."

"I don't think he—"

"You don't know, okay?"

The force in his tone blocked any reply and she backed into the hallway. But she didn't leave. Not yet. Instead, she reached into the purse over her shoulder and pulled out a book—her book. The one with Colin's face, his midnight stare on the cover not all that different than his expression now.

"I, um . . . I wanted to give you a copy of it. Came out in September. Maybe you've already seen it, but . . . "

"I haven't. Broke things off with my agency just a week after this photo shoot." He took the book, examining the front before turning it over to skim the back cover copy. "I remember you telling me about this story. You said I was just like the character in your head."

"I'm working on the second book now. The publisher's given me two deadline extensions already." She watched him trace the raised lettering on the spine. "I honestly don't think I would've gotten anywhere with it if I hadn't wound up in Maple Valley. You were right about the farm—it's a perfect writing spot."

His focus moved from the book to her face, a momentary softening making space for his interest. "You just showed up there? And Drew let you stay?"

"I did, and as for staying, Winnie helped with that."

"Winnie's there?"

He didn't know? What had happened to so thoroughly fracture this family?

But before she could reply, Colin shook his head. "Doesn't matter. Thanks for the book. I'll read it, promise. But whatever Drew came for, it's not happening."

"But he drove all this way."

"He drove an hour."

"In a blizzard. And you're just going to send him on his way?"

Colin backed into his bedroom. "Wait it out downstairs, if you want. I don't care."

And with that, he closed the door.

Maren just stood there, feet rooted to the worn hallway carpet, exasperation-fueled surprise pulsing through her. So that was it? In a daze she retraced her steps and found Drew waiting at the bottom of the stairs. He held up a bundled hand towel.

"Makeshift ice pack. For your head."

She stopped two stairs above him. "My head's fine, Drew. It really didn't hit that hard. What's not fine is that." She pointed behind her. "You and Colin."

He stepped onto the bottom step so they were eye level and lifted the towel-wrapped ice to her forehead. "You've got a bump."

"Drew—"

Though his touch was gentle, his voice was firm. "I tried, Mare. I tried and the same thing happened as always happens. I've got your coat. Let's just go."

She reached for his wrist and removed his hand and his homemade ice pack from her head. "It's blizzarding!"

They stood so close she could almost hear his frustration. Wind rattled the window next to the stairway, and the storm in Drew's eyes flickered. She waited for the tension coiling inside him to let loose—in words or movement or…something.

But the only thing that moved was his stance—from stiff to depleted as his shoulders dropped.

And his only words were soft. "If you'd rather stay here and wait out the storm, I understand. I'll find someplace to hang out, come back and get you when it's over."

He draped her coat over the bannister and was out the front door before she could blink.

Because apparently that was how the Renwycke men handled conflict. Closed doors. Avoidance.

Except that wasn't entirely fair to Drew. He was right. He'd tried.

And she knew him well enough by now to know that was more than simple anger chasing him from the house. Hurt or regret or maybe even something more.

She glanced up the stairs one last time. Nothing—no sound.

She shrugged into her coat and let herself out of the house. The cold instantly slapped against her cheeks, snowflakes like pinpricks and the wind attempting to push her back inside.

She stepped in the tracks Drew's boots had already made, head down and chin tucked into her coat. Not until she reached the truck did she catch a glimpse of Drew's form inside, his forehead leaning into the steering wheel. He jerked up when she opened the door.

And for the first time since they'd reached Des Moines, something like relief seeped into his expression.

* * *

DREW'S WOODSHOP was supposed to be his sanctuary. When he'd moved back to Iowa this August, when he'd wondered if coming home was a mistake and if this carved out piece of property would ever feel like it used to, the little building tucked between the barn and the machine shed had been his one slice of peace.

But tonight not even the smell of sawdust or the humming warmth of the space heater managed to thaw the chilled places inside him.

He scratched a worn piece of sandpaper along the wood surface in front of him, ignoring the cramp in his hand and the ache in his back, a nagging reminder that he'd been sitting in this crouched position too long.

He'd long since lost track of time. After waiting out today's snowstorm in a dinky diner in Des Moines, he and Maren had made the drive home in silence. Maren had tapped away at her laptop while he drove, the freshly plowed interstate nearly deserted.

Black masked the sky by the time they arrived at the farm. He'd walked Maren to the front door before reversing course and coming out here. That had to have been a couple hours ago already.

"Drew?"

He turned as the woodshop's door opened and a whoosh of brittle night air shoved in. Maren appeared, a plate in her mittened hands, and she closed the door with her boot.

Even in the dim glow of the woodshop—only the pale white of a dangling bulb for light—he could see the uncertainty on Maren's face. And all at once, the regret slammed into him. Without meaning to, he'd shut her out today.

And—it hit him now, startling but undeniable—he missed her.

She skirted around Grandpa's old table saw—the one he'd moved from the machine shed. Didn't work nearly as good as the newer one in the corner, but it felt right having it in here.

"You didn't come in for dinner," she said as she side-stepped his tool counter. The aroma of something basily and Italian wafted from the tray. "So dinner's coming to you."

The already small space of the woodshop seemed to shrink as she drew near. The familiar sight of her blue and green striped pajama pants underneath her winter coat drew the closest thing he had to a smile.

She stopped in front of him. "Sorry about the attire. I pumped out a scene in the attic, but it's extra cold up there tonight. My pajamas are warmer, so . . . " She shrugged.

"You should've worked down by the living room fireplace.

"Actually, that's what I was going to do, but when I saw the telltale light of the woodshop and realized you never came in . . . " Another shrug and she nudged the tray toward him.

He took the tray and set it on the counter. "Thanks. Didn't even realize how much my stomach was growling until now." He lifted the plate's covering. "Ravioli?"

"I'd lie and pretend I made it, but Leigh brought it home from The Red Door. I've really got to try that restaurant sometime before . . . "

She didn't finish the sentence, but she didn't have to. She'd only ever intended to stay a couple weeks. And probably now that she realized Colin wasn't coming home . . .

"Actually, Drew, speaking of that . . . I just . . . I wanted to apologize. I've pried—a lot—about you and Colin and I've probably worn out my welcome here. You're probably wondering when I'm going to give you your attic back and—"

"I told you to stay as long as you wanted." He gulped down a bite of ravioli. "And I'm the one who should be apologizing. What you saw with Colin and then how I almost just left you at the house—"

"Except you didn't."

"And then the brooding thing."

Now she was the one to crack a smile. "The totally unfair thing is brooding actually looks good on you. You've got the face for it, the eyes." That tease in her voice, when had he gotten so used to it? "If I try to look broody, it just comes off as pouty."

"Well, pajamas look better on you than they do me. So, there's that. Truce?" He held out his hand.

She took off her mitten before placing her palm in his. "Truce."

He went back to the meal as Maren peeled off her coat, his attention straying back to her while he ate. She wandered the small shop—studied the stacks of measured slabs leftover from the benches he'd made for the city, tried out the lawn swing still waiting for a restaining, and then stopped in front of the old desk he planned to sand and refinish one of these days. The knob had broken off one of its drawers and at least one leg needed replaced entirely.

"Now *this* is a desk."

He finished off his ravioli. "You like it? Used to be in the back of the living room. Grandpa told me once it used to be his Dad's, so you know the thing is old. Can't tell you how many times Mom almost got rid of it."

"I'm glad she didn't. It's a real antique. Like that piano inside."

"And all it needs is a little TLC. I'll get around to it one of these days. Trying to finish Winnie's Christmas present at the moment."

She turned to the project he'd been working on when she walked in. She ran one hand over the smooth wood of the headboard. It curved at the top, spindled knobs at either end. Knowing dawned in her green eyes. "Because she hates the lumpy bed in her room."

"Exactly. Leigh won't let me help pay for a new mattress, so I figure this is the least I can do."

"It's beautiful."

He unscrewed the lid of the Thermos she'd brought with the tray. Not coffee. Hot chocolate? "Thanks. I wanted it to be contemporary enough for Win without looking too modern for the house." He poured a cup of the thick liquid—definitely cocoa. Probably way too sweet for him, but at least she hadn't forced one of her fancy coffees on him.

He motioned for Maren to sit on the stool he'd abandoned when she came in, then dragged over a sawhorse. He found a fresh piece of sandpaper then perched in front of the headboard, posed to continue working.

"Aren't there electric sanders that can make jobs like this go a lot faster?"

He placed the paper against the wood and started rubbing. "Yeah, but it's not nearly as relaxing."

"Relaxing, huh? You might need to prove it."

He shrugged, tore his own piece of sandpaper in half and handed it to her. She held it up to the wood and Drew scooted closer. "You want to go in a back and forth pattern with the grain of the wood. If you go against the grain, any kind of scratch or unevenness will show up more after I stain it."

He placed his hand over hers on the headboard, nudging it into movement.

"And don't press too hard. You shouldn't feel any heat."

"No heat, got it."

Except with the space heater in the corner humming its warmth, the hot meal and hot cocoa in his stomach, he might not be able to follow his own advice. He shed his hoodie as Maren went to work.

"I didn't realize there were so many rules to sanding."

"It's serious business, Grant." The tease in his voice faded into an amicable quiet as they worked side by side.

"Drew?"

His arm brushed against hers as he sanded over a nick in the wood.

"Do you really want to be a farmer?"

He blew on the headboard, sending sawdust scattering. "Of course."

"But look at all this out here. Everything you've done in the house. You could make a career out of building customized furniture. Restoring antiques. Renovating houses. So many possibilities."

The shop light dangling overhead shook as a flurry of wind grabbed hold of the building. The light flickered with the movement.

"Those things sound fun, sure. But none of them are career or financial guarantees. Besides, I've got all this land." He took another drink of cocoa. "And the farm . . . it's a two-person job."

Her sanding stilled as her pause stretched. Her knees knocked against his as she turned on the stool to face him. "You wanted Colin to help. That's why you were so eager to get him home for Christmas? So you could ask him to run the farm with you?"

He looked to the dirt floor, rubbing his thumb over the sandpaper. "I thought if he came home he might remember how much he liked it here. I even thought . . . " He glanced up at Maren. The overhead light painted honey streaks in her brown hair. "I thought seeing you, knowing you were here might help."

She rolled her eyes then. "And clearly we both saw how much of an impact I made. I mean, I probably should've gotten the point a year ago when he never called. But whatever. Better late than never, I guess."

"Colin's an idiot."

At the rise in Maren's eyebrows, he realized he'd said it out loud and good Lord, he wished the words back. Not because he didn't mean them . . . but because of what they revealed.

Colin's an idiot because he let her go.

He took a breath, focus fleeing from her face. Sure, she had the kind of laugh a person didn't get tired of. She constantly made time for his niece—talking about favorite books and reading Winnie's own writing and even going to that marathon of a middle school concert last week. She'd taken a shine to his town, came to church like she was one of the family, and might be the easiest person to talk to he'd ever met.

But she'd be leaving soon.

And anyway, what business did he have thinking whatever it was he was beginning to think when he couldn't even pull his family together? When he had no idea whether his new career would pan into anything?

But it has to.

"Anyway, farming may not be the job either of us planned on, but it's a good life. It was good for Grandpa and Dad. And I would know that Colin . . . " His words wilted as he turned.

He'd know that Colin would be okay.

"You're a good man, Drew Renwcyke."

He stood then, Maren's closeness suddenly somehow claustrophobic. He'd told her she was wrong about Colin. But the thing was, she was wrong about him too.

He reached for the Thermos again, ignored the cup and drank straight from the container. "When I was seventeen, I threw a massive party in the barn."

He turned in time to see Maren's startled blink.

"I know, it doesn't sound like me. But there was a weekend when Grandpa and Grandma and Mom and Dad were all at some church couples things. And I don't even know why I did it." His fingers curled around the Thermos. "Just one of those weird whim things. Pure impulse."

"Like me showing up at the farm after nothing more than a year-old casual invite?"

His grin was fleeting, fading into memory. "Colin and Leigh were in on it. We all invited our friends, thought the worst that could happen is we'd have a mess to clean up before our parents got home. But there was this girl there I was into, so that's where my attention was all night."

He took another breath, gathering the energy or maybe just the willpower to tell the rest of the story. Maren simply waited, sandpaper long since abandoned.

"And anyway, I didn't notice Leigh sneaking off with one of my friends. That's the night she got pregnant with Winnie. She's told me tons it would've happened regardless—that she'd been on that path plenty long. But still. And Colin..." A heavy exhale filled his pause. "He got ahold of some beer...a lot of it. Ended up driving through the yard in one of my grandpa's old tractors. Hit and killed our dog. Which, I'm telling you, that thing was Colin's best friend."

He raked his fingers through his hair, the story's finish squeezing his composure before he'd even uttered it. "But the worst is, Grandpa had a heart attack that night. My parents tried calling us over and over." He felt the glaze in his own eyes, heard the ragged pitch in his own voice.

"Oh, Drew." Maren stood.

"One stupid decision, one night. And I know it was fifteen years ago, but it still . . . "

His voice shriveled then and Maren closed the remaining gap between them.

"Things just never got better. Leigh barely graduated high school, Colin decided he was James Dean or something. I think my Dad resented having to run the farm on his own. I don't know why I'm even telling you—"

But she cut him off as her arms wound around his waist. She buried her face in his shirt and simply waited.

Until he let go of his last reserve and circled his arms around her.

CHAPTER 7

*M*aren woke to the distant sound of a door rattling against its hinges, the murmurs of a pulsing wind.

And someone else's breathing.

Where . . . ?

A toasty warmth wrapped around her, tempting her back to sleep. But confusion tugged her eyes open.

Generous sunlight poured through a lone window, trickling over her surroundings—slabs of wood propped against the wall, tool counter, table saw, headboard.

And then the pillow she had one arm draped over moved. Except . . .

Holy cow. Not a pillow. Definitely. not. a. pillow.

She pitched upward as realization chased away the last of her fogginess. But the movement was too quick—it jolted the swing where she'd apparently spent the night, curled against Drew, sent it and her and Drew toppling backward before she could steady. She landed on Drew's chest with a thump, one leg caught underneath the arm of the bench, Drew's gasped "What the—?" muffled by her hair.

She kicked her leg free and lifted herself up, one palm on the floor and the other on Drew's chest. "I . . . am so . . . sorry."

His slumber-tinged grin drawled across his face. "Attacking me in my sleep, Grant? Really?"

She gave a scoffing laugh and poked his chest before pushing away from him, the chilled floor underneath her barely noticeable. "Let's just acknowledge that was your swing we were sleeping on. You built it. Not my fault if it's not stable."

"You accusing me of shoddy craftsmanship?" Drew sat up beside her, hair tousled and hands rubbing his eyes, sleeping still clinging to his voice. Like a little boy awakened in the middle of a dream.

Except not at all like a little boy. Her breath caught as sunlight sifted over his profile—the lines of his face, the muddy river-blue eyes, the wrinkles in his shirt where she'd spent the night.

"Not shoddy." Her voice was a near-rasp. "Just . . . tipsy."

And then the memories slid in, honey-sweet and heady. Of Drew's arms around her last night after he'd told her his story. Of his feet nudging the swing as yesterday faded into today. Hushed conversation to the tune of the space heater's hum.

They must've simply drifted off at some point.

Drew stood now, and Maren blinked as he extended one hand toward her. She placed her palm in his, let him pull her up and had to level her own breathing all over again when she came up mere inches from him. And that's when she realized she was wearing the hoodie he'd discarded earlier in the evening, zipped halfway up over her striped pajamas.

"So we slept out here?"

She swallowed. "Seems that way."

"Did you at least sleep good?"

She could only nod. Surprisingly good. Her neck should

ache, her back should protest. Instead it was only her common sense that nagged her now, felt the need to remind her that until two weeks ago, she hadn't even known this man who still held her hand. And she had a book to finish and a life to return to and he'd made it clear his family and farm were his focus and . . .

"Mare?"

She met his eyes. "What are the chances we make it inside without Leigh or Winnie realizing we spent the whole night out here?"

"Well, it's Saturday, so if we're lucky, they're sleeping in."

More of last night replayed in snatches. They'd finished sanding Winnie's headboard while trading stories. She'd told him about her book and confessed that maybe the reason she couldn't complete it was the unexpected pressure that came along with a publishing dream-come-true, the worry that it'd be her last contracted book. He'd told her more about how his parents had signed the farm over to him last year. Given him permission to sell it if he wished, do whatever he wanted with the money.

And he'd told her how Colin had flipped over that. Which is why their last time seeing each other—well, second to last time now—had gone so horribly.

"I know he was just hurting. And honestly, I'm surprised Leigh doesn't resent it, too."

Drew had talked more than she'd ever heard him talk.

And she'd wondered—over and over and over—how in the world she was going to tear herself away from this place in a few days.

This place or this man?

"Hey."

His hushed voice drew her gaze once more.

"Last night . . . I don't know how you do it, Maren Grant. Get me to talk, I mean." He glanced down to their linked hands. "But I needed to last night and you somehow knew it and . . . " His Adam's apple bobbed when he swallowed. "And thanks."

His thumb slid over her hand and in that one languid, stretched out moment, she knew. Colin had been a crush. A flighty, fanciful crush born of whim and fueled by daydreams.

But the man in front of her now? She knew him. She *knew* him.

And once she left for Minnesota, snatches of memory, a postcard or two, reliving these last few weeks in the moments before she drifted to sleep . . . none of it would be good enough.

"Drew, I . . . " Her voice trailed as her thoughts stalled.

Just tell him.

Tell him what? That two weeks and one night in a woodshop had convinced her she'd yearned for the wrong Renwycke all this time? He'd think she was crazy.

Crazier than showing up at his house unannounced? Climbing up the trellis?

The woodshop door swung open.

"There you are! Scare a household half to death, why don't you." Leigh's voice scurried in. "Winnie and I couldn't figure out why the coffee wasn't made and—"

Leigh cut off as her vision apparently adjusted to the dim room and she caught sight of the two of them—Drew still holding Maren's hand, the tiniest wedge of space between them.

Drew practically jumped away. "Leigh, sorry. We were working and . . . "

"Uh-huh." Droll amusement edged her scant reply.

The cold of the morning finally began to creep into the shop. Maren zipped Drew's hoodie the rest of the way up. "Yeah, it was . . . we were . . . " *Oh, just never mind.* "Anyway, I have a lot of writing to do today, so…"

She reached for the coat she'd discarded at some point last night. Started for the door, tripped over the tipped swing. Drew's arms jutted out to steady her.

She only allowed the briefest glance of thanks before escaping past Leigh and into the sprawling yard. She took a long, anxious breath tinged with frosty air. Heard the snatches of conversation behind her.

"You spent the night with her?"

"Not like that."

"Drew, you know I—"

Her phone cut through the voices and she plucked it out like a lifesaver, barely registering the name on the display before answering. "This is Maren."

Dayton didn't even bother with a greeting. "How fast can you ditch the frozen tundra of Iowa?"

She halted in the middle of the yard. "Why?"

"Got a call from a professor friend at the University of Minnesota and apparently there's some English department alumni holiday banquet or something happening this weekend. Their keynote just backed out and they're looking for a speaker. Prof knows I work with you, knows you went to U of M. And they'll let you sell and sign books after."

Drew and Leigh's voices drifted from the woodshop. Sunlight glinted off the metal of the machine shed and behind the building, tufts of snow rose and fell like waves, descending into the grove of trees where Drew said he used to spend hours as a kid.

"We'd play hide and seek for hours out there. Once we actually lost Leigh. Turned out she'd wandered out to the west field, started playing house by herself in a corn crib."

"Well, do you want the gig?" Eagerness crowded Dayton's tone. "You'd make my friend's day. Pay is good and that's a ton of people to get your books in front of. Besides, didn't you say you like speaking? Could be a big moment."

She glanced down at Drew's hoodie, its too long arms flopping loose around hers. It smelled like him—that same minty, spicy smell that lingered in the second floor every morning after he'd gotten ready for the day.

A big moment.

The very thing she'd come to Iowa looking for.

"It's just . . ."

Drew emerged from the woodshop, Leigh beside him.

"I think I might be having a big moment right here." Or at least, she was on her way toward one. Because if Leigh hadn't walked in when she did . . .

Goosebumps climbed up her arms underneath the sweatshirt and oh, she had to look ridiculous. Standing in the middle of the yard, one arm hugged around her torso. And smiling—a dopey, toothy, goofy smile.

"You're having a big moment."

"Don't sound so doubtful, Dayton."

"It's just . . . *Iowa.* And anyway, I thought you went there to write."

"I did and I have been. I'll send you some chapters, if you want."

Drew and Leigh reached her then and Drew mouthed something about the cold and how she should get inside and Leigh gave a pointed glance toward the hoodie she wore.

And Dayton let out an impatient sigh. "What I want is an answering on the speaking gig? In or out?"

* * *

"I JUST WANT you to be careful, Drew."

Drew poked a fake tree branch into its spot in the metal center. At least, he'd thought it was the right spot, but the evergreen branch protruded awkwardly. He glanced around the Christmas tree to see his sister holding the tree skirt.

Shoot, he probably should've fit that thing in place before putting the bottom of the tree together.

"Careful of what? Poking my eye out with one of these branches?"

He'd already scraped his arm once and snagged his sweater, too. Served him right for dressing up for a day at home—if a black sweater and his only unfrayed pair of jeans counted as dressing up. Didn't even know why he did it.

It's just, when they'd come inside and Maren had told them about the phone call she'd just received, how she'd actually turned down a speaking engagement so she could stay an extra day or two—*if* it was okay with him—his staid, practical side just snapped. And he'd found himself nodding and smiling like a dolt and then suggesting they put up the Christmas tree today. And now here he was dressed like it was Sunday and shirking his work and listening to Frank Sinatra croon about being home for Christmas.

Maren and Winnie sat in front of the fireplace on the cream-colored rug, sorting through the boxes of Christmas decorations he'd hauled in from the garage.

And Leigh—he glanced back at her—had apparently been watching him watch the others.

"You know what I'm talking about, big brother."

Drew yanked the stubborn branch out. Shrugged and reached for a different one. "Honestly, I don't. But why so serious? It's a good day, Leigh. It's Saturday. You've got the day off. Winnie's happy."

"*You're* happy."

He fit the branch into place. "And that's a bad thing?"

Leigh rounded to his side of the tree, voice lowering. "I want you to be careful about Maren."

Of its own accord, his gaze scooted back to Maren. At some point this morning, she'd traded in her striped pajamas and his hoodie for leggings and some kind of shirt-dress thing with a loose cord belt at the waist. And if he wasn't mistaken, those were Winnie's slippers on her feet.

"What about her?"

Leigh perched on the arm of the wingback chair near the window. "Come on, don't make me spell it out."

"Well, you're going to have to if you want me to understand what you're getting at. Be careful? She's not a wild animal. No claws or fangs." He arranged the wired branches he'd already fit into place, filling in the sparse spots. "She's not a vampire or zombie or whatever paranormal thing is popular right now."

"She's eventually going to leave. I just don't want to see you disappointed or anything. And then there's the fact that she clearly had feelings for Colin when she first showed up here."

"Leigh—"

"And maybe she doesn't anymore, but if that's the case, what does that say about her? She flip-flopped from one brother to the other that quickly?"

He couldn't help another glance Maren's direction, relieved that she apparently wasn't hearing any of this. She and Winnie were laughing over something—probably a clumsy old ornament he or one of his siblings had made in school.

"You're worrying over nothing, sis. And she didn't flip-flop. She went on one date with Colin."

"Yes, and saved the postcard he sent her for a year."

So what? It was just a generic postcard with two lines of scribbling. "You don't know her, Leigh."

"And you do? She's been here two weeks. Like a pet up in the attic who emerges when she's hungry."

He poked another branch into the metal center, not even caring if it was the right spot. "Do you not like her or something?"

"Of course I like her. She's great. Winnie practically dotes on her. I wish my daughter would spend half as much time with me." Leigh rose and handed him another branch. "But I care about you, Drew, okay? And you seem . . . you're so . . . you're wearing a sweater. And you let her talk you into trying that gingerbread creamer this morning."

"You heard her. She was going to heckle me until I gave in. I saved time by trying it." He turned away from the tree, finally giving Leigh his full attention. "I appreciate the concern, little sister, but I'm the one who's supposed to worry about my siblings."

And besides, she was simply reading too far into things. So he'd diverted from his usual flannel for a day. So he'd let Maren doctor up his coffee for once.

So he'd poured out more of his heart than he'd ever meant to last night, let Maren see a side of him few people ever had.

So he'd fallen asleep with his arm around her.

So maybe Leigh isn't seeing things.

"You know, you could've gotten a real tree."

He blinked at Leigh's abrupt change in topic, recognized it for the offering it was. She was letting him off the hook.

"Pine needles make you sneeze like crazy. You were always stuffed up and headachy around Christmas."

"Yeah, but it's already December fifteenth. So it's not like it'd be up that long. And I know it's what you'd choose if Winnie and I weren't here."

Except he might not have decorated at all if they weren't here. If he had this big house all to himself. What would be the point?

Frankly, that's why it'd taken him so long to actually move home after Mom and Dad gave him the place. Until he'd concocted the idea of coaxing his siblings home, he couldn't fathom having so much space to fill.

"The tree might only be up for a few weeks, but the

needles fall off all over the place and we'd be finding them for a month after. I'm fine with this one."

Leigh bit her bottom lip before speaking again. "Actually, Drew, I've been meaning to—"

A burst of laughter clattered from the other side of the room—Maren's. A gap in the branches gave him a view of her waving away Winnie who was tossing loose pieces of tinsel into Maren's hair.

Frank Sinatra faded away, replaced by some other tranquil Christmas classic that reminded him of Grandpa. The slow songs had always been his favorite.

"I've been meaning to talk to you about something," Leigh tried again.

And at that, Drew turned to her once more. She faced the window now, her reflection appearing in the windowpane, a chill sifting from its glass surface. He dropped the last tree branch as the hesitance in her tone awakened an all-too-familiar dread. Had he been so focused on Maren, that'd he'd missed something with Leigh? Was she struggling again with the pills? Or alcohol? Was something wrong with Winnie?

A laugh sputtered from her. "Oh my gosh, the panic in your eyes right now." She shook her head at his reflection next to hers. "Stay calm. I've got my two-year chip. Meetings are helping, that small group at church is really helping—"

"And being here, it's helping?"

Her nod was slow. And weighted with something he couldn't read. She angled away from the window. "It is. Being back in Maple Valley is awesome. I even love working at the restaurant. Seth Walker's a great boss. Oh and his girlfriend, Ava, she's a blast. I'm actually making friends."

He heard the "but" before she said it.

"But I think it's time to start looking for a place in town. There are some cute townhouses on Water Street and—"

"What? Why? I thought you were good here?" The questions bulleted from him. "There's plenty of space. It's rent-free." *I'm here.*

"Winnie and I . . . we're still finding our groove. I need space to really be her mom. I work so many hours and she's got school and even when we're both home, we don't spend much time together." Leigh picked up the branch he'd dropped on the chair, fidgeted with it before going on. "Honestly, it's kind of hard to compete with you."

"It's not a competition." He hated the dark underpinnings in his tone. Even more, the current of anxiety coursing through him. He'd failed coaxing Colin home and now Leigh was talking about leaving?

Couldn't she see he was doing all this for them? Practically rebuilding the house and spending every last ounce of his energy, not to mention his savings, trying to prepare for his new life as a farmer . . . all for them.

"I know it's not a competition, but the fact of the matter is, I don't think Win's ever going to truly depend on me or see me as someone she can count on, when you're the one taking care of us." She placed her hand on his arm. "Please don't be mad."

"I'm not mad, I'm just . . . " Disappointed. And sagging under the realization that eventually it *would* just be him all alone in this big house. That he'd walked away from his life in St Louis for siblings who didn't want to be here and a job he didn't know how to do.

But hadn't he prayed about this? Felt a nudge? Had it all been a mistake? "We're going to need an extension cord for the lights. I'm going to go look for one."

"Drew—"

"It's fine, Leigh. I'm fine. I get it."

He turned before she could read his lie and slipped into the kitchen, Maren and Winnie's voices, the crackle of the fireplace and Bing Crosby's warbling trailing after him.

He pulled open a drawer—the junk drawer, crammed with who knew what. He pilfered through it. No extension cord. He glanced up at the sound of dripping—an icicle outside the kitchen window, melting under a brash sun.

Of course Leigh wants to move. She's always wanted space. And maybe she's right about Winnie. Maybe—

"Drew?"

He heard Maren's slippers padding over the tiled floor.

"Leigh said you need a cord. I borrowed one the other day. My laptop charger didn't reach to the window seat. I can go get it."

He closed the drawer and turned. A couple strands of tinsel still tangled in her hair and she was sliding her feet back and forth over the slippery floor, as if ice skating in place. Her eyes lit with delight.

And he just stood there, one hand still on the drawer knob, wondering how in the world she seemed more at ease in this house than Leigh or Winnie.

And how it was possible—in only two weeks—to feel like he'd known her for a year.

And if maybe, like her parents meeting in a ski lodge during a snowstorm, Maren showing up in Iowa wasn't random, if their easy friendship wasn't happenstance. And if the feeling he was too nervous to name—probably the very thing that worried Leigh and something he wouldn't have thought possible in so short a time—wasn't so ridiculous, after all.

"Drew? The cord? Do you want me to go get it?"

The tapping of the melting icicle filled his pause.

"Do you want to go on a date, Mare?"

She stopped sliding. "What?"

He reached forward to pull a piece of tinsel loose from her hair. "There's a Christmas carnival in town tonight. Just another whackadoo Maple Valley thing, but—"

"Yes."

He fiddled with the junk drawer knob. Opened it. Closed it. "There'll be a bunch of booths and lights and music. And food, tons of it. Funnel cake—that seems like something you'd like. And—"

"Yes, Drew. I said yes."

He clamped his mouth closed. Finally pulled his hand away from the junk drawer, but accidentally brought the knob with it . . . and the whole drawer, off its hinges . . . and everything with it. The drawer dropped and knocked against his leg. Its contents spilled to the floor, rolling under their feet, under the table.

"So it's a date?"

He'd take her burst of laughter as a yes.

CHAPTER 8

For the second time in her life, Maren Grant sat next to a Renwycke brother, bundled under a quilt as glittering snowfall swirled in the air around her and a horse pulled her through a sunset-glazed city street.

Only this time it was the swish of a sleigh's blades through snowy ground that filled the air instead of a clipped trot over pavement. And it was the now-familiar lights of the Maple Valley town square up ahead that beckoned instead of the brick and cement of Minneapolis.

And instead of Colin, it was Drew Renwycke sitting next to her, driving the sleigh he'd found in his barn.

Or, well, attempting to drive. So far the horse pulling the thing had stopped four times and veered off course once.

"I swear I told J.J. I needed a horse that was used to pulling something like this." Drew flicked the reins as the Archway Bridge came into view. "But something tells me Godfrey here is past his prime."

"Or he's just protesting against being named Godfrey." Moonlight brushed over the river's icy ripples and music glided from the square. Christmas lights traced the rooftops and doorways of the riverfront businesses—Coffee Coffee, the newspaper office, the flower shop. She leaned closer to Drew. "Anyway, I don't mind that it's taking awhile to get to the carnival."

"No?"

No, because the longer it took to get downtown, the longer this evening lasted. This enchanted night that so far had all the makings of a date she'd never forget. Almost enough to make her forget the suitcase back in Drew's attic waiting to be packed or the book waiting to be finished or the fact that the bubble she'd lived in for the past two weeks was about to pop.

And it had nothing to do with the sleigh or the snow or the dinner they'd had back at the farm . . .

[Narrator]

I'm sorry, but we can't just skip over this. We're talking candle light dinner . . . in a haymow.

Yes, a haymow.

Drew thought of everything. He brought up a space heater to warm the barn's upper level, spread a quilt over the wood floor, lit candles and strung icicle lights from the rafters.

So basically it was one big fire hazard.

But a romantic one, at that.

And there was pizza. Maren's favorite.

Okay, back to the sleigh ride...

Well, maybe tonight's magic had *something* to do with the sleigh or the snow or the dinner they'd had back at the farm.

But mostly it had everything to do with the man sitting next to her with the winter-ruddied cheeks and the wind-blown hair and the army green coat and—

"Hey, you're wearing a coat."

Drew glanced over, his blue-black eyes lit by contentment. "It's below freezing tonight."

"Don't pretend this is normal behavior for you, Drew

Renwycke. I'm pretty positive this is the first time I've seen you appropriately bundled up since I met you. You're always running around outside in a flannel shirt or one of those puff vest things as if that counts as winter wear."

"That'd be because I'm always hurrying. Trying to get stuff done. Tonight . . . " The sleigh bumped over the edge of the bridge and onto the street that would lead them downtown. "Tonight, for the first time in weeks, I feel . . . relaxed."

"I like relaxed Drew." The words slipped out before she could stop them.

But the way he looked at her then, the shadow on his cheeks unable to hide the laugh lines that deepened as he grinned, she didn't wish them back. They passed under an old-fashioned lamppost, light landing over them for a flicker of a moment.

"Hard to believe you're leaving soon."

His words, though soft, landed with a thud. "We were having such a fun night. Why'd you have to go and bring that up?"

"Don't know. Guess it just keeps hitting me today. How empty the farmhouse is going to be soon. Colin clearly isn't coming home and you're leaving eventually and Leigh's apparently already looking at townhomes."

One block away, the square came into view. Lights and booths and a decorated evergreen, the buzz of laughter and conversation. *Perfect.*

Except for the barely-there whisper of concern in Drew's voice. "Wait, why's Leigh looking at other places? You've got plenty of space."

"That's what I said."

"And after all the work you've put into the place. And it's so pretty out there, like your own little carved out winter wonderland." And she'd wondered more than once what it might be like to actually belong on the farm herself, instead of just temporarily laying claim to the attic.

And there it was again, the reminder that her days in Iowa were coming to a close. Mom and Dad were expecting her for their annual Christmas Eve party and then of course, family Christmas the next day. She had an editor waiting for her book and an agent wondering when she'd be ready with a proposal for more Ethan Whitney books and a school district that expected her to be available after winter break.

I'm not ready.

The horse's gait halted—again. Drew flicked the reins. Nothing.

"C'mon Godfrey, we're almost there."

The horse let out an irritated huff, its mane waving in the wind.

"I think he just shook his head no at you."

Drew's expression was half-amused, half-annoyed. He lifted the quilt and hopped down from the sled. "Maybe I can lead him by hand. I'll walk, you ride." But when he tried to tug Godfrey forward, the horse only stamped its hoof.

"So maybe instead of filling your barn with animals, Drew, you should just save it for romantic dates."

"One stubborn horse defies me and suddenly I'm not an animal guy?" He shrugged, tied the reins around a lamppost and rounded to her side of the sleigh. He reached for her hand. His fingers closed around hers as she stood, his other hand finding her waist.

"I'm just saying, so far it's not looking good for you and horses."

And then she was on the ground, just like this morning in the shed, only inches from Drew, looking up into a face that had at some point—without her realizing it—stolen her affection from the one on her book cover.

"Well, maybe I'm really good with cows."

She blinked away a snowflake that landed in her eyelash and grinned.

"Or pigs. Or sheep. Or goats. You ever think of that?" He let go of her waist, but held on to her hand, steering her toward the square.

"I apologize, Old MacDonald. I shouldn't have underestimated you." How could her steps feel so light with her heavy wool-lined boots warming her feet and her long, belted winter coat? And she shouldn't feel this warm, with the icy air turning her breath white and snowflakes sticking to her cheeks.

"So what do you want to do first? Some of the booths have games—you know, like, throw a ball, knock over some cans, get a cheap stuffed animal. There's probably apple cider and hot chocolate somewhere."

"I want to see your benches."

He led her across Main Avenue. "My benches?"

"You delivered the rest of them a few days ago, didn't you? Let's see where they ended up."

And so that's what they did. For the next ten minutes, they wandered through the square, winding in and out of booths and people, finding each of Drew's benches until they ended at the original—the one where they'd sat while that newspaper reporter took their photo and the mayor waxed eloquent about the downtown beautification efforts.

Just a simple bench sitting under the glow of a lamppost. But it felt like a symbol of something, a sign. The care Drew put into it, the time he'd spent making something for the whole town to enjoy, even while fixing up his house and prepping the farm and doting on Winnie. While watching out for Leigh and worrying over Colin and playing impromptu host to Maren.

And for just a moment—one that lingered soft as the

snowfall—all the echoes of the carnival faded to a mere murmur as she turned to Drew.

"I'm not ready—"

"We'll miss—"

Her blurted words collided with Drew's and she felt his hand tighten around hers. "You first."

"I'm not ready to go. I'm still twenty thousand words from the end of my book, for one thing and I haven't spent nearly enough time in Maple Valley and . . . " And she knew it now. The *what-if* she'd come here to find had shifted. And if she left now . . .

Drew stepped closer, gaze moving from her eyes downward. "And?" he prodded.

The wind grazed over her cheeks. "And what were you going to say?"

"We'll . . . " He stopped, closing the last of the space between them. "I'll miss you."

The hand not encased in his found its way to his arm. "Yeah?" The question came out almost a gasp, barely a whisper.

And as breathy wind swirled around their feet, loose strands of hair tickling her cheeks, Drew simply nodded. He reached his arm around her waist, paused for one breathless moment and then . . .

"Drew?"

Her gaze whipped the direction of the voice as Drew's arm dropped.

And there, rooted beside Drew's bench, the same trench coat he wore on the cover of her book—Colin.

* * *

"CLEARLY, I WALKED IN ON SOMETHING."

Drew blinked—once, twice—as disappointment and disbelief tangled through him.

Disappointment that a perfect moment—the kind Maren might've written about in a book—had snapped in a breath.

Disbelief that it really was Colin standing under the lamppost, arms folded and probing gaze . . . dark.

"You . . . you're here."

Colin dropped his arms. "Yes, but I can see my timing wasn't the best."

His brother had shaved since they'd seen him last. Was that really just yesterday? He'd gelled his hair into some kind of side-swept manicured thing and apparently didn't care what the snow might do to his leather shoes.

"I didn't expect . . . we didn't . . . "

"Obviously." There was something murky in Colin's tone and in the way his focus slid to Maren. "Maren. Good to see you again. I started reading your book yesterday. I saw the postcard tucked in the cover."

She'd left the postcard with Colin? She wasn't carrying it around in her purse anymore?

It shouldn't please him so much.

"Well, we're glad you're here." Drew grasped for the ease he wanted to feel at seeing Colin, but the lingering effects of yesterday's near-fight—of too many years of distance—badgered him.

But that was then. Today can be different.

After all, look at all that had changed in just two weeks. In just twenty-four hours, even. This time last night, he'd sat alone in the woodshop wondering how his plans could've gone so off course.

But sometime today—that moment in the kitchen with Maren or maybe when Leigh told him she planned to move or maybe even before that, when he'd woken up in the shop with Maren—he'd let something go. The need to make sure his siblings' lives were perfect before he moved on with his own.

"You got here just in time. We just got to the carnival. I'm thinking we hit the beverage stand first and—"

"I didn't come for the carnival." Colin plunged his hands in the pockets of his coat.

"Then what did you . . . " But he didn't need to finish the question. Because he saw it—Colin's darted glance at Maren, at their still linked hands. He heard Maren's sharp inhale, felt her palm go limp in his.

He'd come because of Maren?

Not because of. For.

"Anyway, as you were." Colin pivoted.

Maren released his hand at Colin's retreat. "Go on, Drew."

The temptation to pretend the last two minutes hadn't happened, to turn his back on his brother and gather Maren back into his arms, it nearly consumed him. But Maren's eyes urged him otherwise.

So he turned, caught up with Colin in a few steps. "Col, you don't need to leave. Hang out with us. We'll find Leigh and Winnie and—"

Colin jerked to a stop. "She left that postcard in the book. I was sure it meant . . . " He dug a pair of gloves from his pocket and thrust them on. "We went on a date last year. She told you that, right?"

"Yeah, she told me. And she said you never called after that. Yesterday you didn't even remember her at first."

Colin's lips pressed together, his expression taut. "So that was your signal to barge in?"

"Barge in on what?"

Colin stepped up to him. "She came to Iowa looking for me."

"She came to Iowa looking for a place to write. Because

apparently without telling any of the rest of us, you offered up the house as a regular B&B and she took you up on the offer." He nudged his chin into the collar of his coat, the wind dusting snow from the nearby evergreen. Frustration rocketed up his throat. "I can't even believe we're having this conversation."

"Yeah, well, sorry for thinking my own brother would actually stay hands-off in one area of my life. For being serious enough about the possibility of something with Maren to come here."

"Serious? You were serious about culinary school at one point, remember that? And then modeling and then acting. And I can't even count the girls—Maggie and Mel and Ruby and those are just the names I can remember off the top of my head." He ignored the looks from the teens manning a snack booth, the people in line. "And apparently for awhile there you were serious about a job in Des Moines, but sound like that's not going so well either."

He should stop. He knew he should stop.

But now that he'd started, it poured from him.

"And here I thought maybe I could convince you to be serious about the farm. Get you home for Christmas and show you what you've been missing."

"Serious about the farm?" Colin combed his fingers through his hair.

"Yeah, call me crazy, but I actually thought maybe you'd catch the vision for what I'm trying to do here. Stay and help with planting season."

Colin's laughter accompanied the slump of his shoulders. "I *will* call you crazy. Never mind the fact that Mom and Dad gave you the land, not me, *why* in the world would I want to *farm?*"

Seconds stretched, the music from the speakers over the band shell, the buzz of the townspeople, the smell of funnel cakes and cider, all of it crowded in his head until he found his voice again.

"I don't know why you'd want to. Maybe because Grandpa and Grandma poured their heart into this place. Maybe because I thought it could be fun, working together, building something."

"Except I'm not a farmer. And you aren't either."

"We can learn."

"And what? Fake the passion for it for the rest of our lives?" Colin shook his head. "No thank you."

The blunt refusal should've exasperated him, filled him with the same disillusionment Leigh's news had this morning. He'd uprooted his entire life for this.

So why did he only feel a detached numbness?

Colin's focus shifted over Drew's shoulder and realization joined the emptiness: Maren had heard all this. Watched while his dream and plans for the future withered.

"How far has it gone?" Colin's attention was back on him now.

"What?"

"You and Maren? How far? Was this the first date? Because if so, we're even and it's anyone's game now."

His lungs tightened and there, something to fill his hollow emotion. Heat pulsed through him. "Colin—"

But the jarring screech of a microphone cut through the crowd. And up in the band shell . . . a police officer?

"Nothing to be alarmed about, folks, but there's been break-in at the depot. Would the parents of the following kids please come talk to me?" He began rattling off names. Not a big deal. Teens were always camping out in the train cars at the depot. Drew turned back to his brother. "Col—"

A discouraged sigh rattled from him. Colin was already gone. And then . . .

"Winnie Renwycke."

CHAPTER 9

"*L*eigh, you have to calm down."

Drew's sister ignored him, irate footsteps tramping through the snow toward the Maple Valley depot on the edge of town. He'd hated leaving Maren behind at the carnival, but she'd insisted he go. Second time tonight she'd sent him after a sibling.

"Go with Leigh, Drew. I'll get ahold of J.J. and see if he can come pick up his horse."

"But . . . " He'd glanced helplessly at Colin.

"I'll talk to him, too. Smooth things over."

Moonlight drew an eerie outline over the oblong depot building and its span of railroad track that reached into the distance, disappearing into a craggy ridge of bare trees and evergreens.

Out in front, a line of antique passenger rail cars rested on the track . . . one of which Winnie and her friends had broken in to.

"She's not hurt," he called after Leigh. "Nothing was damaged. I heard one of the other parents say Case Walker isn't even pressing charges."

The sound of someone else's car door slamming echoed in the night. "Doesn't exactly make me feel better. I stood in a crowd while a police officer named my kid in front of the whole town." Leigh halted, breaths coming in angry huffs. "She trespassed. She broke into a train car, of all things—"

"Kids have been sneaking into the train cars out here since the depot opened, Leigh. You know that. It's practically rite of passage around here."

Up ahead he could make out Winnie's hunched form, shadowed by the overhang slanting from the depot roof. Several other kids milled around, parents, a lone police officer.

"I can't believe you're not more upset." Leigh's hands were on her waist now. "You, solid and upright Drew Renwycke, who's never done a thing wrong."

"We both know that's not—"

"Whatever, just let me handle this." And with that, Leigh left him in the middle of the depot lawn, her marched steps tracking toward the building.

Like mother, like daughter. Just a couple weeks ago, Winnie had given him the same hurled "whatever" as she marched toward the farmhouse. That'd been the day they found Maren climbing up the trellis.

Drew sighed, his head tipping toward the sky—its span of winking stars an audience entirely at ease. Maybe he should be more upset about this. Fear that Winnie's behavior was more than mild teenage acting out.

But all he could think about was Maren back in the square. How perfectly tonight had started and how off-track it'd ended up. And Colin, who'd seemed almost more hurt than angry when he'd seen them.

"Glad I'm not your niece right now."

Drew turned at the voice. Case Walker—the man who ran

who'd run the heritage railroad station since Drew was eight or nine. Every fall his grandparents brought him and his siblings out here at least once for the fourteen-mile ride. Case would always give a tour of the depot station, the museum, talk about what it was like back when people traveled the country by rail.

Drew had gone to school with Case's kids—sat in home-room with Logan, had a crush in junior high on Kate, played a year of basketball with Beckett. The youngest, Raegan, still lived here in town.

The man's crinkle-eyed gaze turned from the depot to Drew. "Confession: When Officer Marley called me about the kids out here, I was tempted to tell him to leave 'em be. Teens have been camping out in these train cars forever."

"That's what I tried to tell Leigh."

"Then I thought about how cold it's supposed to get overnight—and worse, the ramifications of a posse of frantic parents—and figured we'd better go ahead and handle it tonight."

A parent walked past with a sullen kid trailing behind.

Case actually laughed. "Glad I'm not that kid, too."

Drew didn't know Case Walker well, but he knew about him—everybody did. The man had fought in Vietnam and later worked as an international diplomat. Then he'd had an office at the U.N. until his wife had become sick. He'd moved the whole family back to Iowa, left his illustrious career behind.

Started over for the sake of his family—just like Drew was trying to do.

Or had been trying to do. Before both his siblings made it clear they wanted nothing to do with the farm.

"So you've never done a thing wrong? Did I overhear that right?"

Drew's gaze roamed to Leigh, now standing over Winnie, her frustrated voice carrying over the distance. "Leigh's wrong on that. She's got a case of selective memory."

Case's throaty chuckle rose over the pulsing of the wind. "A certain barn party summer of '99 comes to mind." At Drew's questioning glance, he nodded. "Beckett was there. Longest grounding of his life."

And Drew hadn't been grounded at all. Mom and Dad hadn't had time for disciplinary action—not with Grandpa's funeral to plan. Maybe they'd figured that was punishment enough.

"I've been regretting that party for years."

"Not a big fan of regret myself. It's like walking through life with one hand constantly tied behind your back. Not entirely immobilizing, but hindering all the same."

Drew started to the depot once more, Leigh's voice even louder now. "You've got an interesting way of putting things, Mr. Walker."

"Case. And thanks. I'll have to tell that to my two writers —Kate and Logan. Pretty sure they think they get their word-smith skills from their mom. Maybe they're wrong."

Case clapped one hand on Drew's shoulder and then left him to face Leigh and Winnie. Leigh turned to him with a helpless expression.

He took it as permission to step in and as soon as Leigh moved away, he spoke. "Scoot." He lowered onto the bench beside Winnie.

"She didn't have to yell at me in front of everyone." Winnie's hands, red and wind-chapped, knotted together in her lap. "She's the worst."

"She's not the worst, Win. She loves you." He peeled off his gloves and handed them to her. "Put them on."

"We didn't do anything that bad. Jamie says it's tradition

and that probably all our parents did it when they were kids, too. I bet Mom did, which means she has no right to yell at me. Besides, I've never done anything half as bad as what she's done."

"I know you didn't mean to do anything horrible. But I also know you've gotta stop giving your mom such a hard time. Breaking into the school a couple weeks ago, spending all your time with anybody but her, now this . . . you're hurting her."

"Like she never hurt me?"

A strangled sob cracked Winnie's voice, and Drew reached out his arm to pull her in. "She knows she hurt you. And she's been carrying it around forever."

Walking around with one hand tied behind her back.

His gaze trekked over the landscape, following the metal track that emerged from the snow into the distance. Moonlight scattered through bony branches and landed in the snow in splotches.

"Did your mom ever tell you why she named you Winnie?"

Winnie nodded against his arm, her sigh sending her bangs fluttering. "Something about Pooh or whatever."

"There's more to the story than that. When I was kid, my Grandpa—your great-grandfather—was pretty much my best friend. He's the one I talked to about things. And your uncle Colin, he had this dog. It was named Bacon and—"

Winnie lifted her head. "Bacon?"

"His favorite food at the time? I don't know. But anyway, he had his dog. Well, your mom . . . she had her Winnie the Pooh bear. And, I'm not going to lie, I teased her about it. A lot. But she loved that thing. Carried it with her everywhere. Sometimes at night I'd walk past her bedroom and hear her talking to it."

"So she named me after it. It's cold, Uncle Drew. Let's go."

"All that's waiting for you is a grounding, so you might as well hear me out first." But he took off his coat and draped it over her lap.

"You're wearing a coat." Maren's voice. She noticed the oddest things.

"So your mom had this Pooh bear and she loved it and by the time she was, I don't know, thirteen or fourteen, it was so faded you couldn't even tell what color it was. But every time one of its eyes fell out, she sewed it back in. When its old red shirt ripped, she stitched that up too. She saved it from I don't even know how many trips to Goodwill or garage sale piles when Mom would try to get rid of it. And Dad joked once that if she could take that good of care of a stuffed animal, then one day she'd make a darn good mom."

Winnie's restless shifting stilled.

Another parent showed up for another kid. Over on the far edge of the shoveled boardwalk that rimmed the depot, Case and the cop who'd gathered the parents in town laughed about something.

And then Winnie buried herself against him, one arm reaching across his stomach. And he saw Leigh watching from corner of the boardwalk, read her wounded eyes and the longing in her expression.

She's right.

About Winnie and needing space to connect with her daughter. No, it wasn't a competition. But he was in the way, wasn't he?

He let out a resigned sigh and kissed Winnie's forehead before nudging her to her feet. "Come on, let's go home."

* * *

THE FARMHOUSE WAS dark when Leigh pulled her car into the

gravel drive that circled the house. Drew had expected at least a light or two, some sign of Colin and Maren back from the carnival.

Had they not returned yet?

He climbed from the passenger seat, gaze roving the shoveled drive. Colin's car was sandwiched in between his and Leigh's. But where was Maren's?

Dread heavied his steps as he approached the house, Leigh and Winnie behind him. He found Colin inside, sitting in the living room, only the fireplace for light, down to its last flickers. "Where's Maren?"

Colin didn't turn from the fire. "She packed and left as soon as we got home."

"What? Why? Did you try to stop her?"

"She's a grown woman, Drew. She can leave when she wants."

It didn't make sense. Their date, the dinner, the sleigh ride . . . that almost kiss. Everything had been perfect.

Until Colin.

"What did you say to her?"

His brother stood.

"You can ditch the accusatory tone. I didn't say anything. *She* said she didn't want to be the reason we couldn't reconcile. And that maybe if she left, we'd have the space we need to work things out."

"That's ridiculous."

"The thought of us working things out? That's what I thought, too."

Colin side-stepped him and left the room. Drew pulled out his phone. Had Maren at least called him? He heard Winnie and Leigh's voices in the background—Winnie asking where Maren was and Colin explaining and Leigh's sighed, "I had a feeling this would happen."

One voicemail. He lifted his phone and listened.

"Drew, I'm really sorry…"

He shuffled to the fireplace, toed a log until it dropped and snuffed out the last flame.

CHAPTER 10

"I cannot believe your parents invited Dean to this." Remy hissed her disbelief as she shook out of her lime green coat. "And his new wife? Really?"

Maren took Remy's coat and purse—her usual designated role at Mom and Dad's annual Christmas Eve party. Guests mingled throughout the house—neighbors, church people, long-time friends of the family. The same album as always played on Dad's vintage record player—big band arrangements of Christmas classics—and Mom had outdone herself with the decorations. There was a Christmas tree in every room of the first floor—varying sizes—and the whole house smelled of cinnamon.

"They didn't invite him. Not exactly." Maren led the way to the narrow hallway where a guest bedroom served as the coat drop-off spot. Not until Remy followed her in did she explain. "Mom got to talking to Dean's mom at the Christmas Eve service earlier this evening. They were such good friends back when we were dating. She mentioned the party. Had no idea they'd actually show up with Dean and Bridget in tow."

Mom had apologized to her so many times tonight she'd

lost count. And at least twice Dad had intercepted her before she ended up in the same room as Dean and his wife.

"Just tell me Elaine's not here. I can't deal with Dean's sister tonight. Not on Christmas Eve."

"Promise. She's not here."

Remy walked to the vanity and straightened the red and green headband in her cropped hair. "Well, if you want, we could sneak out that window over there. Go find a party that's *not* crawling with exes."

"I'm fine, Rem."

The sounds of the party drifted under the doorway and Remy's teasing eyes sparked with mischief. "Or better yet, we go out there and start spreading rumors that you just spent two weeks in Iowa with your cover model and it was the most romantic two weeks of your life."

She grinned at Remy in the mirror. "Except that'd be lying and I don't know, something about it being Christmas and all ... doesn't sit well with me."

Remy turned to face her. "Not entirely a lie. When you texted to say you were home, I asked if you got to see Colin. You said yes. I asked if it was as romantic as you imagined. You said it had its moments."

Vague answers about a subject she didn't want to get into via text.

Didn't want to get into at all, really.

Because for eight days she'd been working to convince herself what'd happened in Iowa was just a happy little working vacation tucked into a busy holiday season. And yes, maybe she'd felt ... things. Let herself get carried away by the pretty season and the charming town.

And the really, *really* great guy she'd gotten to know.

But she couldn't stay there. Not knowing what it'd mean for Drew. Colin had finally come home, the one thing Drew had wanted for so long. Such a huge step for his hope of pulling his family back together and getting the farm up and running again.

But she hadn't missed Colin's reaction to seeing them together. And she couldn't—wouldn't—be the thing standing in between their reconciliation.

If she was honest, though, it wasn't only that. It was also . . . well, just the embarrassment of it all. Hearing Colin say out loud that she'd come to Iowa looking for him—it sounded so ridiculous. Humiliating. Sure, Drew might've refuted Colin, but give him a day or two and he'd probably look back and wonder what he was thinking, going on a date with a girl who not even a month ago had still been carrying around a postcard from his brother.

Drew was so grounded, while she was so flighty, fanciful. *Just like Dean said.* And Drew would've seen it eventually.

"What aren't you saying, Mare?" Remy's hands were on her hips.

Instead of answering, she leaned in to hug her friend. "I missed you."

"I missed you, too, but don't think I don't know what this is. Your art of avoidance is slipping."

"I'll try to work on that," she said over Remy's shoulder before releasing her. "Come on, let's go join the party. Mom hired a new caterer this year and the appetizers are amazing. I hid a plate in the pantry."

"Glad to see Iowa didn't change you *too* much."

Maren willed a laugh to the surface and spent the rest of the evening doing the same, trying her best to make conversation and hold her smile in place.

And ignoring the questions that kept itching through her: Had Colin stuck around for Christmas at the farm? Had the church's live nativity—the one she'd heard about during her two Sundays there—gone well? Did Winnie know yet she was getting a new bed for Christmas?

What was Drew doing tonight?

And why hadn't she heard from him?

And what might've happened if she hadn't left in such a rush?

An hour passed, then two. Maren extracted herself from a conversation about Christmas movies and went in search of something to drink. But she paused in the entryway at the sight of Dean knotting a scarf around his neck, ushering Bridget to the door.

Impulse took over then and she found herself hurrying over the foyer's oval Christmas rug and catching the door before it closed behind the couple.

"Dean."

He stopped halfway down the cement steps.

The wreath on the front door jingled as she pulled it closed. The white of the moon spread in a haze over a starless sky.

"Hey, Mare."

Bracing night air cloaked her and she wrapped her arms around her middle. "Hey, Dean, Bridget. I'm sorry I didn't have a chance to say hi earlier."

He glanced back at Bridget, who offered Maren a nimble smile before stepping to the sidewalk. "I'll get the car started."

Dean turned back to her, question or maybe apology in his eyes. "I didn't know you'd be here. My parents insisted we stop by. Sorry if it was awkward or anything."

"No, it's okay. I'm glad our parents are still friends." She shivered against the breeze. Why hadn't she grabbed a coat before following him out? "I just . . . I wanted to say . . . "

She took a pinched breath and let it out before going on.

"I'm sorry if I ever made you feel like my writing was more important to me than you were."

He buttoned up his coat. "That was a long time ago."

"But I never said it. And I'm sorry if I idealized my own

character too much or something. If I ever implied ... or made you feel like ... "

Her words stalled but it didn't matter because Dean's abrupt laughter interrupted her anyway.

"I'm trying to make a heartfelt apology here, Dean."

"I know." He fastened his last button. "But here you are apologizing for your writing dream and your detective guy of all things and it's hitting me how ridiculous we were." At her stare, he shook his head. "How ridiculous *I* was, I mean. I was legit jealous of your main character, do you realize that?"

"That's why I'm saying I'm sorry."

"You do not need to be sorry for my own insecurities, Mare." He shook his head again while pulling on a pair of leather gloves. "Look, yes, I was continually frustrated that you seemed to prefer writing over my company. And I made a big deal of reading your story notes and not digging your main character and all that. But those were just my chosen big ticket items. We had a lot of other problems—smaller stuff, but stuff that mattered."

What? "This is not how I expected this conversation to go."

"I didn't expect we'd ever have this conversation at all. But come on, think about it. We were constantly on different pages. If we'd paid more attention to the little things, we might've been smart enough to call it quits before it got to the big stuff." He glanced back at his wife waiting in the car. "But it all worked out, yeah? I'm married to someone who thinks my vintage car obsession is charming and you've had a book published and ... " He shrugged. "It's all good, right?"

"Sure." Her voice had gone flat. "All good."

He gave her a small wave before backing away and jogging to his car. She watched him drive away, the cold numbing her fingers, but she couldn't make herself turn around. Not yet.

She heard the door unlatch behind her.

"Who left? Who'd I miss saying goodbye to?" Mom joined

her on the top step. "And what are you doing out here without a coat?"

"That was Dean and his wife."

Mom groaned. "Drat. I was trying all night to keep you from having to deal with him. I kept sending your dad to intercept. He must've slacked off."

"Don't scold him, Mom, I'm the one who chased Dean out. Had this silly idea that maybe I should apologize for some things. I don't know, get closure or something." Mom snuck an arm around her waist and she leaned in. "But he basically brushed me off. Told me there was no need to apologize for the big things, when really it's the little things that broke us up. Whatever that means."

Mom tilted her head as Dean's headlights disappeared around the block. "Hmm. Makes sense, I guess."

"Really?" Just bizarre, this whole night.

"Sure, I mean, look at the flip side. It's the little things that make a great marriage. Your father and I? We've had some splendid big moments. But it's the little stuff that glues us together—the way he always knows where I've left my glasses, the post-it notes I still leave him around the house, how he peeled himself away from a half-dozen conversations tonight to make sure his daughter didn't have an awkward run-in with an ex-boyfriend." Mom chuckled. "'Course, then you went an orchestrated a run-in on your own."

Mom steered her around. "Come on. Let's go inside and get warmed up and eventually all these guests will leave and you can finally tell me what happened in Iowa."

"You sound like Remy."

Mom tsked and opened the front door. "I'm your mother, dear. I deserve the details first."

* * *

IF LEIGH HAD to move out, at least she'd picked a good townhouse.

"I can't believe they let us stop over on Christmas Eve night." Leigh turned a full circle in the home's spacious first floor. Her voice echoed off the freshly painted walls and laminate floor—not real wood, but it looked to be in good shape at least.

"That would be the perk of living in a small town." And going to church with the landlord. When Drew had found out what house Leigh was interested in, he realized he knew the owner. He'd talked to Pete at the Christmas Eve program and asked if there was any way they could take a look after the service.

Call it an early Christmas present.

Drew wandered to the fireplace in the corner, crouched and opened the grate near the bottom. "Looks easy enough to light the pilot. Red knob's the gas. Then there's the pilot on/off switch and the button that actually lights the thing." He glanced over at Leigh, who was now checking out the galley-style kitchen. He could write fireplace instructions for her later.

He replaced the grate and stood. "So what do you think?"

"I think it's perfect." She worked her way along the cupboards, opening each one, and then gasping when she opened the pantry door. "It's huge! I've never had a pantry before."

He had to swallow his own rebuttal, the reminder that the farmhouse had a pantry three times the size of the little closet she'd disappeared inside now. And that he'd have more space than he knew what to do with once she moved out.

It'd hounded him for days, the approaching emptiness. The house felt hollow enough as it was, ever since Maren left just over a week ago. Colin might've filled one of the bedrooms, but he was like a ghost in the house—whisking through now and then but more often than not out with hometown friends. Their conversations were stilted. The interactions, minimal.

But he's still here.

Maybe the fact should fill him with hope. But he kept waiting for the inevitable moment when Colin would take off again. Drew had thought tonight—the serving, the live nativity—might make him feel better, tug his Christmas focus back where it belonged. But as he'd stood outside, moonlight sloping over the inclined roof of the makeshift stable, the candlelight and the costumes, the languid strains of "Silent Night," none of it managed to quell the tide of unease churning inside him.

Leigh's happiness now, though, helped at least a little. She hadn't stopped smiling since they pulled up in front of the place. He should've seen it earlier—her hesitation about living at the farmhouse, her need for space. Leigh had always been that way—independent, a free spirit. She'd felt squashed at the farm.

He'd just been too busy trying to decide what was right for her to see it.

"I'm already imagining where I'm going to put furniture. Once I buy some, that is. I'll need to save up awhile longer, but I'm sure I can get some cheap second-hand stuff in the meantime." She tried out a light switch in the kitchen and jumped when it turned out to the be the garbage disposal.

"Or you can take some from the farm. Not like I need everything. You should take the piano, at least."

Apparently he hadn't done enough to mask the dejection in his tone, because Leigh angled around the peninsula that overlooked the rest of the first floor and met him in the narrow dining area. "You understand, right? I love you to death, Drew."

"I know."

"And I know you're dying to ask how I can afford this, but the assistant manager position comes with a raise and I've reviewed my budget plenty. Frankly, the rent's uncannily cheap."

Probably because Pete was giving her a break. The man had a soft heart. And no doubt Seth Walker was being more than generous with the raise he'd granted Leigh. Maple Valley might be quirky, but there was no shortage of kindness and generosity.

"Besides, this change is going to be as good for you as it us." Leigh looked up at him. "You can go back to being the doting uncle who spoils Winnie like crazy instead of having to deal with things like calls from the school and whatnot."

"You realize I'll hold you to that, right?" He zipped up his vest. "She comes asking me for money for expensive concert tickets to that one band she likes, I'm not only getting the tickets, I'm driving her there and buying her a t-shirt and making sure she gets backstage."

"You have my full permission." She watched him replace his fingerless gloves. "Why are you bundling up? I know Winnie's eager for presents, but we haven't seen the second floor yet."

"I know. I thought maybe you'd want to check it out yourself. I'll wait outside."

She just looked at him for a moment, excitement giving way to gratefulness. She pulled him into a hug and promised not to take long.

He was at the door when she stopped him. "Drew?"

"Yup?" He clasped the knob.

"You could call her, you know."

"Who—"

"Don't even pretend. Text, email, show up on her doorstep like she did yours. You've got all kinds of options."

He turned. "Leigh—"

"None of my business, I know, and don't think I haven't noticed how massively hard you've been trying to give me space. Stepping back and letting your siblings figure out their own lives, that's one thing. But giving too much space to the first girl to pique your interest in I don't even know how many years, that's another thing entirely."

If there was a response to be had, he couldn't find it. Not underneath his surprise at how clearly his sister had seen through him. And how easy she made it sound.

And how crazily, incredibly much he missed Maren Grant.

"Just don't wait too long, okay?"

Words still stalled, he only nodded and then let himself out of the house. And then stopped halfway down the sidewalk when he saw the car parked behind his at the curb, the figure leaning against it. "Colin?"

Colin straightened as Drew approached. "Winnie said you guys were here. Well, not *here*-here. She said you were looking at a townhouse and Maple Valley only has a few of those, so it wasn't hard to find you."

"I thought you were with friends tonight."

Colin's gaze dropped to the ground, one foot digging into the snow. "No, uh, actually I went to the Christmas Eve thing at the church. Sat in back." He glanced up. "Hey, remember that time a kid accidentally burned down the stable during the live nativity?"

"That was you, Colin."

"My first taste of acting." His grin faded just a hint. "Huh, maybe it should've been a sign. Anyway . . . " He looked past Drew and took a breath, as if gathering energy for his next words. "I'm getting ready to head out."

"What?"

"Said bye to Winnie at the house. Car's packed, gassed up. All that's left is you and Leigh and—"

"You can't leave. It's Christmas Eve. Mom and Dad are coming in tomorrow and—"

"And that's why I'm going." Colin's stance went limp, hands in his pockets. He slackened against his car. "You know how it is, all the times they've had to bail me out of stuff. I've disappointed them one too many times."

Drew opened his mouth, but . . . he had nothing. No argument, no pleading request for Colin to stay. Maybe he really was turning some kind of corner. Learning to wait instead of rushing in to advise or fix things or whatever.

Learning to hush his own regret and believe the God he was trying to trust his own future with could also be entrusted with his family's.

"I'm just not ready." Colin twisted a glove in his hands. "I'm sorry about the farm. I know you had big plans."

It was the first time Colin had brought it up since the night of the carnival. And for the first time since Drew had made the decision to move home in the first place, something loosened inside him.

Do you really want to be a farmer?

Maren's voice, her question . . . it'd hummed along under the surface for more than a week now. And maybe he could finally really answer it.

No. Did he love the idea of keeping Grandpa's dream alive? Sure. Would it have been great if both he and Colin could've made a living off the land? Yeah, it'd sounded nice.

But would either of them have been happy?

"It's okay, Colin."

"And about Maren . . . "

First time she'd come up, too. Out loud, anyway. But there wasn't a day since she'd left he hadn't felt her absence.

Colin opened his car door, reached inside and pulled out a book. Maren's book. "Early Christmas gift."

"Why . . . ?"

"Spent the last two days reading it. If you haven't yet, you really should."

Colin's face stared at him from the cover. "I will eventually." When he could get its author out of his head long enough to focus on it.

"Just don't take too long."

Same thing Leigh had said only minutes ago. Which was strange, come to think of it—his siblings giving him advice instead of the other way around. "Why?"

Colin rounded his car and opened the door. "Because she wrote you onto the page before she'd ever met you."

He dropped into the car.

CHAPTER 11

The last time Maren Grant pulled up to the Renwycke farmhouse, took in the faded barn and the snow-laced maple tree, the circle drive that wrapped around the front of the house like a gravel grin, she'd half-expected to find the property abandoned.

This time, the signs of life were everywhere. Footprints in the snow and tire tracks on the road. Garland coiled around the porch railing and stringed lights tracing the rooftop.

So why didn't anyone answer her knock?

She tried again, then stepped back, porch boards creaking under her boots. Boots she barely needed as sunshine thawed the air this Christmas Day. If it stayed this warm, snowy fields would turn patchy and that row of icicles over the porch might fall. So much for a white Christmas.

Didn't matter, though.

She didn't need a snow globe landscape or haze of holiday magic. She didn't need white-tipped trees or snowflakes and stars bedecking a dazzling sky.

She did, however, need Drew.

Who didn't appear to be here.

She'd figured it might be incredibly awkward crashing a family Christmas. Had asked herself a hundred times why she couldn't at least wait until the day after to come here. But after she'd poured her heart out to Mom and Dad and Remy last night, they'd practically forced her out the door. In fact, if they'd had their way, she would've left last night.

Dad: *"You're worried Drew will think you're too flighty and fanciful? That's ridiculous. It's one of the best things about you. And if he's a no-nonsense kind of guy, then you're the perfect complement for him. If he's any kind of smart, he'll realize that and like you all the more for it."*

Mom: *"I know you're worried about coming in between him and his brother. But they're grown men, dear. They'll either choose to work out their issues or they won't. But whatever happened between them started long before you came along and you know it."*

Remy: *"Don't be an idiot, Mare. Go."*

So she'd obeyed and every time the worry crept in that she'd be disrupting the Renwycke family's Christmas, she reminded herself that she *had* actually prayed about this last night. And that the best things could happen on Christmas. That Mary and Joseph had made their own trek, probably full of doubts and concerns and…

A voice cleared.

Maren turned . . .

And froze at the top of the porch steps.

Drew stood in the middle of the lawn, arms crossed over a flannel shirt she'd seen him in at least a half-dozen times. No coat. Of course. His quiet gaze was enough to jolt her heart out of rhythm.

"How long have you been standing there?"

"Not long." He stepped toward the porch stairs.

"And you couldn't have announced yourself?" She heard her own huff of annoyance, felt a petulant frown skip over her face.

One that couldn't hope to actually take hold.

Because he just looked so . . .

Perfect.

Drew stopped at the second to last stair, now eye level with her, a half-bemused, half-charmed grin tugging at his lips. "Just wanted to see if you'd go and climb the lattice again. Or maybe try breaking in through a window this time."

"You're never going to let that go, are you?" The question came out more winded than scolding and oh, if every last speck of composure didn't slip from her grasp just then, including the words she'd practiced on the drive down from Minnesota. The ones that'd been building ever since last night.

Or maybe—probably—even before that.

Since that night in Drew's woodshop when he'd spilled his heart. Since she'd seen the way he loved his family.

Since he'd almost kissed her under a winter moon.

"Whatcha doing here, Grant?"

"I . . . because . . . you . . . " Gone were her words and in their place only the clatter of the barn door hitting against its frame in the wind and an icicle dropping to the porch floor.

But Drew's eyes sparked with pleasure anyway and he reached for her hand. "Come on, I've got something to show you."

He led her into the house, through the living room, toward the stairs.

"Where is everyone? I was so nervous about interrupting a family gathering."

He tugged her up the stairs. "Leigh wanted to show Winnie and my parents the townhouse she's going to move into."

"On Christmas Day?"

"Landlord gave us the key last night."

They wound through the second floor hallway and to the

stairs leading into the attic. Drew climbed through first, then grabbed her hand once more to pull her up.

Her gasp filled the room.

She'd grown accustomed to the attic's emptiness—its exposed rafters and hollow shelves and unadorned window seat.

But now . . .

A serene pale blue wrapped around the room and books lined the shelves. A new comforter and pillows—white and lacy—covered the bed. And against one wall, a desk. Wait, she recognized that . . .

She moved to it, took in its curved legs and refinished surface, not a single nick or dent. She spun. "The desk from the woodshop. The antique. When in the world . . . ?" She'd only been gone nine days and he'd done all this?

Drew crossed the room. "Just wanted it to be ready in case a certain author ever showed up on my doorstep again needing a place to write a book."

She blinked away tears that didn't make any sense. Not with such joy spilling through her. "Here I told myself I didn't come here for a big moment. That it was never about one big magical moment anyway but a hundred little moments that all add up to something way more real and . . . and I mean, look at Christmas—Jesus's birth, the grandest moment in all of history and it happened softly and quietly. So I didn't need a big moment, that's what I told myself. And then you go and do this and . . . "

Drew shook his head even while he reached for her hands. "I really have no idea what you're talking about."

"I'm not sure I do either."

He guided her hands around his waist until her fingers laced behind him, then circled his own around her. "Why'd you come back, Maren?"

"Because I didn't say goodbye before. Because I really do

still need to finish my book and this really is the perfect place." She took a breath. "Because I was hoping we could go on a second date, but I refuse to sit around for a year waiting and hoping you'll ask me."

"We can definitely go on a second date." He tipped her chin up. "Right after we pick up where the first one left off."

And then, in the new *new* most enchanted moment of Maren Grant's life, Drew closed the last sliver of space between them and kissed her breathless.

THE END
Kind of.

Just in case you're wondering, Maren finished her book and went on to sign a contract for three more Ethan Whitney books.

Drew sold his farmland to Byron Pratt, but held on to the house and barn and shed and woodshop. He insisted Leigh accept a third of the sale price and sent the other third to Colin.

And then he went into business making custom furniture.

Drew and Maren did indeed have their second date. And then a third. And a fourth. You get the picture, yes? Happily ever after doesn't begin to cover it.

As for Colin . . . I think we'll hear from him again. :)

ONE ENCHANTED EVE

CHAPTER 1

*I*f Rylan Jefferson was lucky, after tonight she'd never have to see Colin Renwycke again.

And if she was very lucky, he'd take his punishment like a man and this would all be over in a matter of minutes.

Rylan perched on the stainless steel island at the front of her culinary classroom, legs dangling over the edge, the heels of her wool-lined boots knocking against its base. Arms folded, she watched as her boss, the private school's owner, Chef Potts—stout, clad in a plaid robe, and clearly none too pleased to have been roused from sleep—rounded the kitchenette workstation where Colin had caused his latest disaster.

Blackened stains marred the countertop. Splatters of meringue and melted ice cream dripped off its edges. Mixing bowls, a sticky frying pan, an abandoned mini blowtorch.

And permeating the air, the scent of burnt rum.

Oh yeah, after three months of tormenting her, Colin Renwycke—undeniably the worst, most undisciplined student baker Rylan had ever tried to teach during her two years at the Denver Culinary Institute—was about to get his comeuppance.

It was all she could do to swallow an eager *finally*.

"What a mess," Chef Potts observed. Hands hidden in the pockets of his robe, snow-white mustache twitching, he released a yawn. Convenient, at least, that the man lived next door to the school. But how early did he go to bed? It couldn't be later than nine now. The evening class, last one before Christmas break, had started at seven. The fire alarms had gone off around 8:30 or so. Chef Potts, looking half-asleep, had arrived at the same time as the local fire department.

Ninety minutes from first egg cracked to complete catastrophe. True to form for Colin.

She refused to look at Colin now, where he leaned with his back against a frost-covered window. Didn't have to, to know what she'd see. Spattered apron, Oxford rolled up to his elbows underneath. Dark hair, light eyes. Blue. Annoyingly so. And they always seemed to be laughing at her, even when he wasn't wearing his obnoxiously dimpled jaunty grin.

Shouldn't a man who must have nine, ten years on everyone else in the class turn out to be the star baker? The one with experienced focus and precision?

The one least likely to heckle Rylan at every opportunity?

Chef Potts, owner of the institute as well as a string of restaurants and bakeries from Denver to Colorado Springs, shook his head before turning to Rylan. "Baked Alaska gone wrong?"

"Exactly." At her resolute nod, her hair clip's last hold gave way and a mess of tangled brown spilled over her shoulder. She blamed the wind, the twenty minutes standing outside the two-story brick building in the biting cold, waiting for the fire department to allow everyone back into the institute.

At least it had been snowing. A gorgeous salting of the landscape, silver in the moonlight. Sometimes when it snowed, when the crisp, mountainous air cleansed her lungs, she could almost believe away the past few years. The lost dream. The broken heart. Almost.

"*Not* exactly." The offender himself spoke up. "Everyone else was making a classic Baked Alaska, yes, but—"

"Because that's what they were told to do," Rylan interjected as she hopped off the counter. The rest of the students, all of whom had gone home by now, had followed the recipe she'd provided. Something Colin had consistently proven incapable of.

"I've made a traditional Alaska a dozen times. I decided to try a variation, that's all." Colin shrugged, just enough remorse in his expression to potentially fool Chef Potts.

But not her. Oh, no. "Chef Potts, this is just the latest calamity—"

"Oh, come on, I think *calamity* is a bit strong." There it was. The taunting smile.

"He's ruined equipment, he's dropped I-don't-even-know-how-many glass bowls, and he's constantly swapping ingredients."

Colin moved to his workstation, planted his palms on the counter top. "Because some of us like to experiment. Unlike *others* who need a recipe card just to boil water."

The urge to chuck a tea towel at him nearly overpowered her. She took a deep breath. Another. And another. Same trick she used while waiting for a soufflé to fall. Her next words were measured, even. "He should be expelled."

There. She'd said it. And quite professionally too, if she did say so herself. None of the livid irritation she felt lacing her tone. Which was important considering it wasn't only Colin's future Chef Potts held in his hands.

The renowned chef and restaurateur had put the word out just last week that he was looking for a head baker for his latest investment—a trendy bakery in Denver's up-and-coming LoHi neighborhood. She'd submitted her résumé so quickly he probably thought she'd had it ready and waiting for just such an opportunity.

Which she had. She was only thirty-four. She had to believe it wasn't too late to reclaim her dream of running her own kitchen rather than spending her days stuck in a classroom.

Longing pulsed through her, heady and intense. How many times did a girl have to watch a dream die before at last discovering an open door?

Oh, please let Potts be my open door.

"You want to expel me?" Colin's gasp intruded. "Wait a second—"

"Chocolate sponge, eh?" Chef Potts cut Colin off. He was leaning over Colin's mess of a dessert.

Colin's helpless gaze swung back to Potts. "Uh, yes sir. I was going for a dark chocolate orange Alaska bombe. Thus, the rum."

Chef Potts nodded. "You were going to flambé it." He reached for a spoon. He was actually going to try a bite of that mess?

"It's December. It's snowing. The mood of the dessert . . . it just kind of demanded it." Colin shoved up a half-unrolled sleeve.

That was his excuse? The mood demanded it? Rylan faced him across the workstation. "You were given instructions, Colin. You didn't follow them. And food doesn't have a mood."

His attention hooked on her for the briefest of seconds. For once, there wasn't a single teasing glint resting in his expression. In fact, she could swear that was pity flickering in his arctic eyes—there and gone in a moment. But it was enough to send a pang she didn't understand on a winding path toward her heart.

Where it found only a closed door. *No room for emotion in the kitchen.* No space for memories. For the long-ago whispered words of another, of one who'd once looked at her exactly as Colin had just now.

As if she couldn't possibly be more pathetic. And so very mistaken.

Brent.

Didn't seem to matter how many times she swept away her dusty hurt. It blew in all over again at the slightest reminder.

"Too much alcohol. That was your only misstep."

She blinked at Chef Potts' declaration, the sound of his spoon clinking in the sink.

"Your flavors are excellent. I'd take that any day over the classic rendition."

Had he forgotten the part about Colin completely disregarding her recipe? Did he remember the smoke alarm, the fire truck, the students all standing around on the lawn while the desserts they'd spent two class sessions working on wilted into melty piles?

"I really am sorry for the mess, sir. I'll clean it all up. I'll pay to replace anything I've broken. There's an extra credit course between Christmas and New Year's, right? I could take that, if it'd help." Colin's glance alighted on Rylan once more. "Just don't kick me out. It took me a long time to . . . I finally have something of a career path and . . . " He ran his fingers down the straps of his apron. "I'd just really appreciate another chance."

Either Colin Renwycke was an impressive actor or, for once, he spoke from a place of sincerity.

Chef Potts looked from Rylan to Colin back to Rylan once more. "I run a strict school. Always have. And I trust my instructors. If you choose to kick him out of your class or give him a failing grade, then he won't be coming back next semester."

Oh, sweet relief. No more trying to teach while Colin cracked jokes under his breath to the other bakers. No more spending an hour after every class cleaning up after him. No more watching him butcher every one of her recipes.

No more begrudging, silent admissions to herself that, honestly, half the time Colin's changes to her instructions resulted in heavenly flavored, if not entirely well-baked creations. He *did* have intuition. He just didn't have the discipline to hone it.

Chef Potts went on. "However, I've popped in on your class enough times to know that with Mr. Renwycke here, you've got a natural talent on your hands. He's creative, has good instincts. A good instructor is usually willing to put up with a few quirks in order to nurture that kind of talent."

A few quirks? Last week he'd spilled an entire bowl of red velvet cake batter . . . *on her.* And then had the gall to insist it was a good look for her.

"Your call, Ms. Jefferson. And Mr. Renwycke?" He shot an appreciative look to Colin. "Be sure to invite me over if you ever try this variation again. Less rum next time. More care with the torch."

Potts started for the classroom door, but stopped halfway there. "Oh, and by the way, Ms. Jefferson, are you free on Christmas Eve?" He cinched his robe's belt. "Before you answer that, let me tell you I received your résumé, and I always start my interview process with a demonstration of some kind. I'm hosting a party on Christmas Eve and would like you to provide an original dessert—a signature recipe."

Rylan's heart thumped. All at once, Colin forgotten, she could taste it—the dream. Her own bakery—well, almost her own. Her own kitchen, her own glass display cases waiting to be filled with her own creations. Sweet, tantalizing. And she wouldn't squander it this time. Wouldn't get distracted. Wouldn't lose it all.

"Absolutely, Chef Potts. Of course. Whatever you want. Whenever you want."

"You don't have holiday plans that might get in the way?"

It seemed almost a challenge. Understandable. Bakeries did some of their best business over the holidays. If she were ever to run one of Potts' bakeries, she wouldn't have the luxury of a Christmas break. "No." No plans at all. Pitiable, perhaps, but it was the truth.

"One recipe. Something with personality. Dazzle me." Then, with a swift nod, he was out the door.

And she couldn't help it—like a child in the snow—the squeal, the clapped hands, the twirl and—

She froze. Colin. Watching her with a mix of interest and trepidation. "Right. You."

"Right. Me. You aren't actually going to kick me out me, are you?"

She grabbed her coat from over a stool. "Why wouldn't I? You've made teaching miserable for three months. If it was just the baking mishaps, it'd be one thing, but the constant heckling?"

He fidgeted with the knot of his apron. "I'm sorry, but I just . . . you just . . . you get your back up against the wall so easily. You get flustered the second someone dares to play around with your recipe. It's entertaining."

She buttoned her coat up to her chin. "Well, I'm not here to be your entertainment, Colin Renwycke. I'll make a decision this weekend and let you know by Monday."

With that, she turned from the room, glided down the first floor hallway, and pushed through the exit into the December night. Moonlight traced the craggy edges of the Rockies in the distance, and winter's frosty breathing brushed over her face. She felt the pitter-patter of snowflakes landing in her hair, on her cheeks.

And something else. Something she hadn't dared to feel in so long. *Hope.*

CHAPTER 2

*S*he'd never say yes.

Colin stood outside the townhouse with the burgundy door and the number 22 in gold letters. Pale brick matched the downy layer of snow blanketing the lawn. Just enough sun peeked through an icy sky to cast the barest glint of color over the residential street.

Sugar Lane. Of course Rylan Jefferson lived on Sugar Lane. It fit her profession, if not her personality.

She'll never say yes.

It was a ridiculous idea, showing up on her doorstep early on a Saturday morning, ready to beg his case. Make an impromptu offer she'd most assuredly refuse. But he was out of options. And out of patience—with his going-nowhere existence, with the never-ending string of failures that was his life.

With himself.

Thirty-one and nothing to show for it. When he'd been offered late acceptance into the Denver Culinary Institute this past summer, he'd thought finally—*finally*—he might be on his way to some kind of productive life. An actual career.

Never mind that he was ten years older than everyone else in the class. He was a late bloomer, that's all. For months he'd been imagining the faces of his family members when he showed up at Christmas and announced how well he was doing.

And now he was about to lose out on their long-awaited approval solely because a surly instructor had decided to dislike him from the moment he singed his first piecrust. A biting wind scraped over his cheeks, blustering a curl of snow from the sloping roof of Rylan's narrow home.

She has to say yes.

Resolute, he lifted his fist and knocked.

Nothing.

He burrowed his chin into the lifted collar of his coat, then brushed the snow off the doorbell and pressed his finger to the button. Once, twice.

No answer.

Instead, from inside the townhouse came a muffled shriek, followed by what sounded like furniture overturning. *What the . . . ?* Another squeal, more banging around.

Either Rylan had found a mouse in her pantry and was chasing it around or she'd thrown an all-night rager that was still in progress. Didn't seem like the partying type, though. Not with those dark eyebrows of hers always in such a slant of disapproval.

But at the third muted yelp, his first tinge of worry rose to the surface. What if there was an intruder in there? Someone could've come in back. Or maybe she had a crazy roommate. What if . . . ?

The crash of splintered glass propelled him into action. He knocked again. "Ms. Jefferson? You in there?" He gave a futile try at the doorknob, knowing he'd find it locked. He looked under the welcome mat, ran his fingers over the doorframe. No hidden key.

His attention snagged on a jumbo ceramic flowerpot. Bingo. He found the key underneath and wedged it into the lock. "Rylan? I'm coming in." He twisted the doorknob and gave it a push. "Don't worry, I—"

A screech whizzed past him, along with something black and furry. A cat?

He stopped just inside Rylan's entryway, stunned gaze taking in the sight in front of him. A coffee table tipped to its side. A shattered mirror that looked to have fallen from the wall. Claw marks on an ottoman.

And Rylan herself, standing in the middle of the living room—bedraggled and wide-eyed. Chestnut hair spilled from a lopsided ponytail and the sleeves of her oversized flannel pajamas—white with little candy canes all over them—draped past her hands.

"You . . . what are you . . . why . . . ?" Her words came in sputtered little gasps.

Do not smile. Do not smile.

He didn't smile.

He *laughed*. A boisterous, impossible-to-contain laugh. Just like so many times in class, except this time there was more nonsensical relief than amusement flooding through him. "I thought you were in here fending off a burglar or something. All that noise was a *cat?*"

She huffed a piece of hair out of her eyes. "What are you doing here?"

"I thought I was saving you, but clearly—" He gestured to her torn-apart room. "You have everything under control."

"You broke into my house!"

She was attempting to point at him, at the open door behind him, but with her too-long sleeve shaking around her finger, it only made him laugh more. So not the way to win her over, but he couldn't help it.

"I didn't break in. I used your spare key. You should probably find a better hiding place, by the way."

"Get. Out." The last remaining chunk of her ponytail fell loose and swooped over her ear.

"That is no way to treat your would-be savior." He reached behind to close the door.

"What are you—?"

"I'm going to help you put your house back together." Like she'd begrudgingly helped him clean up his workstation so many times after class. Probably best not to remind her of that.

Both of her arms raised, flopping sleeves and all, in exasperation. "What about me saying 'get out' makes you think I want your help?"

The crack of splintered glass sounded under his shoe. "We'll probably need a broom and dustpan."

Rylan opened her mouth. Closed it. Then simply whirled and disappeared from the room.

He shrugged and moved farther into her living space, reached down and set her coffee table to rights. Kind of a cool one, really. Looked like it might be made of reclaimed barn wood or something. Actually all the furniture in this room had a unique flair. A rocking chair that was clearly an antique, but with cushions that appeared re-covered with a sprightly green print. Intricately carved fireplace mantle.

Drew would love it all. His older brother had taken the plunge and opened a carpentry business earlier this year. Probably wildly successful already.

Well, if Rylan would give him half a chance, if she'd just hear him out, maybe someday he might be successful, too. No more part-time modeling and acting gigs. No more faking his way through drama school adjunct teaching or a slew of random temp jobs.

He was *good* in the kitchen. He knew he was. Every girl

he'd ever charmed with a candlelit, homemade dinner had told him so.

More importantly, Mom had. Over and over as a kid she'd told him how creative he was with flavors and textures. He'd waffled between embarrassed and proud at her praise. Between thinking baking was a sissy hobby and wondering if maybe there was a reason he so often found himself helping Mom and Grandma in the kitchen rather than hanging out with Dad or Grandpa in the woodshop or cornfields.

Or maybe it was just easier being around Mom than facing Dad's constant gruff disappointment.

Maybe. But surely it wasn't a pipedream to think there might be some kind of purpose for his natural talent and instincts. Where Drew could see a few slabs of wood and envision a desk, Colin could eye an assortment of ingredients and dream up a tantalizing dessert.

If he could just convince Rylan—

"You've got a serious case of wishful thinking if you assume cleaning up my living room is going to impact my decision on whether or not to kick you out of my class."

He turned. She held a broom in one hand and a dustpan in the other. And there went those eyebrows again. Honestly, they'd be an oddly attractive feature if they weren't dipped into such a deep *V* all the time.

"I'm helping you clean up because I'm nice. That's all." *Lie.*

But he could hardly tell her the truth. That, yes, he was here because he planned to talk his way into her good graces. But also because, well, he couldn't sleep last night. He couldn't sleep because he couldn't stop replaying that moment in Rylan's classroom when Potts had asked her about her holiday plans.

Such a simple *no*, she'd uttered. He didn't think she even realized how it'd come out. A forlorn little whisper.

Call him crazy, but he'd actually felt sorry for her. The

churlish instructor with the wild hair had tugged on his sympathy until the idea had hatched itself. He just had to find a way to issue the invitation that wouldn't make it seem entirely daft. Which he was pretty sure it was.

"How did a cat do so much damage anyway? I don't understand how . . . wait. Your cat. I let her outside." What if she . . . he . . . it . . . wasn't an outdoor cat? *Good job, Renwycke. Give her another reason to despise you.*

But Rylan only handed over the broom and dustpan and then flopped onto the couch, as if finally giving up on getting him out of her house. Over the couch hung a large painting of a bridge, its brass frame burnished and bulky. He tossed his coat onto the couch beside her and started sweeping up the glass.

After a minute of silence, Rylan finally spoke. "She's not my cat."

"She's not?"

"I heard her meowing outside last night. Saw her standing on my doorstep, skinny and half-frozen." She shrugged. "I felt bad and let her in."

He stopped sweeping. "You let a stray cat into your house?"

"Hey, she was fine until you rang the doorbell this morning. You freaked her out."

"She could have a disease."

"She was desperate and lonely."

"I don't think cats get lonely." But surprise, surprise, Rylan Jefferson had a heart. Maybe that's what he should do to earn her favor—pretend to be desperate and lonely. He used to be an actor, after all.

Although, would there be that much acting involved?

He gave that taunting thought the solid mental shunt it deserved. He wasn't desperate, nor was he lonely. He was simply . . . determined.

146

This had to work out. For once in his life, he had to finish something he'd started. Give his parents, his sister and niece, his brother a reason to admire him, maybe even eventually come to depend upon him the way they all depended on Drew.

Especially now that Dad . . .

No. He wouldn't go there. Couldn't.

He took a ragged breath and swept up the last piece of broken glass. Finally, he turned to Rylan. Time to level with her. "Listen, I did come over to try to talk you into letting me stay at the institute."

She shook her head. "Not a chance—"

"And to invite you home for Christmas." He blurted it out in a fit of hopelessness. *Crazy, ridiculous idea.*

But there was no taking it back now.

* * *

HE COULDN'T POSSIBLY BE serious.

And yet, there he stood—Colin Renwycke—in the middle of her living room, dustpan full of broken glass in his hand, apparently serious as could be.

"I . . . I think I heard you wrong."

"I don't think you did." He set aside the dustpan. "I'm heading home to Iowa tomorrow. You could come. For a week, two weeks, however long you want."

He wanted her to go to Iowa. With him. It had to be some kind of practical joke.

She jumped to her feet. "I need coffee." But one step in, her oversized pajamas got the better of her. She tripped on one too-long leg of pants and flailed her way to the floor. She landed on both palms.

Her *oomph* collided with a groan the second she saw Colin's outstretched hand ready to help her up. Didn't even have the decency to squelch his smirk. "Now aren't you glad I cleaned up all that broken glass?"

She ignored his hand, lurched to her feet, and willed whatever dignity she had left to show on her face as she budged past him toward the kitchen.

"Cute pajamas, by the way," he said as he followed. "Might've tried buying them in your own size, though."

"They were on sale." And it's not as if she'd ever imagined someone else seeing her in them. Certainly not one of her students. Certainly not *this* student.

Morning sun gushed through the window over her kitchen sink. Her favorite room in the house, this one. All brightness and light—robin's egg blue cabinets and cream quartz countertops. Pale yellow walls and shelves lined with baskets of cookbooks and ingredients.

But now, as she pulled a coffee cup from the mug tree on her counter, Colin's presence behind her seemed to shrink the room. How had he even found out where she lived?

"Pop-Tarts?"

She whirled. He held up the box she'd abandoned earlier when that stray cat freaked out at the sound of her doorbell.

Glee danced a jig over his face. "Miss 'I once owned an award-winning bakery' eats Pop-Tarts?"

She snatched the box from his hand. "I happen to love them, and if you think I'm ashamed of that, you're wrong. Go ahead and mock me."

He lifted one palm to his heart. "Me? Mock you? Perish the thought."

"And how do you know about my bakery?"

"Same way I found your address. I Googled you, of course. Wanted to know what kind of woman I was inviting into my home. Er, my brother's home and—" He stopped.

"What?"

"Your hand. What'd that cat do? Maul you?"

Her gaze swooped down to the row of pink gashes across the hand that now held her Pop-Tarts. She'd barely noticed the stinging, what with the jarring appearance of Colin Renwycke in her house. He in that nice black sweater and those nice dark jeans. She in her decidedly un-nice flannels and makeup-less face. What she wouldn't give for a redo on this morning. This whole semester.

How about the past several years while she was at it?

If she could, she'd rewind to a time before a face so incredibly, eerily similar to the one staring at her now—right down to the ridiculous dimples—had turned her heart inside out. Sent her common sense right out the door. Along with, eventually, everything she'd worked so hard for.

Colin looked from her hand to her face. "Where do you keep your rubbing alcohol?"

She blinked. "What?"

"You have no idea where that cat came from or where it's been. Trust me, you need to disinfect those scratches."

"I know I do, but I can do it myself."

He brushed past her. "It'll be hard to take care of with your left hand. It's your right hand that's injured and you're right-handed."

She marched after him. "Did you Google that too?"

He stopped outside her bathroom, turned so suddenly that she nearly ran into him. Whoa, the man smelled of cinnamon and pine. What'd he do? Take a Christmas-scented bubble bath before coming over?

Yikes, not a picture she wanted in her head. She didn't want Colin in her head at all, dressed or otherwise. Didn't even want him in her house, but it seemed he was bent on taking the full tour.

"No, I didn't Google it. I know you're right-handed because I've watched you stir a hundred batters and knead a thousand doughs. Whatever you think of my skills—or lack thereof—I do pay attention in class."

He actually looked irritated. Maybe even angry. Which made zero sense because *he* was the one who'd barged into her home. Teased her about her pajamas, her Pop-Tarts. Tramped through her space as if being here wasn't all kinds of bizarre.

Great, and now he was digging through her medicine cabinet while she just stood there in the bathroom doorway, tongue-tied and so far past exasperated she might as well give up. Let him explore her closets and bedroom and office next, up and move in if he wanted.

"Well, are you going to come in?"

He motioned for her to sit on the edge of the bathtub. She didn't know what to do but acquiesce. He knelt in front of her and reached for her hand.

She jerked back. What was wrong with her? She was acting like that silly cat—jumpy and out of sorts.

Colin only gave a small smile—surprisingly patient. He pulled her hand forward—surprisingly gentle. He pushed the sleeve of her pajama shirt up and then met her eyes. "Gonna sting just a bit."

She sucked in a sharp breath when he brushed the soaked cotton ball over her scratches.

"You should be more careful of the strays you let into your house, Ms. Jefferson."

Ha, she could almost laugh at the subtext. "I don't even like cats. She just looked so neglected out there on my doorstep."

He finished with her hand, then looked up at her once more. "Look, I know you don't like me. And I know I make class . . . difficult."

"To put it lightly." Was that actually a tease in her tone? Suddenly . . . suddenly she really wanted it to be. Something inside her needed to know she wasn't always the brusque and criticizing woman she'd become. Wanted to believe that she could still joke and smile and laugh.

That Brent hadn't taken all of her.

"But I'm serious about my invitation."

"Why? You don't even know me."

"I've been in your class for three and a half months. I know enough."

"Like?" Why prod him on? Why just sit here while Colin reached for her other hand, observed her palm, turned it over? Looking for more scratches, she assumed. Why not pull away and show him to the door and then eat her Pop-Tarts and drink her coffee in peace?

Why the peculiar desire to see what unexpected thing he'd say or do next?

"I know you're not into fashion. You always wear jeans and hoodies to class under your apron. Unless you know Potts is going to be stopping by, in which case you trade out the hoodie for a sweater."

"Why dress up when I know you're most likely going to spill something on me?" Wow, look at her. She'd teased twice.

"I know even when you're critiquing, you still find a way to compliment students' efforts. The other students, anyway." Still kneeling in front of her, he tossed the cotton ball in her trashcan. "I definitely know you're a stickler for following a recipe."

She laughed—an honest-to-goodness, sincere laugh. She laughed at herself. She laughed at the fact that she was sitting on the edge of a bathtub facing Colin Renwycke. Colin who'd Googled her and shown up at her house out of the blue and tended her scratched-up hand. She laughed at the absurdity of it all.

Colin smiled then. And for the first time since that first

class when he'd butchered his first recipe, the dimples weren't annoying.

She sucked in a breath, looked away. Toward the window behind him, the crystalline sky and glittering snow. There'd been a time when this was her favorite season of the year. When all her hopes and far-flung dreams had seemed vibrant and sparkly as Christmas lights.

"I know you don't have any holiday plans. You said that yesterday. And now I know you don't have a single Christmas decoration up."

She met cobalt eyes that saw too much. "It's only December fifth." Had he noticed the lack of framed photos, too? Did he feel bad for her? Did he think her pathetic?

Did she?

No. I'm just busy with other things. Family and friends and holiday plans—sometimes they have to take a backseat while you're busy rebuilding your life.

Which in her case now meant coming up with a recipe to impress Chef Potts. Well, and teaching that three-day extra credit course at the institute between Christmas and New Year's. Usually the teaching staff drew straws to see which unlucky instructor would get stuck giving up the holiday time. This year, she'd figured she may as well offer. Might give her a leg up with Potts.

Colin's knees brushed hers as he shifted. "I also know you need me."

It was the nudge she needed, a jolt free of whatever fuzzy fog had settled over her since Colin crouched in front of her. "Excuse me?"

"I heard Potts last night. He wants you to create an original recipe. I think you and I both know that's not in your wheelhouse."

The remark landed so hard she jerked, would've fallen backward into the tub if not for Colin's quick grasp. He caught her by the arms, but she pulled away the second she steadied.

"I'm not trying to be mean, Ry—"

"You don't think I can come up with a signature bake?"

"I think you prefer the comfort of what you know. I think that's why I drive you crazy in class."

She pushed his knees out of the way and rose, suddenly desperate for space, for air that didn't smell like a man who spent equal amounts of time in a kitchen and a Christmas tree farm. "I'm tired of hearing what you think you know."

"I can help you. You heard Potts. I'm creative, intuitive, experimental."

She escaped into the hallway. "And clearly humble."

"I know you have absolutely no reason to believe this invitation is anything but a desperate student baker trying to earn his way back into your classroom. I'm sure it sounds nuts. But there you have it." He faced her from the bathroom doorway. "For the record, it's a fun little town—my hometown. Some might even say charming. There's a crazy event or festival every weekend in December. My brother lives in the farmhouse we grew up in. It's huge and recently remodeled and has this great guestroom in the attic."

A charming small town, huh? Maybe if it was a different season in her life, a different person making the offer, the idea might've attached itself to her. Tugged on the whimsy she used to wear like a favorite dress.

"I can help you," he said again. "Come to Iowa with me. The change of scenery will inspire your creativity. I'll give you all kinds of brilliant ideas."

"Again with the humility." But what if he really could help? Hadn't she tossed and turned all last night, doubting her own abilities? She hadn't tried devising a new recipe of her own since losing her bakery. And even before, she'd had trouble trusting her instincts.

If nothing else, maybe accepting Colin's invitation would be better than spending these next couple weeks alone, pretending to be too busy to join her family.

She wasn't actually considering this, was she? She wasn't seriously standing in her hallway, wearing her pajamas, actually thinking about packing a suitcase and ditching Denver?

It was as if Colin could hear her mental gears turning. His face lit up. "Come with me. You'll come up with the perfect recipe, and you might even have a little fun in the process. And you'll be so grateful you won't kick me out of your class." He grinned again. "What could possibly go wrong?"

CHAPTER 3

The lights of the cop car flashed in the rearview mirror of Colin's little Ford. Rylan opened her mouth. Closed it.

"Go ahead and say it." Colin's voice traveled the cramped space between them.

Seven hours in the car with this man and she still hadn't begun to relax. "*Who?* Who gets pulled over in the middle of nowhere for driving too slowly?"

Colin reached over in front of her to close the glove compartment. Never mind all the items that'd spilled out of it when he'd gone digging for his registration and proof of insurance. Sunglasses, old wallet, empty potato chip bag.

That police officer could've passed out from exposure in the time it took Colin to come up with the crinkled papers. All the while, Rylan had huddled against the passenger side door, asking herself for the hundredth time since this morning how she'd gotten here.

Here, at the moment, being the eastern edge of Nebraska, over three-fourths the way into the nine-hour drive from

Denver to some little town with a name she couldn't remember in Iowa.

With Colin.

Colin, who'd gone more and more quiet, almost disturbingly pensive ever since they passed North Platte. Who'd gone from driving ten miles over the speed limit to barely crawling.

"So I'm a safe driver. So sue me."

The cop was back in her squad car running Colin's license. "A turtle could've outrun us."

"I don't think turtles run."

"Colin." His name came out a hiss.

He only folded his arms, his sunglasses shielding his eyes, making it impossible to tell whether he was even a tiny bit upset at being pulled over.

But something was off. Had been for the last hour, at least. It was as if the closer they got to their destination, the more he dreaded their arrival.

Which made no sense at all. Yesterday when he'd charged into her house and somehow wrung from her an agreement to this zany trip, he'd acted as if traveling to Iowa was the most alluring prospect imaginable. When she'd initially—crazily—begun considering his offer to help on her recipe for Potts, she'd thrown out the possibility of him sticking around Denver a few extra days. Working with her there instead of dragging her to Iowa with him.

"No. I'm going to Iowa," he'd said with so much resolve it'd taken her aback. *"I'm leaving tomorrow. It's the holidays. It's important. It's . . . I just have to go."*

It wasn't until later—as she packed her suitcase and tried to convince herself this wasn't the most outlandish decision she'd ever made—that she realized she'd agreed to the trip partially out of curiosity. Who was this man who made a pest of himself in the classroom and had no qualms about showing up at his teacher's house? Who would invite a virtual stranger to his home for Christmas?

Who spoke of Iowa with an equal mix of yearning and something awfully close to desperation?

"Look, if you're still irritated that I didn't turn when the GPS told me to, stop worrying. The back roads are prettier."

The drive *had* been pretty for awhile. But the farther they'd ventured into the Nebraska, the drabber the scenery had become. Snow-quilted rolling hills had given way to flat, beige fields, as if winter hadn't yet breathed over this land. Would Iowa, too, be this . . . brown?

She might feel a little better about this whole thing if she knew anything at all about the man in the seat next to her. What kind of crazy person hopped in a car with a man she barely knew on the off-hand chance that he *might* mean the difference between achieving her career goal and, well, not? Was she that uneasy? That doubtful of her own abilities?

And did she not remember what'd happened the last time she depended on a man to kindle all her hopes and dreams?

"Well, Mr. Renwycke," the cop said, suddenly standing at the window again. Her auburn hair gleamed in the sun. "You have a surprisingly good driving record."

Colin lifted his sunglasses. "That so?"

The officer's smile was wide and brilliant. No way, had she dabbed on lip-gloss back in her car? *Oh, you cannot be serious.*

"So is he getting a ticket or what?"

The officer spared Rylan only the briefest of glances before looking back to Colin, embellished consideration written all over her face. *You've got to be kidding me.* She was going to flirt with Colin. For all the cop knew, Rylan might be his girlfriend or his fiancé or his whatever, and she was still going to flirt with him right in front of her.

So this is how ridiculously attractive people went through life.

Yeah, she could admit it. Colin was handsome. But he was also annoying and smug and . . .

And she was officially off her rocker for even being in this car right now.

"Nope, no ticket," the cop said. "Just a warning and a reminder that sometimes driving too slow can be just as dangerous as driving too quickly." She had the nerve to wink. She tore a piece of paper off her pad, handed it to Colin.

Seconds later, her car disappeared down the road.

"Kind of a good metaphor for life, yeah?" Colin pocketed the warning slip.

"Colin—"

"What the cop said, I mean."

There was an unnatural ease in Colin's voice. Something forced and uncertain. Why were they still sitting on the side of the road?

"She was flirting with you, Renwycke. This is why I've always wished for blue eyes. So I could get out of traffic tickets and library fines and all manner of late fees." Dimples would help too. And something other than untamable brown hair. "I could just flash my baby blues and boom, instant favor."

Colin turned to her, hands in his lap instead of on the steering wheel. "Your eyes are fine."

"Gee, thanks." An approaching dusk teased the edges of the horizon, a few wisps of pink curling into the distance.

"I like hazel eyes. They shift with your mood."

The car's heater gave a raspy huff. "Why aren't you driving?"

He turned away.

"Why are you stalling? Why were you driving like a . . . a . . ."

A hint of amusement broke through his obvious discomfort. "A what?"

"I don't know. I already used the turtle comparison before. I'm trying to think of something else."

"Well, take your time."

"I'm serious, Colin. You seemed almost giddy with excitement when we started out this morning and then all of a sudden you're driving like a sloth—"

"Ooh, good one."

"You're quiet, almost broody. You're kind of freaking me out, and I'm over here wondering if I've made a huge mistake."

He rubbed his palms over his jeans, then finally, surprisingly, pulled away from the shoulder and started forward. "My hometown is only an hour's drive from Des Moines. There's an airport there. You can fly back to Denver anytime."

"Comforting to know you're not planning to hold me hostage." She sighed, leaning her head against the headrest. "I don't usually do impulsive things like this. I don't know you. I don't know your family. I don't know who I'm going to meet when we get there or if they know I'm coming or . . . "

She couldn't have imagined it, his pointed inhale, that almost-wince.

"They know we're coming, right?"

Silence. Other than the sputtering heater. The racket in the engine. She'd eyed the small car with more than a little skepticism this morning when he'd shown up at her house the second day in a row. Wasn't the age of the car that'd thrown her, but instead the question of how a man who had to be a couple inches past six feet could possibly fold himself into the cramped driver's seat.

"Colin, tell me your family is expecting you." The churning in her stomach quickened.

Nothing.

"You're planning to show up at your brother's house, guest in tow, and he doesn't even know? We're just going to barge in? The way you barged into my place yesterday?"

"I didn't barge in."

"Right. You used my spare key and let yourself in. So you must know where your brother keeps his."

"Underneath a porch step. And his name's Drew." His knuckles were white on the steering wheel.

"Does Drew live alone?"

"I think so."

"You think so?"

"My sister and niece used to live with him, but they moved into their own place right after Christmas last year. And my . . . " He took a breath. "My parents retired to Arizona years ago."

"But they'll come for Christmas?"

His Adam's apple bobbed as he swallowed. "I believe so."

He *hoped* so. It was written all over his face.

Or did she only imagine she could read his expression? Like she used to be able to read Brent's?

She couldn't stop a shudder.

Colin flicked the heater up another notch.

"Colin?"

She waited until he glanced away from the road long enough to look at her. A car passed, its headlights spotlighting the tight set to Colin's jaw, the swirl of restrained emotion in his stormy eyes.

No, she wasn't imagining it. There *was* something going on here. She just didn't know what. "Why did you really ask me to come with you?"

For a fleeting moment, she thought he might actually answer.

Instead, with a lurch that made her grab the door's armrest, he steered the car onto a side road, tires throwing up snow and gravel, and then pitched to a sudden stop. "What are you doing?"

He was out of the car before the words had left her mouth. She snatched her gloves from the dash and followed him out. "Are you insane?"

"I just needed a break from your twenty questions."

"They aren't unreasonable questions, Colin. The only unreasonable thing is that I didn't ask them before jetting off to the middle of nowhere with you." She knew she was flinging her arms about. She didn't care. "I don't even know you." She'd already said it once. Again, she didn't care. "I don't know your background or your age or—"

"Thirty-one."

So he was three, nearly four years younger than her. Not that it should matter. "Most of the time I can't even stand you."

At his look of exaggerated offense, she gave an even more exaggerated nod.

"That's right. I said I can't stand you, Colin Renwycke. Because you are one hundred percent the most confounding person I've ever met."

He met her at the front of the car. "You done?"

She heaved a breath. "I'm done. Except if you brought me out here to this remote road to kill me, do it quickly, okay?"

His baritone laugh peeled into the air. "Thank you, Rylan. I needed that."

"Why did you need it? Why have you gone so unnervingly quiet on this drive? Why won't you answer any of my questions?"

He placed his palms on her shoulders. "I'm not going to kill you. I'm perfectly safe to be around. Until you give me a mini torch and then all bets are off." He bent his knees to look into her eyes, his laughter settling. "And I'm just nervous to go home, okay? That's all that's going on here. Maybe you don't know what that's like since apparently you don't have family to be spending the holidays with but—"

"I never said that. I never said I didn't have family." And if he had any idea how much she could understand being nervous about visiting family . . .

"Misassumption on my part, then." The wind riffled through his hair as he studied her for a thin moment. Wasn't he cold without a coat? "It's just important to me that I make a good impression on my family." He dropped his hands from her shoulders and stepped back. "As for my ulterior motive— honestly?—I think you can help me make that good impression."

She felt her jaw drop as realization set in. *Oh no.* No, no, no. *Nooo.* "Oh my goodness, you want me to be your fake girl-friend, don't you? Or your fiancé. It better not be your wife. I am not sharing a bedroom with you, Colin, even if it is just pretend. I am not—"

He was laughing again. All out guffawing. That was a word, right? This was a guffaw if there ever was one. "Rylan Jefferson, you are something else." He actually doubled-over.

"I don't see what's funny here."

"What's funny here is I did not take you for the Hallmark movie type."

"So you don't—"

"Want you to be my fake girlfriend?" He straightened, still laughing. "No. I do not. What do you take me for?"

"But . . . you said . . . you want me to help make a good impression."

"Yes, by not telling my family that forty-eight hours ago I was about to be kicked out of culinary school. By assuring them that I'm actually a little bit okay—good, even—at the whole baking thing. That's it." He twirled his ring of car keys around his finger. "And, you know, if you want to forego mentioning the fact that you can't stand me, that'd be okay, too. Think you can manage that?"

She nodded mutely. She was an idiot.

"Now would you mind getting back in the car?"

She was an *embarrassed* idiot. "I'm not the one who pulled over and stormed out."

Colin's grin would've made that police officer swoon.

She was an embarrassed idiot who had no idea what she'd gotten herself into.

* * *

An eerie quiet and telling cold lingered in every corner of the farmhouse. Where could Drew possibly be?

Colin stared into the empty master bedroom on the second floor, the one where Grandpa and Grandma used to sleep. The one where he'd expected to find his brother after trekking through the rest of the home, Rylan's soft steps behind him.

But no. Just as unoccupied as every other room. Silver moonlight bowed through the window, landing on the quilt he could still remember Grandma sewing. He could almost see her rocking in the chair in the corner, the pattern of squares spread over her lap.

"Colin?"

He didn't turn. Didn't want Rylan to see the plummeting disappointment sure to be making its way across his face. Mom had told him a hundred times if she'd told him once that he wore his every emotion on his sleeve. Probably why acting had never panned out for him.

"Maybe he's at your sister's. You said she lives in town, right?" The old hardwood floorboards of the dim hallway creaked at Rylan's movement.

He managed a nod. "I guess he could be." Didn't account for why the house felt like an icebox, though.

"And didn't you say he's done several home renovations? Maybe he's on the job in a different town somewhere. Or he could be at a Christmas party."

He mustered the closest thing he had to a grin as he turned. "I get the sense you're trying to make me feel better, Ms. Jefferson." Which meant he must not have done a good enough job hiding the distress that'd been growing steadily ever since they'd covered the last stretch of the gravel lane leading to the farm and he'd spotted not a single light in the house.

Be honest. You've been on edge for longer than that. His nerves had started clattering right around the time they passed the Nebraska Panhandle early this afternoon. He should've called. He should've made certain he was welcome. Or if nothing else, ensured someone would be here when he arrived.

He glanced over his shoulder into the bedroom once more. It didn't look entirely abandoned. An old jacket was draped over the rocking chair in the corner. An open book rested facedown on the bed. Wherever Drew was, he was coming back eventually.

Was it at all odd for Drew, sleeping in their grandparents' bedroom? After Grandpa had passed on—a sudden heart attack when Colin was in high school—Grandma had offered the space to Mom and Dad, but they'd never moved from their own room at the end of the hallway. Not until leaving for Arizona.

It struck him now, the oddity of so many people crammed into one house. His grandparents, his parents, Drew and Leigh and himself. But for most of his growing up years, it hadn't seemed crowded. Or if it did, he'd always sort of liked it that way.

"Colin?"

Rylan again. He kept forgetting her. It was this house, these memories. He hadn't realized coming home would feel so very . . . poignant.

He swallowed, pasting on what he hoped was an easy-going smirk. "It appears we're quite without a chaperone, Ms. Jefferson."

Rylan still wore her maroon coat, its belt knotted at her waist. A white knit beret did nothing to tame the tangles of hair reaching past her shoulders. She'd taken off her boots when they entered the house, though, revealing pink and white striped socks below her leggings. "No chaperone? Good thing we're not in Edwardian England, then."

"And that I'm not a rogue."

"And that 'damsel in distress' has never been my style." Her teeth chattered on the last word.

It might be the most amicable conversation they'd ever had. "You're freezing. I'll go turn up the thermostat."

Their footsteps echoed through the house as they descended to the first floor. He spent the next ten minutes bringing their bags in from the car, turning on lights in every room he passed through, taking in all the changes since he'd been here last. The new leather furniture in the living room, fresh paint on the walls. Exposed cedar beams traveled the length of the ceiling and matched the trim around the windows and doorways. Drew's doing, of course. He'd probably built that new dining room table, too.

The sound of cupboard doors opening and pans clanging drew him to the kitchen.

He found Rylan standing on a granite countertop, peering in a high cupboard. Gone were her coat and hat. Instead, she'd wrapped a navy blue afghan kimono-style around her torso and it dangled past her feet. She glanced over her shoulder as he approached. "Doesn't your brother have any muffin tins?"

This time he didn't have to force the grin. "I have no idea. But don't fall, okay? I haven't taken a first aid course in years."

"How am I supposed to make muffins without muffin tins?"

"It's ten o'clock at night, Rylan."

She crouched down on the counter until she was sitting and then slid off, adjusting the blanket tucked under her arms as she straightened. "Late at night is my favorite time to bake. And this kitchen is amazing. And I'm starving."

Gone were the hard edges of Rylan's profile, the tight set of her mouth, even the ever-slanting of her eyebrows. Instead, between the wavy hair fluttering around her face and the near playful curve of her lips, the dancing amber of her eyes and the afghan slipping loose around her—she almost looked . . .

Don't even think it, Renwycke. Because he was the student and she was the teacher. Because for all intents and purposes, she held his future in her wooden spoon-callused hands.

Because she'd probably whack him with said wooden spoon if she had even an inkling of where his runaway brain had almost gone just now, words like *cute* and *adorable* clinking around in there.

He shuffled backward, as if growing the space between them might erase the errant turn of his thoughts. The latest of which was how her red nose and the circles of pink in cheeks —would the heat ever kick in?—only added to her surprise charm.

He inched another step back. Knocked into the kitchen counter.

She grinned.

He looked away, chose instead to study the kitchen she'd called amazing. Of all the work Drew had done on this house, the kitchen had to be most comprehensive transformation. The cupboards were familiar enough that he knew they weren't new, but they'd clearly been sanded and painted. The island in the middle was new; the countertops, the farmhouse style sink, the stainless steel appliances.

"Think your brother will mind if I borrow some eggs? And flour. Sugar. Whatever fruit I can find?" She had her head buried in the fridge. "What are the chances he's got white chocolate chips?"

"Aren't you tired?"

"Nope." She lifted a carton of eggs from the refrigerator. Her afghan dropped as she turned.

He had the wayward urge to pick it up and drape it across her shoulders, then pick *her* up and deposit her in the guestroom bed up in the attic. Insist she get warm and get some rest. They could bake tomorrow.

Instead, he found himself reaching around her for the half-gallon of chocolate milk in the refrigerator door. "Ever use chocolate milk in your muffins? It's amazing."

"No way."

He caught a whiff of her hair. Honey. "Trust me, it'll change the way you make muffins forever."

"But my recipe—"

She jumped at the harsh rap on the back door, would've dropped the eggs if not for Colin's quick movement. He grasped the carton with the hand not already holding the milk jug.

Another knock, this one even harder, and Rylan jumped again, this time latching onto his shirt.

"Who's in there?" a muffled voice called through the door.

He should probably find out who it was about ready to knock the door down, but Rylan still had the front of his shirt bunched in her hand. "If you'll let go . . ."

Her eyes widened as she gasped and released him. Pretty sure it wasn't just the cold reddening her cheeks now. Not the damsel in distress type, huh? He abandoned the milk and eggs to the counter and strode across the room. He pushed the curtain over the door's glass window aside and reached for the nob the second he recognized the face.

"Well, hi, Mr. Pratt."

A blast of icy night air billowed, but the older man on the other side of the door didn't step in. He only stared at Colin, a question in his eyes, the creases around his mouth deepening with a pinched frown.

"It's me, Colin. You know, Drew's brother."

"I know who you are, son. Just don't know what you're doing here. Happen to know Drew's out of town. I saw the lights. Thought I'd better check on the place."

Byron Pratt was his father's age and had farmed the land adjacent to the Renwycke property as long as Colin could remember. "You know where Drew is?"

Byron's silver eyebrows disappeared into the beaver cap covering his forehead. "You don't?"

It was as if he was fifteen again and in trouble for riding a four-wheeler through the ditches of Byron's property. *If only that was the extent of all my wrongs.* His teenage missteps were nothing compared to the rest. "I—we—our visit was a surprise. Can you tell me where Drew is? When he'll be home?"

Wary skepticism tinted the farmer's focus as it moved from Colin to Rylan and back again. "I reckon if Drew had wanted his plans publicized, he would've contacted you himself."

Colin quashed the urge to argue. To point out that he wasn't the public, he was *family*. But he knew what Pratt thought of him. Couldn't even blame him, really. Diana Pratt, Byron's daughter, had gone to at least a couple of the same parties Colin had back in high school. He'd probably made a pass at her at some point or another.

The fact that he couldn't remember doing so didn't mean

he hadn't. Only magnified the reality of what he'd been like back then. And for too many years after.

"Mr. Pratt—"

"I suppose I've no call to be overly alarmed by you being here." Then why did his tone convey the opposite? "Just trying to be a good neighbor to Drew."

"I understand, sir."

"It's only the two of you here?"

Did he think Colin had a stash of partying friends hidden around the corner just waiting to trash the place? "Just the two of us."

With one more glance at Rylan—probably to make sure she wasn't looking for an escape route—Byron tipped his head and retreated.

Colin closed the door, the cold from outside, the cold from inside, clawing through the layers of his clothes. Fatigue settled around him, heavy and cloying.

"I guess we could try making muffins your way."

He heard the cautious concern in Rylan's voice, and when he turned, he saw the same thing in her expression. Discomfiting, the way she was looking at him. As if she could discern every hue of his emotion—discouragement, regret, shame.

"After all, you've got the creativity and intuition. That's what Chef Potts said."

"Actually, I'm kinda tired. Do you mind if I turn in?"

"Not at all. I'm not as hungry as I thought. I'll call it a day too."

He hadn't known her hazel eyes could go so soft. Almost . . . compassionate.

Or he was seeing things. Because Rylan Jefferson couldn't possibly have any cause to feel compassionate toward him.

And if for some unfounded reason she did, Lord knew he didn't deserve it.

CHAPTER 4

"*W*ho do you think she is?"

The curious whisper intruded on Rylan's sleepy daze. Had she ever had such a perfect night of rest? Like sleeping on a cloud, this mattress. A toasty warmth wrapped around her, the snug duvet warding off the chill of the attic.

The attic. At Colin's house. At Colin's brother's house, that is.

The brother who hadn't been here when they arrived late last night.

The pieces of yesterday rambled in as she forced one eye open, then the other. Dust particles danced in the hazy shaft of sunlight spilling in through the window, grating and bright.

I'm in Iowa. On a farm. With Colin Renwycke.

"I guess she must be a friend of Colin's."

A second whisper came from behind her. *Who?* Hadn't Colin said his brother lived alone?

"Think she's his girlfriend?"

The duvet suddenly felt too heavy. Her little nest in this bed, too warm.

"Ha!" A third voice. A scoff. One she recognized in an instant.

"Uncle Colin!" The youngest of the voices had given up whispering.

And Rylan gave up pretending not to have awoken to the ruckus happening in the guestroom doorway.

Last night she'd thought there wasn't a room in this house that could rival the kitchen. But then Colin had led her up to the spacious attic. A peaceful pale blue wrapped around the walls and books lined the white shelves that flanked a cushioned window seat. A mound of white and light yellow pillows were piled on the bed, and edged up to one wall was a gorgeous antique desk.

Colin had mentioned that his brother remodeled nearly the entire house, but it was hard to imagine a man fashioning this space—so feminine and pretty. The second she'd stepped into the room, she'd had the instant desire to pack up all her belongings and simply move in.

Colin, however, had barely given the room a cursory once-over before mumbling a *goodnight* and disappearing down the steps. Too keyed up to sleep right away, she'd settled onto the window seat, staring at the stars glittering in a clear, black sky, wondering how a person who'd seemed so easygoing and unflappable in Colorado could morph into the aching man she'd witnessed in the kitchen downstairs.

She'd thought Colin tense as they approached his hometown. Unquestionably letdown when they'd arrived only to find an empty house. But after that neighbor's terse visit? He'd looked so dejected a maternal instinct she'd never even known she possessed had sparked so forcefully to life she'd nearly crossed the room to hug him.

Probably a good thing she hadn't. It was weird enough

being here, realizing there might actually be more to Colin Renwycke than a careless lack of discipline in the kitchen.

She sat up now, frazzled and wary, uncomfortably aware of how she must look. Yesterday's makeup, what little of it she usually wore, most likely smudged under her eyes. Hair surely a fright.

"So she's not your girlfriend?"

Her gaze snapped to the people in the doorway. A woman that had to be Colin's sister. Her hair was fairer; her frame, slighter. But those eyes. Same delicate, uncanny blue. The girl standing next to her—couldn't be older than thirteen or fourteen—leaned into Colin for a side hug. He'd mentioned a niece, hadn't he?

And Colin. A tease skipping in his eyes. Perhaps the disappointment of last night had worn off some. "I didn't say that."

Didn't say she wasn't his girlfriend?

He was already dressed. Jeans, flannel shirt. His usual five o'clock shadow could almost classify as a beard today. Apparently being on the farm turned him into a lumberjack.

"So she *is* your girlfriend?" This from the teenager.

His facial hair couldn't hide his dimples. "Well, I didn't exactly say that either." He dropped his arm from around the girl's shoulder and strode into the room, way too much amused self-assurance in his stroll. Definitely back to himself today. At least, the self she'd known in Denver.

Before she could so much as clear her throat, he dropped onto the bed beside her. "Truth is, we're still in the 'defining our relationship' phase of our, well, relationship."

She'd roll her eyes if she wasn't so busy trying to catch up with his ever-altering moods. "We do *not* have a relationship." The words came out croaky.

Colin only laughed and shrugged. "You came home with me for the holidays. You're meeting my family. That feels awfully relationship-y to me." He swung his feet onto the bed.

"Oh, speaking of, this is my sister, Leigh, and my niece, Winnie. Leigh and Win, this is Rylan."

She snatched the edge of the duvet out from underneath his legs and pulled it up over her front. "Hi. Nice to meet you." Gritted words. She didn't even look at them. She'd worry about salvaging a second impression later. "Is this how you treat all your guests? Hurtle into their bedroom at the crack of dawn and—"

"It's not the crack of dawn, Rylan. It's like ten-thirty."

She'd slept that long? "Fine, hurtle into their bedroom mid-morning and then lie about their relationship to you?"

"Ha, you just acknowledged we have a relationship."

A laugh came from the doorway. The sister or the niece, she didn't know. The urge to burrow under the covers and refuse to come out nearly overtook her.

"Also, no need to be so modest about your pajamas." Colin's gaze scooted down to her nearly entirely covered form. "I've seen them before, if you'll recall."

To think, she'd been on the brink of feeling some kind of compassion for him last night. "You're insufferable."

"And you're funny when you glower. Little tip: Scowling doesn't work nearly so well for you first thing in the morning. The bedhead completely ruins the effect."

She'd push him off the edge of the mattress if she thought he wouldn't just spring to his feet and laugh all the more. "Colin Renwycke, I really, *really*—"

"Can't stand me. I know." He grinned and hopped off the bed. "All right, fine. Leigh, Winnie, she's not my girlfriend. I'm pretty sure she'd rather have a tooth pulled than date me."

"Try ten teeth and a root canal."

How was it his dimples could become even more pronounced? "Besides, I rarely date older women."

She flung a pillow at him.

"I like her." The sister and niece spoke entirely in sync.

"Go ahead and gang up on me, if you like. Ry could use the help. But as soon as Drew gets here, I'll make sure he's on my side. Where is he anyway?"

Rylan didn't miss the faint hint of hesitation in his voice at the question. Barely there, but there all the same. Which made her think the little show he'd put on just now was less about teasing her and more about distracting himself.

There she went again. Thinking she knew a single thing about this man. Nearly caring about his feelings.

Coffee. She needed coffee. And bad. Just as soon as she put on some clothes and brushed her hair and reminded herself for the thousandth time why in the world she was here.

Because she had less than three weeks to come up with a dazzling dessert for Chef Potts. Three weeks to plot and plan and earn her way back into the life she used to know.

The life where she spent her days in a toasty kitchen rather than a cement-walled classroom in front of students whose dreams were still a blank canvas waiting to be filled.

Unlike her own. Spattered and stained.

Because as much as she hated to admit it, she needed Colin's help.

Because deep down, you hated the thought of spending Christmas alone.

Almost as much as—or maybe more than—she dreaded the thought of spending it with her own family. A familiar ache sliced through her.

"Drew didn't call you?"

Rylan glanced up. It was the sister that'd spoken. Leigh wore her short, blondish hair in twin braids, and a bucket of cleaning supplies dangled from one hand. Had she intended to come up here and clean this room? The teenager beside her held a bottle of Old English and a rag. Probably for the woodwork that traced the room.

Colin shifted. "Uh, no."

"I thought for sure he'd call . . . " The sister set her bucket on the hardwood floor. "Colin, Drew got married on Saturday."

She could almost feel the air whoosh from Colin's lungs. "What?"

She shouldn't be here. This was a family thing. And at the look on Colin's face—surprise and then a veil of melancholy —she was on the edge of feeling for him again.

"I don't . . . I don't understand."

While Colin stammered, she slid from the bed, reached for the coat she'd discarded over a desk chair last night.

"That doesn't make any sense. He got married?"

Leigh nodded as Rylan slipped past. "It was a whim, really. I know he was planning to tell you but maybe he decided to wait until . . ."

Leigh's voice became muffled as Rylan made her way down the attic stairs, each step creaking with age. She wandered through the second floor hallway, not bothering to glance in any of the rooms. She had her coat zipped and her gloves out by the time she reached the first-floor living room. She found her boots where she'd left them last night.

She was out the front door in a matter of seconds. Chilled air stung her cheeks and stole her breath. Bare trees, stripped by the hand of winter, crowded between a weatherworn barn and a metal machine shed glinting under the sun. Not a single patch of snow brightened the brown grass of the yard. Off to the east, dingy fields stretched as far as she could see into the distance.

She hovered in the corner of the porch. So this was December in Iowa. Not exactly the picturesque landscape Colin had painted for her.

Why had she let him talk her into this? Had she really thought he was the key to impressing Chef Potts? Should she call an airline, book a flight from Des Moines?

Every question dissolved into another, each one hinting at the same discordant verdict: She'd made a mistake in coming.

Why, then, the feathery whisper in the back of her mind? She'd felt it last night sitting up at that attic window. She felt it again now, as the morning breeze hummed through the porch lattice and a tangle of leftover autumn leaves tumbled across the yard.

Maybe there's a reason you're here. Maybe you have something to give.

A fanciful thought. A nonsensical thought. All she had to offer Colin was the assurance of another semester at the culinary school. She didn't know his past. She had no wise words or sage advice for fixing whatever must have gone wrong in his family.

She was the last person anyone should look to for righting relationships gone askew. She'd *chosen* to spend her Christmas away from her family, an entire ocean cutting her off from her parents and sisters, the vacation they'd decided to take all together.

The door behind her creaked and Colin's niece came to stand beside her. "I don't understand why the adults in this family can't get their act together. Uncle Drew's okay, but the rest of them? Total train wreck."

The huffy rebuke in Winnie's voice was almost enough to make Rylan smile.

"So if you aren't his girlfriend, what are you doing here?"

Rylan's breath let out in a puff of white. "I wish I knew."

* * *

"He got *married*?"

It had to be the third time he'd gasped the question. Once in the attic. Once on his way down the stairs, after absently realizing Rylan had left the room. Now in the kitchen. And with each asking, more and more pity wheeled into Leigh's eyes.

He couldn't stand it.

"I know he was going to tell you." Bottles of cleaning supplies clunked around in the bucket she carried. So that explained the noise he'd woken up to earlier this morning. He'd assumed it was Rylan banging around in the kitchen already. He'd muttered into his pillow something about her being a workaholic. It's why he'd taken his time rising, showering, dressing. After last night, he hadn't been in the mood to deal with Rylan's rigid obsession with recipe cards and baking rules first thing.

But then he'd heard the voices coming from upstairs, not down. He'd climbed the attic steps to find his sister and niece trying to guess the identity of the woman in the bed.

"Don't be mad, Col," Leigh said now.

He yanked open a cupboard. "I'm not mad."

"I might believe you if you didn't almost jerk that cabinet door off its hinges."

Plates. Bowls. Glasses. No coffee mugs. He refrained from slamming the door, but only because Leigh didn't need another reason to harass him. "Why are you even here?"

"Shouldn't I be the one asking you that? I'm trying to remember when I last heard from you. There was that oh-so-wordy text in July. 'Happy Fourth.' Lovely. Nothing since. No phone calls, no emails."

He flung open another white cupboard door, its frosted glass inserts rattling. There was Drew's attention to detail on display. He'd probably placed every last subway tile in the backsplash under the cabinets with his own two hands, too.

Because he was Drew and that's what he did. Fixed things. As if he actually believed every broken thing could be put back together if he just worked hard enough. Even as Drew had remodeled nearly this entire house last year, he'd put just as much effort in attempting to rebuild their family.

An effort Colin had solidly rebuffed. No wonder Drew hadn't bothered to tell him about his nuptials.

"I'm sorry I didn't keep in better touch."

Leigh harrumphed. "That apology had about as much sincerity as one of those letters Mom used to make us write when we'd fight as kids. I never knew which was worse—Mom forcing us to apologize and tell each other we loved each other in writing or a lecture from Dad."

The mention of Dad made him flinch. Freeze. He abandoned the search for coffee.

The pungent smell of whatever cleaning product Leigh must've used on the sink rose up to clog his throat as he stared out the window. Bleak—that was the only word for the day. Wan sun, white sky.

Leigh's voice softened with her next words. "Colin, about Dad—"

He jerked around. "You never answered when I asked what you're doing here. I thought you and Win moved out."

"We did." Resignation shaded her words as she lowered onto one of the stools around the island. "I thought it'd be nice for Drew and Maren to come home to a clean house. They left in a hurry. This is my only day off this week."

They left in a hurry? "So the wedding wasn't planned?"

Her eyebrows lifted. "Planned? Drew hadn't even officially proposed yet."

So they'd eloped. "I wouldn't have thought Drew capable of being so impulsive."

"Not entirely impulsive. He's been trying to figure out how to propose for months. He already had the ring. But before he could make up his mind how to go about asking, he got the news about Dad and, well . . . " Her whole body seemed to droop as grief pooled in her eyes. "Drew texted me from the airport. Said the news was a wakeup call. Said he never should've waited so long. They stopped in Vegas, got married, then flew down to Hawaii for an impromptu honeymoon."

"Lucky for him Maren agreed." He'd met Maren Grant exactly three times. The first time, *he'd* been the one to catch her eye. They'd even gone on a date. But of course, irresponsible fool that he was, he'd waltzed out of her life as quickly as he'd waltzed in.

By the time he saw her a second time, nearly a year later, she'd met Drew and the rest was history.

That'd been *his* wakeup call. No, he'd never had any real attachment to Maren. It wasn't disappointment that'd triggered his first steps toward a complete life overhaul. It'd been seeing both his brother and Maren so . . . happy. Realizing his own life would never be so put together and settled if he didn't start making changes. Shed his nomadic, partying lifestyle in favor of something resembling adulthood.

No, he hadn't kept in touch well with his family this past year. But that was only because he'd been *trying*. He'd worked three jobs the first seven months of the year, saving up for culinary school. He'd sent off applications to two dozen institutes, applied for scholarships. He'd settled on baking, his eyes on an eventual career as a pastry chef, his hope assuring him that *this* time, *this* plan would work.

He plucked a photo from the fridge, moving its magnet aside. Drew and Maren grinned at him from the glossy print.

"Maren would've married our brother *last* winter if he'd asked," Leigh said. "Personally, I think he was waiting for . . . " She didn't finish. Didn't have to. Her pointed look said it all.

Drew had been waiting for Colin. Waiting for reconciliation. Hadn't given up on his quest to glue their family back together.

Well, I'm here, Drew. I came home.

"Anyway, we've all had our own way of dealing with the news about Dad," Leigh went on. "Winnie's been acting up in school again. I could've sworn that was over with, but just last week she had detention three times. Drew went off and got married."

He forced himself to look into his sister's eyes. The sister he'd all but ignored for years upon years. His life had been a mess for so long, but Leigh's . . . hers had been in tatters. Getting pregnant in high school had only been the start. After that, there'd been nearly a decade of alcohol and pills and treatment centers.

And he'd done nothing. *Nothing.*

Other than continue on with his own reckless way of life. A string of meaningless relationships. Job-hopping from town to town. Broke, more often than not. When his parents finally tired of bailing him out, Drew had taken over for a time.

Just like he'd stepped in to help Leigh and Winnie. Gotten them out of their shabby apartment in Omaha, invited them to move in with him, helped Leigh find a job in Maple Valley.

He was probably already formulating a plan to help Mom and Dad now that their lives had been shaken.

"And you, Leigh? How are you dealing with the news?"

A glimmer of defiance sparked in her eyes, despite the telling circles underneath. "I'm still clean, if that's what you're asking. Not that you have any right."

He didn't. Oh, how he knew he didn't. He lowered onto a stool beside Leigh, wishing for words, wishing for the impossible—to take back the past ten years of his life.

"Alzheimer's. He has Alzheimer's."

Leigh's words were an arrow, sharp and cutting, reaching past his regret and aiming for the pain he'd been refusing to acknowledge for days. Six days, to be exact. Ever since Mom's phone call.

Same day he'd burned the meringue in class. So numb he'd hardly heard a word of Rylan's scolding tirade.

"He has Alzheimer's," Leigh said again. "Dad has Alzheimer's."

"Do you have to keep saying that?"

"Yes. Because that's how *I'm* coping with it. Forcing myself to say it. If I say it enough times, then eventually the shock of it will have to wear off, won't it? It won't be as scary and . . ." Her voice caught and if he looked over, he knew he'd see tears swimming in her eyes.

He should comfort her. He should slip off this stool and embrace her. Or at least lift an arm around her shoulder.

But it would mean forcing away the numbness. It would mean shaking off the dull comfort of his own denial. It would mean acknowledging the anguish that threatened to strangle him if he gave it even the tiniest leeway past what little self-restraint he had left.

He couldn't do it. He just . . . he couldn't.

"I should go find Rylan. How do you feel about brunch?"

"Col—"

"I don't want to talk about it, Leigh." *Selfish. Coward.* Sour, familiar guilt jammed in his throat. He swallowed.

And then fled.

Just left her there in the kitchen and slunk through the house. Past the antique upright piano with the yellowed keys Leigh used to play. Past the sprawling dining room table and around the living room couch. Out the front door.

Cold slammed into him. He gulped like a man parched, lungs stinging from the icy air, and closed his eyes.

"Colin?"

Rylan. He forced his eyes open to see her standing with Winnie on the porch. She still wore those silly oversized pajamas, though her winter coat hid her top half. The wind brushed through her already messy hair.

Winnie looked back and forth between them. The girl must've gone through a growth spurt since he'd seen her—briefly—last Christmas. She had almost an inch on Rylan.

"Are you okay?"

Rylan asked it as if she actually cared. As if he hadn't annoyed her to no end just a few minutes ago back in the attic. As if he hadn't dragged her into this mess solely for his own benefit.

Except, no, that wasn't entirely true. There'd been that strange, inexplicable sense. That moment standing outside her house when he'd honestly thought maybe he was supposed to . . . do something. Help her somehow. Be there for her.

But it sounded even more ridiculous now than it had then. He couldn't even manage to comfort his hurting sister.

"I'm fine," he finally answered.

"You better be." Winnie crossed her arms. "Now that you're home, maybe we can finally have some fun around here. This town is the most boring place *ever*. I thought when Maren Grant got here last year, she'd finally spice things up, being a mystery author and all. But no, she just went and fell in love with Uncle Drew. Lot of good that did me."

Her sarcastic complaints prompted a halfhearted smile.

And he wasn't the only one. Rylan mirrored Winnie's stance—arms crossed, feet rooted—and she pressed her lips around a grin. "Maple Valley is boring? I'm beginning to think you lied to get me here, Renwycke. There's no snow and I haven't seen a single twinkle light or decorated tree. Now I find out the town is boring?"

Somehow, he fought past the emotion attempting to climb up his throat and found a light tone. "Winnie just refuses to see Maple Valley's charm."

"If by charm you mean a thousand antique stores and a bazillion lame festivals. It's the weirdest place on earth."

He planted his palm on Winnie's head. "You're still your delightful self, Win. So good to know some things haven't changed."

Now if only he could find some way to convince his family he had.

CHAPTER 5

*R*ylan Jefferson might truly be the bossiest woman Colin had ever met.

"Careful, Colin. Don't rush it. Roll it slow and evenly."

The thin layer of sponge cake scorched his fingertips through the wax paper. "I know how to roll up a Swiss cake roll." His back tensed as he hunched over the kitchen island—whether from the effort of concentrating on the cake or the weight of Rylan's intensity, he didn't know.

The heat of the kitchen wrapped around him, along with a late afternoon fatigue. Too many anxious murmurs keeping him awake at night, hissing that he might be too late. To reconcile with Drew. To be a good brother and uncle and son. To apologize to his parents.

To finally make his father proud before . . .

Don't think about. Not today.

It'd become his mantra.

"You waited too long after it was out of the oven." Rylan hovered over his arm, the honey scent of her hair mingling with the vanilla fragrance of the cake.

"I waited like three minutes."

"It's going to crack if you're not more gentle."

He'd show her *cracked* if she didn't stop barking orders. Any man who had to share kitchen space with her for any length of time might as well reserve a room at the nearest insane asylum.

Carefully, he rolled the paper-lined cake until it curled into a tight ring. So far this trip home hadn't gone anything like he'd planned. The empty house, the memories. The realization that his brother hadn't bothered telling him about his marriage and his sister resented his year of silence.

But he couldn't change any of that, could he? So instead, he'd thrown himself into keeping his promise to Rylan.

Tried to, that is. Three days of commandeering Drew's kitchen, and he'd discovered Rylan the teacher was no match at all for Rylan the stressed-out baker. He didn't know whether to feel bad for the woman or insist she hitchhike back to Denver. She was obsessed with her recipe cards, with stringent baking technique, with the idea of impressing Potts.

Bossy. Domineering. Perfectionist.

He glanced up.

Cute. She had a streak of flour on her nose and had tucked her hair under a baseball cap that looked more than a little familiar. One of his from when he was a kid?

"See, Ms. Jefferson? It rolled up just fine."

"Would've been easier if you would've done it sooner."

"Yes, well, I was busy arguing with you about how much passion fruit to add to the filling." Which pretty much summed up their past three days—arguing. Bickering. The occasional bout of civil conversation followed by more squabbling.

Okay, fine, it was actually kind of enjoyable. He just wished Rylan was having fun, too.

She studied the roll, a half-eaten Pop-Tart in her hand— because apparently Pop-Tarts were an all-day food to her, not just a breakfast item. Her eyebrows angled under her wrinkled forehead. "Something's not right."

"We haven't even added the filling. You haven't tasted it. You're paranoid."

She flopped into a chair at the kitchen table. "We aren't getting anywhere, Colin."

She hadn't been happy with any of their efforts so far. Not the three-layer mocha trifle they'd made that first day. Not the rainbow of petit fours that'd filled every last inch of counter space yesterday.

"You're too uptight. You need to loosen up a little. Let yourself have fun with this. Trust your instincts."

She looked so desolate. "I don't have instincts. I have knowledge. Baking is science and chemistry. It's finding a formula that works and then making little tweaks to add your own twist or personality."

He flipped off the oven light. "That's playing it safe. Forget tweaks. I think you need to try something entirely new. Get creative, get inventive."

"I honestly don't know if I possess the creative gene."

"But you do. I've been in your house, remember? I saw your living room furniture. It was all unique. Not a single mass-produced Pottery Barn piece in the place. Stop thinking about impressing Potts and start expressing yourself."

She just stared at him.

"All right." He clapped his hands together, flour dusting the air. "Finish your Pop-Tart and find your coat. We're getting out of the kitchen."

"We don't have time—"

"You know the sponge needs to cool for twenty minutes, at least."

"Right, so we should clean up. Do the dishes. Get started on some macaroons. Potts loves lemon, so I'm thinking—"

"Winnie said there's some shenanigan going on in town

today. Let's go check it out. Leigh's working at the restaurant this evening, so we can eat there." In fact, he'd like an excuse to see how Leigh was doing. The couple times he'd seen her since coming home, she'd seemed so exhausted. And yet, she said she loved her job, assistant managing The Red Door, one of the newest restaurants in town.

Sunlight burned orange through the window, beckoning and bright. Yes, they'd been cooped up inside way too long. Hadn't he promised Rylan a picturesque small-town experience? She hadn't even seen said small town.

"I completely understand that you want to spend time with your family. Feel free to head out. But I'm going to stay here."

He was shaking his head before she finished. "I am not opposed to taking drastic measures to get my way, Ms. Jefferson."

"Do you have to call me that?"

He lifted the rolled-up cake. "I will drop this on the floor if you don't agree to a break."

"You wouldn't."

"And then I'll add *more* passion fruit to the filling." Gosh, it shouldn't be so fun watching her tense up. "Oh, and I'll tell Winnie that you're my girlfriend. Give it five minutes and everyone in town will know."

She crossed her arms. "Why would I care what everyone in your town thinks?"

He smirked. "You don't know Maple Valley. Words gets out that there's a new romance brewing and we'll have a wedding planned by the time this cake cools. Every female in town will stop you on the sidewalk to give you advice about what flowers to carry down the aisle and how to wear your hair. I know how much you love attention."

Knew how much she hated it, that is. Winnie had plied Rylan with questions about her family, her baking, her personal life that first day they'd been home. He would've told his niece to knock it off if he wasn't equally as curious about the woman he'd invited here. Not that Rylan had given much of anything away. It was as if she'd had professional training in deflecting questions.

But he could read between the lines enough to know she sheltered some kind of hurt behind the curt exterior she wielded like a shield.

All the more reason to get her out of the kitchen right now. Rylan Jefferson needed more than to find the perfect recipe to secure a new job. She needed . . . happiness. Joy. She was starving for it, whether she could see it or not.

And if he got nothing else right this Christmas break, he'd be the one to help her find it. Time and again, he'd let his family down. It could be different with Rylan. He could make a difference in her life if he tried hard enough. And, at the moment, if he teased hard enough. "Might as well start practicing signing your name *Rylan Renwycke.*"

She bolted to her feet. "You should be so lucky."

He crossed the kitchen until he stood mere inches from her, the cake still pinched between his fingers. "What's it going to be? Ruined cake and wedding plans? Or a quick and much-needed diversion into Maple Valley?"

She eyed the cake. He lifted his pinky, his ring finger.

"I really can't stand you, Colin Renwycke."

He patted her head with his free hand and returned the cake to the safety of the counter. "That's what I thought. Now go find your coat."

* * *

MAPLE VALLEY WAS ADORABLE. Charming, really, even minus any snow. Quaint storefronts, old-fashioned iron lampposts, a Christmas wreath on every door. Poinsettias filled the flower baskets that hung from brass poles on each street corner.

Colin hadn't embellished his hometown's allure.

Nor its eccentricity.

"Colin, it's not that I'm opposed to participating in a town-wide snowman-building contest." She had to take two steps to match every one of Colin's long strides as he led her down the sidewalk toward the town square. "I just don't understand how we're supposed to do it when there's not a speck of snow on the ground."

Apparently this contest was the "town shenanigan" Winnie had told Colin about. The kid really hadn't been joking when she called Maple Valley weird.

There had to be fifty, sixty people gathered on the square up ahead, huddled in groups, buzzing with anticipation. "Are they all just waiting for someone to get up in that band shell and state the obvious—that the event's cancelled?"

Colin's deep laughter glided over his shoulder as he started across the street. "You have so much to learn about this town you've landed in, my friend. Maple Valley never backs down. They've held parades during thunderstorms, pageants during hundred-degree weather. Once at Christmas-time, one of the wise men accidentally set fire to the makeshift stable during the live nativity. Mary and Joseph barely blinked."

Cold air slithered through her coat as she hurried to catch up with him, gaze roving the square. Ribbons and strings of lights threaded through every tree, and Christmas music piped through the speakers hanging over the shell. So this is what she'd missed these last few days of being huddled up in the farmhouse kitchen, oblivious to the weather, the outside world.

Which is where she should be now. "Colin, we need—"

Two steps ahead of her he stopped and spun. "So help me,

Rylan Jefferson, if you tell me one more time we need to get back to work, I'm going to . . . " He scanned the colorful line of businesses enfolding the square then tried to snap his fingers—though his gloves stifled the attempt. "I'm going to go into that Mailboxes Etc., buy a huge cardboard box, stuff you inside, and mail you back to Denver."

"Just as long as you poke holes in it so I can breathe."

Bickering with Colin these past few days had become as second nature as flouring her hands before handling dough. Just as sticky, too. Because it was getting harder and harder to distinguish where her annoyance ended and her amusement began.

Except for right now. Right now she wasn't at all amused by the fact that *he* was the exasperated one for once. She wasn't amused by the way he'd asked her if she was warm enough every two seconds since they'd left the heated interior of his car. She wasn't amused at how he pretended to have some kind of sophisticated aversion to his hometown's collection of quirks while obviously harboring an affection for the place.

And she absolutely wasn't amused at the way the sunlight turned his already impossibly blue eyes the color of an endless summer sky. Not even a tiny bit.

A howl of wind blustered past them, flapping through the striped awnings that stretched from business fronts and spinning an overflowing flower basket. She shivered, burying her chin in her coat's collar and her hands in her pockets.

Colin pressed his lips together. "You said you weren't that cold."

"You said this trip into town would be nice and quick."

"I think the words I used were 'a much-needed diversion.'" He pulled his gloves off one finger at a time and held them out to her.

"I've got gloves."

"Yes, the flimsy kind you can buy for a dollar-fifty. It's twenty-five degrees out. You need better ones. Especially if you're going to build a snowman."

"But there's no snow!" They stood at the corner of the square, her outburst attracting more than a few curious stares. What? Was she seriously the only one confused about how this was going to work? "Besides, what about you?"

"I'll be fine. My manly endurance will get me through." He tapped his foot. "Take the gloves."

She took the gloves. "Manly endurance. It's like you think you're Tarzan or something."

"You don't think I'm manly?" His voice oozed with inflated offense.

She'd just as soon not answer that. Truthfully, living in the same house with Colin for three days had made it unfeasible to see him as anything but. Most of the males in her classes were gangly kids barely into their twenties with skinny arms and zero need for a razor.

Colin was decidedly not gangly. Tall, yes, but more broad than lanky. There were muscles in those arms capable of doing more than kneading dough. And she'd become unnervingly aware of exactly how long he could go between shaves to shift from scruffy to full-on beard.

"Pleading the fifth?" He bent down until they were eye-to-eye.

Had to be his insulated gloves sending shoots of warmth through her. "Pleading to get this over with so we can get back—"

"Don't say it. Remember: Cardboard box. You. Packing tape."

"Good afternoon, citizens of Maple Valley!" The reverberating voice came from the band shell at the corner of the square. Garland and silver tinsel traced the shell's arch. The man with the megaphone at center stage was dressed as Santa.

"That would be our esteemed town mayor," Colin whispered down to her, his breath warm on our cheek.

"He seems jolly."

"You should see him in his Easter bunny costume."

"Your town is weird, Colin."

He grinned. "Yes, but never boring."

The mayor lifted his megaphone again. "I apologize for the delay. We've ordered a supply of synthetic snow, but the truck got a flat tire on the way here. They should be arriving shortly."

Rylan gasped and turned to Colin. "Your town ordered fake snow? Just so they could build snowmen?"

His lips spread, his eyes twinkled. "Told you."

"However," the mayor continued, "one truckload won't be nearly enough for today's event. Thankfully, Louise at the craft store was able to place a rush order on packing peanuts and cotton balls to supplement our building supplies."

Colin's shoulders were nearly shaking with contained laughter. He surprised her then by raising his hand. "Uh, Mayor Milt? When do you expect the truck to arrive?"

"Fifteen, twenty minutes." The mayor lowered his megaphone. "Wait a second. Colin Renwycke? That you?"

"Yes, sir."

Even from a distance, Rylan could see the wrinkles furrowing the mayor's brow. "I heard you were back in town." Not exactly a welcoming tone. "You planning to be here long? Say, through Christmas weekend?"

Colin nodded.

The mayor pointed his megaphone at Colin. "Just you stay away from the live nativity, you hear me, young man?"

Colin laughed and reached for Rylan's hand. "Come on,

since it's going to be a few minutes still, I've got something to show you."

Behind them, the mayor was still talking. "What'd he mean about the nativity?"

"That thing I said about a wise man setting the stable on fire? Balthazar was my first acting gig."

She should've guessed. "Great. I'm living under the same roof as an arsonist. Going to have to start calling you Sparky."

They passed a waist-high cardboard box full of packing peanuts. With his free hand, Colin grabbed a handful, stuffed them in his pocket. "Just in case I have to follow through on my threat to mail you back to Denver. Come on."

He led her to the far corner of the square, across the street, and down a sidewalk stretching past the main downtown area. They reached the end of a block and she followed his outstretched hand to see where he pointed—across another street to where a bridge curved over a frozen river. Wooden planks and metal rails, strings of unlit lights and evergreen twisting around its railing.

"It's called the Archway Bridge. It's not amazing or anything, but I know you like bridges, so . . . " He shrugged and started across the street.

"You know I like bridges?"

"Well . . . yeah. You said something once about the Golden Gate Bridge."

Yes, the day they'd made tarts in class. She'd talked about her trip to San Francisco, how she'd stopped at Golden Gate Bakery and had eaten the best egg custard tarts of her life. He'd actually been listening?

"I saw that painting in your living room. And when we crossed the Missouri River on the way here, you made me stop so you could take a picture of that huge metal bridge. Plus, your phone's lock screen is a photo of that bridge in London."

Tower Bridge. It was on her "visit someday when she had money" list. They were halfway across the Archway Bridge now. Colin stopped, cheeks reddened from the wind and the cold, hands hidden inside his coat pockets.

And she *wasn't* amused—not at all—by the way he shifted his weight from side to side, as if bashful all of a sudden, clearly waiting for her say something. To approve, perhaps. As if it well and truly mattered what she thought of this little metal and wood walkway.

"It's a nice bridge."

"Yes, well." He turned to lean over the railing. "It's no Golden Gate."

"It's pretty." *Nice. Pretty.* Was that the best she could do? For some reason she couldn't possibly comprehend, Colin had taken note of her one admittedly odd interest outside baking. And he'd gone to the effort to indulge her.

Had Brent even once asked her about the framed photos that used to decorate the walls of her old bakery? Sydney Harbor. Pont du Gard. The Brooklyn Bridge. Some she'd visited, most she hadn't.

She moved beside Colin, her shoulder brushing his as she perched her arms on the railing. Colin had told her earlier that this river cut the town in half. That it'd flooded last year, taken out most of the businesses along the riverfront. They seemed to have recovered now—in fact, she'd only noticed one empty space. A cute little storefront with big windows and turquoise shutters.

"Thank you for showing me this. It was really thoughtful of you." A trait she was learning he possessed in surprisingly generous portions.

But why should she be surprised? She hadn't known Colin back in Denver, not really. She'd only ever seen his mistakes in class, only ever taken notice of his latest disaster.

Here in Iowa, he was almost a different man. Layered, a

mystery in some ways. More serious than she would've given him credit for just three days ago. More attentive, too—to their baking, but especially to Leigh and Winnie. Each time his sister and niece had stopped by the house, his entire being shifted into caring brother and uncle mode. He listened, he observed, he poured himself into their every conversation.

"I know you're frustrated that baking hasn't gone well the past few days," he said now. "And I know I basically promised you a Norman Rockwell painting here in Maple Valley. Complete with snow banks and Christmas trees and a thousand lights. I'm sure the lights will come on later when it's dark. But I'm sorry it's so gray and quiet. There should be people ice skating and little kids having snowball fights and—"

She laid her hand on his arm. "I love the bridge. I believe you about the lights. And it'll snow eventually."

Below, glistening swirls of white and silver hid the water's ripples. The echoes of laughter from the town square, the soft lilt of music, summoned.

"Okay, Sparky, if I promise not to nag you about getting back to work, would you please do me the honor of helping me build a synthetic snowman?"

Honestly, if she wasn't a little careful, she could get used to seeing that smile. Maybe even being the one to make it appear.

"Only because you asked so nicely." He held out his elbow and she took his arm.

* * *

COLIN HAD ONLY MEANT to do what little he could to ease the stress coiling Rylan into a high-strung mess. He hadn't realized their afternoon in the square would do so much to relieve the strain of his own taut nerves. He'd known coming home wouldn't be easy—a nosedive into the regret he couldn't seem to outrun.

But who would've guessed Rylan Jefferson to be the cushion that softened the landing?

He pulled a chair free from the restaurant table and waited for Rylan to sit. How was it possible she hadn't argued once when he'd suggested they take immediate advantage of the gift certificate they'd won in the snowman contest?

"I had no idea you were so mannerly, Colin."

"There's a lot about me you don't know, Ms. Jefferson." He helped her scoot her chair in and rounded to his own seat. "Now, one might say after spending the whole afternoon playing outside, we should be back at home, working on yet another of your recipes."

"One might say that."

But true to her word, she hadn't. Not one single time as they built their overly intricate snowman.

The amber lighting of the restaurant—The Red Door, his first time here—did amazing things to her hazel eyes. Added flecks of gold and dancing emotion. She was usually so guarded, refusing to set free anything other than annoyance or sarcasm.

But today he'd seen her playful side. A childlike glee. He couldn't help wanting to see it again. Preserve the bubble of abandon they'd stumbled into this afternoon. If Rylan could put that same kind of carefree creativity into her baking as she did their snowman, she might not be so neurotic all the time.

"Well, I say we deserve dinner out. Our Julia Child snowman was a feat of architecture."

"It really was, wasn't it? I can admit it, Colin—your idea to use my coat as her apron was brilliant."

It'd given him an excuse to play the gentleman once more. He'd insisted she wear his coat, glibly assured her that his masculine body heat would keep him warm. She'd blushed, of all things.

Rylan Jefferson had blushed.

And he'd just stood there for a moment, winter air beating through his sweater, grappling with the realization that she wasn't nearly as stonehearted as she tried to appear. Wondering *why* she tried so hard to appear that way. And how in the world, even swallowed up in his bulky coat, he could find her so entirely appealing.

Entirely inappropriate.

Student. Teacher. He should write it in Sharpie on his palm so he wouldn't forget. Never mind the way she looked at him now, unaware of the packing peanut stuck in her tangled hair, calmly awaiting his next impish, playful comment.

Except, at the moment, he didn't feel at all playful.

"Colin?"

"This building used to be an old bank," he blurted.

She blinked, cocked her head to the side as if unsure of what to make of his sudden discomfort. Yeah, well, he didn't know what to make of it either. He'd come home for the holidays solely to show his family he was doing well now. He'd brought Rylan along as proof, nothing more.

Absolutely nothing. Because he wasn't the Colin Renwycke any longer who messed around with the heart of whatever woman happened to be sitting across from him.

"I sort of gathered that, considering the words 'First National Bank' etched into the stone over the front door." She looked around the restaurant.

He followed her gaze, got the same feeling here that he had walking through Drew's house—that he was getting a front row seat to another man's success, a dream turned reality. He'd thought the outside was impressive, its historic exterior still intact—gray cement accented by the bright red door with the ornate handles. But the inside was just as attractive

—hardwood floors, thick redwood beams crisscrossing overhead to support the vaulted ceiling. Sprawling glass windows gave a gaping view of the town square, currently lit up by the lights he'd promised Rylan—wrapped around every tree and lamppost in sight.

He pointed to the brick counter with a rich wood surface that stretched out at the back of the restaurant. "Leigh told me that brick is straight from Main Avenue. The city decided to pave the street a few years ago. Seth Walker, the guy who owns this place, salvaged the cobblestone." According to Leigh, Seth didn't even know at the time he was eventually going to open a restaurant. Just saw the brick and had a gut feeling.

He wished his own gut feelings were as reliable. More often than not, his instincts got him into trouble. And then his family would bail him out. *Wash. Rinse. Repeat.*

Well, he was done with that. Done. And if Drew ever showed up, he'd be the one with a front row seat . . . to the new Colin. The Colin with a goal, a plan, a career path.

"I've heard about the Walkers."

He handed Rylan a menu from the middle of the table. "Yeah?"

"Leigh's mentioned them a couple times when she's been over. Apparently the restaurant guy isn't the only one who's got a rep in town as a success. Do you know the family?"

A person didn't grow up in Maple Valley without knowing the Walkers. "Everybody knows the Walkers. Everybody loves them." Even the middle son—Beckett. They'd never been close friends, but they'd been at plenty of the same parties in high school. Closest thing the Walkers had to a prodigal, but Beckett was as much adored as the rest of them.

Man, what would it feel like to so easily outpace your mistakes? To know, even if every mess you'd ever made

198

caught up with you, your community—better yet, your family
—would never give up on you?

"Tell me about your family, Colin."

His gaze jerked up. Three days of close quarters and she
could suddenly read his mind?

"I've seen photos on the fireplace mantle. I've met Leigh
and Winnie. But I don't feel like I really know much about the
rest of them. You've told me all about Maple Valley." She met
his eyes over the top of her menu. "But you haven't talked
about your family."

"You haven't talked about yours."

"Yes, but we're not temporarily camped out in my family's
house. My hometown."

He fiddled with his napkin. "I don't know what to tell you.
We're like most families, I guess. We've got our . . . issues. You
already know my parents retired to Arizona. They signed the
house and farm over to Drew. Last year he actually tried to
convince me to help him run the farm, if you can believe that.
But eventually he realized neither one of us was cut out for it.
He sold the land, but kept the house and opened a carpentry
business. Drew's helped Leigh out a lot, too. She's had her fair
share of struggles, but she seems to be doing better now."

Rylan hadn't broken eye contact with him once as he
spoke. There was an unsettling scrutiny to the way she looked
at him. As if she'd heard every one of the details he'd intentionally left out.

My parents retired to Arizona . . . probably because they
needed distance from their two problem children.

They signed the house and farm over to Drew . . . because at
the time, he was the only stable one.

Drew's helped her out a lot . . . been the kind of brother
Colin had never been.

He pulled his gaze from Rylan, settling on the fireplace in
the corner, but it did nothing to relieve the weight of her

study. She was still watching him, he was sure of it, still seeing more than he wanted her to.

But not judging. Not criticizing. Just . . . noticing.

It startled him to his core.

He should toss out a joke, the first roguish comment to come to mind. Tease her about something. Anything.

Instead, he turned his focus back to her and leaned forward, elbow brushing the tabletop as he reached across to finger her hair, free the packing peanut stuck there.

She let out an uneasy chuckle when he held it up in front of her. "How long was that there?"

He dropped the piece of Styrofoam, curled his fingers around his rolled silverware, wished for a glass of water to give him something to do. "I don't know if you've picked up on this, Rylan, but I'm not exactly the standout in our family."

"Different people have different definitions of what constitutes a standout, Colin." She said it so softly he almost didn't hear it over the music of the restaurant.

"I have a lot of regrets. There's no single dark moment in my past that I look back on and think, man, if I hadn't done that one thing or made that one choice, I'd be a different person now. It was a string of little decisions, bad ones that kept compounding until I was just *that guy*. That guy who drank and partied and didn't think about anyone but myself and the next thrill ride." Why was he telling her this? "My dad spent most of my teen years yelling at me, then most of my young adult years lecturing me."

But the silence ever since his parents moved to Arizona was almost worse. As if Dad had finally given up on him.

"I used to think there weren't any long-term consequences to my stupidity, but now that I'm home I see them all around me. Winnie's never going to look up to me the way she does Drew. Leigh would turn to a stranger on the street for help before depending on me. Drew's not even here."

"But you are." Rylan said it with conviction. "Take it from someone who's turned family avoidance into an art form. You're here. That's not a little thing."

"Just starting to wonder if being here is doing any good."

"Give it time. Leigh and Winnie will come around. When Drew gets home, he's going to be fresh off his honeymoon. I would guess that translates into a darn good mood. What better time for a reunion?"

Her assurance was an anchor for his soul. Unexpected and sincere. "You're avoiding your family?"

She unfolded her napkin and dropped it in her lap, then laced her fingers primly on the tabletop. "I believe we were talking about you."

"Yes. Well." He was out of words. Too struck by the surprising comfort of his own honesty and Rylan's heartfelt response in return. He hadn't meant to lay out his background, his mistakes, like place settings on the table. But Rylan had handled his vulnerability as if it were fine china.

Better yet, as if seeing the cracks where he'd been broken, the lines where he'd attempted to glue himself back together, made him something valuable in her eyes.

"I'm, um . . . " He coughed to clear his throat. "I'm surprised a waiter hasn't been by to take our order. Maybe I should go looking for Leigh."

There. Words. A whole string of them. But before he could cobble together any more, Leigh herself appeared through the swinging door leading into the kitchen. She spotted them instantly.

"I'm so sorry. Have you been waiting long? Seth's on vacation and I'm in charge. Our head cook decided to have a baby this week and another one has the flu. So there's a newbie back there trying to single-handedly feed half the town. Two waiters called in tonight because they both had a car accident —with each other. Just a fender bender, but—" She cut herself off with a shake of her head. "Sorry. Freak-out over. Can I get you something to drink?"

Colin's focus swung around the restaurant. Not one empty table. "You've only got one cook tonight?"

"Yes, and I swear he doesn't know the difference between rare and well-done." Her joking tone was a poor mask for the fatigue in her eyes. "Three people have already sent back their orders."

It wasn't fair to Rylan—not any of it. The lack of welcome they'd received at the farm. The un-Christmassy weather. The fact that so far his creativity had done little to assist her.

And now, after assailing her with his woes, he was about to ditch her. But for once, he could do something to help his sister. He'd volunteer to help in the kitchen. "Sorry, Ry—"

"We can help." Rylan interrupted him, not a hint of reluctance in her voice as she stood. "I'm more of a baker than a cook, but I definitely know the difference between rare and well-done."

Leigh's jaw dropped. "Are you serious?"

Rylan stood by his chair. "What are you waiting for, Colin? Come on."

He'd witnessed her impatient foot tapping during every single class for the past three months. Never had he found it as charming as he did tonight.

He rose. *Student. Teacher.*

And for tonight, it seemed, co-chefs.

CHAPTER 6

*R*ylan's arms hadn't felt this heavy, her body this bone-tired since the days of rising at four a.m. to open her bakery.

Two full days of running The Red Door's kitchen ever since Wednesday night and she was exhausted. Drained and wonderfully, inexplicably exhilarated.

The steam of the industrial dishwasher heated her cheeks and her stomach rumbled. Had she eaten anything for dinner tonight? Colin had shoved a plate with a burger and fries at her at some point, but she didn't remember taking a single bite. The enticing smell of the raspberry and chocolate cake they'd served to their last customer half an hour ago clung in the air.

It'd given her an idea for a French crepe cake. She'd never made one before. Mostly because crepes were crepes and cake was cake and why risk ruining two perfect things by putting them together? But certainly Colin would tell her that was an uncreative way to look at things. Maybe if they could finish up here soon—

"It's not fair!"

Winnie pushed through the swinging door that separated the kitchen from the restaurant, her flip-flops slapping against the Tuscan tile floor. She'd heard poor Leigh try to talk her daughter into sensible winter footwear last night. Apparently it'd only prompted another show of defiance because tonight Winnie also wore a tank top.

Leigh straggled in behind the girl. Her usual braids hung limp and loose around her face, like the apron around her waist. "Winnie, everybody else is helping out. Is it so much to ask for you to help clear a few tables?"

"Will you pay me like an actual employee? Or at least give me a better allowance?"

"You know I don't have the money to—" Leigh broke off at the sight of Rylan standing by the dishwasher. "Rylan, you shouldn't be doing dishes. You and Col have cooked the past six meals. That's plenty."

Winnie dumped her backpack on the massive stainless steel counter in the middle of the room. An array of copper pans and utensils clattered overhead.

"Trust me, I don't mind doing a few dishes. I find it weirdly peaceful." She should feel guilty for all the time she'd spent not working on her own recipes. But oh how soothing it'd felt just to *work* in a kitchen. Not to overthink her every move. She hadn't even looked at a recipe card in two days.

Well, not entirely true. When she'd woken up this morning, there'd been a recipe card slipped under the attic doorway—blank, but for Colin's handwriting. *Forecast says it's supposed to snow today. Let's go sledding tonight.*

Dogged man—still trying to give her the idyllic Maple Valley holiday experience. She'd looked out the window at noon. Not a single flurry in the sky.

Thing is, snow or no snow, this past week in Colin's town

204

had done more for her Christmas spirit than she could've possibly imagined. There was that snowman-building contest the other day. The Christmas tunes constantly playing in the restaurant's kitchen. The glow of the town square lights when they locked up at night and walked to Colin's car.

There were the people she was actually starting to get to know by name. Mayor Milt, of course, and Leigh and Winnie, but others, too. Sunny Klassen, the owner of the hardware store, and her husband Lenny. Jenessa, the woman who ran the newspaper, and a man named J.J. who more than likely owned the J.J.'s Stables they passed each day on their way into town.

She'd even met some of the Walkers. Not Seth, the restaurant owner. He was still on vacation with his wife. But she'd met the apparent patriarch—Case Walker—and two of his kids. Kate, the one married to the former NFL quarterback, and Beckett, who'd only recently moved back to Maple Valley after years away.

One week in this eccentric little town and she knew more people by name than she did in all of Denver. Unless she counted her students. But even then, the relationship rarely inched past student-teacher. She might know their names, but that's all she knew.

Except for Colin.

Of everything that had surprised her since arriving in Maple Valley, he was the biggest surprise of all. He'd worked Wednesday night and all through these last two days with a diligence she'd never seen in the classroom. He'd taken on any and every job with an earnest intensity, from manning the wood stove grill to mopping floors to bussing tables.

He's proving something. Perhaps not to anyone but himself. But it was further evidence that she'd been wrong about him all these months. He wasn't incapable or undisciplined. He'd simply needed a greater motivation, something to spur him into focus and action.

Something she apparently hadn't been able to give him as his instructor.

Why that thought should rankle her so, she didn't know. It's not as if she'd ever been on a quest to be a standout culinary school teacher. All the same, how wonderful might it feel to be the spark that ignited someone else's passion?

Not Colin's, of course. *Of course.* But . . . someone.

"I don't think she's even listening, Mom."

Winnie's voice nudged her back to the present.

"Sorry, I was being lulled into la-la-land by the rhythm of the dishwasher." And the unlikely trail of her thoughts.

Leigh propped herself against the glass front of a wall cooler. "I was only saying I wish Winnie would take a cue from you and Colin. You dropped everything to help out here."

"I've got homework, Mom."

"It's Christmas break."

"That doesn't matter to teachers. They're a bunch of Scrooges."

Rylan would laugh if she didn't think it'd only further frustrate Leigh. She felt for the woman. She might not know all of Leigh's story, but she knew enough. Apparently she'd battled addictions off and on, had done several stints in treatment centers. Dealing with a sullen teenage daughter on top of everything else had to be wearying.

Rylan tried to sound encouraging. "Look, Win, if you want to make clearing tables fun, rearrange the napkin holders and chairs and centerpieces. It'll drive Colin crazy." He could call her OCD with her recipes all he wanted, but the man was militant about table arrangement.

Winnie gave an extended sigh and slid from her stool, disappearing through the swinging door a second later.

Leigh took her daughter's place, perching her elbows on the counter and kneading her forehead. "I really don't know what I'm going to do with her. I thought thirteen was hard, but fourteen? It's like someone exchanged my sweet little girl with Oscar the Grouch."

"She's a teenager. A little moodiness is pretty normal, isn't it?" Rylan lifted the dishwasher door, steam clouding around her face. She reached in for a crowded rack of dishes, but yanked her hand back at the heat.

"I don't think Win has any idea what normal feels like. Not with the kind of life I've given her so far. Things are better now than they used to be, but it's still far from perfect. I'm working double-shifts half the time. We hardly see each other."

Enough guilt sagged in Leigh's voice to pull Rylan from her task. She crossed the room and settled onto the stool beside Leigh.

"She's been let down too many times." Leigh's voice was a whisper. "I'm sure she's just in a constant state of waiting for the other shoe to drop. That's why she's so surly all the time. She's waiting for me to . . . "

To slip back into the addiction?

"And I can't blame her because there are days when I'm completely convinced a bottle of Oxycontin would solve everything."

Rylan swallowed. *I'm in over my head.* It'd been one thing being Colin's listening ear the other night. She'd somehow found the right words, and she'd come away from the conversation remembering how good it felt to talk with a friend. After Brent, after her bakery, she'd been so humiliated she'd pulled away from, well, everyone.

Bewildering, really, that it was Colin Renwycke who'd been the one to remind her how much she missed simple friendship.

But Leigh was talking about a potential relapse. That wasn't the kind of conversation you had with someone you met less than a week ago. She should be talking to Colin or a counselor or sponsor.

But you're here. You're the one in the room with her. Don't run away from the opportunity to make a difference.

Again. That voice in her head. The one she knew wasn't her own. "Leigh, I might know just a little what Winnie feels like."

Leigh lifted her head. "You had a deadbeat mom, too?"

"You're not a deadbeat mom. No one who has overcome what you have or works as hard to provide for her daughter as you do could be called a deadbeat." She rubbed her palms over her stained jeans. "And my mom is great. Perfect, really." Just like Dad and Carolina and Dakota. All wonderful. All successful. In their careers, their relationships.

It's why it hurt so much to be around them. Maybe it was childish, but there it was. Holidays had such a bullying way of amplifying all the things that made her different than the rest of them. Bad enough that she couldn't join in on conversations about a spouse's quirks or the latest home repairs, babies or kids or school. But when talk turned to work—whether it was Mom and Dad's CPA firm or Carolina's medical degree or Dakota's travel photography—it was only a reminder of her own once-realized dream now lost.

And the one time she'd brought up the idea of somehow finding a way to open another bakery—Thanksgiving, just last month—there'd been none of the eager questions or encouragement she'd hoped for. Instead, Carolina had said what they'd likely all been thinking: *"Didn't you already try that?"*

Call her a coward, but it was just easier letting the gap grow than continually trying to bridge it, only to be discouraged.

But this wasn't supposed to be about her right now. It wasn't about her family. Leigh was looking at her as if waiting for her to say something helpful. Why couldn't she be better at this kind of thing?

"What I mean is, I've been in that place you described, waiting for the other shoe to drop. Years ago, I owned a bakery. And then I lost it." She took a breath, dredged up her next words from a long-abandoned cavern in her heart. "Just before that happened, I lost a relationship, too. At least, I thought it was a relationship. Brent . . . he didn't feel the way I . . . well, the point is, I thought wrong."

Without the hum of the dishwasher or the muffled voices of patrons, the bustling activity of waiters and plates and oven doors clanging, silence hollowed the room.

"Two of the most important things in my life were gone. Just like that. That was almost three years ago. And after, it was exactly like you said. I was constantly on edge. I kept people at arms' length and I'm pretty sure some of them would describe me much the way you just did Winnie. Like someone had gone and replaced the Rylan they knew with a grouch. But it's just because I was . . . heartbroken, I guess. I kept waiting for the next letdown."

Maybe I'm still waiting.

The thought rolled in like a wave, forceful and impossible to outswim. Was she still shielding herself? Was she still stagnant, stuck in a place of painful caution? Maybe it's why she'd failed to make any close friends in Denver. Why it was easier to travel to Iowa with a virtual stranger than spend Christmas with her family.

But no. No, if she was truly stuck, she wouldn't be working to recapture her dream, would she? "I have something to work toward now. A goal. Maybe that's what Winnie needs—something new to focus on. Something to get excited about. A hobby to pursue or a gift or skill to hone. Maybe it's something you could help her with."

"The way Colin's helping you? He told me you've got a chance to work in a new bakery. He's helping you with a recipe."

"But only so I don't kick him out of my class." She clamped one hand over her mouth. "I wasn't supposed to tell you that." And yet, she was glad she did. Because Leigh had visibly eased, her weary posture straightened and she was no longer rubbing her forehead.

"My lips are sealed."

"From what I can see, you're a good mom, Leigh. Maybe Winnie's just restless."

Leigh let out a breath, less ragged than before. "I hope that's all it is. I don't want to see her repeat my mistakes." She slipped from her stool and turned. "Oh, hey, Colin."

Rylan froze. Colin? She turned on her stool, slowly, to see him standing in the kitchen doorway. How long had he been there?

He pointed over his shoulder as he stepped farther into the kitchen. "Just came to see which one of you told my niece it was a good idea to rearrange all the dining room tables. Though I have a pretty good idea."

Leigh chuckled. "That would be my cue to leave." She brushed past her brother, but stopped before pushing through the door. She turned back to Rylan. "She likes reading. Winnie, I mean. Regular bookworm. And I catch her writing in notebooks sometimes, but she'll never let me see what she's working on." She shrugged. "Drew's wife is an author. Maybe I should see if she'd be willing to talk writing with her or something."

Rylan couldn't look at Colin. The thought of him hearing everything she'd just said . . . "Couldn't hurt."

"And then if that doesn't work, I'll sic her on the two of you. See if she has any latent culinary skills."

"Rylan can teach her to follow a recipe to the T." Colin's voice was a gentle tease.

"And Colin can teach her to break dishes and set off fire alarms."

Leigh pushed through the door, leaving behind an unwieldy quiet. The vulnerability that'd snuck up on Rylan as she attempted to encourage Leigh dawdled now. *Maybe he didn't hear any of it.*

Or if he did, maybe he'd politely ignore it. Pretend he hadn't listened in on her heart as it spilled over. Maybe if she acted nonchalant . . .

She hopped off her stool and moved to the industrial dishwasher. The inside was cool enough now for her to reach in and pull out the tray. Once it was free, she lifted her hands to the sliding door overhead to try to close it. It was high enough she had to stand on her tiptoes.

"You weren't supposed to tell her about me nearly getting expelled."

"Sorry, um, it slipped." Unlike the dishwasher door. She jangled it once more. Wouldn't budge.

She felt Colin's presence behind her and before she could move away, he reached around to grasp the door himself. He steadied himself with his other hand on the edge of the sink, effectively trapping her against the counter.

He had the door down in one sturdy yank.

She couldn't make herself move. Still facing the dishwasher, she waited for Colin to step away.

Instead, hand still clasping the machine door, he paused, breathing measured and words slow. "For what it's worth, Brent sounds like an idiot."

She let out a breath she didn't realize she'd been holding.

And then, with the same strong arm that'd just battled a

stubborn machine, he turned her around to face him. "Now let's go sledding."

* * *

"You weren't lying. It really did snow."

Colin let out a laugh at Rylan's gasped words. "No, I wasn't lying. Generally if I'm going to tell a lie, I try to pick a juicier topic than the weather."

Rylan pulled her nose away from the passenger door window she'd had it smashed up against almost the whole way out of town to the railroad depot they approached now. Her face was the perfect picture of a disapproving matron. "You shouldn't ever lie, Colin. It's very wrong." She turned back to the window.

"You have seen snow before, right? Like, last week back in Denver. And halfway through Nebraska."

"But I've never seen it in Iowa. It's different here."

It was exactly the same. White and fluffy. But he wasn't complaining. He liked this Rylan—all softness and wonder. None of the prickles and sting he'd grown so accustomed to back in Denver.

And the way she'd talked to Leigh back at the restaurant, the honesty and understanding in her voice—he couldn't for the life of him figure out why, but it'd nearly undone him right there in the kitchen doorway. He'd actually had to blink away sudden tears.

Because of his sister's admission of how much she was struggling? Because of what he'd learned of Rylan's own heartbreak?

Or maybe it was the simple and entirely unexpected joy of seeing two people he cared about—apparently at some point in the past week, Rylan had come to fit that description—find exactly what they needed in one conversation. Leigh, a listening ear. Rylan, the chance to step outside her own hurt long enough to share someone else's.

He'd felt uplifted and unraveled, all at once. Yearning and hope stirred together inside him.

Along with something else he didn't dare name, no matter how endearing Rylan had looked with her hair in a knot and her sleeves pushed up to her elbows. No matter how his own awareness had peaked in those moments standing so close to her by the dishwasher.

A few minutes in the cold, a good dousing of snow, would do him good.

"I see the depot!" Rylan lifted one hand to the window. He'd dug the mittens she wore out of the coat closet back at Drew's earlier in the week. "You were right. Everyone in town must be here."

He steered his car into the parking lot of the Maple Valley Scenic Railroad. "That's twice in one night you've acknowl-edged I was right. The snow, the turnout at Depot Hill." The oblong depot, which also served as a museum, was lit up on all sides, a yellow glow in every window and a string of bulbs rimming the roof's overhang. And just like he'd predicted, hordes of kids were already making tracks in the fluffy blanket of snow that covered the hill. Moonlight coasted through the clouds.

Rylan was out of the car before he'd even cut the engine. By the time he rounded the front, snow already half-covered the knit hat she wore over her now-loose hair. He had to blink to keep snowflakes from sticking in his eyelashes. "We probably should've stopped at the farmhouse first to get snow pants or at least layer our clothes."

Rylan shrugged, twisting her scarf around her neck. "Eh, no matter. We'll get wet and cold, but we'll survive."

Was she even the same person who'd scoffed at his every

baking attempt back in Denver? Who'd told him exactly twenty-three times in the past week she couldn't stand him?

"Wait a second." Her mouth drooped into a frown. "What about sleds?"

"I was thinking we'd go bully a couple kids and steal theirs."

She folded her arms. There was the Rylan he knew.

"Have a little faith in me. I didn't come unprepared." He opened a car door and pulled out the two trays he'd stowed in the back seat earlier this evening, soon as he'd realized it was going to snow enough to make sledding a go.

"Did you steal those from The Red Door?"

"Borrowed." Figured it was the least Seth Walker could do considering all the work he and Rylan had put in the past two days. Not that he begrudged the work. Turned out, he loved being out and about in his hometown, seeing familiar faces. Sure, maybe some like Byron Pratt still saw him solely as the kid who'd constantly gotten into trouble as a teen. But plenty of others seemed willing to give him a second—or hundredth —chance.

Made him almost wish he didn't have to return to Denver in January. But no, he'd started down a path with culinary school. He couldn't do what he'd done so many times before —veer off course just to chase a feeling.

"You expect me to slide down a hill on a restaurant tray?"

Colin started toward the hill. "Trust me, it's even more fun than a sled. Because not only do you fly down the hill, you have the extra excitement of trying to stay on the tray. Adds an element of danger."

Rylan's boots made imprints beside him. "Danger isn't really my thing, Colin."

"Poor word choice. Thrill. It adds an extra thrill. We did it all the time in college."

"But I'm not a college kid. I'm in my thirties. My *mid-thirties*."

"So ancient. I'm surprised you don't need a walker."

"I'm just saying—"

He reached for her hand. Just to shut her up. And because she sank into the snow with every step. And because it felt right. "You're not going to get hurt, Ry. You're going to love it. I was right about the snow, wasn't I? I'm right about this too."

She didn't pull away. He didn't know what to think about that.

"You're awfully confident for someone who's broken about every kitchen appliance known to man. If I come out of this with a bloody nose or a broken leg—"

They'd reached the top of the hill. "Then I'll get you to the nearest hospital posthaste. Promise."

Her smile that seemed to come easier and easier with each day that passed gave way to a giggle. "You said 'posthaste.'"

"I think you'll find I have a stunningly expansive vocabulary the more time you spend with me, Ms. Jefferson."

"Well, you've got ten more days to dazzle me with your big words, Mr. Renwycke."

"Ten more days." She planned to leave December 22. Suddenly it didn't feel nearly long enough. At some point in the past week, he'd gone from wondering if he'd made a major mistake bringing this woman to Iowa with him to simply enjoying every minute. Baking, laughing, working alongside each other.

And sometimes when he wasn't teasing, when they weren't bickering, they just talked, too. Over a cup of coffee in the morning. On the way to the restaurant. Late at night when they were beat but too wired to immediately drop into bed.

"Ten days." Rylan repeated her own words. "Ten days until

I have to go back to Denver and impress Potts. Ten days to somehow come up with . . . something."

Worry threatened to shove away her earlier delight. He wouldn't have that. "That's plenty of time for brilliance to strike, Ry. We'll come up with something amazing. Leigh doesn't need us at the restaurant tomorrow. We can get up at the crack of dawn to start baking if you want." He squeezed her hand before releasing it. "But for now, it's time to ride."

He dropped both trays to the ground and lowered onto one of them, folding his knees up to his chest and gripping its sides. Rylan hesitated for a moment before following suit.

"That's a good girl," he said as she shadowed his movement.

"If I die, Colin Renwycke—"

"Then I promise to give a great eulogy at your funeral." And with that, he reached one arm behind her and gave her a solid push.

Her squeal peeled through the air as she went soaring down the hill. Grinning, he pushed himself off with his foot and careened after her. Snow smacked into his face, stinging his cheeks, air barreling past his ears. His eyes closed instinctively, but he forced them open in time to see Rylan's tray swerve and then spin, sending her flying off. A second later, he hit the same bump she had and felt himself roll off his own tray.

His body hit the ground with a thump and a roll, snow seeping down his coat collar and through his jeans.

And Rylan's laughter coming from . . . underneath him?

"Get off of me," she said through giggles muffled by his coat. "Posthaste."

He rolled to his side, his laughter mingling with hers. "I told you it would be fun, didn't I?"

She was splayed on her back, her hat lost in the snow, wet strands of hair clinging to her cheeks. "I think I broke all my ribs," she sputtered. "And I'm pretty sure I have a collapsed lung or two. And I swallowed a gallon of snow."

He rose up on one elbow, tipping the snow out of one ear. "Yes, but all your limbs are intact, so I'd say this was a success."

"I can't feel my face. I'm completely numb."

He grinned as he leaned over her. He tapped her forehead with his glove. Her nose. Her chin. "It's all there, I promise."

She was still trying to catch her breath, from the ride, from the laughter, her chest heaving underneath her coat. She'd lost a mitten and one boot was untied. Her cheeks were red; her lips, nearly blue from the cold.

In that moment, sprawled in the snow, moonlight and mirth waltzing in her eyes, she was, quite simply and undeniably, the prettiest woman he'd ever seen.

You can't go there, Colin. Not with her.

How many times would his conscience have to remind him? She wasn't like the other girls. The ones he'd casually dated and just as casually forgotten. And he wasn't that person anymore.

But that's just it. He *wasn't* that person anymore. Wasn't it possible *this* time, with *this* woman, could be different?

"Colin?"

He could feel the warmth of Rylan's closeness, the sudden slowing of her breathing as he hovered, debated, felt his feeble restraint waning.

"I was just thinking . . . " Did his voice sound as rasped and reedy to her as it did to him? "I was thinking about how you haven't once today told me you can't stand me."

He looked right into her eyes, watched as she swayed between curiosity and delight. "I don't think it's midnight yet. I could rectify that, if you really want."

If he really wanted? If she knew what he really wanted . . .

"Go ahead and say it."

She blinked, swallowed. "Colin Renwycke, I really . . . "

He dipped his head an inch lower. He felt the hitch in her breathing.

"I can't stand . . ." she tried again.

"My brother. Kissing a girl in the snow. Why am I not surprised?"

Shock lanced through him. *Drew.*

CHAPTER 7

$\mathcal{C}$olin would've known where to find Drew even if he hadn't awoken to the strident buzz of a table saw ten minutes ago. Predictable as ever, his big brother.

Scattered footprints already decked the snow-covered lawn, despite the shoveled path leading to Drew's woodshop. Drew's truck was missing from the circle drive that curved around the yard. Perhaps his wife had gone into town.

His wife.

Why hadn't Colin stopped to consider even once this past week that the newlyweds might not appreciate having surprise houseguests when they arrived home? He should've gotten a couple rooms at the local B&B or asked Leigh if he and Rylan could bunk at her place.

Then again, how was he supposed to know they'd come home last night? Apparently Drew had texted Leigh when he'd arrived and realized someone had been camping out in the house. She'd told Drew where to find him.

The rest of the night had been a blur of awkward introductions. Everyone had simply disappeared into different bedrooms once they got back to the house. That is, Rylan into the attic, Colin into his childhood bedroom . . . and Drew and Maren into the master next door.

Definitely not how they must've planned to spend their first night together at home.

The groaning of Drew's saw cut off abruptly when Colin pushed into the shop. "Hey, Drew." The smell of sawdust and coffee engulfed him, along with the warmth of a space heater along one wall.

"Hey."

His brother looked good. More than good. Marriage must do that to a person.

"Leave it to you to already be at work first thing post-honeymoon."

There was a wariness to Drew's smile. That too, predictable. "Maren doesn't exactly love the headboard in my —our—bedroom. I'm making a new one."

He resisted the urge to tease Drew about his slip-up. "You mean the headboard that's been there since Grandpa and Grandma were the ones sleeping in that room? I don't blame her. That's just creepy, man. Tell me it's not the same mattress, too."

Drew rolled his eyes. "It's not the same mattress."

"Good." The tiny space of Drew's shop was cramped with tools, slabs of wood, half-finished projects. "Congratulations, by the way. On the marriage, but also, your business. I've heard rumblings around town. You built an addition onto the depot, put up a building at the orchard."

Drew nodded. "Thanks."

Never one to waste words. Colin stuffed his hands in the back pockets of his jeans. Why couldn't this be easy? Why couldn't they give each other some kind of brotherly embrace and let that be that? That's probably how the Walkers did things.

Yeah, well, you aren't the Walkers. Never had been. That

family was as close-knit as a warm sweater. The Renwyckes were a ball of frayed yarn, so many knots now it'd take more than a casual conversation in a woodshop to untangle the mess.

But he could try. That's why he'd come home, wasn't it?

Drew reached for a mug hanging from a hook on the wall. He poured from the Thermos Colin hadn't noticed until now and handed the cup over. "So the girl?"

Colin sputtered on his first drink. "Uh, Rylan? It's like I said last night. She's my teacher. From the Denver Culinary Institute."

"But what's she doing here?" Drew perched himself on a sawhorse.

It would've been so easy to give the answer he'd rehearsed. The one that made the impression he'd intended all along. *She's got this huge opportunity to work in a trendy bakery, but she needs help and she's seen my creativity this past semester and besides, she didn't have anyone to spend the holidays with.*

Technically, it was all true. So why did he feel the need to blurt out the other half of the story? "I bungled my first semester at the school and she was ready to kick me out until I convinced her give me another chance on the condition that I help her come up with a recipe to impress a big-time chef." The words released in a whoosh.

Drew only cocked his head. Took a drink of coffee straight from the Thermos. "Huh. Not exactly the way she told it this morning."

"You talked to her already?" He hadn't seen her downstairs when he'd come through the house. He'd looked. A little too eagerly.

"She and Maren went into town awhile ago. To the store. Maren insists on doctoring her coffee with half the dairy aisle." He took another swig from the Thermos. "Rylan said you're a star student and seemed to indicate we should all be infinitely proud of you."

She had, had she? No denying a grin at that. "I might've prepped her some."

"I can't believe you dragged a woman all the way from Colorado just to make you look good in front of your family."

Drew saw through him way too easily. And there was just enough guarded criticism in his brother's tone to raise his hackles. "Yeah, well, you don't generally give me much benefit of the doubt."

"Can you blame me? You do remember all the times I've bailed you out of jail, right?"

"Twice, Drew." Once for disorderly conduct outside a frat house. Once after waking up drunk in an alleyway. Did Drew honestly think he wouldn't remember? That the shame didn't still pay him regular unwelcome visits?

"I've paid your rent I don't know how many times. I've helped tide you over when you've been between jobs." Drew had abandoned his perch on the sawhorse. He paced the small space between it and the table saw.

So not how this was supposed to go. "I don't need a recitation of your every Good Samaritan moment."

"You never seem to know what you *do* need, Col."

"Look, if you don't want me here—"

"I didn't say that."

"Well, your welcome home speech could use some work."

Drew halted, heaving a sigh and combing his fingers through his hair. "I just . . . Colin, can you try to see things from my perspective? The first thing I saw last night was you pawing that woman."

"Her name is Rylan and I wasn't pawing her." He hadn't even kissed her. Not yet anyway.

Hadn't stopped him from lying awake half the night thinking of what might've happened if he had. Whether she'd have pushed him away or let the moment stretch. Wondering if she was tossing and turning up in the attic as much as he was down below.

"Then I get two different stories from the both of you about why you're here and I find you're on the brink of being expelled from culinary school." He was pacing again. "And, yeah, culinary school? That's your deal now? You're in Denver? Would it have been that hard to pick up a phone and send an email? Or maybe answer one of mine? Smoke signal, carrier pigeon, anything?"

Colin rubbed his hands over his unshaven cheeks, down his arms, wished he could force himself to meet Drew's eyes. "I wanted to wait until I could tell you honestly that . . . that I was doing well. That things were looking up."

Drew stopped in front of him. "Instead, you almost got kicked out and your solution was to flirt with your instructor until she agreed to lie for you?"

That was it. His coffee mug clanked to the metal surface of the saw's table. "I don't know why I thought it would be different this time. That you'd actually listen instead of tearing me down just so you could be the one to fix me again."

"Colin." A flash of remorse joined the frustration in Drew's eyes.

Too late. He angled past his brother, sidestepped a sanded down chair.

"I'll clear out by the time your wife's back." Didn't know what he'd tell Rylan, but hopefully she'd understand. Or better yet, *not* understand. Because he wouldn't be able to handle it if she suddenly realized how far the gulf between his mess of a life and his brother's really spanned. If she looked at him with the same disappointment as Drew.

The same disappointment he'd seen so many times from Dad.

"You don't have to leave." Drew followed him toward the

door. "You're right, I shouldn't have dragged up everything. Stay. We should talk about Dad—"

He sprung as if attacked, whirling to find himself nearly nose-to-nose with his brother. And then his hands were at Drew's chest, pushing. What was he doing? "Don't bring Dad into this."

Drew stumbled backward. "Colin!"

Why was he now barreling toward his brother, ready to throw himself into a fight neither of them wanted?

He tasted dirt as Drew grappled his way out of Colin's grip and sent him tumbling against the wall. His cheek hit first.

"What is wrong with you?" Drew's voice heaved.

"Drew?" A woman's voice. A flood of light. Maren? "What in the world is going on here?"

Colin lifted his hand to shield his eyes. Oh, please tell him Rylan wasn't there, too.

But of course, it was her voice he heard next. "Colin?"

He tasted blood as his lungs clenched.

* * *

RYLAN HAD DECIDED she liked Maren, Colin's new sister-in-law. Quite a bit, actually. But the jury was still out on the brother.

Way out.

Drew Renwycke sat at the small table in the corner of his kitchen, hunched and far too dejected for a man who'd just returned from his honeymoon.

"I don't understand you, Drew." Maren stood behind him, brushing at the sawdust that clung to his shirt. "You spend a year worrying about your brother. Making me wait for you because you didn't want to get married until you'd magically fixed your family. Then Colin finally comes home and what do you do?"

Rylan hovered in the opposite corner of the kitchen, trying to decide whether to follow Colin's stalking footsteps up the stairs or make herself scarce altogether.

"I threw it all in his face, Mare." Drew dropped his face into his hands. "It's like a decade of wondering when he was going to hit rock bottom . . . it all bubbled to the surface at once. I was a jerk."

Maren glanced at Rylan over her husband's slumped form. "That's a Renwycke man for you. They'll wait an eternity and then, bam, all at once, action."

The barest smile tugged at Drew's lips. "Kinda describes how we got married."

Maren was rubbing his shoulders now, apparently willing to forgive Drew his part in whatever had happened out in that workshop a lot quicker than Rylan was. She'd seen the anguish in Colin's eyes the second sunlight flooded the shop. The hurt.

And a fear she couldn't begin to comprehend. *What is it eating away at you, Colin?* He'd told her about his past, his regret, but there had to be something more.

Maren pressed a kiss to the top of Drew's head. "Just tell me you didn't hit him."

He shook his head. "No. It was barely even a scuffle. Over before it began."

The ceiling creaked at Colin's movement overhead. Shouldn't he get some ice on his cheek? Maren had gone from lightly reprimanding Drew to practically coddling him. Shouldn't someone be looking after Colin?

She crossed the room to the refrigerator, wrenched open the freezer door, and grabbed the first bag of frozen vegetables she saw. Good enough. She started for the doorway.

"Rylan?" Drew's tone halted her. "I'm sorry. I've been a pretty poor host so far."

Maren snorted. "I'll say. You didn't even have creamer to offer for her coffee."

His expression was somewhere between a grimace and a patient grin. The man adored his wife. That much was clear. He reached for Maren's hand over his shoulder as he spoke again. "Colin and me . . . there's a lot of history."

She nodded. Took another step, but stopped again. "He didn't miss a single class, you know." She nudged her head upward. "The whole semester, he never missed. He was never even late. And yeah, he drove me crazy and spilled something at least once a session and messed up recipes like you wouldn't believe. But only because he always had some idea to make things better. He's not afraid to experiment. That's not something all of us can say. Some of us need recipe cards just to boil water." Colin's own words. Who would've ever guessed she'd repeat them—in his defense, of all things.

Drew and Maren wore twin stares.

"And he was really excited to come home for Christmas."

With that, she rotated on her heels and made for the stairs. Let them make what they would of her words. Oh, it was clear Drew regretted whatever it was he'd said or done. Remorse radiated from him.

But couldn't he grasp what a weighty thing Colin had done in coming home? Didn't that deserve some acknowledgement?

She was halfway up the stairs when Maren called her name. "Rylan, wait."

Drew's wife hurried up to her, an urgent plea for understanding in her vivid green eyes. "I know Drew's probably made a horrid first impression on you. But he feels awful, I know he does. He wouldn't get so frustrated with Colin if he didn't care about him so much."

"I get that." And it was obvious Colin loved his older brother just as well. Admired him and craved his respect. "What I don't get is why two brothers who clearly both want to reconcile, would go after each other their first morning in the same house."

Maren let out a breath. "Because they're scared. They got horrible news two weeks ago and they're both just . . . scared."

Horrible news?

The question must've shown on face. Tears welled in Maren's eyes. "Their father was diagnosed with rapidly progressive Alzheimer's. His doctor is saying . . . " She took a breath. "He probably has less than a year."

Oh, Colin. She could feel her heart splinter.

"Drew wanted to fly down to Arizona immediately, but his mom asked him not to. She said they needed some time to digest the news on their own. Instead, they're planning to come up here for Christmas." Maren shook her head. "It's killing Drew. This is something he can't fix. Somehow, our elopement was still wonderful and romantic and all of that, but I'm sure as soon as we got home it all just came crashing back in."

And he'd taken it out on Colin.

That explained the fear she thought she'd seen in Colin's face. It wasn't just the past bothering him, but the shock of the present and the uncertainty of the future. "Thanks for telling me."

Maren blinked away her tears. "I'm glad you're here, Rylan. Partially 'cause it means I won't have to play referee for the Renwycke men on my own. But mostly because I can see you care about Colin. He needs that."

Eight days ago if she'd heard someone suggest she cared about Colin Renwycke, she'd have laughed until her sides hurt, assumed they'd been dipping into the cooking wine. But now?

How could so much change in a week?

She *did* care. Not because he was the means to an end, her hope for nailing that recipe for Chef Potts. Not because he was her student or even because Potts was right about his potential.

But because Colin was a man with a heart and layers she was only now beginning to understand. Because he was constantly *trying*—not just to make a way for his own future but also to give her a real holiday season, to help her prepare for Potts, to make life easier for Leigh in the one practical way he could.

And because where she'd chosen to avoid her family just to escape a few bruised feelings, he'd chosen to humbly face his head-on.

Maren nodded up the stairs. "Go on."

She followed the sound of running water, down the hallway to the second floor bathroom. She hesitated only a moment before knocking. "Colin, it's me."

The faucet squeaked as the water stopped. A pause. Then the door inched open. He must've just washed his face. Water dripped from the ends of his hair, so in need of a trim that it fell over his forehead and around his ears.

He glanced down to the bag in her hands. "Weird breakfast choice."

"For your face." Not that it appeared all that needed. No swelling on the cheek she'd watched hit the woodshop wall.

He took the vegetables from her. "Crinkle cut carrots. Trust you to pick the fanciest of the frozen vegetables." He set the bag in the sink. "But my face is fine. Bit the inside of my cheek so hard it bled, but that's all. I'm fine."

"Colin." She took a small step forward, into the bathroom. Surely she was meant to say something more. Something kind and consoling and helpful. But all she could do was look at him, this man she'd spent so many weeks disliking, and wish away every scrap of hurt that marred his expression like the sawdust on his shirt. "Why didn't you tell me about your dad?"

At her gentle question, his gaze grew even more stricken, the blue of his eyes deepening into a storm of emotion. "I didn't . . . I don't . . . "

She couldn't help it, saving him from words he didn't know how to say. She closed the space between them, reaching her arms around him, and burying her head in the crook of his neck. She felt his shock as thoroughly as her own —his sharp inhale, his surprised stillness.

But before she could ask herself what she was doing, reverse course, and pull away, he released a ragged exhale and pressed into her embrace. His arms wound behind her as a shudder jolted through him.

Or maybe that was her. She really had no idea. Knew only that suddenly and completely, everything felt so very right. Colin's face in her hair and her hands on his back, the burdens he carried and maybe, too, somehow her own, lighter for the wordless sharing.

She didn't know how long they stood there, the floor vent breathing warmth over her feet, the faint scent of Colin's aftershave filling her senses.

"For as many times as you've said you can't stand me, you've got a funny way of showing it, Rylan Jefferson."

His tenor voice slid over her ears like music. She tipped her head back. "It's good for a woman to be a little unpredictable."

The wound in his eyes had made space for wonder. "You are, at that."

He held her gaze so long she could feel her face warm and heartbeat pick up. And every last semblance of logic and restraint fled as he lowered his head, his lips meeting hers. One soft kiss, and then two.

And then his hand behind her was closing the bathroom door and she was pressed against it, her arms clasped behind Colin's neck for a third kiss that stretched until her head swam and heart raced and—

Colin broke away, nearly jumped away. Shock seemed to render him speechless and immovable, the sudden foot of space between them not nearly enough to break the magnet-like pull of what had just happened.

Breathless and dizzy, Rylan could only rasp. "Whoa."

CHAPTER 8

*R*enwycke men, it seemed, didn't talk about things. They didn't talk about scuffles in the wood shop. They didn't talk about years of family discord.

And they especially didn't talk about devastatingly breathtaking kisses that happened in the tiny space of a farmhouse bathroom.

"I don't know whether to feel grossed out or completely enthralled by the amount of butter happening here." Maren stood before the island counter in Drew's kitchen—her kitchen now, Rylan supposed—holding the pastry scraper Rylan had been shocked to find at the back of a drawer. Leigh and Winnie were on the other side, watching as Rylan laid a four-inch by four-inch square of cold butter over the lean dough she'd already rolled atop a floured surface.

Today's baking had turned into an impromptu all-female class on puff pastry making. Rylan's favorite. Sure, a person could opt for the easy route and purchase frozen pastry, save the work of pounding butter and repeated rolling and folding. But it was the work Rylan loved.

"Trust me, the butter is pure magic." She folded the

corners of the dough over the butter and pinched to seal the pocket, mentally reciting the recipe she knew by heart. *Place the beurrage (butter packet) inside the détermpe (dough packet) and fold into an envelope. Turn it over so the seams are down. Roll into a rectangle about twelve inches long by six inches wide.*

"Actually, it's not magic. It's science."

Her gaze darted to the back door where Colin stood with two bags of groceries. More baking ingredients.

In the four days since he'd kissed her—and yes, since she'd kissed him back—he'd been as diligent as ever in aiding her quest to come up with the perfect recipe. He'd made so many trips to the store for ingredients. He'd suggested flavor variations and taste-tested until he had to have a stomachache. He'd been entirely at her service.

Maybe it was just his way of avoiding his brother, but he'd seemed to enjoy the hours on end in the kitchen, laughing when she bossed him around and never once rushing her when she'd stare at her recipe card for minutes at a time. She'd even begun adapting some to his style—the way he took over the entire kitchen when he baked, spread his ingredients from one end of the counter to the other, never putting them away in between steps.

Unlike the quiet she was used to as she baked in her own kitchen, Colin talked as he worked—sharing stories about all his various jobs through the years, drawing her out with questions that somehow didn't feel at all intrusive. She'd found herself telling him about her old bakery in Denver, the years she'd spent saving, the little storefront she'd found the day before her thirtieth birthday and how she'd just known it was "the one."

Two nearly perfect years she'd spent making the space her own, existing inside the bubble of her dream. Until money and the economy and a skyrocketing lease had forced her out. She'd told him all that.

And still they hadn't talked of that kiss. But maybe that was okay. Maybe they'd said all there was to say in those potent moments just after.

"*I . . . you . . . that was . . .* " Colin had said as he backed away.

Perfect? she'd mentally completed for him. *Wholly unexpected but nothing short of remarkable?*

"*Probably completely inappropriate.*"

She'd wanted to melt into the wood of the bathroom door. "*Probably.*"

"*There are a ton of reasons why I shouldn't have . . . why we shouldn't . . .*"

No man should look so charming simply trying to complete a sentence. "*Right. For instance, I'm older than you.*"

He shouldn't look at her like that—with the dimples and the flash of delight in his eyes. Not if he expected her to keep her distance. "*If that's the best reason we've got, we're doomed, my dear.*"

And he shouldn't call her "my dear."

"*I've assured my family you're here as a friend, not anything else. This is exactly what they'd expect from me—taking advantage of a girl behind a closed door. They'll think I lied—*"

"*You didn't take advantage of me, Colin. And I'm a woman, not a girl. I wasn't helpless just now.*" Or at all passive, if he'd recall.

Which it seemed he did, considering the almost smug tilt to the grin he tried to tamp down. He sobered, though, with his next words. "*You're also my teacher.*"

There . . . there was the clincher. He was right. He might be closer to her in age than her traditional students. They might've formed an unlikely friendship in the past days of close quarters and working side by side. But she'd bet every high-end baking utensil in her kitchen there was some culinary institute policy in some employee handbook somewhere that promised repercussions for student-teacher relationships that went beyond, well, a student-teacher relationship.

And so, with little more than a shared look of understanding, they'd stepped into the hallway. Hadn't said another word about it since.

Didn't mean she hadn't thought about it. At night when she was trying to sleep. During the day whenever Colin looked particularly handsome as he kneaded dough or washed dishes.

Right now as he abandoned the bags of groceries and proceeded to give the others a play-by-play of the science to puff pastry making. "What happens is, after all the folding and rolling, you have literally hundreds of paper-thin layers of butter trapped between hundreds of paper-thin layers of dough. When it's the oven, the liquid in the butter and the dough evaporates into steam, the butter melts into the dough, and the steam puffs up the leftover gaps. That's how you get a light, flaky pastry. It's all about evaporation."

He ended up at Rylan's side when he was done. "You see, Ms. Jefferson, I always pay attention in class."

She had to look away from his eyes, lest her stupid heart not listen to her nagging brain and her fingers tremble while she folded her dough into thirds.

"Never thought I'd see the day when I got a science lesson from Uncle Colin." Winnie rocked on her stool.

"If I've heard Rylan say it once, I've heard her say it a thousand times: baking is as much about science as anything. Pure chemistry."

She swallowed as she reached for the French rolling pin, trying to ignore the subtle, but enticing scent of Colin's aftershave.

"Of course, she's not entirely correct."

Rylan paused with her palms pressed over the pin pressed over the dough. "Is that so?"

"It's also about exploring the untested. Trying new flavor combinations. Experimenting. Putting two ingredients together you never would've expected and giving it a go, seeing what happens, even if you don't have a recipe card or a logical, scientific explanation for what you're doing."

She couldn't make her hands move. She needed to roll the dough. Then fold it up and turn it over and roll it again before the butter got too soft. This was a long enough process, what with needing to chill it for a good twenty or thirty minutes every couple turns or so and—

"Speaking of which, I had this idea."

Colin was leaning closer to her now and she was uncomfortably aware of Leigh and Maren watching. Colin's tone was as nonchalant as could be, but surely they could hear her stomach doing acrobatics.

"I know how much you like recipe cards, so I wrote it down. It's in one of those bags." He cocked his head toward the grocery sacks he'd set on the kitchen table. "I can take over here if you want to check it out."

"All right." She handed over the rolling pin, stepped away. Willed her common sense to kick in as she moved to the table.

"Hey, Rylan, I've been meaning to ask you," Maren's voice followed her. "How is it you could ditch Denver for several weeks right at Christmas? You didn't have any family plans?"

"Am I allowed to call you nosy, Mare, or are you still too new to the family for that?"

Rylan grinned at Colin's scolding as she dug through the first bag. He'd already started rolling the dough, the muscle in his arms evident as he made much quicker work of the step than she would've. "It's okay. Uh, actually my immediate family is all in Africa right now. My older sister, Carolina, worked with Doctors Without Borders for several years and she goes back to volunteer at a medical center in Ethiopia at least once a year. This year her husband and kids went with her and my parents got the idea of everyone joining them, doing a safari, that kind of thing. My younger sister, Dakota, and her husband are both travel photographers, so they didn't have to think twice."

No recipe card in the first bag.

"Why didn't you go along?" Leigh asked the question.

"I just . . . um . . . " It was easier to riffle through the second bag than look up. "It wasn't great timing for me. They're actually flying home the day before Christmas Eve, though, so if I want to join them then . . . "

She waited for the next question as she unloaded the grocery bag so she could get to the recipe card she saw at the bottom. They'd want to know about that *if.*

Too bad she didn't have a single answer that didn't sound pathetic. *It's too many happy, successful people in one place. I always feel like the loser of the group.* And of course, there were the inevitable questions: *"Are you dating anyone? Whatever happened with Brent?"*

The sad thing was, she knew her family didn't mean to make her feel as they did. Every one of them had texted or called at some point in early December to ask her to reconsider going to Africa—or at least drive from Denver down to Mom and Dad's in Colorado Springs on Christmas Eve once they were all back in the States.

They just didn't realize the depth of her hurt over the bakery, the extent of her pain over Brent. *Maybe because you're never willing to talk to any of them about it.*

But wouldn't that just make it worse? It was hard enough trying to get through a holiday without constantly comparing her life to theirs. If she opened up about her emotions, they'd surely respond with sympathy. But sympathy too often felt like pity.

And she simply wasn't sure she could handle it.

But Winnie didn't ask the question Rylan expected. "Carolina? Dakota? Why didn't you get a state name, Rylan?"

"Actually my name is Maryland." She pulled the recipe card free and when she glanced up, it was to see everyone looking at her. "Mary would've been the obvious moniker, I guess, but I've always kind of liked to do my own thing."

"Maryland Jefferson." Colin said her name as if just meeting her for the first time, the barest half-smile tugging at the corner of his mouth. He looked to the card in her hand and then back to her. Waiting.

She read the card. *If you'd expel me—just temporarily—you wouldn't be my instructor anymore.*

Her eyes darted to his. Without breaking eye contact, he picked up the flattened dough and slowly turned it over.

She flipped over the card. *And if you're not my instructor anymore, I can ask you on a date.*

The oven was pre-heating. Which meant the kitchen was warm. Which meant maybe Leigh and Winnie and Maren wouldn't think anything of the heat rising in Rylan's cheeks just now.

"Well, guys," Colin said, "after I get this rolled and then folded again, it's going in the refrigerator for awhile. There's not much more to see here at the moment."

He'd effectively dismissed everyone from the kitchen. And she couldn't believe it, but within a matter of seconds, they all emptied from the room. Maren said something about finding Drew out in the woodshop. Winnie seemed to welcome the escape lest she face any further science lessons. Leigh's shift at the restaurant started in half an hour.

Just like that, it was Colin and Rylan and the card in her hands and a *Well?* that seemed to hang in the air.

"Maryland Jefferson," he said her name again.

"My dad's very patriotic." She glanced at the dough. "You should get that in the fridge."

"You should tell me what you think of my latest creative idea."

He reached for a roll of plastic wrap, encased the dough and placed it in the refrigerator, all while she tried to get her brain to work. Expel him. Temporarily. Date. And then he was standing in front of her. "Pretending nothing's changed isn't working for me, Rylan. Just one date. Just to see. Friday night? It'd be fitting—the two-week anniversary of the Baked Alaska incident."

"Disaster, you mean?"

He took the recipe card from her hand and slid it into the front pocket of her apron. "You can call it whatever you want, Maryland. Just kick me out of your class, so I can take you on a date."

She couldn't have said no if she wanted to. "On one condition."

"That I not call you Maryland anymore?"

No, because when it came out of his mouth, it didn't sound nearly as stiff and formal as it'd always felt whenever anyone else said it. "That you talk to your brother."

An unfair request, perhaps, since she'd gone to great lengths to avoid her own family. But anyone with eyes could see he still longed for reconciliation, despite their altercation in the woodshop.

Colin's forehead pinched. "You drive a hard bargain."

"It's what you really came home for, Colin." Part of it, anyway. And oh, she hoped when he saw his dad next week, he'd get whatever else he needed.

"All right, then. So I'm officially—temporarily, let's not forget that part—officially, temporarily expelled?"

She stood on her tiptoes to kiss his cheek. "You're so expelled."

* * *

He was doing this for Rylan.

Maryland Jefferson.

He'd thought it wasn't possible to be any more surprised by the woman. But she was named after a state and she wanted him to talk to Drew. So, he'd talk to Drew. He found his brother in the basement.

"Hey, Drew."

Drew jerked his head up and bashed it on the low slant of a pipe. A musty scent draped in the chilled air of the unfinished space. Cardboard boxes and plastic tubs sat in clusters and piles, turning the basement into a veritable maze. Finally, he'd found the one corner of the house Drew hadn't gotten around to working his magic on.

"Need something?" Drew pried open a large tub, scanned its contents.

Typical Drew question. Tended to think the whole world needed him.

Not helpful, his instant mental sarcasm. He was here to mend bridges. Apologize for however long it took to convince Drew that this time, this change, was for real.

"Maren said you're going to bring up all the Christmas decorations. I thought I'd help." He'd spent two hours assisting Rylan with her pastry first, shaping Palmiers and listening to her complain about how the sugar-rolled desserts weren't nearly dazzling enough.

This demonstration for Chef Potts next week had her so stuck in her own head. She was too close to her every effort, completely devoid of objectivity.

Which is exactly how he'd come to feel about the unexpected about-face in their . . . situation. He'd thought he could wave it off, ignore it, pretend the kiss had never happened. Enjoy their surprise friendship and leave it at that.

Maybe if it had only been a kiss, he could've. But it was probably about time he admit that the bewildering, gradual turn in his feelings toward Rylan—*Maryland*—Jefferson had begun much earlier than that. Probably around week two at the institute when she'd gone on an extended tirade about his marzipan mousse in front of the rest of the class without realizing she had streaks of apricot compote running down her sleeve.

He'd found her harsh and unfeeling and irritating.

And fiery and appealing, he realized now. He just hadn't let himself acknowledge it before.

But even amusement with a heady side of physical attraction might not have been enough for him to rethink the decision to back away from whatever might be happening between them. No, what had him unable to sleep, incapable of focusing, wondering what kind of idiot walked away from a girl—*woman,* she'd been quick to correct him—like Rylan wasn't just the fact that she was prettier than she knew.

It was the softness he'd discovered beneath her prickles. The kindness. The way whenever conversation had turned to Dad these past few days, she didn't push or pry but let him know with simply a look that she was there for him.

Too, her determination. She'd found career success—something he'd never experienced himself—only to lose it all. She'd had her heart broken by some idiot named Brent. And yet, she hadn't stopped dreaming.

"Colin? I asked if you could look in that box over there. I'm hoping it's all the tree ornaments."

Colin shook away his wandering thoughts and stepped around an old upholstered chair, fabric covering torn and faded. This must be where Drew stored the furniture he intended to restore eventually. He found the box Drew indicated and checked inside. "You're right. Ornaments."

"Perfect. Now I just need to find the one with the lights. My wife is obsessed with twinkle lights."

"You like saying that, don't you? 'My wife.'"

Drew's attempt to hide his over-sized grin was entirely unsuccessful. "Guess I do."

"Hey, remember when we made these?" Colin held up two ornaments made of felt and pipe cleaners. Santa and Rudolph.

Drew skirted around an old padded bench that used to sit in the entryway, if Colin remembered correctly. "Yeah, we fought over the hot glue gun."

"And Leigh told on us."

"And then Mom ended up finishing mine for me when I got distracted building a house with the pipe cleaners."

"Guess I'm not the only house-builder in the family." Drew reached for one of the ornaments, the expression on his face reflecting so many memories of the past. So many worries for the future.

"I'm sorry about everything, Drew."

"Colin—"

"No, you gotta let me get this out. My love life depends on it."

Drew cocked his head.

"Kidding. Kind of. But I'm serious. I'm sorry for all the times you had to bail me out—jail and otherwise. I'm sorry about never letting you know where I was or what I was doing. I'm sorry about the parties and the reckless frat boy behavior, the drinking and the girls and . . . " It had all been so stupid at eighteen, nineteen, twenty. But how could he have let that lifestyle stretch so far into his adulthood? "I'm sorry about blowing you off last year when you gave me the opportunity to work the farm with you."

"We were never meant to be farmers, either of us."

"But you were thinking of me, my life. And Leigh. You moved back to Iowa with the sole purpose of helping us get our lives back together, and instead of being grateful you still hadn't given up on me, I pushed you further away." Unlike

Leigh, who'd been smart enough to take the second chance Drew offered.

"I would never give up on you, Colin."

He looked up to Drew. Saw such firm sincerity it nearly undid him.

"Just like I hope you'll never give up on me. Someday I might learn how to stop barging in and thinking I know the answers to everyone else's problems. If there's anything the past couple weeks have taught me, since I found out about Dad, it's that any control I've ever thought I had is flimsy and fake. A false comfort when what I really need is to learn to trust a God who offers something better than answers."

"What's that?" Colin swallowed. He hadn't thought about God in a long time, other than to assume he most likely looked at Colin the way his father had so many times. Sheer disappointment.

"Hope," Drew answered without hesitation.

"That a miracle will happen and Dad will be healed and everything will be fine?" Would Drew be offended by the trace of disbelief in his tone?

Drew only clasped his arm. "Maybe. But also, that even if not, he's still good and faithful and willing to be our ultimate comfort and peace if we'll let him." And then in a move that surprised and completely overwhelmed him, Drew embraced him. "I love you, little brother. I'm sorry about laying into you the other day."

It was over in less than seconds, and then Drew was once again sidestepping boxes and filling his arms with Christmas decorations. He was halfway up the rickety basement steps before Colin could speak past the lump in his throat.

"Drew, I . . . " He swallowed another rising swell of emotion.

"I know, I know, you love me, too. Can you grab that box of ornaments when you come up?"

Drew was letting him off. Saving this conversation—and Colin—from dissolving. But the moment was no less weighty for it. And as Drew disappeared up the stairway, he couldn't help the prayer that mingled with the peace-filled relief filling every corner of his soul.

God, show me how to be like Drew. A man who found the right words when they were needed most. Who made a difference in the lives around him.

A man who was there for his family.

But as he lifted the box filled with Christmas decorations, the thought hit him for the first time: Was it even possible to be the brother and uncle he longed to be—the *man* he longed to be—all the way from Denver?

"Whoa, this wasn't at all what I pictured when you said Sleepy Hollow." Rylan reached for the strands of hair fluttering around her face, the whispers of a gentle wind feathering over her face.

And she'd thought the first half of this date was perfect.

Enchanting. She'd actually used the word *enchanting* to describe the candlelight dinner in the town square's lit-up band shell, a space heater for warmth, twinkle lights and sparkling snowfall for company.

But this?

Colin reached into his car and pulled out a travel mug. He'd stopped at the farmhouse before making the twenty-minute drive south of town. He'd insisted she add another layer of clothing while he prepared homemade hot chocolate.

He placed her mug in her mittened hands. "What did you picture?"

He'd said he was taking her to a place called Sleepy Hollow and her brain had gone immediately to *The Legend of Sleepy Hollow.* "The story of Ichabod Crane. You know, the superstitious schoolmaster who encounters a Headless

Horseman at a cemetery bridge. Always creeped me out. Even the Disney cartoon version gave me nightmares as a kid. I haven't been able to carve a jack-o-lantern since."

Colin chuckled as he hit the lock and closed the car door.

"My childhood fear is a source of delight to you?"

"Everything about you is a source of delight to me."

If he didn't sound so entirely earnest, she might whack him with her scarf. Instead, she let him take her hand and lead her toward the covered bridge that glowed against the starry night thanks to the paper lanterns, hundreds of them, adorning both sides of the winding river. Little blurs of light mingled with the near-dark, their glimmer reflecting over the ice-covered water. Tall reeds of stubborn prairie grass pushed through the snow along the riverbank.

This had to be the same river that ran through Maple Valley. And probably some of the people, couples mostly, who stood in clusters along the riverside were from Colin's town.

"It's beautiful." Her voice came out breathy and awed.

"I couldn't decide whether to come here before dinner or after. Before, we would've had the extra bonus of sunset. Later, however, means fewer people and more lanterns."

"After worked out just fine." They found a spot just outside the bridge's opening and stood with arms dangling over a knotty wood railing—just like they had that day at the Archway Bridge last week or the week before or . . . she didn't know when. At some point, time had come to a stop in Maple Valley.

It was as if she'd slipped into a beguiling little Christmas display inside a storefront window—one that came alive in captivating detail while the rest of the world simply walked by and went about business.

And she was beginning to wonder how she would ever make herself leave.

"Not at all like Ichabod Crane's Sleepy Hollow," she

murmured. Oh yes, Colin Renwycke knew how to plan a date. Which probably made his expulsion from culinary school the most rewarding in the history of educational institutions, culinary or otherwise. "So is there a story to the lanterns?"

"Indeed."

She turned to look at him. Moonlight traced his handsome profile and turned his blue eyes luminous. One day earlier this week when they were baking, he'd confessed that a couple years back, to make ends meet, he'd taken a few modeling gigs. One of his photos had even ended up on a book cover—Maren's, in fact. She had a feeling there was more to that tale than he'd let on.

But it wasn't that story she awaited now as Colin paused, his attention spanning the riverside. "Well? Are you going to tell it? Before frostbite sets in?"

"You're cold?" His gaze darted immediately to her. "You promised me you'd be warm enough."

She was plenty warm. She wore two layers of leggings under her skirt and fur-trimmed boots. Not the most practical attire for an outdoor date in December, but this *was* a date. And for once, she'd cared more about what *she* looked like than some edible creation. She had a new sweater, too, and all the wintry accessories—mittens, knit hat, matching scarf.

"It's either tell me the Sleepy Hollow story or reveal what you put in this hot chocolate." She'd nearly drained her mug already and she'd been heckling him all the way out here for the recipe. She could taste the nutmeg, but there was something else.

"You can be quite petulant and demanding, Maryland Jefferson."

"And you can try a person's patience."

The splendor of his smile could give the riverbank

beauty a run for its money. "All right. Once upon a time, just down the river from a quirky little town called Maple Valley, there lived a man and a woman and their young daughter, Sarah."

A gusty breeze set the hundreds of lanterns flickering. "Once upon a time when?"

"What do you mean?"

"I mean when? Are we talking a few decades ago, pioneer days, pre-Plymouth Rock? When?"

"I have no idea, Rylan. Just sometime in the past."

"But—"

He reached over to lift her scarf over her mouth. "Just listen."

She narrowed her eyes.

"Have I mentioned how much I like your eyebrows? They're thicker than most people's, but in a good way. They're expressive. Especially when you're annoyed. They slant into a perfect *V*."

"Tell the story, Colin." Her voice was muffled by the scarf.

He set his travel mug on the wooden railing in front of them, then reached for her hand. He spoke as if reciting a story he'd heard a hundred times. "Sarah, at the young age of sixteen, fell in love with a boy several farms over named Peter. Love at first sight, if there ever was such a thing. She'd sneak off every night to meet him at the covered bridge not far from her home. But one night, the young couple accidentally fell asleep at the bridge. Sarah's father was livid when he found her and said she could never see the neighbor boy again."

Colin leaned against the railing at an angle, facing her as he spoke, his voice soft as a lullaby.

"Peter, seeing Sarah in a fit of tears as her father dragged her away, called after her. He promised to remember her no matter what. And to come for her on her eighteenth birthday.

Shortly after this, war broke out and Peter went away to become a soldier."

"So this either took place in the early 1900s or in the 1940s."

Colin sighed. "What?"

She pulled down the scarf. "World War I or II. Unless this story dates back a lot further. I meant, I guess we could be talking Civil War or even Revolutionary, but—"

He stopped her with one finger to her lips. "Are you going to let me tell this story or what?"

The humming breeze shaved curling snow from the bridge's rooftop, sent it dusting over them. She barely resisted the urge to forget Colin's story, close the last inches of space between them, find out if a second kiss from Colin Renwycke could possibly rival the first. "Go on."

"Sarah never heard from Peter while he was away. She was positively miserable, but even so, she never stopped believing he'd come back for her, just as he'd promised. When his name was placed on a missing in action list, she refused to pay it any mind. As her eighteenth birthday approached, her one worry was that Peter might not be able to find her. Her family, you see, had moved into town."

Somewhere in the distance, a car's engine rumbled to life, the sound of footsteps in the snow carried on the wind.

"So to make sure Peter would find her, on the eve of her birthday, she came to this bridge and lit hundreds and hundreds of lanterns. Though it was the middle of winter, December 18 to be exact, she spent the whole night at the bridge, wrapped in blankets and awaiting her love. She fell asleep with a peaceful smile on her face.

Colin took a breath and stepped back. "She was still wearing that smile when her family found her the next day, as if within her eternal sleep, she'd finally been reunited with her true love."

Rylan instantly dropped Colin's hand. "Wait . . . *what?* You're saying she *died?*"

"Well, yeah. The soldier died in the war. She died here. The story says they met up in heaven. The bridge got a name and we got nice little lantern tradition that's been carried on every December 18 since."

She was aghast. "That's the worst story I've ever heard."

"It's romantic. It's tragic. Lots of romances are tragic."

"Now I don't know which story to dislike more—*The Legend of Sleepy Hollow* or this one. Is it even a true story?"

"I really don't know." With the resonant laugh she'd come to know so well, Colin kissed the top of her head and then turned back to the river. "So you only like stories with obvious happy endings. I'll try to keep that in mind."

She settled beside him, taking in the lanterns lighting up the riverfront all over again. Fine, maybe the story was a little romantic.

In any case, *this* was romantic. This whole night.

"Hey, Rylan?"

"Are you going to tell me another horrible story?"

"Worse." Uncertainty hovered in his pause. "I'm going to ask you about Brent."

She inhaled a sharp breath. "Why ruin such a perfect night?"

"You don't have to tell me. I just wondered, is all. The truth is, I've dated a lot of girls." He didn't sound proud of it. Not at all. "When I look back, I realize how selfish I was in most of those short-lived relationships. I hate to think there's a girl out there somewhere feeling about me the way you feel about Brent. Not that I assume I know how you feel. But from the one time you've mentioned him . . . "

"Brent led me on for almost two years, hot and cold like clockwork. Unless you did that to a girl, made her believe you envisioned a future with her one day only to bring another girl home the next, it's not the same." She couldn't look at Colin, didn't want to see any of the pity she might find in his eyes. "He looked a little like you, actually."

"Astoundingly handsome, you mean?" he teased.

She'd argue if it wasn't entirely true. "Might be why I was a little hard on you in class right from the start."

"A little hard? Ry, you called my chiffon cake the worst thing you'd ever tasted."

"Because you used baking soda instead of baking powder!"

"Because I was distracted by my pretty teacher!"

He'd thought her pretty? Even back then? She laughed, before sobering. "Anyway, Brent lived in the apartment above my bakery. I cringe when I think about how much of myself I gave him, how long I let it go on. I was constantly emotionally confused. Finally, one day I'd had enough and I asked him straight up if this was going anywhere."

She could feel Colin tense beside her. "I have a feeling I'm very much going to want to hunt the man down when you tell me how he responded."

"He said, 'What do you mean, *this?*' And I said, 'I mean, *us.*' And he proceeded to tell me there was no *us.* There was only today and maybe a few tomorrows, he didn't know. But he wasn't the kind of guy to plan ahead or force his heart a certain direction."

Colin scooted closer to her, slipping his arm around her waist. "Tell me his address. I'll take my mini torch."

Despite herself, she laughed. Had she ever laughed when talking about Brent? Forget laughing—had she ever even talked about him? To anyone? Two years of carrying around the hurt, refusing to let it out. No wonder it'd taken so long to subside.

She leaned into Colin. "I told him far be it from me to 'force his heart a certain direction' but that I couldn't handle being jerked around anymore. I needed him to be in or out. He chose out."

"I stand by my earlier assessment. He's an idiot."

Not even two weeks later, the bakery had closed. Her whole life turned on a dime. A bit like these past two weeks when so much had changed.

Except not at all like these weeks. Back then, she'd felt stripped of purpose and rejected down to her very core. Too, she'd been angry at herself for getting so distracted by Brent that she hadn't realized how precarious the bakery's financial situation really was until it was too late.

But these past two weeks, what had started out solely as a dogged pursuit to revive her bakery dream had turned out to offer so much more. Being here in Iowa with Colin had opened up windows of possibility she hadn't even known to hope for—new friends in Maren and Leigh and even Drew, new places, new feelings.

She'd *never* felt this way with Brent.

"You know, I don't think I've ever really told anyone how things ended with Brent."

"Not even your family?"

"Especially not. I was too embarrassed. I'm not even sure how you managed to get it out of me."

Colin's hands moved to her arms and he gave her a gentle turn until she faced him. "You shouldn't hide so much of yourself all the time, Rylan. You're depriving the people around you of the gift of actually knowing you. Your hurts, your emotion—it's part of what makes you who you are." He cupped her cheeks. "And who you are is worth knowing."

He kissed her then. As feather-light as the snowfall. As gentle as the night air. And the tender voice she'd first heard sitting in the attic window that first night in Iowa and then again the next morning standing on the farmhouse porch, the one that'd wrapped itself around her soul ever since, slipped into a contented sigh. *Yes, there is a reason you're here.*

The second Colin broke away, she buried herself against him.

"Rylan, I know technically this is just a first date," he said into her hair.

"Unless you count the past fourteen days of being in each other's company."

"Right. And I know you have to head back to Denver in a couple days and you've got classes starting up again soon—"

"Not just me. You, too. I have every intention of un-expelling you eventually." She tipped her head, looking for the laughter she expected in his eyes.

Instead, only uncertainty waited for her there. "Actually, that's what we need to talk about—"

His phone cut in, blaring, unwelcome, almost as jarring as the sudden change in his tone. "Sorry, it's Drew. He knows this is a date, wouldn't call unless . . . "

He lifted his phone, frosty air filling the sudden void between them.

And then, Colin's panic-laced grimace. "Leigh's in the ER?"

* * *

Colin's heart hammered as he burst into the ER waiting room. The drive to the hospital had felt like an eternity, worry pulsing with every bump in the road. Nothing, not even Rylan's palm on his shoulder, enough to quell his dread nor the chafing voice drowning all else.

We should've seen this coming. I should've seen this coming.

He, who knew what it was to hit rock bottom. Who knew what it was like to break down. Why hadn't he been paying more attention to Leigh these past couple weeks?

"Colin, over here."

Drew's voice beckoned from over in the corner. He rose from a burgundy-cushioned chair, Maren on one side, Winnie on the other. *Winnie.* His distress was nothing compared to the fear etched into every line on her too-experienced face.

"How is she?" He was breathless as he stopped in front of Drew, vaguely aware of Rylan behind him.

"We don't know. We stopped to pick Win up first. Just got here five minutes ago."

"You said she collapsed at work? That's all we know?"

Drew heard the question he wasn't asking, gave a barely perceptible shake of his head, clearly trying to spare Winnie's feelings.

But it was futile effort. "If it's pills again, I'm done. I'll call DHS myself."

"Win—" Colin began.

"Or I'll come live with you, Uncle Drew." She thrust herself at Drew, the anger in her muffled voice giving way to tears. "I'm just done."

Drew's arms immediately encircled her. Colin could only watch as his brother rubbed their niece's back and spoke calming words in a soothing tone, as if he'd done this a dozen times before. Probably had.

All those years when Leigh was in and out of rehab and treatment centers. When Winnie's life had once again turned inside out. Drew had always been there.

Rylan's hand slipped into his. Had he spoken a single word to her on the way to the hospital? He'd been so close to telling her the thoughts that had been swirling in his head lately. The desire to truly be the brother and son and man he hadn't been for so long. To . . . stay.

Up until this very moment, it had been a longing, just a

fleeting idea. Now, as he watched Drew be the comfort Winnie needed, it became a decision.

The idea of letting go of culinary school had sprouted that day he talked to Drew in the basement—or maybe even before, though he hadn't had the clarity to recognize it. It'd only grown stronger with every day that passed. He belonged with his family. If not here, then down in Arizona with Mom and Dad, doing whatever he could to lighten Mom's burden as she cared for Dad. He'd spent too many years *being* the burden. No more.

But how could he tell Rylan? The fact that she'd reeled the depths of her own vulnerability, told him about Brent, only made it harder. He looked down at their joined hands now. He'd started something he couldn't finish. Again.

Unless I can make her understand. Unless there was a way to hold on to what might be the best thing that'd ever happened to him even while doing what he knew he needed to do.

"Drew Renwycke?"

They all turned as one as an ER nurse approached. Drew stepped forward. "Is she okay? Can we see her?"

The nurse offered a placid smile. "She's fine. Your sister's dehydrated. Cut and dried case of exhaustion. Anemic, too. She needs rest, liquids, and to stop working double-shifts seven days a week."

Colin's jaw dropped as he released Rylan's hand. "She's been working that much? I had no idea."

Winnie shrank into Drew's side. "It's my fault. I need money for a band trip and I told her I want a laptop for Christmas and—"

Drew quieted her with his hand on her back. "It's not your fault, Win." He took a shuddered breath and turned to the nurse. "But that's it? Nothing else?"

The nurse must've been up on Leigh's medical history, because the subtle shake of her head answered the question

Drew didn't ask. "She's been fighting headaches with Tylenol. Nothing more."

Taut air broke free of Colin's lungs. *Thank God.* No overdose. No relapse.

"Now, usually we just take one or two people back at a time, but since this isn't a critical situation—"

"Actually, I'll wait." He blurted it out, awkward with relief. "I just need a sec." He looked away from Drew's questioning glance.

"I'll wait, too."

Rylan.

He had to tell her. Maybe it was the prickling feeling of urgency that crowded the air of the ER. Or the image in his head of Leigh crumpling to the floor. Maybe it was the sight of Drew with his arm around Winnie as they followed the nurse, Maren at his side. The aching, insistent thought that he'd never fully belong until his presence in his family's lives became more than a holiday passing.

"You all right, Col?"

He turned to her, throat clogged and heart already beginning to tear. Her hair fell in wind-tousled tangles over her shoulders and her scarf hung loose around her neck. He was grateful, at least, that they were the only ones in the waiting room.

He reached for the ends of her scarf, his hands needing movement. "I have to stay, Rylan."

"Of course you do. I'll wait out here. However long you need."

"No, I mean, I have to stay *here*. In Maple Valley. I'm going to quit culinary school."

Her eyebrows—always the first feature to give her away—dipped in confusion. She took a step back, the ends of her scarf dropping from his hands. "I don't understand."

"I thought embarking on a career path was going to make

255

me the person I wanted to be. Now . . . I'm realizing all I really want is to be a good brother. A good uncle." *A good son for however long I can.* That last one was too painful to say out loud. "I feel like I can only do that here."

"So after doing all you could to convince me to let you stay in my class, you're going to drop it? Just like that?"

He longed to pull her toward him, let her hear his heart-beat as if that could somehow convey the conviction he didn't know how to put into words. "It's not *just like that.* I've been thinking about this for awhile."

"Not a long while. Not considering I've spent the past two weeks thinking the whole reason I'm here was to secure your spot at the institute."

"You know that's not the whole reason." Frantic desire pushed into his tone. "This doesn't have to change what's happening with us. In fact, it's better. We both know we can't have a relationship if I'm your student. We ignored it pretty successfully earlier tonight, but we would've had to figure something out eventually. This is a big obstacle out of our way."

He could see it happening—the shutters closing in her eyes. "Maybe, but it's only replaced with a new one."

"People make long-distance relationships work all the time."

"For awhile, sure. But, Colin, I can't drop my dream as easily as you're apparently dropping out of school." She fumbled with the buttons on her jacket—unbuttoning, then rebuttoning.

"You can work in a bakery anywhere. Better yet, open your own. If you work for Potts, he'll control your schedule. You won't be managing your own kitchen, you'll be managing his. Wouldn't you rather have your own place again?"

"That's a lot easier said than done. Besides, last time I had my own place, I let myself get distracted and—"

She broke off, but he tasted the bitter realization in her incomplete thought all the same. "This is *not* the same, Rylan. I'm not Brent. I'm not stringing you along and I sure as heck hope you see me as more than a distraction."

"Of course I do," she whispered as she dropped into a chair. Her whole body slumped, her fingers twisting in her lap, her shoulders hunched, withdrawn.

"Don't shut me out, Rylan."

"I'm not."

"You are." He sat in the chair across from her. "You're shutting me out just like you've shut out your family."

Irritation sparked in her eyes. "You don't know—"

"Trust me, I do. I shut mine out from guilt. You shut yours out from embarrassment. And now you're on the brink of shutting me out because I'm making a decision you don't understand."

"Except I do understand." She tugged her scarf away from her neck and it landed in a heap on her lap. "I do. I just don't see how the two of us can move forward when we're going to be missing a main ingredient—namely, being in the same place." She met his eyes. "And I have to wonder, if you can drop school so easily, what's to stop you from dropping me down the road?"

What he wouldn't give to heal the wound so present in her voice. To convince her she could trust him. But how could two weeks of growing friendship and one date overcome all she knew about him? The months of annoying her in class. The erratic past he'd let her in on. Of course she'd see his dropping out of the institute as just another example of his unreliability.

With each passing second, he could feel her retreating further.

"You should go see your sister, Col."

He reached for her hands. "Can't we at least try? Experiment?" He raised one brow, hoping she'd hear the possibility and yearning swirled together in his voice.

But she only pulled away. "I think if anything, these last couple weeks have proven I'm not an experimenter. We haven't come up with a recipe."

Frustration threatened to swallow him whole. "It's possible to take metaphors too far, Ry."

"But if I can't even experiment in the kitchen . . . " She released a shaky exhale and stood. "I just can't handle another broken heart, Colin."

But as he watched her walk away, he was pretty sure it was already too late.

For both their hearts.

CHAPTER 10

*R*ain on Christmas Eve. Somehow it felt appropriate.

Rylan lifted the trunk of her car, her hundredth hasty prayer circling the edges of her strained nerves. *Please let the cakes have survived the drive.*

Bad enough she was late to Chef Potts grand party. If the cakes were ruined . . .

Raindrops tapped the metal surface of the trunk as she surveyed her collection of boxes—five plastic containers in various sizes. She'd arrange the cakes in layers once they were inside.

A sixth carrying case rested at the back of her trunk. The result of a momentary lapse in discipline. A several-hour practice in chasing her creative whim, of trial-and-error baking.

Colin would've been proud.

Colin isn't here.

She ignored the container in the back and instead loaded her arms with the three smallest boxes, then started for the brick Tudor-style house her GPS had led her to. She'd left her

259

townhome in such a hurry she'd forgotten a coat. Sagging gray clouds muted the sunset and veiled the outline of the mountains in the distance. Clumps of soggy snow dotted the pathway to the back door. Per Chef Potts' instructions, she let herself in without a knock.

She'd been back in Denver for four days. Four days of agitated preparation for this night. Four days of wondering when baking solo had morphed from her preferred method to something that felt a little too close to lonely.

Four days of missing Colin. Wondering if she'd made a mistake, letting their kindling bond die down before it'd ever had a chance to fully flame. Leaving Iowa a couple days earlier than planned.

A steamy wave of heat hit her face as she entered the kitchen. The bustling catering crew barely noticed her presence. Christmas music glided from elsewhere in the house— voices, laughter, merriment.

After another trip in the rain to her car, she made space on the counter and went to work assembling and frosting her cakes. No, the flavors weren't surprising; nor the decoration, outstanding. But she was confident she'd pulled off a pleasing creation, all the same. Potts would appreciate the hint of lemon lacing the red velvet tiers, and the silver pearl dragées adorning the outside that looked like tinsel.

Would it be enough to secure a spot in Potts' new bakery?

Someone opened the back door, ushering in a blast of cool air.

Did she even care anymore?

Silly, irrational thought. Of course, she cared. Two years she'd been waiting for this opportunity. Hoping against hope that starting over wasn't a pipedream. That when the bank took away her building and Brent walked off with her heart, there was a new beginning waiting for her underneath the wreckage of one too many endings.

She wanted this. She needed it. There wouldn't be a single question in her mind right now about her desired future if not for Colin.

If not for the poignant reminders waiting around every corner in Denver. When the snow melted and the landscape dulled, she remembered his eager impatience to show her Maple Valley's wintry postcard charm. When she saw families huddled together, moving down the sidewalk, through a grocery store aisle, she remembered what it felt like those stretching couple weeks spending time with Colin's family. When she walked over the Denver Millennium Bridge, she remembered him taking her to the Archway Bridge—in that one little action, proving he saw her in a way no one else had for so long.

And when she heard a reading of *The Night Before Christmas* on the radio on the way over to Chef Potts' house tonight, she could feel all over again the delight of Colin playing storyteller out at Sleepy Hollow.

If it was this hard to put him out of her mind now, what would it be like when she returned to the classroom next week?

"Ah, you finally made it."

She whirled at the sound of Chef Potts' voice. He wore a full tuxedo, black tails, red suspenders and all. He carried a top hat under his arm. Give him a monocle, and he could've played the Monopoly man. "Hello, Chef. Merry Christmas."

He eyed the cake behind her. "I've been curious about what you'd arrive with. Five tiers. I'm impressed."

"Red velvet with a wisp of lemon in both the sponge and the icing." She reached behind her for the tiny, single-serving box she'd brought along. "I made you a sample."

Maybe it was nerves or maybe it was the salty swirl of aromas permeating the kitchen—glazed duck, roasted vegetables—that churned her stomach while she waited for Chef Potts to taste and appraise her cake.

You want this. You need it. You earned it.

She'd followed her recipe to the tiniest detail. She'd focused. Minus the occasional glance at her phone—as if by checking it enough times she might will into existence a call or text from Colin.

But it'd been radio silence since the morning he dropped her off at the Des Moines airport. They'd shared an awkward hug. He'd kissed her cheek and wished her well with her demonstration for Potts. And then he'd leaned down to whisper in her ear. *"Follow your instincts. I know you don't think you have any. But you do. Don't be afraid to surprise yourself."*

Advice she'd ignored until this afternoon when she'd made a last-minute culinary invention, not a recipe card in sight. Went so far as to box up the results and load them into her trunk.

But she'd known all along the red velvet cake was the safe bet.

Chef Potts chewed slowly, his snow-white eyebrows bobbing but his face otherwise entirely unreadable. He swallowed. Nodded. "That'll do."

That'll do?

"That'll do," he said again.

To serve to his guests or to secure her a spot on the list of candidates for his new bakery? "The lemon wasn't too subtle?"

"Nor too overbearing. Appearance is nice." He looked from her to the cake and back again. "I can't say that it's overwhelmingly unique. I confess I was looking for a bit more style, but there's certainly nothing lacking in your technique."

She didn't know which part to latch on to—his tempered praise of her technical skill or his obvious disappointment at the absence of any flair.

This is why she'd needed Colin. If only she hadn't been so distracted most of the time in Iowa.

But would she really take back any of it? Working side-by-side at The Red Door? Sledding on restaurant trays? Taking over his brother's kitchen and in the process, discovering a man who was so much more than he'd seemed?

No. The answer launched through her with such force it almost drew tears. No, she wouldn't take any of it back.

The slamming of an oven door jolted her. Chef Potts offered a noncommittal nod. "Let me do a little thinking and we'll reconnect after Christmas. Good enough?"

It'd have to be. Not exactly the triumphant success she'd hoped for. Disappointment slithered through her.

"You're welcome to stay for the party."

In her rain-splattered top and frayed jeans? "Thank you, anyway, but I think I'll head out."

Chef Potts patted her back as he walked her to the door. "To see family, I should hope."

"You're shutting me out just like you've shut out your family."

Would she ever get Colin's voice out of her head?

She didn't even try to dodge raindrops as she crossed to her car. She settled behind the wheel, key halfway into the ignition.

"Follow your instincts."

She was out of the car once more before she could rethink it. She heaved open the trunk, lunged for the container in back. She ran through the rain to the back door, scanned the kitchen for Potts. No sign of him.

"Don't be afraid to surprise yourself."

She wove around a rolling tray crammed with serving plates, past the industrial stove and out the kitchen door.

She hurried down a narrow corridor, following the escalating strains of a stringed quartet's *Good King Wenceslas*. So many fancy dresses, men in tuxedos, servers carrying trays crowded with champagne glasses. She burst into a rectangular room, all polished woodwork, garland and tinsel.

Potts' jolly chuckle drew her focus. *"Don't be afraid . . . "*

She was standing in front of him in seconds, no chance of reversing course now. "Ms. Jefferson, what are you . . . I thought you'd left?"

"I'm so sorry to interrupt. To barge in looking like, um, this. And to track snow and mud into your house. And . . . " She forced an exhale. "I shouldn't have brought the cake."

"I said it was a fine cake, Rylan." Thinly veiled irritation whirred in his voice.

"Actually, you didn't, but . . ." She shook her head and peeled the lid off her container. "I made something else. I had this idea to make homemade Pop-Tarts and then build something like a gingerbread house from them. Well, not really a house so much as a winter wonderland display. Which I know sounds crazy, but you asked for personality. I didn't make the display, because I wimped out and I didn't follow through on my instincts and I didn't listen to Colin. I should've listened to Colin."

"Reginald, you know this girl?"

The question came from a woman to her right—silver hair, silver sequins on her dress.

"She's a teacher at the institute. For the moment."

No missing that implication. "Won't you just try one?"

Reluctance weighted his movement, but he lifted one of her Pop-Tarts. Her nerves were different this time. Expectant and unhindered, entirely intoxicating.

A slow-spreading expression of pleasure proceeded his swallow. He took a second bite, a third.

"Now *this* is unique, Ms. Jefferson."

She let out her breath. "I realized this afternoon they don't make lemon Pop-Tarts. Or, well, I think they did for a limited time once, but not anymore. And it's a shame because so many people like you love lemon. I don't really, not that much, but somebody could make a grass-flavored Pop-Tart and I'd still try it and—" She made herself stop.

"But this isn't just lemon."

"I added a little rose water, too. I'm always scared to use that because too much is overpowering, but just the right amount—"

"Makes perfection an attainable goal." He fingered his mustache over a knowing grin. "All right, Rylan. You've proven your point. Let's schedule an official interview. Day after Christmas?"

She should nod. She should beam. She should shake his hand and spill out her thanks and agree to an interview whenever, wherever.

"Follow your instincts."

"Actually . . . " She swallowed past the lump in her throat, the sudden rise of emotion. "I think I'm going to be somewhere else that day."

* * *

HE'D NEVER SEEN his father so quiet.

Colin lifted the nearly scraped clean glass bowl from the middle of the table, one lone scoop of Gingerbread trifle still clinging to the edge. "Last call on dessert."

They were crowded around the table in Drew's kitchen, what with the dining room table already set for tomorrow's Christmas breakfast. Leigh and Winnie. Drew and Maren.

Mom and Dad. Looking so much older than last time he'd seen them. New strands of gray tinted Mom's formerly dark hair and the creases in her face were more pronounced. The circles under her eyes, too.

And Dad. Thin and peaked and so very quiet.

You have to talk to him sometime.

He lowered his gaze to the pan in his hand. "Come on, people, speak up. You know I slaved over this for hours." His contribution to the quick family dinner before they all headed out to the Christmas Eve service.

"Yes, brother, and for the record, it's amazing." Leigh laughed as she reached for the bowl. "Do you think the trifle counts as protein? Or the layers of Cognac custard? Or the candied pears? Doctor's orders and all."

His sister hadn't looked better in weeks. After an overnight stay in the hospital, she'd asked Seth Walker for some time off work. Turned out the man was a pretty good boss. Colin had experienced it firsthand just these past few days after hiring on for the length of the head chef's maternity leave.

"I don't think one of Uncle Colin's desserts could ever be considered healthy." Winnie rolled her eyes and drew a laugh.

"Split it with me anyway?" Leigh dished out the dessert.

Winnie had become Leigh's shadow ever since the ER. Leigh had told Colin earlier today that if collapsing at the restaurant was what it took to prompt an attitude change from her daughter, she'd take it.

The Christmas lights shaped like icicles he'd helped Drew hang yesterday glowed outside the kitchen window. Snow fell in wind-blown waves, gusts of winter air hurling against the house. Hopefully they could make it to church and back before this turned into an all-out blizzard.

Was it snowing in Colorado?

He tucked away the question, just like he'd mentally side-stepped a hundred thoughts of Rylan since she returned home. The urge to pick up his phone or, better yet, hop a plane and land in Denver in a couple hours had tugged at him non-stop.

But wouldn't he end up hurting her all over again?

Isn't that, perhaps, why he'd let her go in the first place?

The fear of wounding her just as he had every person sitting around this table at one point or another?

You're not the same man you were.

Maybe not. But he was the same man who, in a manner of days, had gone from begging her to let him stay in her class to willfully walking away. He couldn't blame her for her disappointment. And he didn't want to ruin her Christmas any further by annoying her now the same way he had all those weeks at the institute.

"I don't know if it's the disease or the diagnosis."

Mom's soft voice to his left hooked his attention.

"What's that?"

"Your father. You've noticed how quiet he is. Alzheimer's itself can alter a person's personality. But I think it might be the reality of the diagnosis affecting him as much as anything."

Mom's gaze was on Dad, such profound sadness in her eyes Colin had to look away. But when he braved a glance back, the pain was replaced with a gentle knowing. "You don't have to rehash the past with him, Col. He doesn't need a fancy speech or a host of apologies."

"Mom—"

Her palm flattened over his on the tabletop. "And neither do I. Save your pretty words for the girl you're pining over." At the drop of his jaw, she grinned. "Your new sister-in-law is talkative."

"She was my instructor at the culinary institute."

"So Maren said."

"I brought her home with me."

"So Maren said."

"Then I quit the institute."

"So *you* said."

He'd explained the whole thing yesterday, had honestly halfway-expected Dad to shake his head, make some gruff remark about how he wasn't surprised. How Colin rarely finished what he started.

Instead he'd only clamped his hand to Colin's shoulder and said something about how maybe now he could help Drew farm the land. The land Drew had sold earlier this year. Colin had shared a look with his brother, harsh realization settling like bricks in his stomach.

Dad had left the table and now stood by the sink. His hand was on the faucet but he'd made no move to turn on the water.

"Just talk to him, Colin." Mom patted his hand. "Tell him you love him. The memories from before are going to fade anyway. What we've got left are moments. So give him a good one."

The truth in her words chipped at his heart, and he had to blink to tame the tears that threatened. Christmas spirit was proving hard to come by this year. *But it might be Dad's last.* Another hard blink.

"We can leave this mess 'til after the service," Drew was saying as he stood. He wrapped his arm around Maren's waist, steered her toward the stairway.

"I'll at least clear the table. I'm already dressed for church." Colin rose, stacked as many plates in his hand as he could and joined Dad at the sink. He heard Leigh and Winnie moving behind him, the room eventually quieting.

"Dad?"

His father turned, crystal blue eyes—same shade as his own and Leigh's—pierced straight into him. None of the vague fog Colin had noticed at least a couple times today. No disease staking its claim, at least for this sliver of time.

"What we've got left are moments."

Maybe this was the blessing even in such a desperate prognosis—this opportunity to reconcile. To make an imprint in the present that neither the past nor the future could wash away.

"Dad, I wanted to tell you . . . that is, I've been meaning to say . . . " Why couldn't he find the right words? Mom had said to keep it simple.

Dad took the plates from his hand, lowered them into the sink, and turned. "Do you know what comforts me more than anything as I consider what lies ahead, Colin?" The skin of his hands pulled taut over rigid blue veins. "I am comforted knowing that no matter how I change, no matter what I forget or say or do or don't do, your mother is going to keep loving me. When I'm at my worst, her care and compassion will be at its best."

His voice was lucid and clear, firm and somehow soft. It was a tone he hadn't heard in so long. Another blessing.

"She's going to love me no matter what. Just like she always has. Do you understand what I'm saying, son?"

Yes, he understood. He *understood*. The layers in his father's assurance were a balm for every thirsty depth of Colin's soul. Tears pooled once more, relentless and more needed than he could've possibly imagined.

Another dad might embrace his son. Another dad might spell out the undercurrent coursing through his words.

But this was *his* dad. And this . . . it was enough. "I love you, Dad."

"Good." He turned on the faucet. "Now tell me about this girl I've been hearing about."

His laugh was nearly a garbled sob. "Man, Maren has a big mouth."

"Actually, Winnie's my source, believe it or not. I'd decided my lecturing days were behind me, but if she's as great as Winnie seems to think, I might have to whip out a new one. You're just going to let her go?"

Colin squirted dish soap over the dishes. "Dad—"

"Take a cue from your brother, son. I wouldn't mind seeing another good thing come from this disease. You finding happiness with a good woman? I'd call that a good thing."

Bubbles rose up from the sink. "There are complications. Not the least of which is that up until just days ago she couldn't stand me." Probably couldn't stand him more than ever now.

Dad sighed.

"What?"

"Just trying to decide whether to go into full guilt-trip mode. This might be my last Christmas, so if you want me to have a chance to meet her—"

"Dad! So not ready to joke about this."

His father threw up his hands. "Then stop dragging your feet and—"

"Hey, Colin?" Drew whisked into the room, stopped when he saw them at the sink. "Sorry, didn't mean to interrupt."

Colin wiped his hands on a towel. "No, actually you've got pretty great timing. You're saving me from an inquisition."

Dad chuckled behind him.

Drew ran his hand through his hair. "Just wondered if I could talk to you real quick before church. You and Leigh."

Colin glanced at Dad. "Don't look at me. I don't know what it's about."

Drew grinned. "Don't look so worried. This is one sibling meeting I think you're going to like."

* * *

Dusk had long since hooded the horizon by the time Rylan pulled up to the house. Christmas lights traced the line of the roof and every window watching her approach. She noted the other cars in the driveway. Which meant they were all here, not at church. Not yet, anyway.

Her boots clipped over the shoveled path leading to the front door. She carried her container of homemade Pop-Tarts in one hand. With the other, she pressed the doorbell.

Seconds later, the door opened.

"You came." An overjoyed gasp. Mom's.

And it was followed by her sister's squeals.

And footsteps.

And arms all reaching for her at once.

CHAPTER 11

*I*f Rylan Jefferson was lucky, tonight's class—the last of the institute's three-day extra credit holiday course—would fly by.

And if she was very lucky, her attention wouldn't stray to the workstation on the right, second from the front just like it had the past two nights—expecting, hoping to see a man with a twinkle in his eyes and a dimpled smirk that said he was trying not to laugh.

A mess all around him.

Rylan took a breath and pushed into the classroom. "Good evening, student bakers."

She strode to the front of the room, barely taking in the faces on either side of the center aisle—the most dedicated of her first-semester students. Sure wouldn't have been her choice for how to spend her New Year's Eve. But at least they'd be done in time for holiday parties and family plans.

Speaking of which, Rylan had her pick of gatherings tonight. Dakota and her husband had invited her along to a party over in Fort Collins. Mom and Dad were hosting a gathering at their house down in Colorado Springs tonight.

Funny how much had changed since the night she went home. Since she decided to stop hiding away from her family. Finally let them in.

Rylan set her tote bag on the stainless steel table at the front of the classroom. She already wore her apron. Had already memorized tonight's recipe—Bundt cake, perfect for New Year's since the ring shape could symbolize coming full circle, an ending sliding into a new beginning.

But she'd decided to let the class play with their decorations. For once, she wouldn't provide instruction on how to ornament the cakes.

Oh, how Colin might keel over from shock if he were here.

It should be easy—letting go of Colin Renwycke. After all, she had plenty to distract her. There was teaching, of course, and then there was figuring out what to do next since she'd turned down the interview with Chef Potts. It was probably the most impulsive thing she'd ever done.

But she couldn't bring herself to regret it. It'd been somehow liberating.

A student cleared his throat. Right. Her class. She turned. *Just focus on today, focus on teaching. Don't think about—*

"Colin!"

His name stumbled out as her willful gaze found his face. Right side of the aisle. Second from the front. Twinkle. Dimples.

No mess.

"I . . . you . . . you're not supposed to . . ." Her words were flour and her voice a rusty sifter. Too many pairs of eyes watched as she just stood there, frozen as an icicle.

She'd checked the online class roster. She'd checked it a dozen times, never once seeing his name. He wasn't supposed to be here. He was supposed to be in Iowa with his siblings or Arizona with his parents or . . . or somewhere doing something other than loitering in *her* classroom, watching her with those uncanny blue eyes.

"In the hallway," she finally managed.

"Whatever you say, Teach."

She didn't know which was faster—her feet carrying her from the room or her heartbeat trying to pound its way out of her chest. She heard Colin moving behind her, the thrum of whispers.

She pushed into the hallway, moonlight beaming from the wall of windows opposite her classroom door. Snow fell in tiny tufts of white, draping like cotton sheets over the evergreens standing watch on the institute lawn.

"Almost as pretty as Iowa."

She whirled around at the sound of Colin's voice. "You haven't been here the past two nights. You're not on my class list."

"Because I'm not in the class."

"Then why are you—?"

"Because I know exactly how many days it's been since you last told me you can't stand me and glutton for punishment that I am, I kinda miss it."

He shouldn't stand so close or look at her so . . . expectantly. Patiently. Buoyantly. As if this moment was a late Christmas gift he'd been waiting a week to unwrap.

She reached her hands behind her to fiddle with the ties of her apron. *Too heavy. Too warm.*

Too tight a knot.

Colin had the grace not to grin. Instead, he moved behind her. "Do you know why I applied to culinary school, Maryland?"

Her hands dropped to her sides as he took over with the apron. "I should never have told you my full name."

He didn't miss a beat. "I applied to culinary school because I thought I'd finally found my thing. Everyone else always had a thing." She felt him work the knot at her waist. "Drew with the woodworking. Dad and Grandpa with the farm. Leigh is an amazing pianist, did you know that? That antique piano in the dining room at Drew's—she used to practice on it every day before she quit."

The question of why Leigh quit flitted through Rylan's brain. Another story for another day, she supposed. But, oh please, let Colin's presence here mean there might actually be another day.

Hope, impossible to restrain, rose up from her stubborn heart.

The apron ties released, but Colin didn't move from behind her. "I was wrong, though. Baking makes me happy, sure, and I might even be a little good at it."

"More than a little," she whispered.

"But I don't have the career drive that other people do. That you do. Whatever professional ambition I thought I had, it was all just tied up in this need to earn my family's respect. But it turns out the thing I needed even more, I already had —their love."

Her soul latched onto the peace in his voice, in his words. She should tell him she'd reconnected with her family over Christmas, too. She should tell him how all it had taken was one step, one decision—no more holding back. She should tell him how freeing it'd felt to finally cry to her parents about Brent, talk openly with her sisters. To not just spill her own heart and hurts, but to listen to theirs, as well.

She should tell him everything. But her words were buried under mounting emotion.

Colin finally circled around to her front, gently lifted her apron over her head. "I've been helping Drew some with his start-up. Turns out Winnie doesn't just love reading, but she's super into comic books. I'm taking her to a Comic Con in March. I'm realizing I think I actually get more joy from helping the people I love do *their* thing than I ever have with any of my own botched attempts at some kind of professional ambition." He dropped her apron to the floor and nudged it out of the way with his foot. "Which brings me to this."

He reached into his pocket and pulled out a folded slip of paper. A check? He held it out to her.

"Paying me back for all the kitchen equipment you ruined?" How the joke made its way past her hammering heart, she had no idea.

"Take the check, Rylan."

She unfolded it and gasped when she saw the amount. "Kitchen-Aid mixers are expensive, but—"

He quieted her with a kiss on her cheek. "It's for your bakery, silly woman."

Oh Lord, he smelled like cinnamon and pine, just like always. "I don't understand."

He kissed her other cheek. "Drew sold his farmland earlier this year. Originally he put the money into starting his business, but apparently he always planned to give Leigh and me a cut. That's my cut." His hands slid down her arms to settle on her waist. "He gave it to me on Christmas Eve. And I'm giving it to you."

She couldn't seem to make herself breathe. "You can't give me this. You can't. It's too much."

With a smile nowhere near a smirk—simply, solely, purely hopeful—he pulled her closer. "I know I'm getting ahead of myself, but there's an empty storefront in Maple Valley. It'd be perfect for a bakery. Right across from the river. Turquoise shutters."

She knew that building. She'd seen that building.

"Its windows overlook the Archway Bridge."

"I like that bridge." Really liked it. Might be completely and entirely crazy about it.

"I know it's not the heart of Denver. You wouldn't get the

acclaim you could if you opened a place here. I know it's totally out of the blue and would mean a major move at some point and—"

"Why?" She tipped her head to meet his gaze, trembling with so much elation she could hardly get the word out a second time. *"Why?"*

His arms wrapped around her and he leaned in to her ear, his voice barely a whisper. "Didn't you hear the part about helping the people I love do their thing?"

There was no stopping the tears pooling in her eyes, tracing down her cheeks. The dam broke. "Colin, I have to go teach. I have to go stand up there in front of everyone and be composed and coherent and . . . and there's no way. You couldn't have waited until after? You had to disrupt the class just like always?" She sniffled as his arms tightened around her. "I really can't stand you, Colin Renwycke."

She felt his smile.

"I know, Maryland. I love you, too."

And when he kissed her, the depth of his desire unfurling into every corner of her soul, warm and full of promise, Rylan Jefferson knew she was very, *very* lucky indeed.

Try blessed beyond measure. Enraptured. Enchanted. In love.

And the swirl of snow outside the window, the lights, the stars, the winter moon, none of it was any match for the joy finally at home in her heart.

THE END

Well . . . for now. :)
After all, there's still Leigh's story to tell.

ONE ENCHANTED NOËL

CHAPTER 1

*U*sually on nights like this—with snowfall glimmering under the hazy glow of lamplight, a peaceful hush hovering over the town square—Leigh Renwycke could almost forget.

Could almost believe her new life was her only life and that she'd never crept so close to losing everything.

Usually on nights like this, she could pretend.

But tonight there'd been that voicemail and all the disappointment that came with it.

Leigh zipped up her puff vest and tugged out the hood of the sweatshirt underneath, pulling it over her head, strands of hair spilling from already disheveled twin braids. Pale moonlight bumped into the dark, the row of quaint storefronts lining the street long since silent, shuttered until tomorrow. Snowfall—well, sleet, really, as if the skies knew Leigh's mood deserved a matching sludge—tapped against the pavement, the only sound on this quiet winter night.

That is, in addition to the intruding voice in the back of her head, the one chiding her for applying for that job in the first place. Event planning? Really? The man who'd left the voicemail turning her down for the position had probably had to bite his cheeks not to laugh when he reviewed Leigh's sparse résumé.

Leigh burrowed her chin into the fleece collar of her vest as a hearty wind scraped over her cheeks. Honestly, it wasn't even not getting the job that stung so much as all the reminders that came along with this latest failure.

Who she'd been. What she'd done. How she'd almost—

A crash of shattering glass stopped her cold on the sidewalk.

Leigh's gaze slanted in the direction of the noise, across the town square. A lone shadow moved underneath an empty marquee. Someone was breaking into the old movie theater?

Her indecision stretched only for a moment before action took its place. She pulled her phone from her pocket as she angled toward the theater. White brick wrapped around lanky windows, one of which, if her night vision didn't deceive her, the shadow had just disappeared through.

"Dispatcher. Do you have an emergency?"

Leigh could've picked out the raspy Carol Channing voice from a hundred-person choir. "Hey, Melinda, it's Leigh."

"Don't tell me the smoke alarms went off by accident in The Red Door again." Melinda Parson's laughter barked over the phone. "It's *my* head our esteemed fire chief bites off every time I have to call off his crew when they're already on their way."

"No smoke alarm problems. Promise." Though, to be honest, the days the restaurant's finicky alarms went off tended to be Leigh's favorite. At least those days were interesting. She'd been so happy two years ago when she'd received the promotion to assistant manager of Maple Valley's newest and nicest restaurant. But already the role had proven a little too routine. And her disposition, a little too restless.

Which is always how the trouble began.

But at least this time, all she'd done was apply for an out-of-reach job. No picking up and moving on a whim. No pills.

Leigh forced herself to focus. "I think someone's breaking into the movie theater."

Melinda's snort sounded just as Leigh reached the other side of the square. "What's he going to steal? A movie poster from 2005? I can't even remember what movies came out that year. Is that when that *Pride & Prejudice* remake released? Not the Colin Firth one, but—"

"The theater, Melinda." She peered into the dark. Yep, broken window. Large enough for a person to climb through. "Better send someone over."

"That's some rotten timing. Police department is having their Christmas party early this year. Hate to interrupt, especially considering Chief Sam went all out, for once. Rented the community center and everything."

"Given the circumstances, I'm pretty sure he'll understand being interrupted." Leigh approached the theater, shards of glass littering the sidewalk around her boots.

"I'll call it in. Probably just a teenager with too much time on his hands. You know how teens are, seeing as how you've got one of your own. Not that sweet Winnie would ever get in too much trouble. Now, where are you?"

"Standing right outside the building." While Winnie probably wondered if she'd ever get home. Just the thought of her daughter and their cozy townhouse swept away at least some of the grime of this Tuesday night. Their home might be snug, but between the fireplace and the Christmas tree and the twinkle lights strung around the porch, it was comfy and beckoning.

And almost enough, some days, to drown out the punishing echoes of Leigh's past.

Winnie deserved that. Deserved a happy home and a mom

who smiled. Besides, it was the fifth of December. About time Leigh found some Christmas spirit.

"Well, you just stay there," Melinda said. "Don't go trying to play hero or anything."

Leigh Renwycke. Hero. As if the words could ever fit into the same sentence.

She pocketed her phone, gaze lifting to the wordless marquee above. The theater had closed long before Leigh moved back to town a couple of years back. A shame, for sure, but with Maple Valley being only a short drive from Ames and its nicer theaters, it was understandable.

Still. Didn't give anyone the right to break in. And who knew how long it'd take chatty Melinda to even spit out the news to the police chief once she got ahold of him. Most likely, the trespasser would be long gone before anyone official arrived.

So maybe a little unofficial interference was called for. Leigh could reprimand a teen as good as anyone. Heaven knew Winnie had gotten into her fair share of scrapes in recent years. Melinda probably wouldn't call her "sweet Winnie" if she knew about the multiple missed curfews, that attempted overnight stint in a train car out at the heritage railroad depot—practically a rite of passage for bored Maple Valley teens.

And, oh yes, Winnie had thrown a baseball through the school window two years ago. Seemed the cinema trespasser and her daughter had a little something in common.

Leigh sighed, tipped her hood back and reached for the theater's front door. Locked. Obviously. Okay, so she'd go in the same way the troublemaker had.

She toed a piece of glass out of the way with her boot, then lifted one leg through the gaping window. She hefted herself in with ease, breath white as she straightened inside the theater lobby. It was nearly as cold in here as it was outside. Just as dark, too. And how in the world could the smell of popcorn cling so strongly to the air this many years since the theater's closing?

Lumbering footfalls sounded from overhead. Apparently their trespasser had bypassed the empty concessions counter and gone straight for the projection room. So that was his game—stealing abandoned equipment. Might as well let him know he had company.

"Hello? Who's up there?"

The footsteps halted.

She inched toward the stairway that edged one wall, retrieving her phone and tapping the flashlight app even as her breathing hitched. Possibly not the smartest idea she'd ever had, confronting a burglar on her own. Far from the worst, though. And it's not like whoever it was banging around up there was actually dangerous, right? This was little Maple Valley.

Besides, after the day she'd had, she needed this. Needed the chance to show a little backbone. Be the Leigh she'd been so long ago.

Before the pills. Before the teenage pregnancy. Before the years of wandering from state to state, looking for a life she wouldn't have deserved even if she'd found it.

She climbed the stairs, cleared her throat halfway up. "You should know I already called the police, so—"

The shadowed figure appeared at the top of the staircase, the light from Leigh's phone illuminating his form. *Soooo* much bigger up close. Taller, broader . . .

"You did *what?*"

. . . and with a voice far too deep and much too rich to belong to a teenager.

* * *

SEB MIGHT'VE burst into laughter at the sight of the woman on the staircase—so rigid and alert she'd fit right in on the set of a melodramatic cop show—if he wasn't half-frozen. Why hadn't anyone warned him about winter in the Midwest?

And she hadn't really called the police, had she? He held up his hand to block the glare of the woman's phone. "You going to answer me?"

Instead of replying, she backed down a step.

Seb shrugged and started toward her.

She descended another step. "I'm sure they're already on their way. The police, I mean."

"You really called them?"

"I really did."

"Well, that's . . . unfortunate."

"For you, maybe. But the point is, there's no use in hurting me. Because they'll be here soon." She landed on the ground floor.

He kept following. "Don't be ridiculous. I'm not going to hurt you. But I would appreciate it if you'd stop shining that thing in my eyes."

She was still backing up, holding out her phone like a shield. Honestly, if Seb wasn't chilled to the bone and more annoyed than ever at his grandfather's latest assignment, if he hadn't spent three hours on the road tonight getting lost in the middle of nowhere thanks to his obviously useless GPS, if he hadn't found out only fifteen minutes ago that this town didn't even have a hotel—he'd probably deem this whole situation hilarious.

But he *was* chilled to the bone and annoyed at Grandfather and he *had* spent three hours lost on Iowa's rural back roads only to discover his destination didn't boast so much as a Holiday Inn. So forgive him if irritation overruled his amusement.

The woman gave a flustered *oomph* as she bumped into the

ticket stand behind her. The corner of his mouth quirked. Fine, *almost* overruled.

He reached the bottom step. "If the police are on their way, why don't I hear any sirens?"

She lowered her phone and he had to blink to adjust to the onslaught of darkness.

"Maybe that's on purpose. Maybe they know sirens would spook whoever it is breaking and entering."

He stopped in front of her. "I'm not breaking and entering."

Her head tipped toward the theater entrance behind her. Despite the dark, he could just make out the messy braids framing her face and the whites of her rolling eyes as she poked her mittened thumb over her shoulder. "You broke a window. You entered a locked building."

All right, so it looked suspicious. He really should've waited until tomorrow to explore the theater. But when he'd realized he had no clue where he'd be sleeping tonight, he'd decided he may as well check out his assignment. Grandfather had given him four weeks to complete the task of renovating and reopening this theater. He'd figured he'd see what he was up against.

Hadn't counted on company, though. "To tell you the truth, I'm almost happy to see you. I was beginning to think Maple Valley was a ghost town. Haven't seen a single soul since I rolled in."

"It's suppertime. Everybody's at home around a table."

Families still did that kind of thing? "You're not at home."

"No, because for some ridiculous reason I thought I'd nab me a burglar."

"Not a burglar." Seb folded his arms. Was he smiling? Felt like it, but who could tell with his teeth near to chattering?

"Fine, a trespasser."

287

"Hate to break it to you, darlin', but you're the one trespassing. Not me."

She mimicked his crossed arms. Apparently she'd stopped being intimidated by him sometime in the past couple of minutes. "Darlin'? You sound like a cowboy in an old western. Who are you, anyway?"

He held out his hand. "Seb Pierce."

She ignored his outstretched arm. "Seb?"

"Sebastian Parker Pierce III if you're itching for the full spiel."

"Sebastian? Like that lobster on *The Little Mermaid*? And what do you mean, I'm the one trespassing?"

"You ask a lot of questions, ma'am." He slipped past her, moving to the spot in the lobby where muted light poured in from a streetlamp outside, affording at least a degree of visibility. Enough to notice stains on the carpet, at least. "And I think you mean crab."

The woman turned to face him, but remained rooted in her dark corner. "Excuse me?"

"Sebastian on *The Little Mermaid*. He was a crab, not a lobster. Seeing as how we're in a movie theater, just seems like the respectful thing to do to get our film trivia correct."

"This isn't a game of Trivial Pursuit and if it was, you'd be wrong and—"

"Wanna bet? By the way, assuming you're a local, any chance you know of any hidden-away B&Bs? The lack of hotel was a surprise." He supposed he could drive to a different town, but after so many wrong turns on gravel roads, not to mention his inexperience driving in snow, he'd just as soon stay put in Maple Valley.

"You don't have a place to stay tonight?"

Was that actually the tiniest hint of concern in her voice? And did she ever intend to move into the light? "If you're so inclined to offer me a spare bedroom, I wouldn't turn it down." He couldn't help the teasing drawl that crept into his voice.

Same drawl that had annoyed Grandfather to no end when Seb had surrendered to his summons back in January and returned to California. *"You may have spent fifteen years in Texas, son, but you're no cowboy."*

"Got a pair of boots and a Stetson in the closet that might suggest otherwise." Not to mention a decade and a half of ranch work and the weathered skin and callused hands that came with it.

"Nevertheless, you're home now. You're wearing a suit. You're about to walk into a board meeting. Try to drop the drawl."

He'd dropped the drawl. Because even at thirty-five, standing up to Grandfather's steely-eyed attention proved difficult.

And because of the inheritance. The one Grandfather had promised him at the end of a year's work for the family company. Sort of chapped a man's pride to cower for the sake of cash, especially considering how thoroughly and intentionally Seb had shed the trappings of his wealthy upbringing.

But with the kind of money his only living relative was offering, Seb could make good on his promise to Thad. Save the ranch and the livelihood of the father figure who'd taken him in so many years ago—back when Seb was just a miserable, 20-year-old college dropout, fresh off a Texas-bound Greyhound with no plan and not a penny in his pocket.

Thaddeus Dunlap had changed Seb's life. Seb would do just about anything to return the favor, even if it meant working for Grandfather and his philanthropy board, hopping states and fixing up little town treasures like this rundown movie theater. Seb had contacted Grandfather a year ago simply hoping for a loan, but he'd been offered a windfall instead.

Didn't entirely make sense, given the way Seb had walked

away as a youth, all the years of silence in between. But Seb wasn't about to argue. He'd agreed to Grandfather's stipulations and eleven months later, here he was.

If the woman in the corner was any indication, maybe this final month of playing the dutiful grandson wouldn't be so bad.

"I don't have a spare bedroom," the woman said now.

He made a show of drooping his shoulders. "Pity."

"And if I did—"

"You wouldn't offer it to a stranger. Very sensible of you, if not entirely as warm and welcoming as I'd been led to believe of you Midwesterners." He rubbed his hands together, grasping for what little heat he could.

"Well, I'm sure the police can offer you shelter in a jail cell once they arrive."

"*If* they arrive. They're being awfully pokey about it." He glanced outside. Darn, if that snow-covered town square wasn't very nearly pretty. Might be he'd get to experience his first-ever white Christmas this year. "I truly hate to disappoint you, but I haven't broken a single law tonight."

"I think Chief Ross might feel differently when he sees the busted window."

"Needed replacing anyway. Energy-efficient windows will do wonders for this building's electricity bill."

"Except there is no electricity bill because this theater's been closed for a long time, so—"

Pulsing red and blue lights and the wail of a siren cut her off.

And finally the woman moved toward him. "I told you they'd show up."

But it wasn't the lights or the siren or even the possibility of an impending arrest, however unwarranted, that yanked the gasp from Seb's lungs.

It was the pale wash of lamplight that spotlighted the

woman's blond hair. The heart-shaped face and high cheek-bones. Those ice-blue eyes he couldn't have forgotten if he'd tried.

And oh, he'd tried. For years, he'd tried.

He knew this woman. He'd never known her name or where she was from. But he knew *her*.

"Don't look so shocked," she said, coming to a stop in front of him. "I warned you, after all."

Now she was the one with the tease in her voice. She didn't have any idea, did she?

Breathe, Seb. Before you pass out.

"What's your name?" The question slipped from his lips before he could stop it, all his composure, all his swagger, gone in a moment. "I've always wondered."

"Always as in the past five minutes?"

He heard a car door slam outside, watched muffled colored light flicker over the woman's face. *No, always as in ever since that night in Kansas City.* Since he'd spoken words he'd never stopped regretting. Since guilt had proven a stubborn, unshakable companion, invading not only his waking hours but the occasional unsettling dream, as well.

If he'd had any idea that one day he'd find himself once again standing before the woman from outside that Kansas City bar, he'd have rehearsed his words. Prepared a speech and offered it up without a speck of a drawl.

But all he could do now was stare.

Her forehead wrinkled. Finally, just as an officer stepped through the mess of broken glass, she spoke. "Leigh. My name's Leigh."

Not even the jangle of handcuffs could rip his gaze from her face.

Leigh.

Well, now he knew.

CHAPTER 2

"*I*'m telling you, Drew, it was humiliating."

Leigh paced the length of her older brother's renovated farmhouse kitchen. After that mortifying incident at the theater, she'd finally arrived home only to find the townhouse empty, a note from Winnie on the counter. *Went to Uncle Drew's for supper. Would've texted you . . . if I had a phone. −W*

That daughter of hers—never subtle with her digs.

But Winnie was fifteen. Sarcasm went part and parcel with teenage life. At least they were together and life was, for the most part, stable. Something Leigh hadn't always been able to say. If living a normal mom-and-daughter existence meant she had to put up with a few complaints over not buying Winnie an expensive phone, so be it.

Clanking metal drew her gaze to the kitchen floor where Drew's legs poked out from under the sink, the sawdust on his jeans evidence of a day spent in his carpentry workshop. "Can you even hear me down there?"

Drew's wife, Maren, liked to joke that her husband gave the phrase "strong and silent type" new meaning. Most of the time, Leigh appreciated Drew's quiet nature. It meant she could vent uninterrupted. But now and then, she could use a sign he was still listening.

"I can hear you." Drew reached one hand out from under the sink. "Hand me the wrench, will you?"

She squatted to pluck the wrench from his toolbox. "We had a good five or six minutes before the police even arrived. He had all that time to tell me why he was in the theater. But no, instead he stands around calling me darlin' and arguing with me about *The Little Mermaid*."

Drew twisted whatever pipe needed twisting and finally scooted free. "*The Little Mermaid?*"

"Was Sebastian a lobster or a crab?" Winnie would know, but she was upstairs with Maren, probably hanging out in that gorgeously remodeled attic Maren used as a writing room when she and Drew weren't hosting guests.

Drew had created such an idyllic life for himself here in the home all the Renwycke siblings had grown up in. He'd fallen in love with a successful author, had swept her off her feet and married her, all while fixing up the farmhouse and turning his carpentry hobby into a thriving business.

His was a life marked by wise choices and constant compassion for others. He deserved every little bit of happiness he found.

Drew rose to a sitting position. "Do I look like a man who spends a lot of time watching Disney cartoons?"

Well, no, but neither did Sebastian Parker Pierce III. What kind of name was that, anyway? Didn't at all fit what she'd seen of his appearance when he'd stepped into the faint light of the theater lobby earlier—the unruly hair, the unshaven cheeks, the un-dressy jeans and plaid shirt.

To borrow Maren's phrasing, the man gave the word "rugged" new meaning.

And it should've been Leigh's first clue. A burglar

would've been attired in black. "The point is, I looked like an idiot in front of Chief Ross and his deputy. All it took was one phone call to Mayor Milt to confirm that, yes, the guy has every right to go around busting out the theater's windows. Apparently he's in town to revamp the place so it can reopen."

Drew tipped his toolbox closed and stood. "That's good news."

"I suppose."

"Of course it is. Remember how Dad used to take us to movies on days when Mom hosted her book club?"

Dad. A thread of bittersweet recollection wound through her. Almost exactly one year since the diagnosis. Two months since the funeral. When the doctors had called his Alzheimer's rapidly progressive, they'd meant it.

To be honest, from the beginning, Leigh had thought she'd handled the news better than either of her brothers. Colin had refused to talk about it for weeks, and not even solid, staid Drew had been able to fully mask the depth of his emotion.

But Leigh—she'd faced the reality of Dad's illness head on. If she'd learned anything during her various stints in rehab, it was that denial made a shoddy band-aid. She'd spent more time with Dad earlier this year than in most of her adulthood put together.

But now that he was gone, she couldn't help the guilt-laced questions that needled her whenever Dad came up in conversation: Was it truly peace she'd felt during his final months? The result of the faith of her childhood, rekindling itself as her father approached eternity?

Or was it simply a false comfort? Brought on by the fact that Dad's Alzheimer's meant . . .

It meant he couldn't remember—her worst moments, her bleakest failures. It meant he was the one person in her family who could look at Leigh without recalling all the ways she'd let them down.

What kind of person was grateful for a parent's lost memories?

"Leigh?"

Drew leaned against the island counter, his forearm resting atop his toolbox. Tender concern hovered in her brother's eyes. She'd seen that expression so many times.

"I'm fine, Drew."

"I've heard that for people who struggle with . . . " Drew rubbed his chin, clearly grasping for more words than he was used to speaking. "For people who struggle with what you've struggled with in the past, the loss of a loved one can—"

"I'm not going to relapse."

"I know, but—"

"I haven't taken anything more than a Tylenol in nearly four years. I'm still going to meetings. What do I have to do to convince you—?"

Drew pushed away from the counter, placing both palms on her arms. "Nothing. You don't have to do anything. You're right. I'm just being am overbearing big brother again. I'm sorry."

Now she felt like a bully for cornering him into an apology. Truth was, Drew could've given up on her years ago. Probably should've. But he never had. Heck, he'd been willing to move home to Maple Valley to help Leigh and Winnie start over, had even taken up farming in an attempt to provide for them.

The day he'd finally acknowledged he wasn't cut out for it, sold the land surrounding their childhood home, had been an additional blessing. He'd split the money three ways with her and Colin. Leigh's share was long gone, of course. She'd used it to pay off outstanding debts, buy her first dependable car in years.

But the fact remained that Drew had changed her life when he'd convinced her to leave that cramped Omaha apartment more than two years ago. He'd let her live here at the farmhouse initially and then, when she'd needed her own space, he'd helped her move into the townhouse.

"You don't need to apologize, Drew. I'm just being surly. Hard day."

"Because of the theater intruder."

"Well, that and . . ." She sighed. "I applied for a job. In Des Moines."

Drew dropped his hands. "What kind of job? In Des Moines? You wouldn't really move, would you?"

"Doesn't matter. Didn't get it."

"I thought you liked working at the restaurant?"

"I did. I mean, I do. Most days. But this job would've been event planning. It just sounded so . . . fun, I guess. You know what weird enjoyment I get out of organizing things." She'd honestly thought she'd be good at it. And it wasn't as if the idea had come completely out of the blue. Through her job at the restaurant, she'd catered several weddings in the past year, and she'd helped with a few town events, too.

Mayor Milt himself had personally thanked her for her assistance with this year's summer festival. Of course, he hadn't entirely been able to hide his surprise that she'd actually followed through on the commitment. But could she really blame him? She was the girl who'd gotten pregnant in high school, who'd been caught stealing a doctor's prescription pad the summer after graduation, who'd spent what should've been her freshman year in college at her first recovery center.

Small towns had long memories. Her clingy reputation wouldn't be so easy to shake.

Drew fiddled with the latch on his toolbox. "I'll never forget how you flipped out when you found a label maker in your stocking one Christmas. Or how Mom used to have you plan family vacation itineraries."

"And I'm so crazily detail-oriented, it's not even funny. Event planning just seems like a good fit." Plus, the salary alone was temptation enough. That job could've been the answer to her too-strained monthly budget.

Not to mention her too-familiar restlessness. The kind of restlessness that used to see her continually picking up and moving to a new town, playing piano in a new bar or club. . . popping a new painkiller.

"Don't know what I was thinking, though. I'm not qualified. My employment history is sporadic." *And I don't deserve it.* She dropped onto a stool. "I should be content. I'm lucky to have the job I have."

Drew watched her for a moment before speaking again. "It's good to be content, sis. But there's also nothing wrong with reaching for a dream."

Maybe not, but dreams-come-true weren't for everyone. "It was just a random whim. That's all."

Before Drew could respond, pounding footsteps barreled in. "Mom, check this out!" Winnie bounded into the kitchen. Her almost-white hair, same shade as Leigh's, poked out every which way from a messy bun atop her head.

"Hello to you, too. Ready to head home?"

Winnie thrust a paper at Leigh. "Not until you look at this. It's a summer writing program at the University of Iowa. Maren thinks she could help me get in."

Leigh glanced at the paper. Maren always indulged Winnie's bookworm tendencies and writing aspirations. Leigh appreciated the attention both Maren and Drew showered on Winnie, even as she couldn't deny the twinge of envy she sometimes felt at Winnie's obvious admiration for her aunt and uncle.

But then, Leigh hadn't given her daughter a whole lot to look up to over the years.

And—she skimmed the information about the writing program—it seemed she was about to let her down again. Maren might be able to get Winnie into the program, but no way could Leigh pay for it. Nine hundred dollars?

She swallowed. Hard. "Win, this is so cool, but—"

The door at the back of the kitchen flung open, ushering in a blustery cold and saving Leigh from so quickly eroding Winnie's enthusiasm. Her other brother's grinning face appeared. "Hey, guys." Colin tramped into the kitchen, tracking snow with him, the door still open behind him. "Hope you don't mind, Drew, but I met a newcomer in town and might have offered him one of your many spare bedrooms. Seems he got to Maple Valley only to discover there's no room at the inn. Or, well, no inn at all. Except for the Everwood B&B, but we all know that place is too creepy for words."

Colin kept rambling in his usual boisterous mode, but Leigh stopped hearing him the moment a second figure stepped through the door.

You've got to be kidding me.

Sebastian Parker Pierce III. Coatless, with red cheeks and red ears and snow in his hair.

And a shocked expression that surely matched her own.

* * *

"I swear, I didn't know."

Seb followed Leigh out the door he'd come in only minutes ago, a wintry chill wrapping around him the moment he stepped into a farmyard blanketed in white. What had started out as sleet earlier tonight had firmed up into a fluffy snow that sparkled under moonlight.

Picturesque, but he really should've been smart enough to invest in a coat before showing up in Iowa. In December.

Leigh's boots printed the snow as she marched toward a car he assumed belonged to her. She'd ordered the girl who was basically her exact replica to come along with. But so far, Seb was the only one who'd trailed out of the house after her.

And why he had, he didn't even know. All he knew was since seeing Leigh in that theater, he couldn't shake the feeling that he was here in Maple Valley for reasons that went beyond some dilapidated, old theater.

"I didn't know you'd be here," he said again. "I didn't know Colin was your brother. Didn't know him at all until we met at the coffee shop." Seb had been desperate for something to warm himself up after standing around in that freezing theater, explaining his situation to an amused officer while the police chief gave Leigh a half-teasing, half-scolding lecture on taking criminal matters into her own hands.

Special mock emphasis on *criminal*.

Which probably accounted for her less-than-pleased reaction to seeing Seb again. Unless . . .

Unless she'd remembered. Recognized him from that night in Kansas City. A blast of cold shoved through the thin cotton of his shirt.

Leigh stopped halfway to her car, turned. This woman looked so much healthier than the one he'd encountered five years ago. Her formerly gaunt frame had filled in with curves her winter layers didn't hide. And he'd seen in that bright farmhouse kitchen that her skin was no longer a sallow shade. In fact, her cheeks had turned downright rosy at the sight of him.

But those eyes . . . they were still a blizzard of emotion. Too many layers to sort out on the spot, but he was keen enough to recognize an undercurrent of hurt when he saw it.

A hurt he'd contributed to once upon a time. Something he well remembered, even if she didn't.

"You're staring at me again. It's unnerving." She reached into both pockets of her vest, pulling out her mittens.

"Sorry, it's just . . ." Should he bring up their chance encounter outside that seedy bar? Would the coincidence of their second meeting bowl her over the way it had him?

Or maybe it's not a coincidence.

What if being here in Iowa, running into Leigh again, was some unexpected answer to prayer? He'd wished a thousand times to apologize to the downtrodden woman he'd so heartlessly berated that night. He couldn't take back his razor-sharp, judgmental words, but if he could just let her know how much he regretted them . . .

Well, this was his chance.

So why the hesitation coiling through him?

Leigh jabbed her hands into her mittens. "It's just what? The police chief didn't tease me enough? You want to finish the job?"

"Of course not."

"Good."

"Although . . ." He let the word dangle, his drawl creeping in again.

Her eyes flashed.

And he just couldn't help it—the barest of smiles. "You have to admit it was a little funny."

She folded her arms over her zipped-up vest, snowflakes dancing in the air around her and dissolving into her hair. "I don't have to admit anything."

"What would you have done if I'd been an actual dangerous robber? You didn't have a weapon. And though I'd never stoop to calling a woman weak, I am about three times your size—"

"Slight exaggeration, perhaps?"

"Regardless, I really don't think we'd be equals in hand-to-hand combat."

She dropped her arms. Then folded them again. Dropped them.

"Try stomping your foot, darlin'. It'll make you feel better." Truly, someone ought to slap a piece of duct tape over his running mouth.

"You call me darlin' one more time and I'll—"

The slam of the kitchen door interrupted her. Shame. He wouldn't have minded hearing the rest of her threat. Wouldn't have minded at all.

"Maren's going to call you sometime, Mom." The girl breezed past him. "About the writing program."

"Oh. Great."

Leigh's tone flat-lined. But if her daughter recognized the instant distress flooding her mother's features, she didn't show it. Just continued on to the car and flopped into the passenger seat.

Oh, the memory that induced. Same girl, only years younger with eyes closed. Asleep in a different vehicle in a different town . . .

It just can't be a coincidence.

While disbelief gnawed at him all over again, Leigh bit her bottom lip. Just how many concerns pressed down on this woman? Clearly she'd risen above the circumstances Seb had found her in years ago, but anybody could see she still shouldered a burden or two or twenty.

And the urge to lighten her spirits, even if only for a moment, couldn't be denied. "You care to finish that threat now, ma'am?"

Her attention snapped to him once more. "Look, Sebastian Parker Pierce III, I don't know why you're in town or how long you'll be here—"

"Four weeks. Just long enough to spruce up the theater

and see it reopened." Although from what he'd seen so far, albeit in the dark, that place needed more than a sprucing. It'd take far more work than any of the other projects Grandfather had assigned him.

Just so long as he got it done by the end of the year. It'd mean working through the holidays, but no matter. Not as if he'd be missing some joyous family gathering. Grandfather had never spent Christmas Day celebrating when Seb was a kid. He reckoned that hadn't changed any in the years since.

"So is that what you do? Like, for a job? Fix old theaters?"

"Only temporarily." Something close enough to interest flickered over Leigh's face that he went on. "My grandfather is an entertainment lawyer in Beverly Hills. Has more money than he knows what to do with. He gets his yearly charitable tax deductions by making grants to small towns all over the place to restore old cinemas, community theaters, auditoriums, that kind of thing. For the past year, I've been working for his philanthropy board—basically just traveling wherever they tell me, overseeing whatever project they're funding." Or in this case, singlehandedly carrying it out.

"And when you're not breaking into theaters?"

He grinned. "I work on a ranch in Texas."

"So that crack I made about you sounding like a cowboy in a western—"

"Not all that far off." Would knowing as much jog her memory? Last time she'd seen him—only time until tonight—he'd been wearing the Stetson Thad gave him on his twenty-fifth birthday.

But still, there wasn't a hint of recognition on her face.

"Look, I really can find another place to stay. Before I met your brother, I'd been planning to drive on over to Ames. But Colin said that was crazy. He's mighty persuasive, your brother. One minute I'm ordering a large French roast, trading small talk with a stranger, the next I'm following the guy to a farm."

"That's Colin, for you."

"He must not know about his sister's vigilante tendencies, though, because when I told him about the woman who tried to apprehend me at the theater, he didn't make the connection."

Her eyes narrowed. "Go on inside, Mr. Pierce. Before you get frostbite."

"Something tells me you wouldn't be all that upset to see me lose a few fingers or toes."

Her saucy grin felt like a reward.

"Maybe. Maybe not."

With that, she turned and marched toward her car. Her headlights beamed into the night, casting a glow on a lineup of outbuildings and evergreens ribboned with snow.

Seb didn't even feel the cold as he watched her drive away.

CHAPTER 3

*S*omeone should have warned Seb about Maple
Valley—the cold, the snow, the quirkiness.

As evidenced by the crowd currently gathered outside the
theater. It was barely eight a.m.!

"Oh yeah, that's asbestos."

On his hands and knees, Seb turned away from the sight
of the townspeople clustered on the sidewalk outdoors. Drew
Renwycke perched on the top rung of a ladder in the same
corner of the theater lobby where Leigh had stood in the dark
last night. Today vivid sunlight splayed over every surface—
the cracked glass of the concession stand counter, peeling
striped wallpaper, the faded carpet Seb was currently pulling
up. It'd seemed like a good place to start.

Drew pointed to the smudges of gray visible on the wall
underneath ripped paper. "You're going to want to do something about that."

Asbestos. As if he didn't have enough to do to get this
theater in shape before Grandfather's deadline. He'd headed
to the theater at the crack of dawn this morning and already
his to-do list was overwhelming. The marquee out front

needed better lighting, new chairs in the sole auditorium were a must, and he didn't even know where to start with the projection and sound equipment upstairs.

The plastic tarp covering the window he'd broken the night before flapped in the wind, voices drifting in from outside. "What's up with the audience?"

Drew climbed down the ladder, eyeing the gathering on the other side of the generous windows Seb *hadn't* broken. "You've been in town almost fourteen hours. Surprised it took this long for a crowd to form."

Seb stood, hammer in hand. "It's really that exciting? The theater reopening?"

"Yup."

A man of few words, this Drew Renwycke who'd unexpectedly become Seb's host. Seb had offered multiple times the previous evening to find somewhere else to stay. The other brother—Colin, who was apparently only living at the farmhouse temporarily until his upcoming wedding—had mentioned a B&B. Said it was eerie, but surely he exaggerated.

Then again, Colin had also warned him that both his presence and his purpose in town were sure to cause a splash, and considering the gathering outside, he hadn't embellished that. So maybe the B&B was as bad as he claimed.

Regardless, Drew had waved off his repeated offers to relocate. *"We've had a guest in the attic for the past two holiday seasons. Might as well make it a third."*

Frankly, odd as it felt to intrude on someone else's home, Seb was grateful. That attic was a masterpiece of reno-work. Beautiful built-ins and hardwood floors, a cushioned window seat underneath an octagon of glass that overlooked the spacious farmyard. There was even an en suite bathroom that Drew had put in this past summer.

The man clearly knew what he was doing. He had a vision

for his home and his talent.

How different from the way Seb's own adulthood had shaken out. He'd never had real career aspirations, had only known he didn't want his grandfather's kind of life. When he'd finally gotten brave enough to ditch college and the pre-law major Grandfather had insisted on, he hadn't known what to do next. The bus he'd hopped to Texas? Nothing more than the rash impulse of a young man with no direction.

But these days, he tended to look back on that Greyhound ticket as one of God's greatest gifts. He may only have bought it because it was the first bus out of the station, but it'd landed him in Thad's path. Soon, he'd found himself with a whole new life.

Maybe, in a small way, meeting the various Renwycke siblings last night was something similar. Stumbling into Colin had landed him not only a place to stay, but a connection with someone who probably knew more about what this old building needed than Seb did. Drew's eyes had actually lit up when he'd offered to come look over the theater with Seb.

"The bones of the building are just fine," Drew had declared when they first arrived. *"It looks like a lot of work, but really, most of it's just cosmetic."*

Of course, that was before he'd found the asbestos.

Drew moved his ladder out of the way now. "Better paste on a smile. You've got company."

A man with white hair, bushy brows, and a mustache to match, pushed through the front door and made a beeline for Seb, one hand outstretched from a winter coat unzipped to reveal a sweater vest underneath.

"Sebastian Pierce, yes?" The man's handshake was as exuberant as his tone. "Mayor Milt. Pleased to meet you."

"Uh, pleased to meet you, too." Longest handshake of his life, this was.

"I can't tell you how thrilled we all are that you're here. That's why everyone's gathered outside. Don't worry. I won't make you go out there and give a speech or anything."

"Unfair." Drew's voice sounded from behind the mayor. "He made me give a speech two years ago and all I did was donate a few benches. You're renovating an entire theater."

The mayor finally released Seb's hand and looked over his shoulder. "Not unfair at all. Mr. Pierce is new to town. You, my boy, are a Maple Valley native." He turned back to Seb. "And anyway, certainly you'll give a speech at the grand reopening. Might as well save up any grandiosity for the main event."

"Grandiosity?" And wait a second. Grand opening? Main event? "Mr., uh, Mayor . . . I think there might be some confusion here. I'm here to do some renovations. That's it."

The mayor was shaking his head before Seb finished speaking. "Renovations *and* a reopening celebration. It's right here in the grant agreement." He reached into the inside pocket of his coat, pulled out a rolled-up stack of papers, and handed it to Seb.

That was the logo for Grandfather's foundation at the top, all right—Pierce Philanthropic Foundation for the Arts.

"Take a look at the second page," the mayor urged.

Seb flipped the top page over. It was all he could do not to groan out loud when he read the last paragraph. Really? No one on the philanthropy board, not even Grandfather, had bothered to fill him in on the extra requirements of this last job? It wasn't enough that they'd asked him to perform a miracle on a decrepit building in less than a month? He also had to host a grand reopening?

"Friday, December twenty-second, should work just fine. Evening would be good."

What? That wasn't even three weeks away. Not a chance. "I really don't think—"

"I can't tell you how grateful we all are to the Pierce family." The mayor nabbed Seb's hand again for another vigorous shake, his gaze swimming over their surroundings. "You have your work cut out for you, but I've no doubt you're up for it."

Seconds later, the man disappeared the way he'd come, a bluster of frigid air whooshing in before the door closed. Seb just stood there for a moment, hammer dangling from the hand the mayor hadn't nearly squeezed the circulation from.

Drew spoke up from behind him. "He can be a little much, our mayor. And he *really* loves any excuse for an event."

Seb rubbed his stubbled cheeks, thoughts jumbling too quickly to keep up with. Should he call Grandfather? Tell him there was no way he could plan an event on top of everything else? Should he beg out of this assignment all together?

"Seb?"

He blinked. "Sorta wish someone had told me party planning was part of this gig. I thought I'd have all the way through the New Year to fix up this place. The twenty-second is only two and a half weeks away."

"But honestly, you're just looking at some new paint and new carpet and nicer furniture. It'll go faster than you think."

Seb combed his fingers through his hair, turning to see the crowd still outside. He lifted his hand from his head, gave a frustrated little wave.

They waved back. Every blasted one of them.

"This is one peculiar town." He turned once more, only to see Drew leaning against the staircase that led to the projection room, one thumb hooked through a belt loop, a grin teasing the corner of his mouth. "What?"

Drew straightened, reaching for the jacket he'd slung over the stairway railing. "I'm about to kill two birds with one stone." Drew tossed him the second coat, one Colin had loaned Seb. "But you're gonna want to work on your brown-nosing skills on the way over."

"On the way over where?"

"To find Leigh. Only you can't tell her it was my idea. Drives her crazy when I try to fix things."

"What idea?"

Drew only grinned.

* * *

LEIGH HAD to find a way to break the news to her daughter.

She skimmed the paper Winnie had handed her in Drew's kitchen for what had to be the tenth time. Each time she'd hoped the writing program registration price might magically transform into a manageable amount. But no, it was the same dismal number staring back at her each time.

There's just no way.

She folded the crinkled page and stuffed it in the pocket of her restaurant apron just as Winnie waltzed into The Red Door's kitchen. The tantalizingly sweet aroma of maple syrup clung to the air, along with smell of coffee and their head chef's famous blueberry pancakes, the most popular item on their breakfast menu.

If only Leigh were half as good at making the pancakes. Shan had called in sick this morning, which left Leigh manning the griddle. Soooo not her forte.

She poured a circle of batter onto the sizzling surface. "Shouldn't you be on the way to school already?"

Winnie dropped her backpack on the stainless steel counter in the middle of the room. "After I get a coffee refill."

The urge to suggest Winnie was too young for such an ardent coffee habit climbed up her throat, but she swallowed it before it could make it past her lips. If a caffeine dependency was the worst routine her daughter ever established, Leigh should count herself grateful. Besides, picking her battles seemed to be the key to mothering a teen.

Which is why she also refrained from remarking on the weather being much too cold for the flimsy leggings Winnie wore under a denim skirt with a frayed hem that only reached halfway to her knees.

But she couldn't nix telling Winnie the writing program was a no-go. Maybe she could've scrounged up nine hundred dollars if she had a few months, but according to the flier, registration was due January fifteenth. Better to tell her daughter now before she spent another day with her hopes up.

Leigh took a breath. "You've got that history test today, right?"

Coward.

Winnie nodded as she filled her travel mug. "Uncle Drew helped me study."

He always did.

Leigh abandoned her bowl of batter and walked to the massive fridge. She pulled out a bottle of French vanilla creamer and delivered it to Winnie. "Third period?"

"Fourth." Winnie doused her coffee with creamer until it was the color of sand.

Leigh draped one arm around her daughter. "I'll be thinking of you." The phrase *praying for* had almost come out instead. But the words still tasted a little too foreign.

She'd started going to church again since moving back to Maple Valley, but hers was a tentative sort of belief. She tiptoed around the faith she'd grown up with, certain God was there, but not nearly as certain she was the kind of person He listened to.

"Thanks, Mom." Winnie leaned up to kiss Leigh's cheek.

The surprise of it was enough to upend her. "What was that for?"

Winnie's wispy bangs nearly reached her eyes. "For being a good mom. I know I'm not always the easiest kid. And you're probably sick of me heckling you about getting a phone." Winnie turned, reached for her backpack and slung it over her shoulder.

Later. She'd tell Winnie they couldn't afford the writing program later.

Wimp.

Winnie stopped at the kitchen door. "Oh, speaking of which, Uncle Colin said he has an old iPhone I can have if I want. It's like three versions ago, but it's better than nothing, right?"

Leigh closed her eyes. She loved her family, but sometimes their helpfulness only made her feel like she was coming up short when it came to raising her daughter. Now even Colin could provide what she couldn't? Colin, who'd spent plenty of years competing with her for the role of the black sheep of the family. She rotated to face Winnie. "Win—"

"I know, I know. I don't need a phone. It'll just distract me from school and writing and blah, blah, blah."

"Good thing it's not a vocabulary test you're taking today."

At least Winnie laughed. "See you tonight, Mom."

She whisked from the kitchen, the sound of chatter and clinking dishes drifting in behind her.

And the smell of burning batter. Shoot.

Leigh dashed across the kitchen and yanked her spatula from the bowl of batter, sending specks flying. She pried the spatula under the charred pancake, smoke billowing around her face. Lovely, just lovely. If the smoke alarms went off again, she'd never hear the end of it from Melinda.

She scraped the ruined pancake free then reached behind her to unknot her apron. She scrambled onto the sprawling steel counter in the middle of the room and lifted her apron over her head, waving away the smoke before it could reach the detector.

Which is exactly where Seb Pierce found her when he

sauntered through the kitchen's swinging door only seconds later.

She didn't even try to hide her groan. But it came out more like a sigh, sending straggling strands of hair fanning around her face and tickling her cheeks. And here she'd thought she just might be able to avoid the man during his stint in town. After all, The Red Door was on the opposite side of the square as the theater. As long as she stayed over here—and away from Drew's place—she'd have her bases covered.

So she'd hoped.

"Not the warmest greeting I've ever received in my life," Seb said as he moseyed toward the center of the room. "But not the worst, either. Worst was this time I walked into a cattle barn and found myself being welcomed by an escapee longhorn with an ax to grind. Your greeting wasn't quite so bad as that."

Leigh stopped waving her apron. "Did you just compare me to a *cow*?"

Seb lifted one shoulder in a haphazard shrug. "Said cow might prefer the term bull. I survived the ordeal, just in case you were wondering."

"I wasn't."

"I've got a pretty scar to prove it. Took thirty-seven stitches to patch me up."

"You mean the bull actually—" She clamped her lips shut. Nope. She had pancakes to remake. Sebastian Parker Pierce III could find someone else upon whom to hoist his tall tales.

"Can I help you down?"

With such obvious amusement plastered all over his face? She didn't think so. Rather than clasp his outstretched arm, she dropped her apron in his hand instead and climbed down on her own.

Only to find herself inches from his flannel shirt.

She lifted her gaze. The flecks of amber in his hazel eyes fairly twinkled as he grinned down at her. "Good morning, by the way."

She snatched her apron from his hand and brushed past him. "What are you doing here?"

"Thought I was coming over for a little polite conversation. Maybe some breakfast—"

"Then you should go out to the dining room and let a waiter take your order." She reached for her bowl of batter.

"—but that was before I saw the state of your kitchen," Seb finished.

"It's not *my* kitchen. I'm just filling in." And doing a lousy job of it, to boot. She glanced behind her in time to see Seb's darting gaze—from the batter-speckled wall behind the griddle to the charred remains of her last pancake attempt to the pile of dishes no one had bothered to put through the dishwasher just yet.

He returned his focus to her. "Will you bite my head off if I offer to help?"

He asked the question so sincerely she couldn't even make herself scowl. "I only bite off a person's head after he's led me to mistakenly believe he's engaged in criminal activity."

Seb stepped between her and the griddle. "If I were the exacting type, I might point out that a more accurate account of our previous interaction would include very little leading-on from me and quite a bit of jumping-to-conclusions from you. But as it turns out, I'm *not* the exacting type." He reached for the bowl in her hands. "I am, however, exceedingly skilled at making pancakes."

"And not at all self-assured."

His grin only widened before he turned to the expansive griddle. "Now, for starters, you've got the heat way too high. And the batter's too soupy."

"It's our chef's recipe."

"Well, your chef isn't here. I am."

And Leigh still had no idea why.

Nor did she have any idea why she didn't just make him leave. Certainly didn't have a thing to do with the creases at the corners of his eyes when he smiled. Or his smile itself. Or the way his drawl was just the slightest bit charming—not that she'd ever admit it. Not in a hundred years.

"Fine. But you'll have to wear a hairnet."

* * *

WELL, Drew had told Seb to brown-nose. Hopefully an hour over a hot griddle counted.

Who could've known those early years of ranch work, back when he'd still been low enough on the totem pole to be assigned kitchen duty, would eventually do him some good?

Leigh came shuffling into the kitchen, arms loaded with empty plates. "Breakfast rush is over. We survived." Blond hair spilled from a hapless ponytail and the sleeves of her white shirt were rolled to her elbows. Did she know she had blueberry stains on one arm?

And how could she not remember him? Every detail of their chance meeting five years ago was burned in his brain. The way her blue dress had hung too loose over her thin frame. How she'd smelled of alcohol and trudged with head and shoulders down.

How she'd flinched when he'd laid into her about leaving her daughter in the car.

"Something wrong?" Leigh emptied her load into the nearby sink now.

Seb had been in Kansas City for a cattle auction that night. Only reason he'd been outside that bar was to drag one of Thad's younger cowhands back to their hotel. But when he'd seen a little girl asleep in a car, he'd had to do something. He'd been on the brink of calling the police when Leigh had approached.

And that's when he'd lost it, had given a virtual stranger a far worse tongue-lashing than he ever would've given that unruly cowhand.

Later that same night, he'd tried to justify his actions. Thad had suffered a major heart attack only days earlier, he'd reminded himself. Seb's nerves had still been raw from the fear of losing the only true father figure he'd ever known.

But he should've stopped himself from taking it out on the woman. Even if she had left her child in a car. On a busy street. In a dangerous part of town.

He'd stayed awake far too late last night wrestling with the question of whether or not to tell Leigh they'd met before. On the one hand, it seemed cowardly not to. Maybe even dishonest. But on the other, if she'd entirely forgotten the encounter, what was the good in bringing it up? Maybe she'd been too inhibited for his words that night to even sink in.

Maybe they hadn't played and replayed in her mind all these years the way they had in his.

What kind of mother are you? How long were you in that bar anyway? If this is how you take care of your kid, you don't deserve—

"Seb?"

She'd moved to his side now, her forehead scrunched and honest-to-goodness curiosity on her face. Maybe even concern.

"Something wrong?"

He coughed, wished his own words away. "Only thing wrong is my growling stomach. And this last pancake ain't gonna be enough to stop it." He scraped the last of the batter from his bowl and dropped it on the griddle.

"You haven't had breakfast? You didn't have to stay all this time, Seb."

"I wanted to help."

"You could've at least let me know you hadn't eaten." Leigh tucked her hair behind her ear. "Let me make you some scrambled eggs or something."

What a change from the glaring woman he'd found atop the counter when he first walked into the kitchen. Truth be told, he liked both versions. "You really don't have to."

"I'd like to. It'll give me a chance to prove I'm not entirely inept in the kitchen."

"Never thought you were inept." No, as a matter of fact, while she might have burned a few pancakes before he'd arrived, in the past hour she'd more than displayed her managerial skills. She'd kept meal orders moving in and out of the kitchen, secured a substitute chef for the lunch shift, handled an inventory delivery, and pitched in with dishes and table-bussing in her every free minute.

Made him all the more certain of the genius of Drew's idea. It was probably about time he pitched it to Leigh.

He flipped the last pancake with a flick of his wrist, then turned to face her. "Listen, I'll take you up on the scrambled eggs, but first, can we sit for a sec?"

One corner of her mouth quirked. "Don't tell me your feet are tired."

He whipped off his hairnet. "Spent fifteen years working on a ranch, Miss Renwycke. Herding cattle, fixing fences, mucking stables. Worked my way up to foreman by the time I was twenty-seven. An hour on my feet in a kitchen is nothing."

"Your humility is inspiring." She plunked atop a stool near the steel island counter.

He waited until the pancake was ready, then freed it from the griddle and took a seat on a stool next to her. "Now then—"

"Aren't you going to eat that pancake?"

"Business first, food second."

"Business? What business could you and I have to discuss?"

His knees bumped into hers as he rotated on the stool to face her. "You ask a lot of questions."

"You said the same thing when I caught you breaking and entering. Only that time, you tacked on a *ma'am*."

"Wasn't breaking and entering."

"And I'm not having the strangest sense of déjà vu right about now, Sebastian Parker Pierce III."

The woman was exasperating.

The woman was *pretty*. From those pink cheeks on down to her sensible black shoes. "I've got a proposition for you, Leigh. One I think you might like."

She lifted one eyebrow.

"Maybe proposition isn't the right word. But we can help each other, you and I. Hear me out?"

Not until she shrugged and gave a noncommittal "I'm listening," did he let out the breath he hadn't even realized he was holding.

"I hear you're interested in event planning."

"My brother has a big mouth." She pressed her lips together.

"I'm under strict instructions to pretend he has nothing to do with this." Which is why he and Drew had parted ways at the restaurant's front doors, after Drew's coaching on the way over.

"She just got turned down for a job yesterday," Drew had said. *"So her pride's probably hurting. Make it clear she's the one doing* you *a favor and not the other way around."*

Easy enough, considering she actually *would* be doing him a huge favor if she agreed to coordinate the grand reopening.

Which was probably another tally for the side of *not*

reminding Leigh of their first meeting. If she did remember that encounter, no way would she say yes to the plan.

And right now, as he looked into those impossibly blue eyes of hers, he suddenly craved her yes for a whole host of reasons that had very little to do with the theater—not the least of which was the fact that for the first time in years of bachelorhood, here was a woman who, to put it much too mildly, piqued his interest.

"Here's the thing, Miss Renwycke. Turns out I've got an event to plan in addition to a theater to renovate, and I reckon I'm just not up to the task. Especially now that my timeline has just diminished."

"An event?"

"To celebrate the reopening of the theater. Except it seems somebody somewhere along the line forgot to put it in my job description. But I'm going to be way too busy attempting to perform a miracle on that building to throw together an actual event. So I'd rather ask for help than make a mess of things on my own."

At some point during his talking, she'd pulled a piece of crinkled paper from her pocket and she clutched it now. "I don't have a lot of experience. Or, well, any. Not technically. But I am good with organization and details and—"

"Don't have to convince me. I just saw you in action."

"You'd actually pay me?"

She's going to say yes. He shouldn't be so pleased. He really, really shouldn't. "Name your price."

She glanced at the paper in her hands before looking up at him.

And if he'd thought her pretty before, that smile now . . .

You're a fool, Seb Pierce.

"Nine hundred dollars."

CHAPTER 4

$\mathcal{M}$aybe Leigh should've let Seb take a few drinks of coffee or at least bite into his pastry before showing him the binders. All four of them. Complete with color-coded dividers.

Seb stared at her from across the little table in the Sugar Lane Bakery, the only available seating when they'd arrived at the packed shop. It'd been three days since she'd agreed to plan the theater's grand reopening, and this was the first chance she'd had to sit down with the man to present her ideas for the event. She looked from the binders to Seb and back again.

Perhaps she'd gone a little overboard.

"I just, um, really like putting ideas down on paper." In clear, twelve-point, sans-serif fonts . . . on three-hole-punched paper . . . organized according to category—theme, decorations, menu, entertainment, budget.

"This looks like a lot of ideas on a lot of paper," Seb finally said, reaching for his pastry, one of Colin's signature items.

Colin and his fiancé, Rylan, had opened this bakery only months ago and already it'd become a fixture in Maple Valley.

Pristine white walls contrasted with the dark walnut, wide-planked floors that matched the exposed beams overhead. Glass cases displayed all manner of colorful treats.

They'd named the bakery after the street Rylan used to live on back in Denver. Back before, as Rylan put it, Colin had upended her entire life. She always tried to glower when she said it. Could never actually pull it off.

Those two were so gooey-sweet together they could give their own baked goods a run for their money.

"Also, it seems you've got a thing for binders," Seb added.

She glanced at Seb once more. No plaid today. Instead he wore a tan sweater that matched his sandstone eyes. According to Drew, the man had worked twelve-hour days since Wednesday. Only reason he'd taken time to meet this morning was the need to be out of the way while an asbestos removal team took over the theater.

"I actually get a little jealous each year when it's time to buy Winnie's school supplies," she confessed. She tried and failed to suppress a yawn.

Seb grinned around a bite. A good sign. Hopefully it meant he didn't think she was a complete nutcase.

Unlike Winnie, who'd taken one look at the stack of binders this morning and muttered something about her crazy mother. Well, she wouldn't be so quick to mock when Leigh eventually told her she could apply for that writing program. She'd almost spilled the beans that first day, right after Seb agreed to her financial terms.

But she didn't actually have a check in hand just yet and anyway, it'd be more fun to give Winnie the news on Christmas morning.

Who'd have thought that first night when she caught Seb busting into the theater that he'd turn out to be her own personal Santa? It wasn't only the fee they'd agreed on that had brightened her entire week, but the chance to test out her event planning skills. See if that random whim might not be so random, after all.

In the past two years, Leigh had watched both her brothers jumpstart new and successful careers. Maybe it wasn't such a pipedream to think it was possible for her, as well.

And she had Seb to thank.

"Listen, Seb—"

"Hey, you didn't use my full name, for once."

A patron jostled past their table and Leigh's Americano sloshed over the edge of her mug. She grabbed a napkin. "I just wanted to say thanks for hiring me. It means a lot to me. More than you know." She wiped up the spilled liquid, surprised and more than a little uncomfortable at the depth of her own sincerity. "I know the binders are probably overkill, but I really want to do a good job."

When he didn't reply, she forced herself to meet his eyes. Kind, studying eyes. There was a potency to his patient scrutiny, enough to make her squirm even as she couldn't rip her gaze away. Why the tiniest niggle of familiarity just now?

And moreover, what could he possibly see in her to look at her that way? As if she were a book with pages worth turning. If he could see what the former chapters of her life held . . .

"How much sleep did you get last night, Leigh?"

She blinked at the unexpected question. "Say what?"

"You ordered a triple-shot Americano. You've yawned four times since we sat down." Seb tapped the top binder. "Just how late did you stay up last night working on this?"

"It wasn't that late."

He pinned her with a disbelieving stare.

"I'm not lying. It wasn't late when I finally went to bed. It was early . . . this morning."

There he went studying her again as he downed the last

bite of his pastry. Only after he'd swallowed and gulped a drink of his coffee did he finally look away. She didn't have time to ponder why she felt so relieved because he immediately opened the first binder. "All right, let's see what kept you up to all hours."

She spent the next fifteen minutes talking him through each binder, reviewing her ideas, enduring—or maybe actually enjoying—his amused quips at all her color-coded organization. First there was her winter wonderland-themed binder—a little cliché, but probably the most doable of all her ideas, although the Rockin' Around the Christmas Tree theme was a close second as far as ease of execution.

Her favorite, though, was the classic Christmas film concept. They could decorate the lobby with posters for *It's a Wonderful Life*, *Miracle on 34th Street*, *White Christmas*, all the classics, and set up a photo booth in one corner where guests could dress up in costumes and have a black and white photo taken. They could decorate with clapperboards and movie reels.

The idea was perfectly apropos for a movie theater reopening, and it'd give Leigh a good excuse for forcing Winnie to watch her old favorites.

Finally, Seb leaned back in his chair, arms crossed. "I'm a little confused as to why this reopening needs a theme. Don't get me wrong, all of this is impressive."

Leigh finished off her raspberry cream cheese flip and shook the sugar from her hands. "You say 'impressive,' but somehow I think you mean 'absurdly detailed.'"

"Couldn't it be both?"

He had a dimple in one cheek. How had she not noticed that before? "Fair enough."

"I just wonder if you're making the planning of this thing a little harder than it needs to be. The event is only two weeks from last night. I was assuming you'd keep it simple—appetizers, Christmas music, maybe a tree in the lobby."

"Seb, this is Maple Valley."

He lifted his coffee mug. "And?"

"And events are a big deal around here. Did you not see that snowman-building contest happening in the square yesterday? Have you noticed all the posters for WinterFest? Tonight there's an actual ice maze out at the Jaminski ranch—"

"What's an ice maze? Wait, there are ranches in Iowa? I thought it was just cornfields around here."

She laid her palm on the top binder. "The point is, yes, your event needs a theme. Believe me, I know Maple Valley."

"I do believe you." He moved his chair as the line stretching from the bakery counter grew.

"Then trust me, too. Appetizers and a tree are so not enough."

"I do trust you, Leigh. I trust you completely." He lowered his mug, something in his expression deepening, as if his words came from a tucked-away place inside.

"Why?" It came out before she could stop it. But hadn't she been wondering for days? Hadn't she asked herself at least a dozen times why in the world he'd entrusted this task to someone so totally untried and untested? "You don't even know me."

"The thing is . . . " It was the first time she'd seen him struggle for words, but she knew the look from so many conversations with the quieter of her two brothers. There was something he wanted to say, only he had no idea how to say it. "That is, the truth is . . . "

The crowded line reached past their table and someone bumped into the back of Leigh's chair. At the jolt, her coffee cup slipped from her hands, sending liquid spewing onto her shirt and over the table.

Over her binders! Her pretty, pretty binders. The classic Christmas film one got the worst of the splash, its cover dripping and coffee seeping inside.

"Are you going to cry?" Seb's look of inflated worry was almost enough to snap her from her shock. "Please don't cry."

"I'm not going to cry."

He swiped a napkin over the damaged binders then stood, snatching all four from the table. "Let's go."

"Go where?"

"There's a restroom in this place, isn't there?"

He bolted through the crowd and all she could think to do was follow him. He pushed into the men's room, holding the door with a look of impatience.

"It's the men's bathroom."

"But there aren't any men inside, save for me, and I promise not to relieve myself in your presence."

"I guess that's . . . comforting?" She shrugged and stepped in. "But why—"

She didn't have to finish the question. Seb dropped three of the binders on a counter and then elbowed the hand dryer, holding the fourth binder open underneath.

And she couldn't help it—the smile, the laugh, the tingle of illogical delight that thoroughly eclipsed all the facts of this moment. Like the fact that she was standing in a men's bathroom. With a coffee-stained shirt. While operating on only a few hours' sleep.

"You don't have to do that." She had to raise her voice to be heard over the humming dryer.

"I do. The Christmas movie theme is the obvious choice, so we can't let your binder succumb to a coffee-induced death."

She moved to his side and separated two damp pages. "You're pretty much one surprise after another, you know that, Sebastian Parker Pierce III?"

"Back to my full name, is it?"

She opened her mouth to reply, but nothing came out. Not one single quip. So she simply turned another page. And then another. And another. Until enough quiet moments passed that she could almost convince herself those hadn't actually been flutters in her heart or her stomach or wherever at the sight of Seb attempting to save her painstakingly organized binder.

Or at least, if they had been flutters, it'd been about the binder, not the man standing next to her whose subtle, woodsy cologne could do serious damage to a girl's common sense.

"So tell me about this ice maze."

Before she could answer, the bathroom door opened.

They both burst into laughter at Colin's gasp.

* * *

"Holy smokes, it's actually a maze made of ice."

Seb stared at the frosty walls of white that rose up in front of him and stretched into the distance. Twilight teased the horizon in pastel tendrils. Next to him, Leigh adjusted to the pink knit cap she'd pulled over her blond braids.

"Of course it is. What'd you think of when you heard the words *ice maze?*"

He'd thought . . . well, he didn't know what he'd thought. But it turned out Leigh Renwycke hadn't at all been exaggerating this town's stance on events. The maze, this whole place, it was . . .

Enchanting. That was the only word for it. From the inviting cinnamon scent of apple cider to the evergreens draped in lights to the faint strains of Christmas music floating in the air. Clusters of townspeople filled the rural grounds—an actual ranch with stables and horses and everything, right here in Iowa.

No, it wasn't nearly as sprawling as Thad's land down in Texas, but this property—J.J.'s Stables, according to the wood sign they'd passed under when they'd arrived at the ranch—was apparently undergoing a revival of sorts. Leigh had told him on the way here about the woman, a Sara something-or-other, who'd moved back to Iowa earlier this year to take over her family's land. Apparently she planned to run horse camps in the summer and provide animal therapy and other counseling services throughout the year. Kind of a cool idea, if anybody asked him.

He turned to Leigh, a full day's worth of satisfaction winding through him. The sound of her laugh when her brother walked into that men's room this morning—he'd carried it with him throughout the rest of the day as he checked up on the asbestos removal team, placed rush orders online for paint and carpet . . .

Endured a dozen irritating texts from Grandfather. Turned out the man didn't approve of Seb's hiring an event planner. Well, Seb would pay the nine hundred dollars from his own pocket, if need be.

It was worth it to see Leigh Renwycke happy.

He'd been so close to telling her about their first meeting back at the bakery this morning. Had opened his mouth and even found the first few words. But the rest of them just wouldn't come.

And no way was he about to ruin this evening by bringing it up.

"Awfully nice of you, by the way, showing a former urban-Californian-turned-isolated-Texan what a Saturday evening in Maple Valley looks like."

Behind Leigh, children lined up in front of a fence,

standing on tipped-over apple crates to pet horses. "Actually, if I recall, you invited yourself along."

"Really? Don't reckon I remember it that way."

She stopped at the corner of a towering red barn. "Let's review: After Colin found us in that bathroom, he broke the news to me that his fiancée wasn't feeling well and wouldn't be able to come to the maze with me tonight. You said, 'If you're short a date for the evening, ma'am, I can happily fill in.' I said, 'Don't call me ma'am.' You said, 'So you prefer darlin'?' Next thing I know, I'm waking up from a much-needed late afternoon nap to find you ringing my doorbell."

He grinned. "You skipped the part where I shoveled your sidewalk while you got ready."

Frankly, he hadn't known why she needed to "get ready" at all. She'd looked plenty cute with her sleep-mussed hair and smudged makeup. Not that he'd have dared to say it.

"Fine, that was nice of you. Thank you." She nodded.

He nodded back. "You're welcome."

"But just in case there's any misconception happening here, I only let you come along so I could prove to you how seriously Maple Valley takes its events. This—you and me right now—this isn't a date." Her mitten flopped as she waved her hand back and forth between them.

"Wouldn't dream of assuming it was."

She grabbed a lantern from a nearby table and started toward the maze.

His phone buzzed in his pocket. Again. Didn't have to look to know it was his grandfather.

Seb swallowed a frustrated sigh. Grandfather had micro-managed every one of the past twelve months' assignments. Made him feel like the man was just waiting for him to bungle things up. Not for the first time, Seb wondered what would happen if he *did* make a mess of things. Would Grandfather cut him loose? Renege on the promised inheritance?

The thought alone was enough induce panic. He needed that money. He couldn't just stand by while Thad lost his land and his livelihood. Disease had swept through their herd two years ago. They'd still been digging their way out of debt at the time, crippling medical bills after Thad's heart attack years earlier having depleted the man's savings. The loss of the herd had only deepened the financial hole.

"Where'd all the ice come from?" He asked it solely to distract himself—from thoughts of Grandfather, of Thad's struggles, of the very real possibility of the ranch that'd become Seb's haven reverting to a bank.

A group of teens raced past, leaving a mess of prints behind as they disappeared into the structure.

"This is what I've been trying to explain, Seb. Maple Valley goes to great lengths and expends obscene amounts of effort to carry on our tradition of ceaseless and creative town events."

"By which you mean . . ."

The lantern that dangled from her hand creaked as she lifted it. The light splayed over her face—cheeks and nose red from the cold. "By which I mean, the ice was trucked in. Just like we shipped in fake snow when last year's snowman-building contest unfortunately collided with a December heat wave."

"Think anyone in town ever stopped to consider that maybe the reason Maple Valley couldn't afford to keep its theater open was because all its money went to stuff like this?"

She handed him the lantern. "That's the kind of logic we don't tend to employ all that often in these parts."

A gentle gale skimmed a dusting of snow from the top of the ice wall as they entered the maze. They walked in silence for a few moments, distant music and the voices and laughter of others filling the quiet.

And then he started telling her about Thad. Didn't really know why other than it just felt natural—talking to Leigh, telling her about his life before this past year, about the man he'd run into outside that bus station in Texas and how it'd changed everything. He told her about Thad's heart attack and his wish that the man would slow down some.

Which made him wonder, as he had plenty often before, if he'd done the right thing in going to Grandfather. The money would hopefully help save the ranch, but what good would that do if Thad worked himself to the bone in the meantime? Seb had checked in with his stand-in foreman every month to make sure Thad wasn't overdoing it, but it rankled him something fierce not to be there himself.

He paused at a fork in the maze, waiting for Leigh to lead the way. Her footsteps crunched in the snow as she turned right. "But I don't get it, Seb. If you were so happy on the ranch, why'd you leave it to work for your grandfather?"

"Let's just say, I needed the money." It'd taken all the gumption he could muster to make that initial call home, to ask Grandfather if there was any chance of receiving some financial help. He'd expected a cold brush-off.

But no, Grandfather had summoned him to California and laid out his deal.

No doubt he hoped a year of carrying out the foundation's grunt work would entice Seb back to the family fold. That is, if a grandfather and a grandson with years of gaping distance between them counted as a family.

But Seb had known his Grandfather's life wasn't for him from the time he was a teen. Nor was living in the shadow of cement and chrome skyscrapers.

Working with Thad on the ranch, though? That fed Seb's hunger for freedom. Not that cattle roundups or even riding trail felt like some special calling or anything. But if it meant fresh air and a sky that stretched in unending blue, if it meant a sense of belonging he'd never once felt in boarding school or Grandfather's pristine parlor, then he'd happily spend the rest of his adult life in the saddle.

"It's about Thad, isn't it?" Leigh tipped her head to look over and up at him, her steps slowing. "You needing money—it's not for you, is it?"

A couple holding hands turned a corner and passed them by. "You're very astute, Miss Renwycke."

"And you're very transparent when you talk about Thad. You love him like a father."

"He's been more of one than Grandfather ever was." At her glance, he answered the question she didn't ask. "My parents died in a car accident when I was a toddler. I don't remember them." He heard the lack of emotion in his own tone. Maybe it seemed odd, the way he could say the words without a crack in his voice or even a wince.

But it was all he'd ever known, this parent-less existence.

Until Thad.

"My dad died two months ago."

Leigh said it so softly that at first he almost missed it. Might have missed it entirely if she hadn't stopped in the middle of the pathway. Her pink cap sat lopsided on her head and she just stood there for a moment, looking small and sad under the last waning light of dusk.

"Were you close to him?"

"Not really. Our whole family . . . we sort of fell apart a long time ago. Drew's been trying to put us back together in recent years."

She started walking again and it was just about the most natural thing in the world to reach for her mitten-covered hand.

She didn't pull away. "Mom's back in Arizona now. She and Dad retired there a few years ago. She's coming home for Christmas, though."

There was something so peaceful about walking beside Leigh. Reminded him of long nights camped out under the stars in Texas, only Thad for company and the ease of unhurried conversation. "I'm sorry, Leigh."

"No, I'm sorry for turning Debbie Downer on you. I'm supposed to be introducing you to the wonders of Maple Valley."

They reached another split in the maze. He was the one to halt this time, to turn and face her. "You've already done so."

"The ice maze is great, isn't it?"

He didn't mean the ice maze and maybe she knew it. Because there was a breathless quality to her voice and she tugged her hand free. But she didn't inch away from him, nor did she look away.

You should tell her. You should tell her right now.

He should bring up Kansas City before he gave in to any one of the irrational impulses gliding over him right now. Like the urge to touch the lock of hair that escaped her cap or . . .

"Leigh!"

Colin's voice stole the moment from him. Leigh's brother's steps sent snow spinning into the air. His mouth was curved in a frown.

Confusion flooded Leigh's face. "Col—?"

"It's Winnie," he sputtered, skidding to a stop in front of them. "She's on her way to the hospital."

CHAPTER 5

*L*eigh burst into the ER a woman on a mission.

A *guilty* woman on a mission. How could she have left her phone in the car? Apparently Drew had tried calling her repeatedly before finally sending Colin to search for her at the ice maze.

The hospital's fluorescent lights glared overhead, reflecting on the shiny floor beneath Leigh's feet. Only too late did she realize she should've stopped on the entryway rug to shake the snow from her boots. The wet surface sent her slipping and sliding, and if not for Seb's steadying arm, she'd have lost her balance entirely.

"Try to calm down, Leigh."

In any other situation, his deep voice might've been a soothing cadence.

"My daughter rode in an ambulance to the hospital. Without me." A car accident. Only it didn't make sense. Winnie had been at home when Leigh left with Seb. Leigh had tried talking her into coming along to the maze, but her daughter had insisted she had studying to do.

Leigh's boots skated underneath her again and Seb's arm

slid the rest of the way around her waist. "You heard Colin. He said Drew said there weren't critical injuries."

But there *were* injuries. Leigh should've been here half an hour ago. No, she shouldn't be here at all. She should never have left Winnie alone tonight.

"Can I help you?"

Leigh blinked, a nurse's face or maybe a receptionist coming into focus from behind a desk rimmed by red and silver tinsel. "Winnie Renwycke. I'm her mom. Where is she?"

"I'll need to see some identification. Patient confidentiality, you know."

"Are you serious? She looks exactly like me. And she's under eighteen, so you can take your patient confidentiality and—"

"Leigh." Seb again. With that same calm tone in his voice.

But maybe it was working this time. Because she took a deep breath, reached for her purse, managed to fumble around until she found her driver's license. It seemed to take the woman behind the desk an eternity to look from the license to her computer monitor and then finally nod.

"All right, Ms. Renwycke. Your daughter's getting her arm x-rayed right now. I'll let you know when you can go back."

Leigh's purse thudded to the floor. "You mean I can't see her now?"

"Not while she's in the x-ray room."

"But—"

"If you'll just take a seat."

The urge to yank the tinsel from the woman's desk nearly got the best of Leigh. But Seb's hand at her elbow steered her away first. He led her toward the huddle of chairs in the waiting room, the jingle of a holiday movie playing on the TV in the corner grating on Leigh's already taut nerves.

Apparently Seb could read her mind. Because the first

thing he did after seeing her seated, was locate a remote and mute the television.

"I should be with Winnie."

Seb sat down next to her. "You will be. Soon."

"How can they keep a mother from her child?"

"Actually, I'm impressed they didn't shove a bunch of paperwork at you. Insurance and all that."

Drew had probably taken care of it already. Because he was Drew. Because that's what he did.

Her blurry gaze fastened on the speckled floor. "I hate hospitals." Hated how they made her feel. What they made her remember. The lies she'd told one doctor after another over the years. The coveted prescriptions she'd clutched every time she left.

All because she'd dated the wrong boy in high school. A football player with a knee injury and painkillers to spare. She'd complained of a headache one night, and he, impatient to get to a party, had tossed her the bottle. A couple pills later and she'd never felt better.

But the temporary high had led to a lifetime of lows. Truthfully, much as she wanted to, she couldn't blame Winnie's father, wherever he might be these days. He might've offered her those first two pills, but she'd been the one to swallow them. To keep going back for more.

"I had Winnie in this hospital. When I got pregnant, my parents wanted me to give her up for adoption."

She didn't know why she said it, and Seb's silence stretched until she had to look at him. Certainly he'd realized, hadn't he? That she'd been a teenager—barely older than Winnie—when her daughter was conceived?

"I'm too selfish to regret the decision to keep her. I love her too much. Doesn't mean I don't wonder, though. Her life could've been so different. She could've had a dad who was actually around. She could've had a stable childhood instead of . . ."

Instead of being dragged from town to town while her mother did whatever it took to get the next orange bottle. Instead of being routinely dumped on relatives whenever Leigh decided to get clean for awhile, try a new rehab program.

"Leigh—"

"Whatever nice thing you're about to say in an attempt to comfort me, please, just don't. If you really knew me, knew all the things I'd done . . ."

She felt a warm hand close over hers, just like out at the maze. Only this time there was no mitten, and she could feel the callused skin that spoke of strength and hard work. It didn't make sense, the way his presence wrapped around her like an embrace now. She'd only met him days ago. He shouldn't have this effect on her.

But she allowed herself the trifling comfort of leaning her head on his shoulder anyhow.

She didn't know how many slogging minutes passed as she sat like that. At some point, Colin joined them. And eventually, finally, Drew appeared in the waiting room, his shirt untucked and relief sliding over his face. "Good, you're here."

Leigh jumped from her chair. "How is she? Where is she? What happened?"

And there was Seb again, standing at her side, holding her hand once more.

"She's fine, Leigh. Broken arm, but—"

"You call that fine?"

Drew's attention hooked for the barest moment on her hand in Seb's. "It could've been so much worse. If you'd seen the car—"

"Whose car? And where? Why wasn't she at home?"

Drew took a breath, patience in his eyes. "Apparently she

went to the library with a friend. They studied for a couple hours and then he drove her home, but they hit a patch of ice. She used an officer's phone to call me."

He? He who? And wait . . . "She called *you*? Why didn't she call me?"

Clearly Drew didn't have an answer. Or if he did, he couldn't bring himself to acknowledge it. He only tilted his head toward the hallway he'd entered from. "They're going to cast her arm in a few minutes. You can go back and see her first. Down the hall, fourth room on the left."

Leigh nodded, so much more than guilt churning inside her now. She slipped her hand free and moved to the corridor.

"Leigh?"

She paused at Seb's voice.

"I can wait for you."

She closed her eyes, humiliation twisting its way into the company of the rest of her stormy emotions. She'd spilled too much moments ago. He'd seen too deep.

And to top it off, he'd just heard the same thing as she had —that after a car accident, on the brink of an ambulance ride to the ER, her daughter had chosen to call her uncle instead of her mom.

She glanced over her shoulder. "That's all right."

"You'll need a way to get home," he reminded her gently. "I can leave my rental and get a ride home with Drew."

She nodded, accepted the keys he held out, and turned without another word.

She found Winnie where Drew said she'd be—in an exam room sitting atop a paper-covered table. She rushed to her daughter's side, resisting the urge to pull her into a hug, settling for a kiss above her ear instead. "Win, I was scared half to death."

Winnie leaned away, her broken arm encased in a sling,

purple circles under both eyes and hair hanging limp around her shoulders. "I'm fine, Mom."

"There's blood on your shirt."

"That's Ty's. He scraped his forehead helping me out of the car."

Leigh's heart galloped. "Ty? You were with a boy. What were you doing with a boy? Where is he now? Does he even have a license?" And why—*why*—hadn't Winnie called her?

"Mom—"

"I want to talk to Ty's parents. Better yet, I want to talk to Ty." She should stop. She knew she should stop. But all her worry and all her fear took control. "You're not old enough to date yet, Win. I've told you that a hundred times."

Winnie slipped from the exam table, paper crumpling and a wince scrunching over her face at the movement. "He's my science partner. We were studying."

"That's why you called Drew instead of me, isn't it? You didn't want me to know you were with a boy."

"I can't believe you'd even accuse me of . . . whatever you're accusing me of." Winnie threw her uninjured arm in the air. "I'm not *you*, Mom."

All the breath fled from her lungs, leaving not one solid thought in its wake. Leigh sank, stiff, mute, into the hard chair in the corner. Tension fogged the quiet.

Until a nurse arrived to escort Winnie to get her arm casted. Winnie only nodded and followed the nurse from the room.

* * *

"I'm worried about her, Drew."

Colin's voice drifted from the woodshop just a short walk from the Renwycke farmhouse. Seb paused outside the shop, light spilling from its windows and the smell of sawdust wafting in the cold night air.

The ride from the hospital in Drew's car had been quiet. After four days in the man's house, Seb knew silence wasn't unusual for the man. But it'd been different tonight. Drew had seemed edgy, anxious.

Turned out he wasn't the only one. Colin had arrived at the house only minutes after Drew parked in the driveway. He'd disappeared into the shop on the heels of his brother.

Seb had paced the farmhouse kitchen for a good ten minutes before finally wandering out to the woodshop, propelled by his own concern and the echoes of Leigh's words in that ER waiting room. When she'd told Seb he didn't really know her, he'd felt the pain she still carried. Down deep in the marrow of his bones, he'd felt it, and the brunt force of it bruised him still.

All he'd wanted to say in that moment was that he *did* know. Maybe not everything, but he knew more than she realized. It'd been obvious from her tremors and glassy eyes the night he first met her that she struggled with some form of substance abuse, and just from comments he'd heard here and there in the past four days, he'd picked up on the fact that her life had only stabilized in recent years.

It was both too little and too much, all the bits and pieces swarming around inside him. Mostly, he just wanted to make Leigh feel better. Somehow, some way . . .

"Winnie's going to be okay." Drew's voice, muffled by the woodshop door, was only slightly deeper than his younger brother's.

"I know she is. It's Leigh I'm concerned about. Shouldn't one of us have stayed with her at the hospital? Just in case . . . you know."

"She's been clean for over four years now, Col. Just being in a hospital isn't going to send her spiraling."

He shouldn't be standing here eavesdropping. Seb either needed to make his presence known or trudge back to the house.

"I called Maren," Drew added. "She left her book club to go to the hospital. Leigh didn't want us to stay, but maybe she'll let Mare."

"It's not just tonight that worries me." Colin sighed. "She's restless. She applied for a job in Des Moines without telling anyone. Since when is she an aspiring event planner?"

"She could be plenty successful at it." The sound of sand-paper against wood joined their voices.

"Being successful isn't the same thing as being happy, Drew. It's you and the farm all over again. You were ready to throw aside your real passion to become a farmer because it felt like the logical thing to do when Mom and Dad deeded the land over to you. But you wouldn't have been content. You're a woodworker. Leigh's a crazy talented pianist. She's a free spirit. She comes alive when she plays."

Leigh played piano?

"And you think her free spirit's trapped in Maple Valley?" Sincere curiosity tinted Drew's question.

"Might not be Maple Valley so much as single parenthood and a job she has no real passion for. And now she's planning some event for your houseguest? When she's already got so much on her plate?"

Cold billowed around Seb. Should he not have asked for Leigh's help with the theater reopening?

But no, it had been Drew's idea in the first place and Leigh was legitimately excited about the whole thing. Besides, she was a grown woman, capable of making her own decisions and—

His phone blared into the quiet.

Drew's sanding stilled.

Great.

Clomping footsteps joined the sound of his ringtone and the woodshop door swung open. Drew gawked at him from inside. "How long have you been out here?"

"Not long." He couldn't feel more awkward if he were standing out here in only his britches.

"Well, come in." Drew opened the door wider.

A haze of warmth—probably from the space heater in the center of the room—folded around him as he stepped inside, gaze flitting from a varnished rocking chair to an unfinished cradle.

Colin hopped up. "Coffee? It's decaf. Because Drew's an old man and can't sleep if he has caffeine after three p.m."

Drew dropped his sandpaper atop a counter crowded with tools. "Mock me all you want. I sleep like a baby."

Colin reached for a Thermos. "And snore like a machine. So says Maren."

"Kinda wish you and my wife hadn't become such good friends."

Seb had gotten used to the brothers' interplay in recent days. It was enough to revive the wish he'd always had as a kid—for a sibling, a playmate. He had a feeling Drew would miss Colin's presence when he got married and moved out.

He accepted the cup Colin handed him. "Have to confess, I might've heard some of your conversation just now."

"Don't tell Leigh we were talking about her." Colin perched on a sawhorse in the corner. "She hates it when we butt in too much. She likes her space."

"I just don't think you need to worry that planning a theater reopening is too much for her. I think you're underestimating her. She's more than up for it. She made these binders and already has theme ideas and—"

"You've known her four days, Pierce." Colin folded his arms.

"Colin." Drew's voice held the slightest hint of warning.

Colin ignored him. "I'm just saying, maybe four days is enough to buddy up to her, even move into handholding territory, but I think we know our sister a little better than you."

Now Drew looked at him with more than a little speculation, too. He didn't speak, but with that Renwycke, sometimes the silence said enough.

And right now, Drew's silence said his younger brother wasn't the only one with questions about the nature of Seb's relationship with Leigh. Which was crazy, because there was no—

His phone rang again, startling him enough that he nearly spilled his coffee. He'd ignored it last time, assuming it was Grandfather. But what if it was Leigh?

He set his mug on the sawdust-covered floor and pulled out his phone, still feeling the stares of Drew and Colin. He glanced at the screen. Thad?

He glanced up. "Sorry to interrupt what I think might be about to turn into an interrogation about my intentions, but I need to take this."

"Did you know she was in the hospital at this time last year being treated for exhaustion?"

Colin's question halted Seb's movement, his phone still ringing in his hand.

"She collapsed at work. Drew and I were both convinced she'd relapsed."

"Colin." Drew grimaced.

"What? At least we were wrong. But she was dehydrated and dead on her feet from working so much overtime at the restaurant." He slid off the sawhorse.

Seb's phone quieted. "Why are you telling me this?"

"Because you came in here telling us not to worry when you don't know the whole story. Leigh's had a lot harder time

341

of it than you probably realize. I don't dislike you, Pierce, but if you hurt her—"

"I'm not going to hurt her."

Except that he already had. And if guilt had nipped at him before, it was eating him alive now.

His phone dinged, signaling a voicemail.

Finally, Drew spoke. "She's our sister, Seb. We both have our own way of showing we care."

Yes. Drew worked behind the scenes to help her land a job. Colin went on the offense.

He lifted his phone. "I should go."

Drew nodded.

Seb wound his way to the door, skirting around a pile of two by fours, and stepped into the cold. He stopped in the middle of the farmyard, wintry cold pummeling him from every direction. He was only supposed to be in Maple Valley to renovate a theater. Two weeks and he'd be saying his farewells.

But this place, these people, this family—somehow in such a short time they'd drawn him into their world more fully than he ever could've imagined.

And Leigh . . . what was the use in denying it? She'd gotten under his skin. Burrowed all the way into his heart, if he was honest. Maybe a person shouldn't be able to do that in only four days, but she'd had more than four days. For five years, she'd camped out in his memories. For five years, he'd wished for a second chance.

Now that he had it, was he blowing it?

Stars winked from a midnight sky so clear and sprawling it reminded him of Texas. He tapped his phone and lifted it to his ear to listen to Thad's voicemail, lumbering through the snow as he did, his breath white in the air and his fingers numb. At the first sound of Thad's voice, his image flooded Seb's mind—ruddy cheeks filled with weathered creases, thin lips under a hawkish nose and angled brow, permanently bronzed skin.

Until the man's words stopped him in his tracks.

"I know you're not going to like this, son. But Stephanne Smith made me an offer for the ranch. A mighty good one. I'm seriously considering accepting."

CHAPTER 6

*T*he incessant banging coming from the theater projection room made it nearly impossible to be heard.

"Sorry about the noise, Seth."

Leigh handed her boss, Seth Walker, owner of The Red Door, a printout of the menu she'd finally settled on for the theater's reopening. In between shifts at the restaurant, she'd spent hours each day and night this week working on event plans—a convenient distraction, if nothing else.

Five days since the accident and the chill between mother and daughter hadn't come close to thawing. Leigh had tried talking to Winnie, had stood outside her bedroom door for nearly an hour that first night, but it was as if Winnie had shut down. Leigh had finally given in this morning, told Winnie she could apply to her writing program, in hopes it might clear the air.

But even that wasn't enough.

She just wished she knew what had brought on the cold front. Yes, Winnie was a teenager, and yes, they'd had mother-daughter scuffles in the past. But this was different.

"Wish I could say this place looks great," Seth said now, his attention roving over the theater lobby. Seb had pulled out all the stained carpet and removed old wallpaper, but cracked walls still awaited fresh paint and the concessions area had been completely gutted. He only had a week and a day to pull off the rest of the renovation.

But apparently the lobby wasn't a priority this evening, not if all that thumping around upstairs was any indication. What was Seb doing up there anyway?

The few times she'd seen him this week, the man had been nearly as stand-offish as Winnie. Not rude, but not all that amicable, either. No teasing. And he hadn't called her darlin' even once.

If that wasn't a sign that something was off, she didn't know what was.

"My brother always says reno sites generally look their worst before they can start looking better." Leigh side-stepped a pile of unopened paint cans. "Which I'm sure you already know, considering all your work on the restaurant."

Leigh hadn't been living in Maple Valley back when Seth Walker had turned the old First National Bank building into the stunning restaurant it was today. The outside still had a historic look—concrete and brass and that bold red door. The inside was all rustic warmth and amber lighting, with unique touches all over the place.

Only a year older than her, Seth was as much a fixture in Maple Valley as The Red Door—just like his slew of cousins and his uncle. They were a close-knit clan, that Walker family. Drew had told her once he used to wish their family could be as tight as the Walkers. It's why he'd moved back to Maple Valley, had done his very best to coax his siblings home.

"Oh yeah, there were times with the restaurant when I was convinced it'd never stop looking like a construction site."

Seth glanced down at the paper Leigh had given him. "Anyway, the menu looks great. Won't be a problem at all."

Leigh squatted in front of the paint cans. Ooh, she liked this rich evergreen paint Seb had picked out for the walls. But why hadn't he asked anyone for help with the painting itself? "I hope it's not awkward that I took on this extra job, Seth. I'm not cutting back on hours at the restaurant or anything."

Seth pocketed the menu. "Not awkward at all. Frankly, I've been wondering if the day might come that I'd lose you. I'm already dreading it."

"Why would you lose me? Wait, you don't think . . ." Was this another case of her dogged reputation tainting her present? "I'm not going to flake out on you, I promise."

Seth's laughter echoed in the hollow room. "Not what I'm concerned about. You're the hardest worker around, my friend. Heck, if I wasn't overly attached to the place, I'd step away and make you The Red Door's manager. I'm not worried you're going to flake out, Leigh. I'm worried you're going to get a better offer elsewhere and I'm going to be left without my crackerjack assistant manager."

Leigh turned slowly in her crouched position, angling enough to see the look on her boss's face. A look that told her he meant every word he said. "Wow. Thank you." He couldn't know how much she'd needed to hear something like that, especially after these past days with Winnie.

Days when it seemed like, once again, she just couldn't get it right.

A thud shook the ceiling overhead. Seth tipped his head. "Think someone should go check on that guy?"

Leigh stood, brushing dust from her knees. "I will. I've got party plans to discuss with him anyway. But we're set on the menu?"

"I'll do a food and supplies order today and line up a catering crew."

"Sorry it's short notice. I was waiting on budget approval from Seb." Who, if she had to guess, had been waiting on approval from his grandfather. Maybe that accounted for all the noise upstairs. She'd spent enough time with him in recent days to pick up on his less-than-ideal relationship with the man.

Made her a little sad, to be honest. She may not have been close to her parents through most of her teenage and young adult years, but at least she'd had a chance to mend the rift between them before Dad passed. Didn't erase those lost years, though.

She saw Seth out the front door, then crossed the lobby and climbed the rickety stairs toward the projection room. Seb didn't even look over when she nudged her way in.

Instead, facing away from her, he gripped the edge of a shelving unit with both hands and pulled. Hard. Enough that she could see the outline of muscles in his back, pushing against the fabric of his shirt.

She glanced away, taking in the cramped room. A ratty old couch took up one wall—must be where the projection room attendee used to lounge while movies played. Another wall contained a horizontal glass window that overlooked the theater, currently empty of chairs.

The rattling shelves pulled her attention back to Seb as he yanked the whole unit clean from the wall. Her "whoa" finally captured his attention.

"Oh. Hey. Didn't hear you come in."

"You were too busy showing those shelves who's boss."

Shouldn't he make some jokingly arrogant comment right about now? Ask if she was impressed at his strength? Where was the swaggering cowboy from last week?

"Don't need the shelves anymore. They used to hold all these film reels. This is probably one of the last, non-niche theaters in the country to go digital." He gave a cardboard box a shunt with his foot, pages of yellowed paper spilling out, then moved to inspect the wall behind the shelves. "A fact Grandfather didn't realize when he green-lit this project. The man has enough money to buy a small island, and yet he's upset he's going to have to shell out a little more for a digital projector. He's called me two times a day every day this week."

"Seb, has it occurred to you at all that maybe your grandfather . . . well, could it be that he just wants to talk with you, to reconnect or something? And maybe he's using this as an excuse?"

He jostled the shelving with his movement. "It's a nice thought, but that's not really the way my grandfather works. He's not into bonding. He's into giving orders and making sure they're being followed."

"And that's why you're stomping around up here, going all He-Man on the shelves?"

She could almost make out his dimple when he peeked through the shelving at her. "I was making that much noise?"

"I was starting to wonder if you were going to come crashing through the ceiling."

"Might as well have. I already have an impossible amount of work to do. Why not add replacing a ceiling?" He came out from behind the shelves, brushing bits of drywall from his hair and clothes. "How's Winnie's arm?"

"Her arm is fine. How are you?"

He moved to the window, tapping the projector that sat on a metal tray that suspended from the ceiling. "Isn't it kind of crazy to think that just ten, twelve years ago, the way movies are produced and distributed was entirely different? Think about how much film it took to get one single movie in theaters all over the country. Hundreds of thousands of dollars to produce enough reels just for one flick. Now everything's distributed on hard drives and encrypted USBs."

"So this super pleasant mood you've been in for days, the stomping around and ripping out shelves with a lot more force than necessary . . . we're just not going to talk about it?"

"Maybe I'm in a bad mood because I'm sad about the decline of 35-millimeter film. Maybe I'm a cinema purist who misses the magic of the old days."

She knelt to collect the papers that had spilled out of the cardboard box he'd tipped over. "Or you're just enjoying being a man of mystery and—" She cut off at the sight of the music notes on the first page she picked up.

"Whatcha got there?"

She swept up the rest of the pages. Sheet music, all of it. And with the strangest names—*Stealthy Escape, Remorse, Comedy Excitement, Verdict.* All looked to be composed by the same person—J.S. Zamecnik.

Seb moved to her side, his nearness almost as jarring as the papers in her hands—the notes, the clefs, the half and whole rests. Longing rose up inside her, making its escape from a padlocked room in her heart and spreading until it reached her itching fingers. Five years since she'd let herself so much as touch a set of ivory keys.

Five years since that gig in the bar in Kansas City.

Since that stranger in the cowboy hat—

Like so many times before, she slammed the door on the memory.

Seb pulled the top paper from her hands. "Oh, wow."

"What is it?"

"They're all silent film cues." He knelt down to riffle through more of the papers on the floor, and she caught more titles as he did—*Wings, Old Ironsides, The Wedding March.* "Some of these are full scores."

"It's all movie soundtrack music?"

"Not exactly. Way back in the early 1900s, pianists or full orchestras would play along to silent films. Sometimes they improvised, sometimes they had snippets of music to fit specific scenes—like the ones you're holding. And sometimes they had full scores. Zamecnik did loads of cues and accompaniments for silent films."

"I had no idea you were so up on your cinema history, Seb."

He stood. "Grew up next door to Hollywood, remember, and my boarding school had a special emphasis on arts and entertainment." He looked up from the paper. "But this theater can't possibly date back to the time of silent movies."

Leigh shrugged. "Maybe whoever used to work here was a movie buff. Maybe he collected old film paraphernalia."

Seb glanced from the pages in his hand to the pages in hers. A grin he'd held at bay for too many days now sidled over his face. "We should show a silent film at the grand reopening."

Why did she get the feeling she wasn't going to like the direction he was going with this? "We're showing *It's a Wonderful Life*. It's already out on the marquee."

"I can change that easily enough. All we need is a piano." He met her eyes. "We've already got a pianist."

Wait, how did he know . . . ? "No, we don't."

"I heard Colin say you play."

"Used to."

"Actually, I think the words he used were 'crazy talented.'"

She dropped the sheet music in the box and swiveled. "I'm telling you, I don't play anymore, Seb."

She must've said it too harshly, because Seb didn't respond. She watched his reflection in the glass window—the way he opened his mouth and then closed it again, the questions, the lines of confusion in his forehead.

Why did this moment feel suddenly familiar? As if she'd seen his face in glass once before?

"All right."

At his simple concession, she turned to face him. They'd switched roles somehow. She'd come up here convinced Seb was upset, but now she was the one flustered and unsettled.

And he was the one with a soft look of concern. No, more than concern—understanding. Which was so . . . nonsensical. Maybe they'd spent a fair amount of time together in the past week. Maybe that night at the ice maze and then those minutes at the hospital had seemed weightier, more significant than usual for a pair who'd been strangers just days before. And yes, she'd seen him every day this week and they'd shared snatches of conversation and he was staying with her brothers.

But he didn't *know* her. He couldn't hear the way her nerves quickened at the thought of playing piano again. The way her conscience hissed. The way her past threatened and her restless spirit tempted.

Other than those little glimpses she'd given him in that hospital waiting room, Seb didn't know the old Leigh. He'd only seen the new-and-improved version. She aimed to keep it that way.

Although why it mattered so much to her . . . well, she'd rather not think too hard about that.

"How are things with Winnie?" Seb asked after a quiet moment. "You said her arm is fine, but everything else?"

How did he know to ask that? "Not great."

He dumped the rest of the sheet music into the cardboard box and carried it to a corner. "You got plans tonight, Leigh?"

She shook her head. For the life of her, she didn't understand this man.

"If I can get this dusty old projector working, how do you feel about a movie night?"

* * *

SEB HAD CALLED it an hour and a half ago—no way would Leigh make it all the way through the movie. Not when her eyelids had started drooping barely ten minutes in.

She was curled into the corner of the couch he'd dragged down from the projection room, legs tucked underneath her. She'd toed her shoes off at some point, and they sat on the cushion between them.

Seb leaned back on his side of the couch, wishing he'd been able to doze off as easily as Leigh. Had he slept more than four or five hours a night even once since returning Thad's call last week?

"You can't sell, Thad. You love that land." It was the first thing he'd said when Thad picked up.

"Hm. I reckon I was kind of counting on a 'hello, how are you?' before you started scolding me, son."

"Thad."

"Fine. We'll skip the chit-chat. You know I'd rather sell the land than lose it to the bank. And you also know Stephanne. She's a good rancher. She said she'd hire on all my men, you included."

Sure, Thad's nearest neighbor was a good sort, but that wasn't reason enough to let go of his home. *"I'm almost done working for Grandfather. Can't you just hold on a few more weeks?"*

"Seb, this isn't your responsibility. I never asked you—"

"You didn't have to."

Round and round they'd gone, and when the call had finally ended, Seb was nowhere near certain he'd convinced the man to hold out. It had translated into too many restless nights since. Didn't help that Grandfather had been checking in twice a day to assess his progress on the theater.

He thought he'd done a fine job of hiding his burden, but Leigh must have seen right through him. He'd suggested the movie as much to distract him as her.

He still couldn't believe he'd even gotten that projector

working. Couldn't have done it without the YouTube videos Leigh had found on her phone. From there, they'd just had to decide between the few reels he'd found lying around the room.

Leigh had nixed *Jaws,* declared *Star Wars* too long, and said she'd hated *E.T.* since her first viewing. *Princess Bride*, it was.

Not that she'd seen much of it at all. Movie credits rolled now and Leigh's hair fanned around her face as she breathed.

He leaned over. "Hey, Sleepyhead. Time to wake up. Movie's over."

"I'm not sleeping." Her muttered words accompanied the barest of movements, her head lifting from the corner of the couch, only to sink back down a moment later.

"I'll forgive you the lie since you're probably sleep-talking and have no idea what you're saying."

She didn't even bother opening her eyes. "I know exactly what I'm saying."

Felt like the first time he'd smiled in days. Suddenly all he wanted was to make this night stretch. Go place another reel in that projector—didn't even matter which movie—and settle on the couch once more.

Only maybe this time he'd move Leigh's shoes and take their spot. Let her lean against him instead of the edge of the couch.

And it was thoughts like that only adding to his insomnia these days. *You're a thirty-five-year-old man, not a fifteen-year-old kid with a crush. You have a job to do and an inheritance to earn and a ranch to save. You have no business falling for a woman whose name you only learned nine days ago.*

Even if she was adorable when she tried—and failed—to stay awake.

With a sigh, he pulled himself to his feet. "Fine, then. You keep not sleeping and I'll go turn off the projector."

His footsteps reverberated on the hard floor. Hopefully by

this time tomorrow night, his new chairs would be installed. He needed to get moving on the painting, too. Carpet should arrive on Friday and . . .

Tomorrow, Seb. Let it go until tomorrow.

Within minutes, he'd cleaned up the projection room and locked it behind him. When he returned to the theater, he found Leigh sitting up and pulling on her shoes. "Told you I was awake."

"Whatever you say, darlin'." Even as the word rolled off his tongue, he shook his head. Honestly, since when did he go around calling women *darlin'*?

Since coming to Maple Valley, that's when. And he *didn't* call women darlin'. He called Leigh and Leigh alone darlin'. And it was ridiculous and he should stop.

"That's a good sign," Leigh said now as she stood.

"What's a good sign?"

"You said darlin'."

He held out her coat. "Thought you didn't like that."

"Yes, but the fact that you haven't said it in days had me worried." She shrugged into the coat and then turned. Her eyelids were still heavy from the sleep she denied and the curl of her lips drew his stubborn gaze. "I thought something must be seriously wrong."

If anything was seriously wrong, it was his own foolish brain. The way it had him standing here in a darkened theater, thinking maybe the past months had been worth it if they led him here. That maybe moments like this in a peculiar little town in Iowa made up for all the nights he'd slept in hotel beds in the past year—missing Thad, missing the ranch, missing the life he couldn't wait to get back to.

That maybe he wasn't as eager to return to that life as he'd been just a week ago.

You're a fool, Seb Pierce. It'd become his ever constant, heckling refrain.

"Something *is* wrong. Can't you tell me what it is? Is it stuff with your grandfather?" Leigh lifted her hand to touch his cheek.

At her touch, in nothing more than an instant, he was defenseless. Desire he'd done his best to ignore simply took over. He turned his head just enough to kiss the inside of her palm and then wrapped both arms around her. He felt her sharp inhale, heard the tiny gasp that followed. But when she didn't pull away, he took it as his sign.

He lowered his lips to hers and kissed her before his conscience could send up a flare. And before the annoying voice in the back of his head could get a word in edgewise or call him a fool again, he tightened his hold and deepened the kiss. Her lips were soft and her skin smelled like vanilla and man, did she fit perfectly in his arms.

Only when he was out of breath did he make himself break away. At which point something must have snapped for Leigh, because she instantly backed up a step. She stared at him in the dark, her panting breaths matching the rhythm of his heart. Holy smokes, what had he just done? Should he apologize? Kiss her again?

"What. Was. That?"

"I'm . . . sorry? I mean, if you want me to be sorry, I guess I'm sorry." He zipped up his coat. Unzipped it. "Except if I'm honest I'm *not* sorry because that was a heck of a kiss and if I'm really honest, I think we should probably do it again at some point and—"

Panic flooded her features. "I can't deal with this right now, Seb. What time is it? I should be home. Winnie's probably wondering where in the world I am." She hurried past him.

"You don't have to run away from me, Leigh. I'm not going to throw myself at you." Not again, anyway.

You're really, really *a fool, Seb Pierce.*

He trekked after her into the lobby. "Leigh—"

She'd halted midway to the front door, mouth gaping. "You've got to be kidding me."

He followed her pointed gaze to the lofty windows he'd had installed last week. Snow. Sheets and sheets of white blurred by a wind that hurled itself against the building. *Oh boy.* "I've never seen a blizzard before, but I've seen my fair share of dust storms. If this is anywhere near as bad . . ." He wouldn't be driving out to Drew's place anytime soon, that was for sure.

Leigh pulled out her phone.

"What are you doing?"

"Calling Winnie to make sure she's at the house. She better not be out in this."

From what he heard of Leigh's end of the ensuing conversation, her daughter was home. She pocketed her phone less than a minute later.

"Guess we'd better hunker down."

Leigh tossed him a glance. "You can, if you like. But home is only a four-block walk. I can brave it."

He glanced out the window again. He couldn't even see the streetlamp only feet from the theater entrance. "Are you crazy?"

"No, I'm hardy. I'm an Iowan. I can handle a little snow, Seb."

"But—"

"You can come with if you want." She pulled her pink cap out of her coat pocket.

"I can?"

"Trust me, even if the snow lets up in the next hour, as long as the wind keeps up, you won't want to be on the road. And I'm not going to just leave you stuck here all night. Can you handle a blustery walk?"

"I can handle it."

She looked doubtful.

"Those dust storms I mentioned? I rounded up eleven escapee cows in one once. Could barely see a thing."

She rolled her eyes as she fitted her cap over her head. "Was that before or after your thirty-seven stitches?"

He wiggled his fingers into his gloves, thankful all over again to Colin for loaning him the winter wear. "It'd be nice if you'd try to be a little more impressed by Texas tales, ma'am. You could at least pretend." Another gust of wind slammed against the building. "Are you sure you don't just want to wait this thing out?"

She shook her head.

He sighed. "As you wish." He buttoned up his coat. "That was a *Princess Bride* joke, by the way."

"I didn't sleep through the *whole* thing."

"Then you admit you slept through some of it?"

She marched toward the door. "Now I'm tempted to kiss you just to shut you up."

"I wish you would," he muttered, finishing with his coat and trailing after her.

She stopped with her fingers wrapped around the door handle. "Ready?"

This night had taken so many unexpected turns. Might as well go traipsing through a blizzard to top it off. "Ready, if you are."

But she didn't push open the door. She waited there for a moment, absently touching her lips and looking up at him, a sudden and charming shyness mixed in with her unmistakable curiosity. "When I asked you what was bothering you before, you suggested the movie. And when I asked you again, you kissed me. If I ask you a third time . . . ?"

"You're very persistent, Miss Renwycke."

"And you're elusive."

Oh, did he want to kiss her again. Something fierce. "Thad

wants to sell the ranch. But he loves that place, and I can't stand the thought of watching him give it up."

She bit her lip for a quiet second, then leaned toward him and kissed his cheek. Sweet, but oh-so-swift, and why it should affect him even more than that kiss from before, he didn't know.

She grabbed his hand and pushed her way out the door. "Let's go."

CHAPTER 7

*I*t was a shriek from downstairs that jerked Leigh from sleep the next morning.

Winnie?

Seb.

Leigh shot out of bed. "Shoot, shoot, shoot, shoot . . . " She scrambled to throw on a robe over her flannel pajamas. She should've insisted Seb take her bed last night. Winnie finding her mother sleeping on the couch wouldn't have been nearly as shocking as a finding a man down there.

But when she'd suggested it, Seb had refused and she'd been too cold from the walk home to argue. She'd stopped by Winnie's bedroom on the way to her own, but her daughter had already zonked out. Apparently she hadn't felt the need to stay awake long enough to make sure her mother arrived home safely.

Leigh stuffed her toes into her slippers. She should've woken up Winnie. Warned her about the man camping out downstairs.

A man who'd *kissed* her last night.

That really happened, didn't it?

Leigh cinched her belt robe so tight it pushed out a cough. What was happening to her life? Ten days ago, it'd been so calm and routine. And now?

She paused in her doorway.

Now everything in her orderly little world had tilted.

And the scary part was, she liked it. The warm feeling pooling in her stomach, she knew it too well—that familiar thrill that interrupted a restless season. But thrills had only ever led her down the wrong path before.

"Mom!" Winnie barreled down the hall.

Leigh hadn't even heard her come up the stairs. "Honey, sorry, I was just on my way down to—"

"To give me CPR after I stopped breathing? There's a man on the couch!" Winnie's backpack thumped on the floor, her casted arm hanging at her side, the other fisting her waist.

Right. It was a school day. But surely with the blizzard last night, there was a late start this morning. "Win—"

"I can't believe you got on your high horse with me about Ty, who—*again*—is just my science partner, when you're staying out to all hours and bringing men home."

"It's one man, not men, and I didn't 'bring him home.' Not the way that unnecessary tone of yours is implying. There was a snowstorm. It wasn't safe to drive."

Winnie just shook her head, her messy bun flopping from side to side. Clunking movement coming from downstairs let her know Seb was up and about. He'd only seen her little home in the dark last night. Did it look better or worse in the light?

She'd been so proud of this place when she first moved in. Fresh beige paint on the walls, two full bathrooms, even a little fireplace in the living room—it'd felt like a paradise compared to the cramped apartments she and Winnie had called home for so many years.

But Seb came from a wealthy family. He'd most likely

grown up in a mansion with Greek columns out front and a pool in back. And he'd spent the past fifteen years living on a big ranch in Texas. Her townhouse must look like a prairie lean-to in comparison.

But why was she worrying about this now, with Winnie's spearing vexation aimed straight at her?

"I'm sorry I didn't warn you in time." Leigh attempted a light tone. "At least you're dressed, right? Not like you went down there looking like I do at the moment."

"If you expect me to laugh about this, Mom, you're even more clueless than I thought."

"Winnie, I said I'm sorry, but this attitude has got to stop."

Winnie stomped down the hallway. "You don't even know why I'm really upset."

Leigh hiked after her. "Then tell me. I've been trying to get you to talk for days. I know you think I overreacted about the car accident, but can you understand that I was scared?"

Winnie whirled outside her bedroom. "You applied for a job in Des Moines, Mom."

Leigh halted. Blinked. "What? How did you—"

"You left the file with your cover letter open on the computer. I found it Saturday while you were at the ice maze with that guy. Were you planning to just pick up and move without giving me any warning at all? Like when we moved to Sioux Falls? And Kansas City? Omaha?"

"Win, of course I would've talked to you before—"

"You already work constantly, and now you're spending all this time with some guy? Probably an old boyfriend, right? He looks familiar." She gripped the knob of her bedroom door, her back to Leigh. "What am I supposed to think, Mom? Feels like we traveled back in time. I'm just waiting to find a bottle of pills hidden behind the coffee cups in the cupboard or under a couch cushion."

Every word out of her daughter's mouth was another

splinter in her heart. "I had no idea you felt this way. I promise, Win, you don't have to worry about this stuff."

Winnie swiveled enough for Leigh to see her face. "Do you know how many times I've heard you make that same promise? I stopped believing it a long time ago."

If there were tears in her eyes, Leigh couldn't feel them, not with the numbness spreading over her now. "Win—"

The door slammed before Leigh could even get out her name.

For a long moment, Leigh couldn't make her limbs move. Should she knock? Force her way in? But what could she say to soothe her daughter's wounded heart? Winnie had every right to feel what she did.

She turned, slippered feet carrying her back the way she'd come, toward her room or maybe the stairway. She didn't even know.

All she knew was Winnie was hurting and she didn't know how to reach her and . . .

And suddenly she was back in Kansas City, leaving that seedy bar and hating herself for what she'd done.

No. Don't remember. Not now.

She choked on the memory, desperate to swallow it. But hurt hauled it from her broken heart, all the details she'd tried so hard to forget. How she'd called everyone she knew that afternoon, trying to find childcare so she could perform that night. Just one short gig. Just an hour at the piano. Sing a few songs, collect a paycheck.

Feed an addiction.

But no one had come through for her. She hadn't wanted to leave Winnie at the apartment alone. Not with the kind of neighbors they had. So she'd brought Winnie along and had just . . . just left her in the car parked at the curb of a busy street. What kind of mother did that?

The messed-up kind. The kind who deserved jail time

So said the man who'd happened upon her ten-year-old that night. A stranger who'd seen her kid's face plastered to a chilled window as she slept. Who'd been on the brink of calling the police right as Leigh exited the bar, probably smelling of smoke and alcohol.

He'd lashed into her, every one of his incensed words so justified that Leigh just stood there and took it. Couldn't even look him in the eye.

"She's a child. *You left her alone in the car? I'm not even from Kansas City, but it doesn't take a genius to tell this is a horrible part of town. Did you think for even a second about what could've happened to her? I've been waiting here for ten minutes trying to decide what to do.*"

And the worst part . . . the part that rang so horribly true:

"*If this is how you take care of your kid, you don't deserve her.*"

"Leigh?"

Seb. He stood halfway up the staircase, so much concern in his hazel eyes, it was almost too much for her.

"H-how much of that did you hear?" It took effort to get the words out, memories still thrashing around inside her—from five years ago, from five minutes ago.

"Most of it," he admitted. He climbed the rest of the stairs. "Are you okay?"

She swiped the back of her palm over her eyes before her tears could escape. "What Win said about the bottle—she meant painkillers. Oxy, Vicodin, those were my favorites, if you're wondering—"

He shook his head as he approached her. "I wasn't."

"I should've known that's what she's been worried about. Why wouldn't she? Any time I got clean before it never lasted. So why wouldn't she see a mess waiting to happen when she looks at me? Why shouldn't she expect . . ."

Any other explanation she might've tried to get out was muffled by Seb's shirt, same one he'd worn last night, as he pulled her into his arms. Finally, she stopped trying, her tears replacing her words as she let herself cry.

* * *

"YOU'RE MAKING SUGAR COOKIES? At nine-thirty in the morning?"

Seb pulled a batch of cookies from the dated but functional oven in Leigh's compact kitchen, warmth wafting over his face. If he'd expected anyone to eventually join him in the kitchen, it was the woman whose fridge he'd raided to find the cookie dough in the first place.

Not her daughter.

But there Winnie stood at the edge of the kitchen, backpack over one shoulder again, just like before—when she'd walked into the living room only to squeal when he popped up from the couch.

He set the pan on a counter. "There comes a point in every man's life, Winnie Renwycke, when he realizes that he's an adult and he can eat whatever he darn well pleases for breakfast."

She made a sound somewhere between a snort and a grunt and let her backpack slide down her arm. "I have a two-hour late start today."

"So I assumed." He turned away, opening one drawer after another, looking for a spatula.

Honestly, he wasn't that keen on making small talk with the girl. Not after the way he'd heard her talk to Leigh. But it had to have been a shock to Winnie, finding him on the couch earlier. This, too, must be weird—him making himself at home in their kitchen.

But no way was he leaving until he made sure Leigh was okay.

The sound of running water drifted from upstairs, which

meant Leigh must be in the shower. Earlier she'd cried in his arms until she'd been entirely spent. He hadn't known what to do other than simply stand there and brush his fingers through her hair. Give her something to hold on to while she gave in to a storm of emotion he had a feeling she'd been bottling for days.

Or maybe much longer.

No one should have to hurt like that.

What he wouldn't give to take it all away. Convince her that no matter what her daughter said, she wasn't a mess. She wasn't the sum of her past failures. She was strong and she was resilient.

And he was so far past pretending what he felt for her was anything less than life-altering. Maybe it'd happened too fast, but it'd happened all the same. He'd fallen for her. Hard. And it changed everything.

He'd spent half the night on that couch last night trying to convince himself their lives weren't entirely incompatible. That just because he lived and worked in Texas and she in Iowa, they weren't doomed from the start.

You're a fool, Seb Pierce.

Winnie cleared her throat. "Try the cylinder on the counter."

Sure enough, a metal spatula poked out from the clutter of utensils. "Thanks." He liked this little kitchen. Just like the rest of the house—at least, what he'd seen of it so far—it reflected the family who lived inside. Photos of Leigh and Winnie, Leigh's brothers and their significant others, and an older couple he assumed to be Leigh's parents crowded the fridge. But true to form for organized Leigh, they were arranged in straight lines with magnets centered at the top of each picture. A plant with dangling leaves sat in the windowsill over the sink alongside a line-up of Christmas figurines.

In the living room, a Christmas tree was decked out with

homemade ornaments Winnie had most likely made over the years. The couch was old and a little lumpy, but turquoise and white pillows perfectly matched the colors of the artwork on the walls.

"So are you going to lecture me or what?"

Winnie's question pulled him from his thoughts. "Don't think I know you well enough for that."

"But if you did . . ." She raised her eyebrows in a challenge.

Like mother, like daughter. "If I did, I'd tell you to cut your mom some slack. I know you haven't had it easy, but neither has she. And I've never met anybody who tries as hard as she does at basically everything." Winnie opened her mouth, but Seb went on before she could reply. "And you may not love that she works so much, but I hope you know that every penny she's making planning an event for me, she's putting toward that writing program for you."

He'd learned that little tidbit from Drew the other day. Made him respect Leigh all the more.

By the look on Winnie's face, she'd had no idea.

"I probably shouldn't have said that. If you could pretend I didn't, I'd appreciate it."

Winnie just stared at him from eyes so like Leigh's it was uncanny. He gripped the spatula and started freeing cookies from the pan, lining them up on a cooling rack he'd found in a cupboard next to the oven. Was he completely overstepping here? Raiding their kitchen? Scolding Winnie like . . .

Well, like a father, he supposed.

"I don't hate her, you know."

He abandoned the cookies. "Of course you don't. Reckon you even like her quite a bit. You could just do a lot better job of showing it."

She tipped her head to the side. "And I *reckon* I'm not the only who likes her."

"If that was an attempt at a drawl—"

"It was an attempt at figuring out your intentions toward my mom."

She could spar as good as Leigh. He pointed the spatula at her. "Already been through that with her brothers, young lady. Now do you want a cookie or what?"

She shrugged. He took it as a yes, nabbed a napkin from a holder on their small kitchen table and placed a cookie inside. "I saw frosting in the fridge."

She shook her head. "Bus will be here soon."

"Tell me something, Winnie. What's the deal with your mom and playing piano?"

She chomped into the cookie. "I'm not here to be your information source. You want intel so you can date her or something, you're going to have to look elsewhere. Try talking to Uncle Colin. He's the chatty one in the family."

"It was a simple question."

She shrugged. "I don't know why she doesn't play anymore. I know Uncle Drew wishes she would, though. You've seen that ugly antique piano in his living room?"

"I've seen it." But ugly? All that upright needed was a new keyboard to replace its old, yellowed keys and a good dusting and it'd make a gorgeous home furnishing, even if no one ever played it.

"He's been trying to get Mom to take it ever since we moved out. She's the only one who ever stuck with piano lessons, he says." Winnie shrugged again. "Mom insists we don't have room for it, though."

Was that the only reason? She'd sure stiffened when they'd found that piano music in the projection room.

"It's kind of sad, I guess. I think . . . I think maybe music is Mom's happy place."

Footsteps sounded on the stairs. That'd be Leigh. "Listen, Win, you go out there and hug your mom before you leave and I'll give you a second cookie."

367

She rolled her eyes. "Bribes don't work on me, Mr. Pierce." She swung her backpack over her shoulder and flounced from the room.

He couldn't help inching to the edge of the kitchen, glancing down the hallway to where the staircase met the front entryway. Leigh slowed near the bottom of the steps, wet hair straggling over her shoulders.

Winnie met her at the door. "Mom, I'm . . ."

He watched as Winnie shuffled from foot to foot. *Come on, kid.*

"It's all right, Win. I know you've got school. We can talk tonight."

One second stretched into two, which stretched into three.

And then, finally, Seb let out a relieved breath as Winnie tucked herself against her mother. Only for a moment. But surely it was enough. For now, at least.

He returned to the cookies, listening for the sound of Leigh's padding steps, trying to pretend he wasn't anxious to see her. To make sure the emotion that'd swept over her an hour earlier hadn't left her too ragged.

"You made cookies? At nine-thirty in the morning?"

He whipped around. She leaned over the peninsula counter that jutted into the room. Her eyes were clearer now, and if she'd bothered with makeup, he couldn't tell. She wore an oversized sweatshirt over black yoga pants. She made the outfit look as good as if it were her Sunday best. "Your daughter said the exact same thing."

"My daughter who just hugged me. Did you have something to do with that?"

"Don't look at me. I've just been in here playing Mr. Kitchen."

She reached for a cookie. "And digging through my fridge and cupboards, apparently."

"Am I in trouble?"

She grinned. "No, but you can never tell Colin you found store-bought dough in my fridge. My pastry chef brother and his professional baker fiancée would go into a collective shock if they knew."

He rounded the peninsula, coming to a stop in front of her. "Dunno, Leigh, I saw what I saw. Then again, depending on what you offer me in return for my silence . . ." His sentence trailed off into a shrug and a wink.

"You're a flirt, you know that?" She brushed past him to open the fridge, pulled out a container of frosting, and then plucked two butter knives from the open dishwasher.

He took the knife she handed out. "I'm not, though. A flirt, I mean. Not usually."

"You just winked at me." She uncapped the frosting and dug her knife in.

"I have no idea why. I never do that."

She spread a slab of red frosting over a cookie. "You've called me darlin' so many times I've lost count."

"Must be something I picked up on the ranch."

"You tease me constantly and whenever you do, your drawl gets more pronounced. You're like the little boy in Sunday School who's always pulling on a girl's braid." She frosted a second cookie. "Also, you kissed me last night. Maybe it was just a kiss but still . . . it was a kiss."

Yes. That. He'd wondered when it would come up. What she'd say. What he'd say. Whether anything needed to be said at all. *Idiot.* Of course something needed to be said. Except wouldn't it be easier to skip all that and just kiss her again?

"Are you speechless, Seb? Did *I* actually get under *your* skin?"

"You're not under my skin at all. I'm just focused on doing a good job with this frosting."

The cookie crumbled right in his hands.

She had to clamp one palm over her mouth to keep from laughing. He shook the crumbs from his hands then turned to face her, one hip leaning against the counter. "Feeling pretty good right about now, Miss Renwycke?"

"A little. Yes."

"Well, then, this is probably a good time to tell you you've got red frosting on your face." As quick as a blink, he lifted his hand and brushed her cheek with his thumb. She went so still, he could swear he heard her heartbeat. Or maybe that was his. "I'm really not a flirt, Leigh."

"No?" Her voice had gone tinny.

"Not with anyone else anyway, but with you . . ." He let himself do what he'd wanted to do so many times—tuck a strand of hair behind her ear. "And that wasn't just a kiss last night."

"I know." Her eyes searched his. "But Seb—"

"I had a feeling there was a *but* coming."

"We barely know each other and I've got Winnie and you've got the theater and . . . " She inched closer to him. "There's so much you don't know about me."

"I know enough."

"But you don't. Those things Winnie said . . . I do jump into things too quickly. It always happens when I'm restless and I just . . . I don't want to mess up again." For once it wasn't guilt or shame or worry in her voice, but simple, solid resolve. "Could we maybe just, I don't know, press pause on . . . on whatever this is? Just for a little bit? 'Til after the theater reopening, maybe? After Christmas? Take some time to think?"

It was a good idea. A wise idea.

Except that after Christmas, he was supposed to head home to Texas.

Yet all he wanted to do now was ignore that particular

complication. Ignore all of them. All he wanted was to close the last sliver of space between them and—

But she'd asked for space. She'd asked for time. A gentleman would give it to her. He forced himself to back up a step. "We can press pause for as long as you need to, Leigh."

And he'd pray—something he hadn't done nearly enough of lately. That's what he should've been doing about Thad and the ranch, too. Praying instead of spending days worrying.

Leigh's gaze was locked on him. "You understand why? You know it's not that I'm not . . . I mean that I . . . it's not as if I'm not interested . . ."

"For the record, you're making this awfully hard on me, darlin', blushing like that and all."

Despite her own words of restraint, she stretched onto her tiptoes to kiss his cheek just like she had last night. "Don't call me darlin'."

"I should get to the theater." His voice came out sounding scratchy.

She grinned.

And the delight of that moment, her smile, her kiss, his awakened heart, it stayed with him as he tore himself away from that little kitchen, shrugged into his coat, and thanked her for putting him up for the night. It stayed with him as he trundled into the post-blizzard cold and walked the four blocks to the theater, where he found his car almost entirely buried. It stayed with him as he unlocked the theater door and let himself into the building . . .

All the way until he saw the man in the lobby.

Grandfather.

CHAPTER 8

*D*id Grandfather really mean to see this thing all the way through to the end?

Seb stepped inside the theater's newly painted lobby, the lingering smell of paint almost lost underneath the scent of buttery popcorn from the new machine he'd tested last night. Except for a small break for church on Sunday, he'd worked from dawn 'til dusk in the days since the blizzard and his grandfather's sudden appearance. Every day, he'd assumed Grandfather would tire of inspecting Seb's work and head home to California.

But there he stood again this Wednesday morning, scrutinizing the line-up of candy in the spot-free glass case that fronted the concessions area.

"Leigh thinks we should've given the Reese's Pieces top billing in the display, but I overruled her. Junior Mints, all the way."

Grandfather straightened, his suntanned skin almost too smooth under a coif of white hair. "I'm here for the projector test." Gruff, stilted words.

Seb bit back a sigh, shaking the snow from his coat. "As

am I."

With no more acknowledgement than that, they started toward the projection room.

This is how it'd been since Grandfather arrived in Iowa on Friday. A wooden handshake. An overly formal greeting. And then the rapid-fire questions had begun. Questions about the budget, the digital projector, why the new carpet still leaned in plastic-wrapped rolls against an unpainted wall.

Well, he'd finished painting two days ago—thanks to everyone in the Renwycke family, even Winnie. They'd surprised him on Saturday, showing up at the theater with bags of donuts and bagels from Colin's bakery, cups of coffee in cardboard carrying cases, and extra paint rollers. They'd spent that whole day working together. Then on Sunday afternoon, Leigh had come by on her own. They'd painted—and talked about everything under the sun—until midnight

On Monday, Drew had helped Seb install new carpet, and yesterday, the digital projector and sound system had finally come in.

To think, at this time last week Seb had been half-convinced this project would never be completed on time. The whirlwind was nearing its end.

So why was Grandfather still here?

Seb spent the next sixty minutes standing by, useless in the cramped space of the projection room, while an A/V expert fiddled with the new Sony projector. He only paid minimal attention. After all, he wouldn't be the one operating this equipment at the grand reopening or any other day. Hiring was already underway for a theater manager and a crew of employees to keep this place running once the Pierce Foundation pulled out. In the meantime, Mayor Milt had coaxed a theater owner from a couple towns over to help with the movie screening at the reopening on Friday night.

"You look tired, Sebastian." Grandfather still wore his black trench coat, buttoned all the way up to his neck.

It just didn't make sense—Grandfather coming all the way to Iowa. Unless . . .

Unless there'd been something to Leigh's offhand sugges-tion last Friday. *"Could it be that he just wants to talk with you, to reconnect or something? And maybe he's using this as an excuse?"*

But if Grandfather wanted to reconnect, why had he insisted on staying in a hotel in Ames rather than taking up Drew on his offer of a room at the farmhouse? Why had he declined each time Seb asked if he wanted to grab lunch or dinner at The Red Door?

"Restoring a rundown theater in less than three weeks will do that to a person," Seb said now. Truthfully, he *was* tired. Not so much from the work, but from all the spinning thoughts that refused to quiet at night. Thoughts of Thad and the ranch. Thoughts of Leigh. Thoughts of his own future.

Fifteen years in Texas had been enough to convince him that's where his future lay. Up until a couple of weeks ago, he hadn't once considered not returning to the ranch after this one-year hiatus.

Even now, despite all the feelings for Leigh that swirled inside him, after so many hours cooped up in this building, he longed for open land and the call of coyotes. He missed the comfort the came from waking up each day confident in his purpose, the sense of belonging he'd always felt in Texas.

Thing is, lately he'd started to feel that same sense in Maple Valley. People knew his name. The barista at Coffee Coffee knew his standard order. He could walk down the riverfront and exchange greetings with familiar faces. And the way the Renwyckes had banded together to help him with the theater—that meant something to him. Even Winnie had seemed to warm to him in recent days, trading barbs as she painted with her good hand on Saturday, making fun of his drawl.

And Leigh . . .

There was a moment every evening in Maple Valley just as dusk dusted the landscape in its last colors before nightfall, a hush that seemed to whisper over the town square as the sun slipped into its bed. And then it happened—those old-fashioned street lamps released their glow. Twinkle lights that traced the borders of buildings and draped over trees blinked to life.

That's what Leigh Renwycke had done to him. His quiet, peaceful life on the ranch had seemed enough before. Until an unexpected flush of light illuminated his world with new possibilities.

"You off in la-la-land, son?"

Son. It sounded so different coming out of Grandfather's mouth than it did Thad's.

"Is there something more you're waiting on?" His reply came out more curt than it should've.

"Excuse me?"

"Why are you here, Grandfather? You seemed fine overseeing projects from afar every other time. Were you that sure I was going to make a mess of this one?"

The A/V guy cleared his throat. Grandfather narrowed his eyes and moved to the door. He stopped underneath the doorframe, impatience lifting his brow.

Seb didn't hold back his sigh this time, but he followed all the same.

"There's no need to get churlish with me." Grandfather tossed the words over his shoulder as he descended the stairs.

"I'm sorry. Like you said, I'm tired."

"Maybe it hasn't occurred to you that now and then I like to see firsthand the fruits of my labor."

His labor? What more had he done than write a check? He

hadn't even been the one to review the hundreds of applications his philanthropy board received each year.

Seb reached the bottom step, stifling words that would do no good. No point in antagonizing Grandfather. Theirs was a relationship fated for distance since the day Seb had traded in a college education for a life several states away.

Or more accurately, since the day after day after day in Seb's childhood when Grandfather had made it more than clear that Seb was a responsibility he'd never asked for.

Leigh's optimistic suggestion had been a nice one. But she had a family who'd welcomed her back with open arms after years of distance. His had never been a family in the first place.

"I'm sorry," he said again, solely to appease Grandfather and hopefully end this conversation.

But then Grandfather surprised him by placing one palm on Seb's shoulder. "It doesn't have to be like this, Sebastian."

"What doesn't?"

"You think my checking in on you is a sign I don't trust you. Perhaps I simply decided it was time to see for myself what you're made of. You've proven to me in the past few days that you can oversee a project and keep to a schedule and make things happen."

His mumbled "thank you" was infused with confusion. Surely that was Grandfather's version of a compliment. But shouldn't the past months of completing one assignment after another have proven Seb's capabilities already?

Grandfather dropped his arm and stepped away. "There's a place for you on the Pierce Foundation. Long-term. You asked why I'm here—that's why. I'd like you to take charge of the foundation. I can assure you, you'll find the salary and benefits package quite attractive."

Seb's throat went dry, but he forced his expression to remain neutral. He crossed the room, angled behind the concessions counter and reached for a box of Junior Mints. He'd restock later. "Grandfather, that's very kind of you, but—"

"I don't need a decision now."

Yes, but Seb had an answer now. A very clear answer. He couldn't move to California. He couldn't join his grandfather's world—wear a suit everyday and work in an office building.

A glint hardened in Grandfather's eyes. "Don't make this decision the same way you hopped that bus when you were twenty. Don't throw this away the way you threw away all I offered you then."

Seb ripped open the candy box. "You mean a law degree I never wanted and a career I was absolutely not cut out for?"

He shouldn't have said it. It made him sound like the ungrateful youth he'd been back then.

Grandfather's expression darkened. "I'd watch your words, son. You may not want the life I can offer you, but I happen to know you want my money."

A piece of candy stuck in his throat. "We made a deal."

"I want better for you, Sebastian. Your parents would've, too." He pulled a pair of leather gloves from his pocket.

How would Seb know what his parents would've wanted? Grandfather had refused to talk about them all throughout his childhood. Well, other than to remind Seb that his father had been set on following in Grandfather's footsteps, getting a law degree, joining the firm.

Seb's heart thudded. Grandfather wouldn't actually back out of their deal, would he? If he didn't come through with the inheritance, Seb had nothing to offer Thad. And with Thad already considering an offer on the ranch . . .

"Grandfather—"

"All I ask is that you consider it."

Not until his grandfather reached the theater door did Seb free the question he couldn't hold back. "Why?"

Creases that hadn't been there before lined Grandfather's forehead now.

"We've never been close," Seb went on. "You never seemed to want me around. I figured it was a relief to you when I walked away. Why do you want me to come back now?"

Grandfather's eagle-eye attention bore into him. "Because you're my grandson. And I'm your grandfather. For all the ways we've disappointed each other, I'd like to think that counts for something."

* * *

"You know what the Christmas tree is missing?"

Leigh squealed at the unexpected voice, whirling to thump Seb with her bag. "You scared me half to death!"

His laughter bounced off the walls of the lobby. The grand reopening was still two days away and much of the decorating wouldn't happen until tomorrow night or Friday morning. But she'd decided to get an early start tonight. She'd coaxed Drew and Colin into helping her set up the sixteen-foot Christmas tree—fake, but it looked plenty real. She'd spent the past two hours arranging and decking out its branches.

Maren had invited the whole family plus Seb out to the farmhouse for dinner and everyone else had left at least thirty minutes ago, but Leigh hadn't been able to pull herself away from the tree just yet.

"I'm here to retrieve you." Seb picked up her bag, frowning at the weight of it. "Your brothers are worried you're going to pull an all-nighter here. What's in the bag?"

"My binder, of course." The one with the to-do list of final preparations for Friday night's event. She faced Seb, hands on her waist. "What's the Christmas tree missing?"

Maroon and gold ribbons twisted over the tree's branches and glitter-covered bulbs glistened under the light of the chandelier that dangled from the lobby ceiling.

A far cry from the tree at home—the one crowded with rainbow-colored twinkle lights and Winnie's homemade ornaments. Leigh might have messed up plenty over the years as a young parent, but she'd managed to save every pipe cleaner candy cane and felt Rudolph Winnie ever made.

Seb sidled up to her, his presence radiating warmth and the faint, musky scent of that cologne that always did a number on her senses. He must've cleaned up at the house before coming back to town for her. The tips of his hair were damp and he'd traded in one plaid shirt for another. "Popcorn," he said. "In the movies, they're always showing people threading popcorn over a string and hanging it over a tree."

"I've never seen the point of putting popcorn on a tree when you could just eat it instead." Although, this *was* a movie theater. Maybe this one time it would've made sense. Shoot, did the tree look too formal? Perhaps she should reconsider—

"I was kidding, Leigh."

"But maybe it does need popcorn."

"It's perfect. It belongs in a magazine or something. You've done an amazing job on everything so far and all the final details are going to fall into place. Promise."

"I wish I felt as confident as you." No matter how many times she reviewed her to-do list or revised the itinerary for the reopening, she couldn't shake the feeling she was missing something.

Seb took hold of her elbow, gently steering her toward the door. "You're a miracle-worker. If I'd been left to plan the event on my own, a) I never would've made progress on the renovation, and b) I would've let down your whole town."

"I'm just organized and detail-oriented, that's all."

"And talented and creative." He held out her coat. "And particularly captivating when you're ordering people around."

She *had* spent half the evening bossing around her brothers as they moved the tree from place to place until she was satisfied with it in its current location. Lucky for her, they'd put up with it.

Seb, too, had been at her beck and call—carrying in boxes of decorations from her car, climbing a ladder to place the angel atop the tree. He'd carried out her every instruction and hadn't once made fun of her for constantly referring to the to-do list in her binder. He had faith in her. He valued her.

And maybe it was pathetic, but she couldn't get enough of that feeling—the feeling that she was needed and respected and appreciated.

Only that was a whole lot more than appreciation flitting over his face at the moment as he watched her pull on her coat and wind her scarf around her neck. How many times had she caught him looking at her like that this week?

Too many and not enough.

She felt a familiar blush crawl over her cheeks. He only grinned and looked away.

Was it really possible she'd only known this man a little over two weeks? They'd spent so much time together, especially in recent days. He'd seen her in tears last week, had been exposed to at least some of her weaknesses and failures. And none of it seemed to turn him away.

What really got to her was how much Winnie seemed to like him. She'd gone from railing at Leigh after finding Seb on their couch to insisting he sit with them at church on Sunday. She'd lightened toward Leigh, as well, since their morning quarrel on Friday. She hadn't exactly apologized for her words, but there'd been that hug and a few moments of mother-daughter camaraderie in the days since.

"So what if I would've refused to come with you?" she asked now as she dutifully followed Seb toward the exit. "Would you have dragged me out of here?"

"Yup. Would've picked you up and carried you out if I'd had to." He opened the lobby door, her bag still over his shoulder. "And I reckon I would've enjoyed it."

"In that case, for your sake, I apologize for not putting up more of a fight and—"

She broke off, a gasp slipping from her lips at the sight outside the theater. A sleigh? And horses. And a quilt folded on the seat. And snow and stars and a full moon and . . .

And Seb barely restraining his pleasure at her surprise. His hazel eyes danced under the light of the marquee above.

"You . . . how . . . ?"

"You insisted on sleigh rides around the square during the reopening. I figured we'd better test it out. I admit, I don't know if it's technically on your to-do list, but it seemed like a good idea." He reached for her hand.

"You know how to drive one of these?" Freshly fallen snow crunched under her boots.

"Uh-huh. Of course, I had to spend a good forty-five minutes this afternoon convincing that Sara woman who owns J.J.'s Stables that I do, in fact, know my way around horses, and then another twenty minutes driving this thing around her yard to prove I could handle it."

He helped her onto the bench at the front of the sleigh, settled the quilt around her legs, and picked up the reins.

"You really are one surprise after another, Sebastian Parker Pierce III."

"You've said that before. I hope it's a good thing."

He didn't know how good. It was as if God had answered a prayer she'd never been bold enough to pray—sent Seb to liven up her world. She loved Maple Valley, she did. She loved her picturesque little hometown in all its wintry, snow globe charm. But with Seb's arrival, the snow globe had tipped upside down and everything looked different now.

And she didn't know what she'd do when he went back to Texas.

He gave the reins a shake and the horses started forward, their whinnies breaking into the quiet, their breath white in the cold night air. They passed under garland draped between two streetlamps, the sleigh's blades scraping through slushy snow.

Moonlight traced Seb's handsome profile—cheekbones that stood out over his stubbled jaw, slightly crooked nose, lips she'd let herself think about a few too many times in these past days.

"Seb?"

He steered the sleigh around a corner and toward the riverfront. "Yep?"

"When do you go home?"

He flicked the reins, a stillness in his wayward gaze. "Haven't exactly bought a plane ticket yet."

"Oh." A simple word. A small word. But did he hear all the half-formed questions it held?

"Got an interesting offer from my grandfather today, actually. He wants me to move to California and work for him long-term. I wouldn't actually do it. Big city life was never for me." He seemed to loosen his grip on the reins. "But it made me think . . . that maybe a lot of things I've been sure about aren't so certain as I thought."

"Are you going for cryptic or just a little vague?"

His light laugh rang into the quiet. "Never mind. I'd rather not think about any of that tonight anyway. Not California or even Texas or really anything other than right here and now."

She tucked her arm through his as the river came into view, starlight skating over ice. "You want to stay inside the snow globe."

He glanced down at her. "Huh?"

She didn't answer, simply nestled closer to his side and decided to pretend right along with him that nothing existed outside this moment. This perfectly peaceful, perfectly exquisite moment.

She gazed at the star-studded sky and drank in the lights of her sleepy town. And when the lights trailed away as they neared the edge of town, she stuck out her tongue to let snowflakes land and memorized the sound of Seb's chuckles. And when buildings gave way to rolling white fields and tangled groves, she closed her eyes and wished for the sleigh to slow.

"You're not falling asleep on me, are you?"

Seb's deep voice lulled over the horse's clomping gait.

"No."

"Good, because I think your sister-in-law has this whole evening of pizza and games planned. Oh, and by the way, I promised Winnie a ride in this thing."

"She'll love that. She's turned into a pretty big Sebastian Pierce fan lately."

"She's a smart woman."

"Please don't call my little girl a woman. In my head, she's still five with pigtails." Up ahead, the fuzzy lights of the farm-house peered through the trees. "Hey, Seb? Can I tell you about an idea I had?"

"Of course. Do you have it all laid out in binder-format?"

She elbowed him and laughed and shook her head. "Haven't gotten that far yet. But I was thinking about the reopening and Maple Valley, in general, and how many events we have year-round and Mayor Milt is always trying to harangue more volunteers into helping out and, I mean, maybe it's a far-off pipedream or something but—"

"Yes, you absolutely should start your own event planning business."

"You just stole my thunder."

"You were taking a long time to get there and we're almost to the house."

Yes, unfortunately. She was so far from ready for this ride to end. Just like she wasn't at all prepared for Friday evening to be over and Seb to leave and life to go back to normal. Surely that too-familiar restlessness hovered at the ready, just beyond the borders of her current happiness. "It's risky, starting a business. And I have a good job now. I'm grateful for it. And on my best days, I'm content. But other days . . ."

Seb waited for a moment before speaking. "You know, wishing for something different or something more—that's not always a bad thing, Leigh. Being a little restless? Sometimes that's God getting you ready for whatever's next."

Perhaps. But how did a person know that restless nudge was God and not just her own faulty nature?

Maybe by waiting and praying and listening.

Maybe by choosing to believe that God heard and cared about the desires of her heart . . . even when she didn't feel like it, when it didn't make sense. She'd been so convinced for so long that hers weren't the kind of prayers God heard, that she wasn't the kind of girl He listened to.

But if her parents could forgive her, if her brothers could continually accept her, if Seb could look at her the way he kept looking at her, even knowing what he now knew about her background . . . how much more might God care for her?

All too soon, Seb steered the horses into the farmyard, pulling up in front of the house. He hopped from the sleigh, his shoes sending snow flying, then reached up to help Leigh down. She landed in front of him. "Seb?"

"Yes, Miss Renwycke?" He folded the quilt she'd used over his arm and replaced it on the seat.

"I wish I knew how to thank you."

"I'm glad you liked the ride."

"Not just the sleigh, Seb. Thank you for letting me plan your event."

"I don't think I 'let' you so much as begged you."

"Thank you for the movie the other night and for talking to Winnie the next day. Thank you for . . . for seeing me." Oh how silly that must sound. But she meant it. She meant it so very much. "I love my family and I know they love me. But I also know they can't just forget the person I used to be. There are things they can't help but see when they look at me, but you . . . you're like Dad was this past year and I know that's horrible to say, to admit that it was a relief, watching at least some pieces of his memory drift away. It's horrible but . . . "

She needed to make herself stop talking. She needed . . . oh, she didn't know what she needed, but she knew what she wanted. And he was standing right in front of her wearing an expression she couldn't begin to read.

"Leigh—"

She clutched his jacket before he could say anything more, pressing her lips to his. His shock lasted less than a second before he clasped his arms behind her, kissing her back so thoroughly she lost track of every last thought.

Until suddenly he broke away. "What about pressing pause?" He rasped the question.

"Changed my mind?"

And then he was kissing her again. Her feet were off the ground, her hands sliding from his chest to wind around his neck. Did a door slam in the distance or was she hearing the clamor of her heart?

"Is it finally my . . . "

Winnie.

Leigh yanked herself away from Seb, breathing hard, turning so quickly she might've slid on the slippery ground below if not for Seb's steadying hand.

" . . . my turn?" Winnie finished.

Her daughter gaped, feet planted in the snow, arms dangling at her sides.

"Win, I can explain—"

"What is there to explain? I knew you liked each other, but ..." Something shifted in her expression. Surprise turned to disbelief as her attention locked on Seb. "I just figured it out."

"Figured what out?"

She could hear Seb still breathing heavily behind her. Could feel her own pulse practically galloping.

"You were there." Winnie stepped closer, words directed at Seb. "You were in Kansas City. I saw you."

The cold she'd barely felt earlier scraped over her cheeks. "What?"

"Winnie." All Seb said was her daughter's name. But how could one word be filled with so much ...

Dread?

She turned to him. "Seb?"

"I was asleep, but I woke up when I heard yelling outside the car. It was you. You were yelling at my mom."

The color drained from Seb's face. What was Win saying? There was no way. No way at all.

But Seb's eyes—a hundred emotions swirled there at once. *No. It's impossible.*

"You didn't have all the scruff then and you were wearing a cowboy hat, but it was you." Certainty filled Winnie's tone. "I don't know why I didn't see it before. Maybe it took seeing you in the dark or something?"

It can't be him. I would've recognized him.

But would she have? She'd had tremors that night, so desperate she was for her beloved pills. And in her shame she'd barely looked at the man. She'd seen his reflection in the window, but ...

A gasp pushed its way free. That night in the theater,

when she'd seen Seb's face in the glass of the projection room, felt that jolt of familiarity.

She met Seb's anguished gaze. *He knew.*

He'd known all this time. Or maybe not the whole time, but he'd known before now. That much was clear.

"Leigh—"

Before the sob gathering inside could climb up her throat, she ran.

"This is your night, Leigh, and you're missing the whole thing."

At the sound of her brother's voice, Leigh straightened at the front of the theater auditorium. Tiny lights bordered the narrow red carpet that ran the length of the aisle. Polished sconces with frosted glass were the room's only other source of light—pale light, at that.

But it was enough to make out Drew's form standing just inside the door, a garment bag slung over his shoulder. Hers, most likely. She should've changed out of her faded jeans and hoodie long ago. But she'd realized, just as the lobby doors opened half an hour ago to eager community members, that no one had placed the goodie bags on the auditorium's plush new chairs.

So she'd disappeared into the theater to complete the task herself.

Or maybe *escaped* was the better word. She might be missing out on the festive atmosphere of the lobby right now —the music, the laughter, clinking glasses and the tantalizing aromas of The Red Door's catered meal. But at least there was no Seb in here.

"Everything going smoothly out there?" She pulled a red and green plastic bag from the cardboard box she carried. How many hours must Colin and Rylan have spent making so many Christmas treats to fill these bags? Each one included an oversized, immaculately decorated sugar cookie.

For which they definitely wouldn't have deigned to use refrigerated store-bought dough.

And of course, there came Seb's smiling face to mind again.

And there went her stubborn heart, clinging to the image before her brain could banish it. Just like it had every time the man dared to enter her thoughts in the past forty-eight hours

Two full days and the sting of realization hadn't worn off.

Instead, the memory she'd tried so hard to forget for so long, words that had shattered the last of her dignity five years ago, caught her in an inescapable vice grip all over again. If she'd slept at all the past couple of nights, it'd come in fitful scraps that did nothing to soothe her turbulent state of mind.

"It's going really well," Drew said now as he moved down the aisle. "Turnout is insanely good. I think Seth Walker is having some trouble with the warming plates on the catering table, but other than that . . ." He stopped in front of her. "Your event is a complete success, Leigh. People can't stop oohing and ahhing about the decorations and the food and everything."

Another bag. Another chair. Her box was almost empty and nearly every chair accounted for. She'd be out of excuses for hiding away.

Drew followed her down the front row. "You should be out there."

"I'm the party planner, Drew. I'm supposed to be behind the scenes."

"You're supposed to be wearing this dress and mingling with guests and soaking up well-deserved compliments."

The faint strains of *Jingle Bell Rock* drifted in from the lobby. "I'll join in the fun soon enough." At least now that the party was underway, it'd be easier to avoid Seb. Ignoring his calls and texts throughout Thursday had been easy, but eluding him this afternoon as they readied for the party was a different story. He'd tried to talk to her several times. But each time, she'd found a conveniently urgent task to complete or errand to run.

She reached the last chair and placed the last goodie bag on the seat. Exactly the right number of bags. Thank goodness all the details of this event hadn't crumbled as thoroughly as her broken hopes. Had it really been only two days ago that she'd let dreams of a whole new life carry her away? Dreams of a potential new career laced with the giddy prospect of romance. Dreams that had felt so real for awhile there . . .

Foolish dreams.

"He's a wreck, you know."

Her attention snapped to her brother. His tie hung loose and crooked around his neck. Maren would love that. She got a kick out of Drew's haphazard attempts at dressing up.

"Both Mare and I were awake 'til after midnight listening to Seb pace around the attic Wednesday night and last night was no different. I don't know what happened between the two of you, but the man is on the brink of frantic." Drew traded the garment bag for her empty box. "And for the record, it was all I could do the other night to keep Colin from pummeling him. Neither one of us is big on seeing our sister in tears."

At least that's all they'd seen.

Unlike Seb.

The force of realization pounded through her all over again. Seb, the one man she'd thought saw only the new Leigh, had witnessed her at her very worst five years ago. All this time, he'd known who she was. What she was. What she'd done.

He'd known and he hadn't said a word.

She could've lost Winnie that night. If the unsafe neighborhood hadn't done it, that phone call to the police Seb had almost made would've. Child Services would've gotten involved. She could've been in danger of losing custody of her daughter.

The thing is, as much as Seb's words had wounded her that night, they'd also saved her. They'd caused her to recognize her rock bottom for what it was. She'd finally gotten serious about finding real, long-term help.

The garment bag draped over her arm weighed her down. She lowered onto a cushioned chair, a goodie bag crinkling underneath her. "I just ruined someone's cookies."

"Maybe if you talked to Seb, you'd both feel better." Drew sat beside her.

"You don't know the full story, Drew."

"So tell me. Let me be your brother, Leigh. Let me in."

So much tender concern filled Drew's voice, his gentle gaze. What had she ever done to deserve a brother like this? Like both of them. Time and time again, Drew and Colin had forgiven her failures. Time and time again, they'd welcomed her back with open arms. Drew had paid for her rehab programs, and in this past year, Colin, with his own wayward, partying days behind him, had done all he could to make up for lost time.

Her brothers had watched out for her long after Mom and Dad had cut her loose—something she'd never once blamed her parents for. They'd needed to let her go, to stop enabling her poor choices. Thank God she'd finally been able to get clean and they'd reconnected before . . .

Dad.

"I was relieved, you know. When Dad stopped remembering things . . . I was actually relieved." The moment the confession slipped free, she wished it back. How could she admit something so shameful? But once the words were out, they didn't stop. "For awhile there, I wasn't his daughter who'd made a mess of her life. I wasn't the addict who got pregnant in high school."

Drew shifted in his chair. "Leigh—"

"While everyone else was grieving his illness, I was secretly relieved that he saw me in a way no one else possibly could." Her garment bag slid to the floor. "And then Seb came along and I thought . . . "

She'd thought wrong.

She stood abruptly, trapping emotion that threatened to climb outside her skin. No. This wasn't the time. She should go check on the event. Make sure Seth had the catering table under control. Review the checklist in her binder. She should locate Winnie, too. The movie was scheduled to start in half an hour and—

"Leigh."

And she should change before doing any of that. Tonight the people of Maple Valley would get a taste of the new-and-improved Leigh. She'd put on her dress and show her face in the lobby and if anyone happened to compliment her on an event well-planned, she'd kindly smile and accept the praise.

Tomorrow. She'd think about Seb and Dad and all the ragged pieces of her broken heart then.

She swiped her garment bag from the floor.

"Leigh, please—"

"You're the one who said I should join the party." She started up the aisle, bag over her shoulder.

"But I want to help."

She picked up her pace. "You can't fix everything, Drew." She was out the door before he could try to stop her again.

Stealthily avoiding partygoers, she hurried into the restroom and huddled in a bathroom stall, trading her work clothes for the burgundy dress she'd found in the back of her closet earlier this week.

She was nearly ready when the sound of the bathroom door opening reached through the stall. She heard the clip of high heels, the swish of skirts, voices . . .

Her own name.

"Leigh Renwycke? Really? I thought she was a waitress?"

Leigh's breath caught.

"I'm as surprised as you are. She works at The Red Door, yes, but apparently she coordinated this whole shindig."

Someone turned on a faucet. "Did you hear about her daughter's car accident?"

Leigh's breathing hitched.

"Mm-hm. She was with the Carter boy. Ty, I think. If I were his parents, I'd put a stop to whatever's going on there fast as lightning. I mean, you remember Leigh in high school, don't you? Wouldn't surprise me if her daughter—"

Leigh burst out of the stall. "If my daughter what?"

Both women stared at her from the mirror in front of them—round eyes, gaping jaws, shock dissolving into hasty regret.

Regret she wasn't about to give them time to voice. She fled the bathroom, abandoning her discarded clothes, the empty garment bag. She willed herself to harden, to smile, to blend into the lobby's swirling colors and gleeful crowd and—

"Leigh!"

Seb's voice wrapped around her, squeezing, choking . . .

Tears clouded her eyes until all she could see was the Exit sign, its red letters suddenly her only escape.

* * *

"LEIGH, WAIT! PLEASE!"

Seb couldn't do it any longer. For two days, he'd tried—he'd *tried*—to give Leigh the space she clearly wanted. But the second he saw her hurry into the lobby, all his patience and all his prayers—that somehow he'd find a way to undo all the damage he'd done, the pain he'd caused—all of it evaporated.

"Leigh!"

He said her name so loudly this time that people clustered around nearby tables turned to look.

Tables Leigh had so meticulously prepared with deep red tablecloths and star-shaped glitter confetti, candles and centerpieces. This whole foyer spoke of her hard work—the menu in chalk on black clapperboard, the ticket stand turned photo booth, old film reel curled like ribbon with tinsel over the staircase banister.

"We need to figure out what to do about these warming plates, Seb."

Seth Walker's voice intruded. The owner of The Red Door and his catering crew had prepared the perfect feast, thanks to Leigh's planning. But their serving dishes were growing cold, which might not be such a big problem now considering most of the crowd had eaten and would soon filter into the theater for the showing of *It's a Wonderful Life*.

But when the movie was over, the caterers were supposed to serve a warm dessert.

He gave a frustrated glance toward Leigh's pathway to the exit. She wouldn't really ditch the party altogether, would she?

And where was Grandfather? The man still hadn't shown

his face at the event. He'd stopped by the theater yesterday while Seb was helping set up tables in the lobby. He'd asked Seb again about taking a job with the foundation.

Seb had thanked him for the offer, but firmly declined. Even with all that had happened with Leigh, with all his inner turmoil, all the exasperation on Grandfather's face, he'd still harbored the faint prospect that maybe Grandfather would understand. That even though Seb was saying no to the job, they could still muddle their way toward some kind of reconciliation.

"You're my grandson. And I'm your grandfather."

Those words meant something, didn't they?

But then, if Grandfather couldn't even be bothered to show up tonight . . . Seb had felt his phone vibrate a few minutes ago. Maybe Grandfather had called and—"

"Seb?"

He blinked. "I don't know what to tell you, Seth. All the outlets worked earlier. I never did have an electrician come in to look at the wiring since everything seemed to be working just fine."

Seth sighed, one palm rubbing the back of his neck and the other hovering over a serving dish that was probably supposed to be steaming. "You got any extension cords? Other outlets are obviously working, and it'd be easier to use an extension cord than move the tables."

Mayor Milt was walking toward them now, his red sweater vest a perfect match for the bowtie at his neck. Right, he expected to Seb to get up and give a speech.

But the only person Seb had words for at the moment was currently disappearing out the front doors.

"Extension cords—janitor's closet. I know there's at least a couple in there."

Seth nodded, and Seb took the opportunity to abandon his post before the mayor could reach him. He wound through the crowd, tossing out forced grins as people greeted him by name, patting his back, complimenting the theater.

Why couldn't he dredge up even an ounce of satisfaction on this night—a night when he should've been celebrating? He'd completed his task. His work for Grandfather was finished and his role here in Maple Valley had come to an end. He could go back to Texas and save the ranch and—

A blast of bitter cold spiked his skin as he stepped outside.

And there stood Leigh, under the glow of lamplight—no coat, no mittens, no boots. Just a classy burgundy dress that pulled in at her waist and flared to her knees. Her hair was knotted at the side and from this angle, he could just make out the glint of the simple gold locket she wore around her neck.

She was beautiful and she was breathtaking. "Leigh." Her name slipped out on a hushed whisper.

She refused to face him. *But she isn't stalking away. That's something.*

In the distance, the sleigh they'd nestled in two nights ago whisked a group of teens around the square. Music from inside coasted into the night air. Goosebumps trailed up Leigh's arms as she hugged them to herself. He pulled off his suit jacket and rounded to her front to settle it around her shoulders.

That's when he saw the tears.

If regret and remorse had needled him repeatedly these past two days, then this pierced him so sharply he simply couldn't help it—couldn't help lifting both palms to her cheeks, swiping at tears with his thumbs, tilting her head until he could look into her eyes. "I'm so sorry."

He poured his every raw emotion into the three words. And when it didn't feel like enough, he said it again. "I am so very sorry."

He felt a sob wrack her whole body as cold air scraped his

lungs. He closed the space between them and pulled her head to his chest.

"That night in Kansas City—I was a fool. Thad had just had his heart attack and it's not an excuse, I know that. But I have never stopped regretting the way I took it out on you. If I could go back—"

"You s-should've told me." Her muffled voice shook, her arms hanging limp at her sides.

"I know."

"Y-you were supposed to be the one p-person . . . the one person who saw me differently."

His arms tightened around her. "I do see you differently, Leigh. I see your strength and your resilience and—"

"You see the woman who left her child in her car outside a bar."

Icy air tightened his lungs. "Leigh—"

She pulled away from him so quickly it left his arms hollow and his voice useless. She swiped the back of her hand under her eyes, smudging her makeup and damming her emotion as if by force of will. "You should've told me. I'm not a weakling, Seb. I could've taken it." She turned away from him. "Or did you think the same thing as my brothers and Winnie and apparently everyone in this town?"

He angled around her. "I don't know what you—"

"That I'm just one bump in the road away from falling into addiction again?" His jacket slid off her shoulders, dropping into the snow at their feet. "It's never going to matter what I do, is it? My family's always going to try to shelter me out of worry and this community is never going to forget."

"You know what? Maybe this is part of your problem." Frustration wriggled in. "You're so worried about how your family sees you. How this town sees you. How I see you. But if you ask me, the real issue is how *you* see you."

"No one did ask you."

How could she look so stunning, even with windblown hair and anger cramping her expression? When she took a step back, he took a step forward. "Your past is part of you, Leigh, whether you like it or not. But you're so busy running away from it, you can't see all the ways it's shaped you into the woman you are today." He took a breath. "A woman I . . . "

She stepped back again, bumping into the streetlamp—just like she'd bumped into the ticket counter that first night in the theater.

"A woman you what?"

He closed the space between them, his silent pleading surely showing on his face. "A woman I think I might love."

He heard her breath catch. Felt her rigid posture give way. "You can't love me, Seb. You've only known me seventeen days."

That she knew the exact number of days probably shouldn't fill him with so much illogical hope. "I've only known your name for seventeen days. I've known *you* for five years." *Please look at me, Leigh. Please believe me.*

When she lifted her gaze, hope became courage. None of this made sense—how quickly he'd lost his heart to a woman he never thought he'd see again, how suddenly she took precedence over his no-show grandfather or even Thad. But what had started as a flutter of a feeling that first night in Iowa had fanned all the way to life. God had led him here as surely as he'd placed him on that Greyhound fifteen years ago.

"I started loving you a long time ago, Leigh, whether I realized it or not. Maybe all I knew of you then was a hurt I didn't understand. But now I know the rest of it—I know your hopes and dreams and determination. I know you'd do anything for your daughter, and I know you have a musical gift that's probably begging to be set free one of these days. I know you love details and three-ring binders and that you're as pretty in pajamas and a bath robe as you are this gorgeous dress."

"Seb—"

"Please, can you give me another chance?"

It was as if the very air around him held its breath—not even a whisper of a breeze or a dusting of snow over the sidewalk.

Until startling darkness budged in.

The marquee went pitch-black. The light pouring from the theater windows disappeared. Drifting music ceased.

He wrenched his gaze from Leigh's face to stare at the veil of murky shadows. What had just happened?

And then his phone vibrated again.

* * *

Chaos had already erupted inside the theater when Leigh rushed in. She blinked, trying to make her eyes work in the dark. Someone bumped into her as somewhere near the back of the lobby, Mayor Milt's voice called out for everyone to calm down.

She found Colin first.

"Turns out Seb really should've had the wiring checked. Seth plugged an extension cord into a power strip and suddenly, *poof*, no power at all." He tugged her free of the rush of foot traffic toward the exit.

"If it's a blown fuse, can't we just find the fuse box and flip a breaker or something?"

Drew's voice came from behind her. "If it was only a fuse, I don't think the whole building would've gone dark."

So that was it? The party had ended before it'd barely begun? All her work, all those hours of planning and decorating . . .

A crash sounded from across the room. Had someone just

knocked over a catering dish? And where was Seb? What had possessed him to answer his phone at a time like this?

"Sooo . . . do we all just go home now?" Colin scoured the unlit space. "How am I supposed to find Rylan in this circus?"

Leigh should find Winnie. What was the point in staying? The event was ruined and it was too dark now to take down decorations. Seth would need help cleaning up the catering space, though, and— "The goodie bags! We could at least make sure people leave with those. If we hurry—"

Drew snuck his arm around her shoulder. "Half the crowd is gone already."

And the other half was laughing as if this was all some big joke.

As if tonight, all of it, hadn't thoroughly wrung her heart dry.

"Leigh?"

She felt Drew's arm stiffen at her back at the sound of Seb's voice.

"That phone call . . . I have to leave. It's Thad. Another heart attack."

The last of her fortitude waned into nothing. "Oh, Seb—"

"I don't know why Grandfather didn't show tonight, but if you happen to see him . . ."

It was as if Seb didn't even notice the pandemonium around them. His eyes were glazed; his voice, numb.

And then he was just . . . gone.

CHAPTER 10

"*Y*ou could always go to Texas, you know."

Winnie's whisper from the other side of the bed they shared tugged Leigh from a near sleep. Leigh's mom had been the one to insist everyone in the family stay overnight at the farmhouse on Christmas Eve. *"So we can all wake up on Christmas Day in the same house and have break-fast in our pajamas. Like we used to when you were all kids."*

It'd been so good to see Mom smile tonight. Made it at least a little easier to paste on her own grin earlier this evening as they filed into their usual row at church for the candlelight service. To mouth her way through *The First Noël*. To pretend.

"Did you hear me, Mom?"

Leigh turned onto her back in the king-sized bed in Drew's remodeled attic. A little weird, really, settling under its white duvet, knowing Sebastian Parker Pierce III had slept here for two and a half weeks. "I heard you."

"I know you miss him."

"We became good friends really fast. He was . . . a lot of fun."

"Mom."

There was a little too much knowing tucked into her daughter's voice. "Fine. He was more than a lot of fun. But he has a whole other life in Texas, Win, and I've got a life here, and some things just aren't meant to be."

But at least she'd heard from Seb. Thad was okay. The heart attack hadn't been nearly as serious as his previous one. But Seb hadn't known that when he'd left Maple Valley in such a panicked hurry. And when they'd spoken on the phone the next day, she could tell the scare hadn't worn off.

She'd waited to see if he'd bring up their conversation outside the theater just before the ensuing commotion. What would she have said if the power outage hadn't interrupted? Would he have re-asked his question after everything calmed if he hadn't been called away to Texas.

"Please, can you give me another chance?"

Winnie sat up. "Could you be a little more cliché?"

Her daughter's real life voice crowded out the memory of Seb's. "Could you be a little more sarcastic?" Leigh tugged at the duvet. "If you've really got your heart set on boy talk, then maybe you should finally tell me about Ty."

"I've already told you—"

"That he's only your science partner. I know. But you're forgetting one vital fact: I was fifteen once. I gave that same line to your grandmother at least a dozen times." She grasped at the mental distraction. "Plus, I saw him signing your cast at the theater reopening. We're talking sparks."

"Whatever." Winnie flopped back against her pillows. "I'm going to sleep."

"Now she's sleepy."

"Goodnight, Mom."

Leigh turned to her side, gaze drifting to the octagon window that peered into the night. Wispy clouds muted the moon and a barreling wind sent rooftop snow blowing over the window.

You could go to Texas.

No, she really couldn't. For one thing, expensive airfare just wasn't in the budget. For another . . . she couldn't run after Seb.

She couldn't run after him because it'd be like all the other times she'd run. To a new city. A new gig. A new prescription.

Any new thrill to momentarily quiet her restless spirit.

Somehow she had to find a way to be content with the life God had given her. She had a job and a home. She had a daughter who'd finally settled into her school. She had her brothers. She should be happy.

She *would* be happy.

"You know, wishing for something different or something more —that's not always a bad thing, Leigh. Being a little restless? Sometimes that's God getting you ready for whatever's next."

Seb just couldn't stay out of her head. She hadn't realized at the time how closely his words had mimicked Drew's from a few weeks ago.

"It's good to be content, sis. But there's also nothing wrong with reaching for a dream."

She flopped onto her back once more.

"Mom?"

She turned over to face Winnie. "Hmm?"

"That day after the blizzard—"

"It's okay, Win."

"It's not. I never said I'm sorry. I should've said it. I was just . . . mad. And scared, I guess."

Leigh reached over to tuck a piece of Winnie's hair behind her ear. "I know. And I'm so sorry I've given you so many reasons to be scared through the years. But I want you to know, I am always going to be here for you. I understand if you have worries. I understand if you don't quite trust me all the time. But I'm here for you. Always." She watched her daughter blink in the dark.

"I love you, Mom."

"Love you, too, Win."

Winnie suddenly sat up. "I promised Drew and Colin I wouldn't say anything, but I can't wait. Let's go downstairs. I have to show you something."

"But it's so toasty in here."

Winnie was already sliding on her slippers. "Trust me."

Leigh gave an embellished groan as her bare feet touched the chilled floor. She grappled around in the dark for her fleece robe. "If we wake everyone up and they get mad, that's on you."

Winnie only laughed.

Leigh followed her down the attic steps, through the second floor hallway and down another staircase. The house creaked with their movement and outside, a hefty gale moaned into the night.

Winnie padded into the living room, where Drew and Maren's massive Christmas tree swallowed up one corner. She plugged in its string of lights and then stopped in front of the old upright piano where Leigh had spent so many hours as a child. Nicks and scrapes marred its dark wood and one leg of the bench underneath had been super-glued more times than Leigh could count.

Maren had covered the top of the piano with a red and green Christmas runner, upon which she'd set up a Nativity scene Leigh remembered from childhood. Grandpa Renwycke had carved the stable himself and Grandma had collected the figurines inside from thrift stores around the county. It was a mish-mash of a scene, but Leigh had always thought that made it all the more special.

"What did you want to show me?"

Winnie pointed to the closed piano. "This." She lifted the lid.

And Leigh gasped. The keyboard was a line of sparkling white and smooth black. No yellowed keys or missing ivory pads.

"It's tuned, too, and the pedals even work again."

"What . . . who . . .?"

Winnie reached for a wrapped gift sitting on the bench. "This goes with it."

"I don't understand."

"Open the present."

She tore the paper away, let it fall to the ground, and stared at the three-ring binder in her hands.

"Look inside," Winnie commanded eagerly.

She cracked the binder. Sheet music? Complete with plastic page protectors and color-coded dividers and . . .

And a scribbled note on a yellow Post-it stuck to the inside cover.

Just in case you ever decide to play again. —Seb

Tears pooled in her eyes, blurring his scratchy handwriting. This wasn't just any sheet music. They were the crinkled pages from the theater, those musical scores from old silent movies.

"Colin said if he was going to restore the piano, he should have the wood sanded and stained and all that, too," Winnie said now. "But Seb said no. He said each dent in the wood probably has a story and he'd never want to sand that away. He said all the nicks and grooves are part of what makes the piano beautiful." Winnie shrugged. "Which I think is kind of weird."

Leigh blinked, tears escaping down her cheeks. "It's kind of wonderful."

Winnie folded her arms. "Now will you admit you should probably go to Texas?"

Laughter burst from her lips as she moved to the piano and lowered onto the bench. "I don't know about that."

But she did know one thing: She was, finally and so very happily, ready to play again.

A teardrop landed on Middle C as she placed her fingers over the keys.

* * *

"I'VE RECEIVED some mighty fine Christmas gifts over the years, but getting to leave that stuffy hospital on Christmas morning is the best one yet."

Seb steered Thad's old Ford truck onto the gravel road that led to the ranch. Potholes shook the truck and his visor did little to shade his squinting eyes from a beady sun. So much for that white Christmas he'd anticipated.

But for all the ways his insides churned at all he'd been forced to leave behind, coming home to Texas had been the right thing to do.

Except *home* no longer felt such a certain thing anymore. But maybe that would change when he walked into the ranch house and plopped his suitcase on the bed. Maybe when he saw the Christmas tree Thad had no doubt cut down with his own ax and smelled the scent of pine, maybe then his soul would settle into this life once more.

After all, since returning to Texas, he'd spent all his days at the hospital and all his nights in a nearby hotel. Only made sense to feel a little like a windblown tumbleweed.

"You take a vow of silence or something, son?"

Seb followed the curve of the road, the sprawling ranch grounds coming into view. The truck's A/C rasped from open vents. "Figured I didn't need to talk what with you doing so much yammering." He adopted the easygoing tone and accompanying repartee he knew Thad expected.

"I had a tube in my mouth for a day and doctors poking and prodding me ever since. Excuse me if I'm enjoying the ability to express myself once again."

He nearly flinched at the image that came to mind—of Thad as he'd been when Seb first arrived at the hospital. The tubes and machines and his nearly transluscent skin. The stark white walls of the hospital room had closed in on him as he stood there beside Thad's bed, listening to a doctor say how lucky they'd been.

Luck didn't have anything to do with it, Thad had asserted as soon as he could speak again. Pure miracle, he'd said.

"I don't think it's a coincidence that Stephanne Smith just happened to stop by that day or that she happens to drive like a maniac. Got me to the ER faster than an ambulance ever could."

Yes, Stephanne Smith. The woman from the neighboring ranch who wanted to buy Thad's land. Seb hadn't found a way yet to bring up the topic.

Or maybe he simply hadn't wanted to.

Thad's doctor had insisted on keeping him for two more nights after that first night. Since it was his second heart attack, they'd wanted to run a slew of tests, monitor him for a couple of days.

"At the risk of sounding like a nosy old woman, you do realize, I hope, that one of these days I'm going to insist on a full rundown of your time in Iowa." Thad squirmed against his seatbelt. "Complete with romantic details."

Dust clouded outside his window as the truck jostled over another pothole. "What makes you think—"

"My ticker momentarily gave out, Seb, but my intuition is as hearty as ever."

Seb pulled onto the ranch grounds, the sight of the rustic log house and its wraparound porch a sure sight for sore eyes. This place was all the comfort and security and belonging he'd longed for as a kid. This place had changed his life.

Thad had changed his life. Two and a half weeks in Iowa couldn't overshadow that.

No matter how strangely and strongly that little town tugged at him. No matter how much one resident in particular had staked a claim in his heart and mind and even his dreams.

This *was* home. He glanced at the man sitting next to him. It had to be. Because the doctor had been clear—Thad couldn't go back to his normal pace any time soon, maybe not ever. He had to step back from the rigors of ranch life.

Which meant Seb had to pick up the slack.

Which meant somehow he had to figure out how to quell the ache pulsing at the edges of his heart. Or simply learn to live with it.

Seb braked and turned off the ignition. "Merry Christmas, Thad. We're home."

"So that's how it's going to be? Just going to ignore my prying?"

He opened his door, Texas warmth clambering in. "Reckon so." His shoes landed in the dirt and he rounded the truck to help Thad out. Probably to the man's credit that he didn't brush off Seb's steadying hand as he stepped down, nor argue as Seb kept his pace slow to match Thad's as they approached the house.

"We do need to talk, son. Not just about whatever it is that has you so squirrely and tight-lipped—"

"I'm not squirrely."

"On edge, then. And don't argue with your elder. But we need to discuss the ranch."

The porch's floorboards rattled under their feet, and Seb reached for a key he knew he'd find over the doorframe. "It's Christmas Day, Thad." He pulled open the screen door, slid the key in the storm door's lock and pushed his way in. "Let's just enjoy the holiday and being back home and—"

His words skidded to a halt as he took in the ranch house's long living room. Where was the tree and the scent of pine? Why all the boxes scattered across the hardwood floors? That beige and blue rug that had rested in front of the stone fireplace since the day Thad brought Seb to his new home was now rolled up and propped against the wall.

Thad's soft footsteps sounded behind him as he stepped over the threshold. "This is what we need to discuss."

Seb whirled to face the man, disbelief rasping his voice. "Tell me you didn't sign any papers." This couldn't mean what he thought it did.

"I knew if I didn't do it while you were gone, you'd possibly talk me out of it."

No. *No.* "I'll go talk to Stephanne. Maybe we can still undo it. She's kind and reasonable and—"

"And she's the new owner of this house and all the surrounding property. I'm glad of it. She'll do right by it." Thad moved a box from an old wingback chair.

His chair. The one he always sat in by the fire while Seb lounged on the brown leather couch. How could he do this?

"This makes no sense, Thad. You've spent your entire adult life building this ranch. It's your home. It's my home. I know you need to slow down, but I can pick up the slack. I've got my inheritance now, so we can hire on extra help."

Grandfather had wired the money on Christmas Eve. No explanation as to why he'd missed the theater's grand reopening.

Seb had tried not to feel the familiar rejection.

Thad shook his head as he lowered into the chair. "You don't understand, son. I'm ready for this. I've been ready for a long time—since my first heart attack, if I'm honest. Of course I love this land and this house, but I'm sixty-three. I'm ready to slow down and more than that, I'm ready to enjoy some of the things I've missed out on during so many decades of being tied to this land."

"Like what?" The question came out sounding as confused and helpless as Seb felt. All this time, all these months, he'd worked for his grandfather for the sole purpose of saving Thad's ranch. What was the point of any of it now?

He sunk onto the couch, now covered in a white sheet.

"I'd like to travel. I've actually been jealous of you this past year, did you know that? I'd like to see some sights."

"But where are you going to live?"

"Actually, this is part of what sold me on Stephanne's offer. We're going to swap houses. She's got that much smaller, much newer home on her property and she's not going to need it anymore once she moves in here. She's deeding it over to me, while keeping all the surrounding property. I'll have a place to land whenever I'm not traveling."

"But . . ." So many questions, so many arguments tumbled through him, but frustration clogged his throat.

Thad leaned forward, his green-eyed gaze vivid despite his clinging pallor. An urgency infused his voice. "I did this as much for you as for me, Seb."

"I don't . . . that doesn't . . . it doesn't make any sense." He forced the words out.

"It does. I know you love this ranch, but I think your reasons for loving it have very little to do with the actual place or the lifestyle or the job. You love it because you found a new life here. You love it because I'm here. But step outside that for a moment." Thad's pause stretched. "You were running away when you came here. And there's not a day I haven't been grateful that running led you to me and this ranch. But I think perhaps it's time you consider running *to* something. Something of your own this time. Thirty-five isn't too old to ask yourself what you'd like to make of your life. If ranching is it, then great. Stephanne's ready to hire you on immediately. But if there's something else, anything else . . . consider it a favor to me. I don't want you feeling trapped here the way you did in boarding school growing up."

Seb lifted his gaze. "I've never once felt trapped here."

"I won't be your burden, Seb."

Exasperation propelled him to his feet. "You're not—"

"And I absolutely won't be the excuse you use to stay in one place while your heart's in another."

He stared down at Thad—this man who knew him so very well. After all the loneliness of his youth, God had surprised him with a father.

And perhaps now He was surprising him with something else.

Finally, he dropped onto the couch again. "You're kind of annoying sometimes, Thad, you know that?"

Thad chuckled before leveling Seb with a look that urged him to pay attention. "Look, you can stay as tight-lipped as you want about whatever woman it is who clearly has you tied up in knots, but I can tell you this: Whoever she is, she's not your grandfather. I may not know a thing about her, but I know *you*. And there can't possibly be two people in this world dense enough not to recognize you for the gift you are."

It was so ridiculously good to laugh. "Come on, old man. Let's scrounge up some Christmas dinner."

The last one they'd share in this house. But somehow, it no longer felt like an ending.

CHAPTER 11

"*N*ow, I know the theater's reopening event didn't go quite as smoothly as planned, but that was an electricity glitch, a fluke."

Mayor Milt tilted his head toward the binder open in front of him on the table near The Red Door's entrance. Leigh folded her hands in her lap, willing herself not to fidget. Even though it was four days past Christmas, holiday music still played over the restaurant's speakers and decorative stockings still dangled over the crackling fireplace in the corner.

She caught Seth Walker's eye as he delivered heaping plates to a couple on the other side of the restaurant. His nod of hopeful affirmation stilled, at least for a moment, her flurry of nerves—a match for the blustery sight outside The Red Door's long windows. Snowflakes tussled under a brilliant December sun, the windy breath of winter bowing the trees in the town square.

She forced her attention back to Mayor Milt. Hopefully it wouldn't take him too much longer to review her proposal. She did have somewhere else to be soon.

But she couldn't rush him. Maybe this was a fanciful proposition. Maybe the mayor would shake his head and tell her the city simply didn't have the funds to hire an event coordinator, even part-time.

But she had to try. Seth had even given his blessing, telling her if she needed to cut her hours at the restaurant or resign altogether, he'd completely understand—as long as she always hired The Red Door whenever she needed a caterer.

"We have at least two major events every month here in Maple Valley—more during the summer and Christmas-time. That's a lot of work for you and the Chamber of Commerce and a scattering of volunteers to pull off each year." She unwound her hands and ran clammy palms over the leggings Winnie had given her for Christmas. Red with black and white music notes.

Not a print she'd have picked out for herself. But if wearing them made Winnie happy, she could do it.

Although maybe she should've taken her attire into account before meeting with Mayor Milt. Maybe she should've opted for something businessy instead of the denim skirt and black sweater she'd paired with the leggings.

But then she'd have had to change into something more comfortable before heading to Des Moines. No way did she want to sit through a flight in a business suit.

"This is impressive, Leigh." He flipped through the binder.

It should be. She'd catalogued every event Maple Valley had hosted in the past year and had gotten her hands on budgets for as many as she could. She'd outlined potential cost-savings, ideas for revitalizing old events, anything she could think of to recommend herself.

"I know hiring someone to coordinate events is an extra expense, but having one person consistently at the helm can also lead to less expense in the long run. I can look for special deals with vendors, bundle tasks and projects, all while saving you the time and effort of scrounging around for volunteers."

The mayor fingered the ends of his curling mustache. "It's certainly an interesting prospect."

"I'm sure you'll have to talk to the City Council." She rustled up her resolve for one final pitch. "But I hope you'll seriously consider it. I think I could be a true asset to Maple Valley."

She closed the binder and pushed her chair away from the table, ready to let the mayor get on with his day. She needed to get on the road soon, too.

But his palm on top of the binder stopped her. "You're already an asset to Maple Valley, Miss Renwycke. I do hope you know that."

She met the older man's kindly eyes. For all his boisterous ways, how had she never noticed his compassionate side? She swallowed past a lump in her throat. "Thank you."

He patted the binder. "And if you don't mind, I'll hold on to this. I can't guarantee we can find a full-time salary in the city budget right away, but that's always something we could work up to."

Leigh couldn't have squelched her oversized grin if she tried.

"Plus, I am plum worn out of being in charge of every crazy shenanigan we come up with in this town." At her burst of laughter, Mayor Milt rose. "And no, you don't need to point out that most of the shenanigans are my idea in the first place."

She stood, as well, reaching for the bag slung over the back of her chair.

"I'll be in touch." He leaned forward. "And don't be afraid to get your hopes up. I can be very persuasive with the Council. I talked them into that ice maze, after all, didn't I?"

"Which I reckon is one of the most impressive things I've ever seen."

The unexpected voice, complete with a drawl she'd missed so very much, froze Leigh in place. She held her bag mid-air, couldn't make herself turn or speak or even shiver at the blast of cold barreling in from the restaurant door Sebastian Parker Pierce III must've just come through.

"Why, Mr. Pierce, you've returned." Mayor Milt swept her binder from the table and skirted around her. "Thank you, by the way, for hiring that electrician to look into the theater's wiring after the, ahem, misfortune at last week's event. That was certainly an above-and-beyond gesture. Wasn't part of the grant agreement."

Leigh's heart thumped. What was he doing here? Seb was supposed to be in Texas. Why wasn't he in Texas? What about Thad and the ranch and—

Finally, her limbs unlocked and she whirled, her bag landing in a clump at her feet.

And then she froze all over again at the sight of Seb's hazel-eyed gaze and his dimpled smile and . . . and his coat. The man had finally gone and gotten himself a winter coat of his own?

Somehow in her periphery, she was aware of Mayor Milt's attention swinging back and forth between them. "Well, I have places to be."

Just like that, he whisked away, bells she hadn't heard when Seb entered jarring her with their chimes now.

"Was he carrying one of your binders?"

"What are you doing here?"

He moved toward her, shrugging out of his coat as he did. "Is that all the welcome I'm going to get?"

"You're supposed to be in Texas."

"But I'm not." He stopped in front of her, tossing his coat on a chair. "I'm right here."

"I can see that, Seb. I'm not blind." But she was shaking. And not exactly breathing. "It's just . . . I was planning . . . I was going to . . . there was this cheap ticket . . . and I . . . "

Seb placed both hands on her shoulders. "I'm trying to follow you, Leigh. Really, I am. But it'd help an awful lot if you'd complete at least one sentence."

He was standing too close and he smelled too good and she couldn't think.

She backed away and reached for her bag. "I was going to go to Texas."

His eyes widened. "You were going to go to Texas?"

Sort of nice not to be the only flustered one all of a sudden. "I kept telling myself it was too expensive, but then Winnie told me she'd skip that writing camp in the summer if I'd use the money to go to Texas. And obviously there was no way I was going to do that, but when I realized how serious she was, I started looking at flights. I found this super cheap airline and they'd don't let you take hardly any luggage but that doesn't matter because I only really needed to bring this one thing." She pulled out another binder.

Seb blinked. "Okay, that was maybe a few too many complete sentences at once."

"Look at the binder, Seb."

"Leigh—"

"Please. Just look." Before she lost her nerve and the last weakening grasp she had on her composure. If she didn't get ahold of herself, she'd laugh or cry or most likely both, so overwhelming was the happiness, the hope, that flooded her now.

He might not be back for you. Maybe he's just here to check on the theater. Maybe . . .

For once, she silenced the droning voice on the brink of telling her she didn't deserve this man standing in front of her.

Instead, she listened to the voice she'd finally heard on Christmas Eve when she'd lowered onto that piano bench and touched beckoning keys. The one that hushed into her spirit promises of a love that had never once waned. A love that had come into the world two thousand years ago on that first Christmas.

A love that had been waiting patiently for her return.

She'd played for an hour that night, waking up everyone in the house. No one had complained. She'd switched from the binder full of movie music to playing Christmas carols. And as she played and everyone gathered around, as Maren heated up hot chocolate and Drew lit a fire, it'd struck her that God was making something beautiful of the Renwycke family.

Drew had let go of the need to stitch everyone else's life together and had embraced his own, finding new love and a new dream along the way. Colin had stopped trying to prove himself and had instead poured himself into simply being who he was—a son, a brother, a baker, and now, a soon-to-be-husband.

Mom was healing and Winnie was growing up and Leigh . . .

Leigh was standing in front of Sebastian Pierce right now with her hope quite literally in his hands.

With every page of the binder Seb turned, his smile grew. Only four pages. It's not as if she'd needed the binder at all. But it'd just felt . . . right.

Finally, he looked up. "Created a job for me, did you?"

"It's . . . it's kind of a thing I do now. Figured as long as I was creating one for myself, I might as well help you out as well." And it'd been easier than she could've possibly imagined. One visit with Sara, the woman who owned J.J.'s Stables, was all it had taken to convince her that Seb could be an asset to the woman's blossoming plans for the property. He knew horses, he knew ranch life. Hiring a full-time ranch foreman would allow Sara to focus on the animal therapy and horse camp side of the business.

They'd worked up a job description, a salary and benefits package, everything.

It was crazy and presumptuous and she still couldn't quite believe she'd done it. But she had. And then she'd bought that plane ticket with the intention of showing up in Texas and presenting the job opportunity to Seb in person.

But now he was here and she was . . . just plain incapable of saying another word until he hurried up and told her what he was thinking and let her know whether or not she had completely overstepped and for heaven's sake, explained what in the world he was doing here.

He closed the binder and set it on the table, his eyes never leaving her face.

"Aren't you going to say something?"

"I don't think so."

"But—"

"I'm going to kiss you, Leigh Renwycke. That's what I'm going to do." He pulled her into his arms before she'd even processed his words. "And then we can talk about that perfect-sounding job and how cute those leggings are and whether you liked my Christmas present—"

"I did." The breathless words barely escaped her waiting lips.

"—and how Thad can't wait to meet you. He's waiting at Drew's house, by the way."

"I thought you were going to kiss me."

His breath was warm on her face when he laughed. "I missed you something fierce, darlin'."

And then, finally, he kissed her. And it wasn't the sound of the murmuring wind or the crackling fire she heard, nor the

Christmas music or even the sudden burst of applause from restaurant patrons she'd forgotten about entirely.

It was her heart humming along to a love song better than any she'd heard before.

She slid her arms around Seb's neck just as he broke their kiss and leaned up on her tiptoes to whisper in his ear. "I'm so happy I can't even make myself scold you for calling me darlin'."

There wasn't a better sound in the world than his laughter. "As it should be, darlin'. As it should be."

THE END

ACKNOWLEDGMENTS

Writing this Christmas novella series over the past few years has truly been one of the most fun experiences of my writing journey. There's just something about sitting in front of the fireplace and dreaming about charming little Maple Valley at Christmas-time...about snow and twinkle lights and made-up people who feel so awfully real...and about romance, of course!

Writing a novella isn't nearly as intense a process as churning out a full-length novel. But it still takes work, and I'm oh-so-grateful to the people in my life who have helped make these Christmas stories possible:

Mom and Dad—I'm writing this acknowledgment page while sitting in your house, drinking your coffee, soaking up your loving presence. Thank you for everything.

Grandma and Grandpa—Because I just know that one of the major reasons I'm an author today is because of your encouragement over the years.

Susan May Warren—I don't know if you'll remember this, but I told you my idea for *One Enchanted Christmas* at a conference several years ago and you basically said I *had* to write it. Thanks for spurring me on.

Hillary Manton Lodge—The cover for this collection is so pretty I can't even handle it. Thank you soooo much.

Terri Simmons—Thank you bunches for your proofreading help...and also for talking books so often with me at the office!

Readers—You are the reason one Christmas novella turned into a full Christmas collection! Your encouragement —and emails and messages asking when Colin and Leigh would get their own stories, when the collection would be available in paperback, etc.—helped me put my nose to the grindstone and churn out these stories. I am blessed beyond words each time I hear from one of you. *Thank you* for all the ways you make my heart happy.

And, of course, I'm so grateful to God for giving me a love of stories in the first place...and for writing the best Christmas story of all.

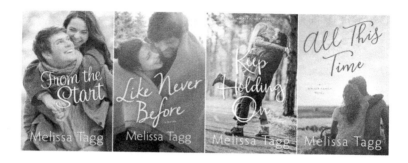

All This Time

Raegan Walker thought Bear McKinley was gone from her life for good. But when he returns to Maple Valley with two children in tow, she'll have to face the fears that have held her captive for far too long.

Plus, don't miss the FREE prequel novella:

Three Little Words

ABOUT THE AUTHOR

MELISSA TAGG is the author of the popular Walker Family series, the Where Love Begins series and the Enchanted Christmas Collection. She's a former reporter, current nonprofit grant writer and total Iowa girl. Her spring 2016 release, *Like Never Before*, was named to one of Publishers Weekly's Top Ten lists and her fall 2017 release, *All This Time*, is a Romantic Times 4.5-Star TOP PICK. When she's not writing she can be found hanging out with the coolest family ever, watching old movies, and daydreaming about her next book. Melissa loves connecting with readers at www.melissatagg.com.

www.melissatagg.com
melissa@melissatagg.com

Made in the USA
Coppell, TX
27 November 2023

24789552R00256